# Cousins at War

# Cousins at War

*by*

## Doris Davidson

First published in Great Britain in 2005 by
Birlinn Ltd
West Newington House
10 Newington Road
Edinburgh EH9 1QS

Reprinted 2008

*www.birlinn.co.uk*

ISBN10: 1 84158 416 9
ISBN13: 978 1 84158 416 4

British Library Cataloguing-in-Publication Data
A catalogue record for this book is available on request
from the British Library

Typeset by Initial Typesetting Services, Edinburgh
Printed and bound by CPI Cox and Wyman, Reading

# Part One

# Chapter One

*January 1940*

As in most cities, the west end of Aberdeen is home to the upper class – the professors, surgeons, solicitors, bankers, et al. – and also to those with less remunerative occupations who have been fortunate to inherit sufficient money to meet the rates demanded annually by the council for the privilege of dwelling there. The Rubislaw Dens – North and South – are two of the most prestigious streets, quietly impressive and lined by magnificent granite houses, where the owners keep themselves to themselves. Neighbours are not in the habit of running in and out to borrow a shilling for the gas meter as they tend to do in the tenements of the east end, and if any fall on hard times, or are beset by misfortune, they do not broadcast it. Appearances must be kept up at all costs.

The Potters lived in the broad, sweeping arc of Rubislaw Den North. Martin was a solicitor; his wife, Hetty, had been an Ogilvie before their marriage; seventeen-year-old Olive attended Miss Oliver's Private School for Girls – high fees and an expensive green uniform; Raymond, fifteen come April, was at Robert Gordon's College for Boys – high fees and an expensive navy and gold uniform. They were a typical family of their district.

3

On the afternoon of 1 January, 1940, Olive Potter ran up the wide curving staircase in something of a temper. She had looked forward so much to the dinner her mother was giving for all the family for New Year, and things had not gone as she had planned. She was wearing a brand-new dress, a green crêpe-de-Chine, with short puffed sleeves, which her mother had said in the shop wasn't suitable for this time of year, but she had got her own way in the end, as she always did. The bodice was moulded round her, with ribbons stitched in a V just below the neck then sweeping down underneath her full breasts and tying in a bow at the back. She had borrowed her mother's make up, taken extra trouble with her hair and knew that she was looking her best. All of this effort had been for her cousin, Neil, but he had scarcely looked at her, and Raymond had put a match to her fuse by saying, in that sarcastic way he had, that she looked as cold as a fish on a marble slab. She had been cold, but she didn't want to admit it.

When she reached the landing, Olive threw open her bedroom door with such force that it banged back against the wall, but she grabbed it and slammed it behind her. They would all hear and she didn't care. Why couldn't Neil have been nice to her for once? Their mothers were sisters, and for as long as she could remember she had been sure that he was the boy she would marry some day, but he had never shown one iota of affection for her.

Flinging herself on the bed, she pummelled the pillow in frustration, her fair hair swinging round her neck, her oval face pink and scowling. Why couldn't he see that she loved him? He was just ten days older than she was, but he had no time for her. Even when they were quite young, and had been taken on those boring family picnics, Neil had preferred to play football with Raymond rather than play games with her, and she could still remember how annoyed she had been, but as she grew into her teens she had realised that all boys of that age were shy with girls. They were both seventeen now, however, so how much longer would it be until he grew up?

Turning on to her back, she wondered if she was stupid to love a boy who had no prospects – even when he was finished his apprenticeship, he would just be a mechanic – but once they were married, she would make him find something better. He was good with his hands, and she had brains, so there was no reason why they shouldn't set up a business of some kind. Yes, they would be married one day, she was quite determined about that, and it would be no use him trying to wriggle out of it. The thing was, she didn't want to wait too long. If she could just get him on his own, he was bound to succumb to her charms and fall in love with her.

A soft tap on the door made Olive sit up. She didn't want to see anyone, but if it was her father, he would haul her downstairs no matter what she said, so she tried to keep her pique out of her voice. 'Yes? Who is it?'

'It's Patsy. Can I come in?'

'I suppose so.' What did Neil's sister want?

'Dinner's out,' the younger girl said, apologetically, as she came in, 'so I said I'd ask you to go down. Why did you run out like that?'

Never having had much time for Patsy, who was too much of a goody-goody, Olive didn't hide her annoyance. 'It's none of your business!'

5

'I know it isn't, but I can guess. You've got a lovely new frock on, and Neil didn't say anything about it.'

Mollified by Patsy's admiration of her dress, Olive gave a sigh. 'He wouldn't notice if I'd nothing on at all.'

Her fifteen-year-old cousin gave a little giggle. 'I bet he would, but he still wouldn't say anything. He's shy with girls, you know.'

Olive stood up then. 'I may as well come down with you.'

Martin glowered at his daughter when the girls went into the dining room but Hetty said, 'Olive, I've put you next to Neil, and Patsy can sit beside Raymond.'

For the duration of the meal, Olive was much happier. Neil couldn't avoid answering her when she talked to him, and if he showed more interest in the conversation going on around them at times, it was only because he felt shy with her. At least he felt something.

'I miss Ishbel and Peter and the children,' Hetty remarked, as she and her sister Gracie cleared away the first course dishes. Ishbel, their youngest sister, had only recently moved to New Zealand to join Flo and her family, who had been there for some time.

Gracie nodded. 'Me too, but Peter was set on it, and it's just as well they went in May, for they couldn't have gone once the war started. It's likely they saw the New Year in at Flo's, so at least Ishbel was with one sister. It's sad to think we're the only two Ogilvies left in Aberdeen now . . . but Ellie's just in Edinburgh and Donnie's in South Norwood.'

When her parents were seeing the visitors off at the door – Auntie Gracie said not to bother going out because it was

too cold – Olive went up to her room. Her window overlooked the driveway where Uncle Joe had parked his car
and it gave her a chance to have one last glimpse of Neil
and hear if he said anything about her to Patsy. She was
rather ashamed of her tantrum now, and hoped it hadn't
put him off her. It was Joe Ferris who passed the remark as
he jiggled his key in the frozen lock of the car door.
'Olive's getting a lot worse as she gets older. She's a right
spoiled brat.'

Gracie gave a loud 'Ssh!' but her husband paid no heed
to her warning. 'It's Hetty's fault, though, for always
giving in to . . . hah! That's it, at last.' Opening the door,
he slid into the driver's seat to let his family in.

Olive closed her window and walked over to switch on
the light. She didn't care what Uncle Joe thought of her,
but it wasn't nice to be called a spoiled brat, and she
should try to curb her temper in future.

As Joe drove off, Patsy turned to her brother. 'I know
why Olive took the huff, and it wasn't Raymond's fault.
She'd a new dress on and you didn't tell her she looked
nice.'

Neil snorted. 'She'll have to wait a long time for that.
She's a blinking pain in the neck, always has been.'

Their mother looked round from the front seat. 'Olive
has a vindictive streak in her, Neil, so you'd better be
careful how you treat her. Don't say anything nasty to her.'

'I can't help how I feel about her. She's off her head.'

The Ferrises' home in King Street was far removed from
the luxury of Rubislaw Den, but it was the only place Joe
had been able to find a suitable shop when the council
condemned his premises in the Gallowgate, and it was

better than some of the other tenement-lined streets. A wide thoroughfare, it ran almost due north from the Castlegate to the bridge over the River Don. Their first-floor flat, above a butcher and a few doors along from Joe's grocery shop, had originally been meant to have a kitchen, parlour and two bedrooms, but Neil and Patsy were too old to share, so their parents slept in the parlour and the only public room was the kitchen.

None of them had relished the idea of sharing the lavatory on the half-landing with the other first-floor family, but it wasn't too bad, after all, and Mrs Mavor never missed her turn in cleaning it. All six tenants used the outside wash house, which was awkward for Gracie after having one to herself for so long, but being able to put up her ropes on the four clothes poles on the patch of grass in the backyard was better than having to zig-zag them across the wash house, as she'd had to do before, and her washing had a lovely fresh smell when she took it in. Unfortunately, her turn came only once a week, so, in between, she had to rinse odds and ends in the kitchen sink and dry them on the pulley that let down from the ceiling. But the neighbours were very friendly and stuck rigidly to the rules about outside cleaning, so that the entrance lobby, the passage out to the back green and coal cellars, even the stairs, were all kept spotless.

As usual when she went home after visiting Hetty, Gracie started talking about her sister's lovely house. 'It's not that I'm jealous of her,' she said, when Joe pulled a face, 'for I wouldn't be happy living in the West End. I'm a down-the-towner, as Olive sneers about some folk. It's what I was born and what I'll be to the day I die, and I'm not ashamed of it. We're every bit as good as the toffs, and my family has never had to do without. You get three good meals a day, your clothes are washed and ironed, I put your shoes into the shoemaker to be soled or heeled as soon as they need it. I defy any mother in Rubislaw Den to do any better.'

'Nobody's arguing with you,' Joe exclaimed. 'I don't see what you're getting so het up about if it's not jealousy.'

'It's not! It's just . . . oh!' Gracie broke off, then said, a little sheepishly, 'I suppose I *am* a bit jealous, but not the way you think. You work a lot harder than Martin and you haven't got half what he's got.'

He patted her hand. 'I've got everything I want, lass – a lot more than Martin. I've got a home I can relax in, not a showpiece, contented children and a better wife than any man on this earth.'

'Oh, Joe,' she sighed happily then remembered that their son and daughter were still in the room. 'It's time you two were in bed, and get that grin off your face, Neil.'

Neil was still grinning as he went out, but when he came up from the lavatory, he heard his father saying, 'Don't fly off the handle at me, Gracie, but I couldn't help noticing the size of Olive's breasts,' and was so taken aback that he waited to hear what else might be said. 'They're bigger than yours ever were,' his father went on, 'even before you had the kids.'

'You're a dirty old man,' his mother laughed. 'I know mine are sagging a bit, but just you keep your eyes off hers.'

'A man can't keep his eyes off what's flaunted in front of him, but that's not what I meant. She's too conscious of

9

her body, and she's going to use it to land some man in trouble some day. Oh, don't worry about me, I'm not roused by her, but Neil . . . ach, I'm speaking a lot of rubbish! It's all that drink Martin forced on me.'

'You didn't need much forcing.'

'Maybe no', maybe no', but it's only once a year. Still, I think we should call it a day, what d'you say?'

Hearing his parents moving, Neil scuttled into his bedroom before they caught him eavesdropping. He, too, had seen how Olive's new dress had emphasised her breasts and had been a little alarmed by a strange feeling every time his eyes fell on them, but his father didn't have to worry about him. He had never liked her; she gave the impression of looking down on other people but always gave him a come-hither look which was a complete waste of time, for he couldn't stand girls of any kind. Boys – well, most boys – could talk about football or something else he was interested in, but girls babbled on about trivialities, and Olive was worse than any of them. He would have to be careful not to let her get him on his own, though, for she was so cunning that she could trap him into saying whatever she wanted him to say, even if it was the last thing on earth he'd meant to.

A few days later, almost wishing that he hadn't given them the money to go, Joe listened with half an ear to Gracie and Patsy telling him how well the A.R. Whatmore Players had performed *Charley's Aunt* that afternoon, and when they ran out of things to say he observed, 'Rationing starts on the eighth, and Jim and me are going to be tied in knots worrying about coupons as well as serving.'

10

Gracie, more interested in her rare visit to His Majesty's Theatre, brushed this triviality aside. 'It'll maybe not be as bad as you think,' and Patsy added, 'You've said yourself that the war's not going to last long.'

'It looks as if it's going to last longer than I thought,' he admitted, 'and you'll change your tune, Gracie, when you just get the bare rations.'

This put a different complexion on things. 'You'll surely let your wife have more?'

'No, I'll be in trouble if I give anybody more than their share, and I can see some of my regulars falling out with me for not letting them have as much as they want.'

His wife came dangerously near to falling out with him the following week when he brought up three pounds of sugar and informed her that it was their allowance for the week. 'It's not enough!' she exclaimed, in disgust. 'I need five pounds, sometimes six.'

'Three's all you'll be getting now.'

Gracie looked at him accusingly. 'You take four spoons in every cup of tea and so does Neil. That's more than a pound each in a week. What about Patsy and me? And puddings?'

'You'll just have to cut down.'

The tables were turned next day when Gracie gave Joe his supper. 'One haddock?' he gasped. 'That's not enough to keep body and soul together.'

'Fish is up in price,' she told him, triumphant at getting her own back, 'and I could only afford four.'

Both Neil and Patsy hooted with laughter at this, and Joe said no more.

As the weeks passed, Gracie, like all housewives in Britain,

11

became adept at spinning out the rations. A thin scraping of butter was all she allowed on toast; the deep sugar spoon in the bowl was replaced by a small teaspoon, and Joe and Neil were shamed into taking only three per cup, because she had stopped taking any at all. Milk puddings were never as sweet as her menfolk liked them, but they didn't dare to pass any comments and soon became so used to the taste that they cut themselves down to two spoons in their tea.

Neil had done a year and four months of his apprenticeship as a motor mechanic, and Patsy had started as an office girl with an insurance firm when she left school last summer, but their wages were so small that their mother was still on a tight budget. It took all Gracie's ingenuity to clothe and feed four on what Joe gave her, and she had to wait until he handed it over on Saturday lunchtime before she could buy in Sunday's dinner, but they certainly never starved.

His mother sometimes wished that Neil had found some other kind of work, his workmates sounded such a rough bunch, and her feelings were strengthened when he came home one day in high spirits. 'We'd all a right laugh this morning. You know I told you a new apprentice was starting? Well, he got the usual works from the boys. First of all, old Crookie . . .'

'Crookie?' Gracie looked puzzled. She thought she knew all the men's names by this time.

'Dougie Cruickshank, you've heard me speaking about him. He's a grim-faced bugger . . .'

'Neil!' The reprimand shot out from his shocked mother. 'I don't allow swearing in this house, you should know that.'

'Sorry, Mum, I forgot. As I was telling you, Crookie's a grim-faced . . . blighter, but he's an awful joker, and he told Harry, that's the lad that started today, to go and ask the storeman for a left-handed screwdriver and . . .'

'I didn't know there were left-handed screwdrivers.'

'There aren't, that's what was so funny, and the storeman played along with Crookie. He sent Harry to ask the foreman for a long stand and promised to have the screwdriver looked out when he came back.'

'What do they use a long stand for?'

'Och, Mum, you're as ignorant as Harry. He stood for about half an hour beside the foreman before it dawned on him they were making a fool of him, but he took it in good part. All new apprentices have to put up with things like that.'

'I don't think it was very nice of the men to do that.'

'It's just for a laugh, Mum.'

'Taking the rise out of a young boy doesn't sound much of a laugh to me, and I'm not sure if that's a decent place for you to be working. I just hope the men don't teach you any more bad language.'

'Ach, Mum!'

Neil's lunch break lasting only three-quarters of an hour, he had to go back to work before Patsy and Joe came in at one, but Gracie recounted the incident to them and was quite put out when Joe roared with laughter. Patsy, like herself, was sorry for Harry, although her father told them it was the usual practice for time-served tradesmen to play pranks on new apprentices.

'I'll never understand men's mentality,' Gracie declared, making Joe laugh even louder.

13

Neil was not in a good mood when he came home for lunch at twelve, two days later. Gracie took one look at his lowering brows and said, 'What's wrong with you? Were you at the end of the teasing today? Now you'll know what it feels like.'

'It wasn't anything like that. It's Olive. She was waiting for me when I came out, and she was determined to walk home with me, though I told her to get lost.'

'I told you not to be nasty to her, Neil.'

'It didn't bother her. I wouldn't let her put her arm in mine though she tried to, but the lads were all laughing at me for walking up the road with a schoolgirl, and I bet I'll get a right earful when I go back.'

'She'll not bother you again if you've upset her.'

'She'd better not!' Neil said, darkly. He'd been mortified to see the bottle-green clad figure waiting for him outside the yard. 'She looked like a top-heavy cucumber with feet,' he spat out in disgust.

When Patsy came in, she was so excited about her promotion from office girl to junior typist that Gracie said nothing to Joe about Neil's upset, but she worried all afternoon in case Olive was getting too fond of him. He wouldn't find it easy to brush her off, and she might cause trouble.

At teatime, Neil cuffed his sister lightly on the cheek when he heard her news. 'Good for you. You'll soon be in charge of that office.'

Anxious to know what had transpired after the interlude at lunchtime, Gracie asked him, 'Did anybody say anything when you went back?'

His face split into a grin. 'Nothing I wasn't expecting. I

14

just laughed when they said I was cradle snatching, and they soon got tired of tormenting me.'

'Aye,' she agreed. 'That was the best thing to do.'

Joe and Patsy were loud in condemnation of Olive when they learned what she had done, but Neil said, 'I was rattled at the time, but I've cooled off now, and I don't think she'll come back. It's the first time she's seen me in my dungers, and the look on her face was enough to make a cat laugh. Her nose crinkled up like she'd touched a dollop of shit.'

Joe slapped his thigh in glee. 'Olive's easy scunnered if she can't stand the smell of a wee bit grease. You should be glad she came, if it put her off you.'

'That's what I was thinking myself,' Neil laughed.

'You haven't washed your hands yet,' Gracie reminded him. 'I'm not wanting oil all over the tablecloth.' She, too, was glad that Olive had been 'scunnered'. She had often moaned herself about having to wash Neil's dungarees and how long they took to dry, but not any more.

Olive was disgruntled. Neil had made it quite clear that he wasn't pleased to see her, and it had been a mistake to go, in more ways than one. She shouldn't have worn her uniform; he had been embarrassed that his workmates – horrible dirty men who had leered into her face – were seeing him with a schoolgirl; and worse, he wasn't so handsome when his face was all streaked with grease. She had been nauseated by his filthy overalls when she tried to slip her arm through his, and had been relieved when he shook her off. She would have to insist that he changed his job before they were married, because she couldn't face having

15

a mechanic for a husband. It would be much too degrading.

The thought of him being her husband cheered her up. If he had a white collar job, it would be sheer heaven to wait for him coming home each night, to let him take her in his arms and kiss her, to have his soft hands running over her body. Absolute bliss! And she was sure it would come to pass, some day. She would just have to figure out another way to get him on his own before she could start working on him.

Furious at the butcher – meat rationing had been introduced on 11 March – Gracie took it out on her husband. 'It's all a trick, if you ask me. One and three-quarters pounds per person per week, he said, but I need something for a dinner and a supper every day. Then he'd the cheek to say we'll get nothing but mutton or rabbit for a wee while.'

Neil screwed up his face. 'Not mutton? Yeugh!'

'Things are getting tight,' Joe said, cautiously.

Gracie was not appeased. 'What right have the Ministry of Food to tell folk what they can and can't eat? How can wives feed a family on what they're allowed? It's like the loaves and fishes all over again. If this war goes on much longer, we'll all be skeletons.'

'It's a good way to keep slim,' Patsy smiled, 'and there's always plenty of tatties.'

Gracie tutted. 'They used to say tatties were fattening, and now they're telling us they're good for you. They just say what they like.'

After tidying up, Gracie vented her anger on the balaclava she was knitting for the 'Comforts for the Troops'

16

campaign, her needles flashing in and out as fast as the needle of her mother's Jones sewing machine. It was very old, marked 'By appointment to Her Majesty Queen Alexandra', but still worked as good as new. She had turned a pair of sheets yesterday, splitting them up the middle where they were worn thin and stitching the side edges together.

By May, Gracie was even more angry at the Ministry of Food. 'It said on the wireless that the sugar ration's to be cut, and the butter's to be halved.'

Joe rolled his eyes. 'You don't need to tell me. It's bad enough just now having to explain to folk that money doesn't matter these days, without the rations being cut down. How will old wives understand they can only get half a pound of sugar and a quarter of butter, when they see I've got more in the shop? And it's not just food. They've to contend with other things as well. I was sorry for one poor old soul this afternoon. She must be over eighty, and she'd been caught in that crowd that wrecked Mosely's meeting at the Castlegate. She was in a real state, she thought the Jerries had come.'

'That Mosely!' Gracie exclaimed. 'Him and his black-shirts, they're just din-raisers.'

'Aye, you're right there.' Her husband was pleased that he had taken her mind off the cut in the rations. He had to put up with his customers moaning at him all day, and he wanted peace and quiet to read the evening paper when he came home. He lifted his head and smiled when Patsy walked in, but his peace was shattered when Neil appeared minutes later.

'I want to join up,' Neil told him, 'but I've to get your permission, Dad.'

Joe's eyes darkened. 'Well, you're not getting it.'

Gracie, halting in the act of dishing up the supper, came over to the table with the serving spoon in her hand. 'Neil, what are you thinking about? You can't join up. You've still to finish your apprenticeship.'

'I could finish it in the army.'

Joe thumped the table with his fist. 'You're not going in the army, and that's final.'

'I'll be called up in a year or so, anyway,' Neil pointed out, indignantly, 'so what's the difference?'

'You've just said it,' Joe thundered. 'A year or two. The war could be over by that time and you wouldn't need to go.'

'I want to go!' Neil roared.

Putting her hand on her brother's arm, Patsy said softly, 'Calm down, Neil. You'll never get anywhere shouting at Dad like that. Why don't you finish your apprenticeship first, then see how you feel about joining up?'

He turned to her earnestly. 'All my pals are in the forces already, the last one signed up today, and I want to do my bit too.'

'I know how you must feel,' Patsy sympathised, 'but think of Mum and Dad.'

'It's them I was thinking of, them and all the other mums and dads. The army needs young men like me.' He looked at his father again. 'Once I'm eighteen, I won't need your permission.'

The determination on his face made his mother's heart turn over, and Joe muttered, 'If you still feel the same way when November comes, I won't try to talk you out of it, but I'd like you to think it over carefully before that. The wartime army's not a bed of roses, no matter how exciting you think it'll be. Ask any old soldier from the last time.'

Aware that his father was meeting him halfway, Neil said, 'I'm sorry I flew off the handle at you, and I promise to think it over, but I'm sure I'll still feel the same in November.'

When she learned that Neil was intending to join up when he was eighteen, Olive made up her mind to put more pressure on him. She couldn't let him get away without giving her some guarantee that he'd come back to her. Once he was in the army, he'd be out of her control, and she wouldn't know what he was getting up to. Surely she could make him fall in love with her in six months? The problem was . . . how?

# Chapter Two

In June, the newspapers and wireless reported the evacuation of Dunkirk, the last British troops leaving from Cherbourg, as the *Press and Journal* stated on 1 July. Most of the 51st Scottish Division, however, were left behind to fight a rearguard action and were taken prisoner. This was a bitter blow to Aberdeen, the home of the Gordon Highlanders. It was the first real indication that the war was not running well for Britain. There had been several air raids in the city, of course, but the 612 Squadron from Dyce usually managed to divert the enemy bombers before they reached the coast, and the Aberdonians had had a false sense of security. Now most families had or knew someone who had escaped from, or been lost at, Dunkirk or who was a prisoner in the enemy's hands and the war was affecting the citizens for the first time.

Gracie Ferris was deeply thankful that Joe had refused to give his permission for their son to join up when he wanted to. 'Neil could have been one of the men that were killed on the beaches if you'd let him go,' she said one night.

'He wouldn't have finished his infantry training yet,' her husband told her, 'and maybe this business'll have made him think twice about going.'

On 9 July, the headlines – with the intention, no doubt, of giving hope, but actually giving rise to renewed fears in all minds – screamed MEN OF DUNKIRK RE-EQUIPPED – READY FOR BATTLE OF BRITAIN. Gracie, positive that Neil had seen sense about volunteering, was more upset that the government was speaking about taking all garden railings to make munitions, although there were no railings in her part of King Street. 'It's interfering with people's privacy,' she said to Joe.

'They wouldn't be left alive to enjoy any privacy if there was no munitions,' he reminded her. 'There's word of Hitler going to start an invasion.'

Joe rushed in one lunchtime a few days later brandishing the *Press and Journal* he had bought that morning. 'Listen to this, Gracie. It says, IF THIS IS DER TAG, WE'RE READY.'

'Der tag?' Gracie looked perplexed.

'German for "the day",' he explained. 'It means that we're ready for the invasion if this is the day, and they say the rumours about 600,000 invaders coming are just moonshine.'

'Thank goodness for that. Now, when are you giving me the extra two pounds of sugar we're supposed to get for making jam? I could maybe get berries from the Green on Friday.'

Shaking his head, Joe muttered, 'Do you not have anything in your head at all except your stomach?'

On 12 July, a gorgeously warm day, Neil was using a wire brush to clean the plugs of an Albion when he heard a crump-crump sound as if bombs had fallen some distance

21

off. Hardly able to believe that the enemy would attack in the middle of the day, he turned and looked uncertainly at the time-served mechanics who seemed to be as non-plussed as he was. 'What's happened to our Spitties?' one of them asked, of nobody in particular, and another man answered, 'I bet they're chasing the Jerries back now.'

In the next instant, the scream of descending bombs made them fling themselves down on the cement floor just as the explosions came, in quick succession and so close that Neil could feel the workshop floor reverberating under him.

When the next series of bombs fell, they seemed to be much farther away, so he sat up – his teeth chattering, his body aching from being gripped in to make a smaller target – and gave a low, slightly hysterical giggle at his own stupidity. His legs were shaking as he got up, and he hoped that no one saw him when he leaned against the lorry for a moment. This was no way for a future soldier to behave.

Patsy crossed King Street, walked down Mealmarket Street, up Littlejohn Street and down Upperkirkgate, going slowly to get the benefit of the sunshine. She heard a few bangs, but as she wasn't far from a munitions factory, she assumed that something must have gone off accidentally and she carried on up Schoolhill. When she came to the gate to the 'Trainie Park' as her father called the Union Terrace Gardens, she thought of going down the steps and walking along the paths to her office, but a glance at her watch told her that she didn't have time, so she cut through the slip road past the statue of William Wallace as she normally did. She was turning into Union Terrace when an aeroplane, flying very low, appeared from nowhere. One of ours, she thought, and didn't halt, but a loud, staccato burst of machine-gun fire made her stop in her tracks, the red-hot tracer bullets dancing along the pavement only inches away from her.

'Get doon! It's a bloody Jerry!' The man's yell came from behind her, and a shove in the small of her back knocked her to the ground. When she got her breath back, she saw that a tramcar had pulled up between stops, and that the passengers had all jumped off and were running to shelter in a shop at the other side of the street.

In a minute or so, the man at her back shouted, 'Look! The Spitfires are efter him.' Feeling safer now that the German pilot's attention was fully occupied in trying to save his own skin, they stood up to watch, and people came running out of shops and offices to see the toy-like planes darting back and forth beside the bomber, forcing it away from the area, an area congested with people in the busy lunch hour.

A great, triumphant shout arose from massed throats. 'He's going down! He's down! They've got him!'

The whole incident had taken less than five minutes, but it was something that Patsy – and all the other people there – would never forget, and when the quiet voice spoke beside her, she was startled. 'I hope you werena hurt when I shoved you, but you coulda been killed, you ken.'

Turning round, she saw him for the first time – a slight, short, oldish man with glasses, in white overalls splattered with all the colours of the rainbow. A painter, she thought, in wry amusement. She'd been saved from death by a painter. 'I didn't really take in what was going on, and I'm glad you pushed me down. Thanks very much.'

He grinned at her. 'Nae bother, lassie. Now, are you sure you're OK? Hiv you far to go?'

'Just along there a wee bit, at the other side.'

'So long, then, it's been nice meetin' you.' Tipping his cloth cap, he walked away, whistling.

She had to smile at his matter-of-factness after the drama they had witnessed, but she dusted down her skirt with her hands before finishing her journey, her wobbling legs soon regaining strength. The other watchers dispersed, too, still talking excitedly – as they would for years to come to those who would listen – about their hair-raising experience.

When she heard the noise of bombs exploding, fortunately not too close, Hetty Potter's first concern was for her husband, who worked in the centre of town. Her children had gone on a picnic to Hazlehead Park on the outskirts of town, and would be well away from any enemy activity – or so she believed.

Raymond was barely inside the house when he burst out, 'Me and Olive had to dodge among the trees at Hazlehead or else we'd have been machine-gunned.'

'Oh, God!' Hetty gasped, then looked sceptical. 'It's not true. You're just trying to give me a fright.'

'It is true, Mum,' Olive said quietly, 'and when we were coming home on the tram, we heard men telling the conductor that they worked in the nurseries at Pinewood, and they had to jump over a dyke to save themselves.'

The Pinewood nurseries, where young trees and shrubs were cultivated for selling, were situated just behind the Park, so Hetty realised that her children were telling the truth, and she sat down with a thump, her face chalk-white. 'You should have come home right away. I thought you were safe, but . . .' She wrung her hands in agitation.

'Mum, we're OK,' Olive assured her, 'and it was all over in a few minutes.'

Raymond grinned. 'It was kind of exciting while it lasted though, and I don't think he was aiming at us anyway.'

On tenterhooks until Martin came home, Hetty flew into his arms as soon as he appeared. 'Are you all right?'

'I'm fine,' he assured her, 'but a lot of men were killed at Hall Russell's. The boiler room got a direct hit. I'd an appointment to see one of the directors at four, to explain some of the legal jargon on a contract they have from the War Ministry for some naval boats, and I didn't know they'd been bombed. When I got there it was absolute pandemonium.'

Hetty was silent for a moment, then she whispered, 'What if you'd had to go in the forenoon? You'd have been there at the time the bombs fell.'

'But I wasn't, thank God.'

Raymond, who had been waiting in suppressed excitement to tell of his lucky escape, took the opportunity of the slight lull to say, 'We were in the thick of it.'

Olive could tell that her father had been badly shocked by what he had seen. 'It was nothing, Dad. We got a scare, but I don't think we were in any real danger.'

Mrs Mavor, Gracie's neighbour on the same landing, came to her door in the afternoon. 'Did you hear aboot the folk that was machine-gunned in Union Terrace at dinnertime? Doesn't your Patsy work there?'

Gracie's heart raced uncontrollably. 'Her office is about halfway along . . . oh, I hope she's all right.'

Regretting having upset her, Mrs Mavor tried to reassure her. 'You'd have heard by this time if she wasna.'

'I suppose so.' Gracie, grateful for her concern, gave her a cup of tea, and having been warned, was more able to face the other tenants in the building when they came to tell her the same thing. They were only being neighbourly after all, rallying round her as they would to anyone in trouble. But even although Mrs Mavor stayed with her for almost an hour, she felt nauseous until Patsy came home, unharmed but eager to tell her mother what had happened.

Gracie was horrified when she heard how close her daughter had come to death, and when Joe came in with the news that Hall Russell's shipyard had been bombed, and that the single aircraft had caused mayhem all over Aberdeen, she telephoned to ask Hetty if any of her family had been hurt. 'Olive and Raymond were machine-gunned, as well,' she told Joe in a few minutes, 'but they weren't hit either, thank God. Oh, that damned German, putting the fear of death in folk.'

Knowing how much his wife was against even the mildest of swearwords, Joe let it go. It just showed how upset she was.

Neither that night's *Evening Express* nor the following morning's *Press and Journal* reported the full story, which spread by word of mouth, exaggerated a little more each time it was passed on. Gracie's conviction that this would put the final nail in the coffin of Neil's plan to join up was very wide of the mark. Her son was harbouring a deep hatred of the enemy for this act of barbarism and was all the more determined to enter the fight against the Axis powers.

Over the next few weeks, as the newspapers reported repeated attacks on London, Gracie felt anxious about her brother and his family. Croydon was one of the places mentioned that had been severely hit by bombs, but with so many enemy planes shot down, she believed that the Germans would abandon their fruitless attempts to force Britain's capital to its knees. It came as a shock, therefore, when she received a note from Donnie's wife, Helene.

Thursday.

Dear Gracie and Joe,

I hope you don't mind, but I'm taking Queenie away from the bombing. We have had air raids nearly every night for weeks, and we hardly get any sleep. We're taking the night train on Friday, and we'll arrive in Aberdeen early Saturday morning. I'm sorry not to give you more warning, but I don't want to wait any longer.

Love as always, Helene.

'It must be terrible for them,' Gracie wailed, returning the letter to the envelope, 'and Donnie should give up his shop and come up here with them.'

Joe shook his head. 'It's all very well saying that, but the newsagent's is his livelihood and he's worked hard to build up a trade. I wouldn't leave if I was him, but I'm glad he's had the sense to get Helene and Queenie away.'

Gracie's mind had already jumped ahead. 'I'll have to give them Neil's room – I'll give it a good going over –

27

and he can sleep on the bed-settee. I'm sure he won't mind in the circumstances and it'll just be for a wee while.'

'No, Gracie, it'll be longer than a wee while. Look, I can sleep with Neil, Helene can sleep with you, and Queenie and Patsy'll manage on the three-quarter bed.'

Although it was into August, Saturday morning was cold and misty – the damp even seemed to pervade the glass roof of the Joint Station – and Gracie and Patsy were both shivering after only ten minutes. After another half hour, Gracie began to panic. 'Maybe the train's been bombed. For all we know, they could be lying dead somewhere.'

Patsy gripped her mother's icy hand. 'They'd have put up a notice here if the train had been bombed or announced it.'

'No, they wouldn't. We're always being told careless talk costs lives.'

'It's not the same thing,' the girl said, patiently, 'but I'll go and ask, if you like?' The stationmaster came out of his office at that moment, so she ran over to him. 'Excuse me. Can you tell me about the London train, please?'

The man's stride did not alter. 'Two and a half hours late at Newcastle, but the last word we had was that it had made up twelve minutes since then.'

'Thank you very much.' Patsy turned and walked back to her mother to relay the information. 'Two and a half hours less twelve minutes, that's . . . just over two and a quarter hours, and we've been here three-quarters of an hour, so it'll be an hour and a half before they come. We can't stand here – we'll be frozen to the spot. Will we go home and come back?'

Gracie shook her head. 'It's hardly worth it, and we might miss them.' After pondering for a moment, she burst out, 'I

28

know! We'll go to the fish market and get some fish. Helene says the fish down there's never as fresh as it is here.'

'Good idea.' They linked arms and made their way out on to Guild Street, Gracie's feet protesting after standing for so long in one place.

What Gracie called the fish market was not the proper fish market on the quay, where trawlers landed their catches and fish merchants bid for them, it was part of the New Market, a conglomeration of various kinds of shops under one roof. Downstairs from the main arcade, with an entrance from The Green, a number of stalls – manned by the wives of fishermen from the small coastal villages – sold fresh fish of various kinds, and each woman who shopped there patronised her own favourite stall. Patsy could tell no difference between them, and smiled when her mother made straight for the one she preferred.

There followed a long discussion on which particular fish was best that day, and how many she would need to feed six, which led to an explanation of why she was buying more than she normally did. After that, the other woman said that her sister was still in London, but that she was speaking about coming to Aberdeen, too. Finally, Gracie decided to buy some filleted haddock, and while her change was being counted, she said, 'I thought we were bad having to stand so long in that draughty station, but you're worse, having to work with ice-cold fish all day – in a draught, as well.'

The woman gave a roar of laughter. 'Och, I'm used to it, and it's nae so bad as what I did when I was a young lassie. A bunch o' us used to follow the herrin' fleet, an' we'd to stand on quaysides in Yarmouth an' Lerwick in a' kinds of weather to gut the fish. I dinna cut my fingers to bits now – well, nae so often. Cheerio, an' I'll see you next time.'

'There's always somebody worse off than yourself,' Gracie observed, as she and Patsy went through the open gateway out to The Green – where, at the beginning of the thirteenth century, William the Lion had a palace, and where, a century later, Edward III's army defeated the city's inhabitants. The rich merchants of olden days sold their wares on The Green to any passing travellers, but granite setts – or cassies, as local people called them – had long since replaced the grass, and although the square was lined now by small shops, it was let out to outlying farmers on Fridays and Saturdays.

'We've still plenty of time,' Gracie went on, 'so we could take a look round some of the stalls for a wee while.'

Because The Green market mainly sold fresh produce – fruit and vegetables, eggs, butter – which Gracie could get from Joe, she bought nothing, but spent half an hour in comparing prices. When they reached Rennie's Wynd, she said, 'Maybe we should get back to the station, Patsy. The train could have made up some more time.'

They had been waiting for only about seven minutes when it steamed in, and the doors clattered as the passengers came off. There were so many carriages that it was fully another three minutes before Helene and Queenie neared the barriers, their wan faces pinched, their eyes dark-circled and deep in their sockets. They brightened and hurried forward when they saw Gracie and Patsy, and as soon as they passed the ticket collectors, Gracie enveloped them both in her arms.

'What a nightmare of a journey,' Helene gulped. 'We had to stop outside Peterborough for ages . . . they were

30

being bombed somewhere near . . . and again just outside York. I thought we'd never get here.'

'Give me your case.' The significance of the single small suitcase escaped Gracie, she was so glad to see them in one piece. 'You're here now, and that's what matters.' She fell into step with Helene, behind their daughters. 'There's been some raids here, as well, but nothing like you've had in London, so the roses'll soon be back in your cheeks.'

Helene hesitated. 'I'm not staying. I promised Donnie I'd be back on Tuesday morning. I only came with Queenie.'

'You can't go back! Be sensible.'

'Gracie, leave it for now. I don't want Queenie any more upset than she is.'

'Sorry. I didn't mean . . . I should have thought.'

Nothing further was said about the return to London until after the two girls were in bed, then Helene turned to Joe. 'I've told Gracie I'm leaving Queenie here and going back on Monday night. I can't leave Donnie on his own, and we've to take our chance, that's all. If we go, we go together.'

Joe frowned. 'What about Queenie? Have you thought what it could do to her if she lost her mother and her father in one fell swoop?'

Helene's hand went up to her brow, as if trying to massage unwelcome thoughts out of her head. 'Donnie and I have gone over and over it, Joe. He wanted me to stay here, but I love him. Can't you understand?'

'You mean you love him more than you love your daughter?'

'It's not like that at all. I do love Queenie, but I could live without her if I knew she was safe, but . . .' Her hand dropped to wipe a persistent tear. 'If anything happened to Donnie, I wouldn't want to go on living, either.'

Forcing out the words through her tightened throat, Gracie said, rather stiffly, 'You'd have to, for Queenie's sake.'

'It's for her sake I'm doing it – she'll have more chance of survival up here, and if anything should happen to Donnie and me, she'll have you. If she stayed in London, she could be at school when . . . and she'd have nobody – my parents are too old to look after her. That's why I . . .' She stopped, biting her lip, and added in a trembling voice, 'It was a difficult decision to make, Gracie. Please don't make me go over it all again. I love my daughter as much as you love yours, but . . .'

'Aye,' Joe put in, gruffly. 'Well, we'll all pray that it never comes to it but if it . . . we'll look after Queenie.'

'I can't understand how any mother . . .' Gracie began, but Joe didn't let her finish. 'She's trying to give Queenie a chance and it's her decision, whatever you think.'

Helene's eyes met her sister-in-law's, beseeching her to try to understand, and after a prolonged pause, Gracie said slowly, 'I won't say any more then, and I promise we'll look after Queenie if the worst comes to the worst.'

Joe smiled at his wife. 'I'll put the kettle on for a cup of tea, and we won't speak about it again.'

Over tea, Helene told Joe and Gracie of the nights on end spent in a concrete shelter with neighbours and how the trauma had been eased by little incidents such as one old man forgetting to put in his false teeth and having to be restrained by the wardens from going back to his house to get them. 'In the morning, there was a huge hole in his roof, and part of his chimney had fallen on his bed. The glass with his teeth in was lying on the floor, and if he'd gone back for them he could have been killed.'

Helene purposely didn't tell them that her house had also been damaged in that raid, but went on, 'Bill Tompkins, two doors along, died a year before the war and Dot, his wife, keeps his ashes in a casket on her mantelpiece. She takes it with her to the shelter, and she always says, "On the day he wed me, he promised he'd look after me for the rest of my life, and I'm not letting the crafty bugger off now, war or no war. Anyway, I don't want Jerry scattering my old man all over South Norwood." What a character she is, Joe, keeps us all in stitches.'

Gracie found it impossible to believe that people could laugh when bombs were falling all around them, and Helene, aware of what she was thinking, said, 'We'd all go mad if we didn't joke about it.'

Gracie looked repentant. 'I'm sorry, Helene, I didn't know how bad things were for you. How can you . . .?'

'We have to put up with it, there's nothing else to do.'

'You must be tired,' Joe said, suddenly. 'You'll be ready for your bed.'

'I haven't slept in a bed for so long, it's going to feel queer.' Helene yawned unexpectedly and gave a giggle. 'I am tired, though. Goodnight.'

However queer it was for Helene to be in a bed again, she slept until almost lunchtime the following day and Gracie left her undisturbed. In the afternoon, they paid a brief visit to Hetty, surprised that Queenie, although a few months older than Raymond, was so much shorter.

The three women talked for over an hour, while Queenie sat beside Olive, uncomfortably aware that this cousin was not as friendly as Patsy. At last, Gracie said, 'We'd better go. Patsy promised to have our supper ready at six.'

As they walked the short distance to the tramstop, Helene said, 'You didn't say much, Queenie. Auntie Hetty must think you're very shy.'

'Olive didn't say anything, either.'

Gracie patted her niece's head. 'Och, don't mind Olive, she's a stuck-up wee monkey. If nobody's paying attention to her, she goes in the huff.'

After teatime, Joe said, 'Gracie, what about a tune to buck us up?' He had bought the old piano secondhand years before so that his children could learn to play, but Gracie had turned out to be more musical than either Neil or Patsy, although she'd never had lessons. 'She plays by ear,' Joe went on, proudly, 'anything you like.'

'I'm sure Helene doesn't want to . . .' Gracie protested.

'I'd love a sing-song,' Helene smiled. 'In the shelter, we sing all the old music hall songs . . . "My Old Man", "Down at the Old Bull and Bush", that sort of thing. One of the men always takes his harmonica with him, and he's ever so good.'

'Please, Auntie Gracie?' Queenie pleaded.

Gracie would have preferred not to – she hadn't played a note since her father died over a year and a half before – but she sat down on the piano stool and let her fingers run lightly over the yellowing keys. 'I'm not all that good, but here goes.'

After giving them her own favourites – 'When Your Hair Has Turned To Silver', 'Silver Threads Amongst The Gold', 'Won't You Buy My Pretty Flowers' – she turned round. 'Play some of your songs, Patsy. Queenie doesn't know my kind.'

Patsy's repertoire consisted of songs currently popular on the wireless – 'Roll Out the Barrel', 'Run Rabbit Run', etc. – for which she had bought the music for sixpence a sheet in Woolworth's. While the others sang – Joe and Neil joining in lustily – Gracie sat back in her chair, wondering mournfully when they would see Helene again . . . if they would ever see her again.

She started as Joe nudged her. 'Cheer up. Everything'll be all right.'

On Monday afternoon, when Helene said she wanted to show Queenie a bit of Aberdeen, Gracie did not offer to accompany them. It was only right that they should be on their own on this last day, for they might not see each other again for a long time. When they came back, they were in high spirits, although Helene's eyes were perhaps a little too bright and Queenie's cheeks a fraction too red. Gracie could never get over how unlike they were. Helene's hair was as black as it had ever been, her complexion almost as dark as a gypsy's; Queenie had fair skin like her father, though his hair was ginger, and hers a blondie-gold. They quietened down during tea, and by seven o'clock, when Helene had to leave for the station, they were both on the verge of tears.

Helene hadn't wanted anyone except Joe to go with her, but Gracie knew that Queenie would not forgive her if she wasn't allowed to wave her mother off, so only Neil stayed at home. When the inevitable, dreaded moment arrived, Helene waited until the last possible second before giving Queenie a quick hug and going into a carriage. Gracie came forward to put her arm round the girl and Patsy held her hand until the train was out of sight.

35

Joe blew his nose loudly. 'I know you three lovely ladies are going to argue about who's going to take my arms, so . . .' He linked arms with the two girls, and Patsy felt a surge of love for her father for putting the smile back on Queenie's face. He would be fifty in a few years and his hair, what was left of it, was steely grey. If she ever had to go away from home, she would miss him as much as she'd miss her mother. She could understand how Queenie must feel, and she would do her best to make her feel part of their family.

When they went into the house, Neil said, 'I'll sleep on the settee in the kitchen, Mum, if you want to give Queenie a room to herself.'

It was Queenie who answered. 'I don't want to put you out of your bed. Thank you for the offer, but I'd rather share with Patsy.'

Neil did not argue. He was still planning on going into the army when he was eighteen, and he wouldn't have long to wait now. Once he was away, Queenie might take advantage of the empty room. Once he was away – he couldn't wait to get away, for Olive had been a proper pest lately. She didn't meet him outside his work, thank goodness, but she had taken to lying in wait for him on his way home at teatime, and going on about how much she liked him and asking how much he liked her. It was awful, and what could he say? If he told the truth and said that he hated her, it would cause a row between their mothers, and he couldn't chance saying that he liked her, otherwise she'd hang round his neck for evermore. Up to now, he'd got away with mumbling things like, 'I'll have to go or I'll be late for my tea,' or pretending not to have heard and speaking about something else, but she was so determined to trap him that she wouldn't always be so easily brushed off.

# Chapter Three

No great damage had been done in Aberdeen since Queenie had arrived, and the bombs that had fallen had been nowhere near King Street, but when an alert sounded, her stomach churned, her mouth went dry and she knew that she would never forget the terrors of the Blitz. Helene wrote to her every Sunday, assuring her that the enemy planes ignored their street now and, although the girl did not believe that one street could escape for so long when the rest of London was being razed to the ground, her haunted eyes had gradually cleared, her hollow cheeks filled out and her smile was more genuine.

She had been fifteen in April, and could have left school last year, but her parents wanted her to continue her education, and Gracie had enrolled her at the Central Secondary School; it was run by the council, but her aunt had said that it was as good as any private school, and she had done well in the six weeks since she started. At first, she had found it hard to understand the Aberdonians, particularly when they spoke quickly, but she had grown used to the flat vowel sounds and the guttural consonants and was amused when her school friends told her that she was the one who spoke 'funny'.

Apart from missing her mother and father, she was enjoying her enforced stay in Aberdeen. Uncle Joe and Neil teased her constantly, but it was all in fun, and they laughed when she gave back as good as she got. Patsy treated her like a real sister, listening to her opinion when they discussed things, helping her to experiment with new hairstyles, and making up her face in the privacy of their shared room. Being an only child, she had often felt lonely at home, but she had plenty of company here and only Auntie Gracie made her feel as if she were being tolerated rather than loved.

Not that anything had ever been said, Queenie admitted to herself as she walked home from school one afternoon. It was her aunt's manner, an expression on her face when she didn't know anyone was watching her, that suggested she wasn't very happy with the arrangement; and it wasn't always there, just occasionally, mostly when she was tired.

Passing the familiar little grocer's shop, Queenie put her head round the door and called, 'Hi, Uncle Joe.'

No matter how busy he was, Joe Ferris always took time to smile and wave to her and she carried on contentedly to the house. 'I'm home, Auntie Gracie,' she said, as she threw her schoolbag through her open bedroom door.

'So I see,' Gracie grunted, then turned with the hint of a smile. 'You'll be needing a cuppie to keep the wolf from the door till suppertime?' She couldn't treat Donnie's daughter as she did her own though she had tried, for she had nothing against the girl herself. She still felt angry at Helene for going back to London, that was the whole trouble.

'I'll make it,' Queenie said, brightly, lifting the kettle from the stove and taking it over to the sink. 'I don't know what you've got in the oven, but it smells delicious.'

'Och, it's nothing much. Just a little something I made up out of my head.'

'Brain stew?'

Gracie couldn't help laughing. 'Aye, that's it. Brain stew with dumplings.'

Giggling, more at the unexpectedness of her aunt's little joke than her actual words, Queenie carried the kettle back and lit a gas ring. 'Miss McFadden said my French was above average,' she volunteered, as she took two cups and saucers out of the cupboard. 'She said I should concentrate on that for one of my Highers when the time comes.'

An involuntary thrill of pride shot through Gracie. 'Well, I always knew you were a clever lassie.' Realising that this was the first time she had ever praised the girl, she added, 'I maybe don't show my feelings like your mum, but it's just the way I am. I'm going to miss you when you go home.'

Queenie's eyes lit up as she turned to hug her aunt. 'I'm going to miss all of you, too. Sometimes I feel I don't want to go home, I love being here, but I love Mum and Dad more. Do you understand what I mean?'

Embarrassed at the sudden show of affection, Gracie pushed the girl away. 'I understand and it's only natural. Now, are you going to let that kettle boil dry?'

Grinning again, Queenie filled the teapot and studied her aunt while she waited for it to infuse. She knew that Gracie was younger than her mother, but she looked much older. Her mousey hair, shot through with grey, was pulled back off her face, emphasising the gauntness of her cheeks. She was very thin, but maybe that was because she sacrificed most of her rations to make sure everyone else had enough to eat.

Poor Gracie, Queenie thought, love for the woman coursing through her as never before. Even with the ten shillings her mother sent every week for her keep, her aunt must have a hard struggle to make ends meets, not like Auntie Hetty, who had no worries about money. She had lovely Axminster carpets in every room except the dining room which had Wilton, while the floors in King Street just had congoleum squares with surrounds stained dark brown. At Rubislaw Den, the mahogany furniture reflected like mirrors, but Gracie's was a dull oak, solid but old-fashioned, and not really pleasing to the eye. Her curtains had been bought by the yard from Cameron's in Broad Street, she had told Queenie once, and she had run them up herself on her Jones sewing machine, but Hetty's had been made to measure by Galloway and Sykes, a furniture shop in Union Street which was so high class that Gracie had said she never dared to set foot inside it, adding, with a little laugh, 'Even the wee cushions sitting on the fancy suites in their windows are beyond my purse.'

Hetty's husband was a solicitor, of course, Queenie mused, not a small shopkeeper, so they had a big salary coming in and would have to keep up the same standard as the people he worked with. It was no hardship for them to send Olive to Medical School, and she seemed to be enjoying it though she hadn't been there long. Raymond, the same age as she was herself, was still at Gordon's College, so he was probably going on to the university like his sister. Her mother and father had never mentioned that for her, but surely the war would be over and she would be back in South Norwood by the time she was old enough for the decision to be made.

'The lassie's fitted in well,' Joe observed one night.

Gracie smiled. 'She was a bit quiet at first, for she must have missed her mum and dad, but she soon bucked up.'

'She's a wee comic sometimes, imitating her teachers and her school chums, she fair brightens the place up.'

'And she never loses her temper, though you and Neil tease the life out of her. Patsy and her are real pals, as well.'

'Aye, well,' Joe said, proudly, 'Patsy gets on fine with everybody.'

One Sunday, the Potter family arrived at King Street just after lunch. The visit had not been arranged and Olive was delighted to find Neil at home – he usually contrived to be out when he knew they were coming – but her pleasure dimmed as time went on, because he was too intent on cracking jokes with Queenie to pay any attention to her. When she had first learned that their London cousin was to be living with the Ferrises, Olive hadn't been too bothered. Queenie was a kid, only fifteen, and presented no challenge as far as Neil was concerned. She had been disconcerted when she first saw the girl, although she had been sure that such a chocolate-box prettiness wouldn't appeal to Neil. Seeing them laughing and sparring with each other today, however, was more than just disconcerting, it was down-right upsetting. It was probably all innocent fun but it was easy for fun to become serious.

'Neil,' she said, loudly to make sure he heard, 'have you seen any good films lately?'

There was a slight frown on his face as he turned to her. 'Nothing startling. Have you?'

41

'I haven't been to the cinema for ages, but I wondered if there was anything you would recommend.'

Her 'hoity-toity' manner of speaking had always irked him, but he caught his mother's cautioning eye and went across to sit beside Olive. 'There's a Fred Astaire–Ginger Rogers on next week, I think, if you like them. It's been here before, and it's quite good.'

Knowing that he was interested in dancing, she smiled. 'I might go to see it, if I can find someone to go with.'

He didn't rise to the bait. 'Get Raymond to go with you. He likes them as well. Don't you, Raymond?'

'I like them,' Raymond muttered, 'but I don't like going to the pictures with her.'

'Why don't *you* go with her, Neil?' Joe's solution was met with a grim glare from his son.

'I saw it the last time it was here.'

The brief silence was broken by Patsy. 'I'll go with you, Olive, if you want?'

'Don't bother,' was the frosty answer.

Angry at her husband for making the suggestion, and at her son for being so rude in his refusal, Gracie turned hastily to Hetty. 'There's a sale on at Watt and Milne's just now, and they've got corsets from five shillings a pair.'

Her sister was most indignant. 'I don't need new corsets. The ones I have are firm enough, it's this old skirt that's all out of shape.'

Martin and Joe were talking about football, so Raymond and Neil thankfully joined in. Olive was staring straight ahead with a face like thunder, and Patsy winked at Queenie and shrugged, as if to say, 'Never mind her, she's sulking.'

It was fury that was consuming Olive, not pique. Neil had insulted her in front of everybody but she would make him pay for it.

When Martin said they would have to go, they all stood up and Olive was amazed to see Neil tickling Queenie when she passed him on her way to get the coats from her bedroom. It was as if he couldn't keep his hands off her, and Olive's heart felt crushed by a heavy weight. He might not be in love with the girl yet, but it was more than likely that he would be soon, if he carried on like that. What could she do to prevent it? Neil would be angry if she said anything to him, but warning Queenie might be a good idea. She would say that she had a prior claim to Neil, that they had an understanding, and the Londoner was so young that she would take it as gospel and discourage him.

Two days before his eighteenth birthday, Neil again tackled his father about joining the army, and this time Joe merely said, 'You haven't changed your mind, then?'

'No, I'm more determined than ever.'

'Aye, well, that's it, I suppose.'

Gracie did not interfere. Her husband, although he was an easygoing man as a rule, could dig his heels in if he felt like it, and her son was old enough to know his own mind. It was hard for her to let him go but she couldn't tie him to her apron strings for ever. In any case, it was four against one, because Patsy and Queenie were on Neil's side, thrilled because one of the family would be in the armed forces.

Only two weeks after his medical, a large envelope arrived for Neil. 'I've to report on the second of December at

Chilwell in Nottingham for training with the Durham Light Infantry.' Excitement was building up inside him. His dream was coming true at last.

'I thought it was the Ordnance Corps you'd joined,' Gracie observed, puzzled.

'They've to do their infantry training first,' Joe said, 'and he'll be sent to the Ordnance Corps after that. They'll not turn down mechanics, though they've just done two years of their apprenticeship.'

'It's all more experience,' Neil pointed out. 'I was told they'll teach me about all kinds of vehicles.'

'They haven't given you much time,' Gracie moaned. 'Just two days?'

'It's long enough,' Joe told her. 'Tell your foreman when you go in that you'll be stopping work tonight. You can go to Rubislaw Den tonight after teatime, and that'll let you have a free day tomorrow to let you do whatever you want.'

Neil would rather have slipped away with no fuss, but his mother would be disappointed if he didn't say goodbye to her sister. 'Mum, you'd better phone Hetty to let her know I'll be coming, but don't tell her I've got my marching orders. I want to surprise them.'

'I'm never sure if it was a good idea getting the phone in here,' Gracie remarked. 'I don't mind the neighbours using it if they need a doctor, but sometimes they take advantage and speak to their friends for ages. One or two, mentioning no names, just come to be nosey.'

Joe laughed. 'They wouldn't find out much when the phone's in the lobby?'

'Oh, they pop their heads round the kitchen door to tell

44

me they're finished. It's just an excuse to see if I've got anything new. Fat chance of that!'

Neil did surprise Hetty Potter that night, when he told her when he had to leave. 'Already? My goodness, they didn't let you have much warning, did they?'

'That's what Mum said, but it's better like this. I didn't say anything to her, but I'm really looking forward to it.'

'You young lads,' his aunt smiled. 'You can't wait to get away from your mothers, can you? Thank heaven Raymond's too young to go.'

Her son looked at Neil with envy. 'I'll join up as soon as I'm old enough. I just wish I could be going with you.'

Olive was less enthusiastic; she had hoped that Neil would not have to go for weeks yet, and she still hadn't succeeded in getting him to say he liked her. Doing her best to hide her dismay, she told him that she was pleased for him and kept a smile fixed firmly on her face.

Martin, who did not come home until nearly eight o'clock, also turned out to be envious of Neil. 'I've been thinking of offering my services, but I'm probably too old.'

'I should think you are!' Hetty burst out, indignant that her husband could even think of going. 'You'll be forty-one in three months, and you did your bit in the last war.'

Martin shrugged wryly. 'Not for very long, but I won't do anything about it just yet.'

'One of the lads who used to work with me joined the Royal Artillery a couple of years ago,' Neil remarked. 'He's been in Egypt since before the war, the lucky blighter, seeing the world at the army's expense.'

'You'll probably see too much of the world before

45

you're done. On the other hand, you could meet a lovely girl, like I did, thousands of miles from home.' Martin smiled fondly at his wife.

Neil grinned. 'I'd forgotten you were in the ANZACs, but I won't be looking for a wife for a long time. I'm too young.'

'Don't you believe it,' Hetty laughed. 'Martin and I were both only eighteen when he came to Aberdeen – and we fell in love as soon as we saw each other.'

Finding it difficult to believe that this middle-aged man and woman had once been young and in love, Neil muttered, 'I suppose I'll find the girl for me some day.'

Olive felt as though a knife had twisted in her heart. The girl for Neil was sitting less than three feet away from him, if he only knew it. 'Will you write to me?' she asked.

For a second, his brows came down, but he answered with a light laugh. 'I might drop you a few lines if I get time.'

He was so offhand that she could have shaken him. 'Well, I intend writing to you, anyway, once I know your address.'

The slight frown was there again but, luckily, her father said, 'You'll be glad of letters, Neil. I know I was.'

Olive hoped that her cousin would kiss her goodbye at the door, but he just shook her hand, as he did to her parents, so she turned and went inside with tears in her eyes.

Taking out his wallet, Martin fumbled in it for a moment, then said, 'Take this for luck. You'll likely be glad of an extra bob or two.'

'There's no need for . . .' Neil began, but his uncle forced a note into his hand. 'Thanks very much. I suppose I will be glad of it.'

With a wave, he walked down the path, waiting until he was out of sight of the house before he opened his hand, and was delighted to find that his uncle had given him a fiver, not a pound as he had thought. Good old Martin!

Hetty closed the front door and turned on her husband, her voice acidic. 'You weren't really serious about joining up, were you? They wouldn't want you at your age, and besides, what about me?'

'If you're going to quarrel, I'm going to bed.' Olive ran upstairs. It hadn't bothered Neil that he wouldn't see her for a long time. Why couldn't he realise that she loved him? Would he miss her when he was away? Did absence really make the heart grow fonder? She could only live in hope that it would, and she did have the photo of him that her father had taken in the summer. She looked across at the wooden-framed snapshot – a head and shoulders close-up. The lack of colour didn't matter; she knew that his wavy hair was the colour of milk chocolate, that his eyes – crinkled against the sun – were blue though they looked dark enough to be brown. His determined chin was square, his face more round. He was so good-looking, so manly, that the girls would flock round him like bees round a honeypot, but none of them would get him – he belonged to Olive Potter.

Walking to the tramstop, Neil let out a gusty breath, quite relieved that Olive hadn't tried to get him by himself. She usually tried to get all his attention, and he'd been a bit worried that she might monopolise him for the whole evening once she knew that he was going away so soon. She had always rubbed him up the wrong way and he couldn't help feeling so antagonistic towards her, though it wasn't very charitable. She could be classed as pretty, he supposed, with her long fair hair and sky-blue eyes, but he didn't like bossy girls. He wasn't really ready for girls of any kind yet, but when he was, he would want to be the one to make the running, and he didn't fancy making it with that boa constrictor. Once he was out of her smothering reach, he would feel free.

Gracie looked up when her son came in. 'So that's all your goodbyes said now, is it?'

'Yes. Martin gave me a fiver for good luck and Raymond said he's going to join the army when he's old enough.'

'Oh!' Gracie exclaimed. 'I hope the war's over before he's old enough to fight – he's only fifteen.' She hesitated for a moment, then said, 'Did everything go off all right?'

'Yes. Martin said he'd thought of offering his services, but I don't think Hetty was very pleased.'

It was Olive's reaction that Gracie was interested in, but she didn't ask. Hetty would tell her the next time they saw each other. 'Your father went to bed about ten minutes ago, and Patsy and Queenie went about nine. They want to be up in time to see you off at the station.'

Neil pulled a face. 'I don't want any of you coming to see me off, Mum, I'd feel a proper twerp if my mother and my young sister and my cousin were . . .'

'But . . .' Gracie stopped. Her son would be in uniform soon – a soldier. 'All right, if that's how you want it. Now, off to bed with you.'

Breakfast was early the following morning, but no one ate much – Neil was too keyed up, his parents, sister and cousin too sad – but Gracie still had to issue a mother's

48

caution. 'Look after yourself, remember, and don't leave your clothes all over the place like you do here. There won't be anybody there to pick them up after you.'

'I know that. I'm not helpless, for God's sake.'

Patsy, recognising that her brother's sharpness was due to emotion, not bad temper, tried to help him out. 'Aren't you getting excited, Neil? I know I'd be, if it was me.'

Her tactics worked – the antagonism vanished. 'A wee bit, but I'm looking forward to it. It's like starting out on an adventure. I don't know what's in front of me, and . . .' The boy's defences broke. 'Oh, Mum,' he gulped, 'you don't need to worry about me. I'm old enough to look after myself.' He drew his hand hastily across his eyes. 'I'll have to go now, but I'll write as soon as I can.'

Disengaging himself from Gracie's hug, he shook hands with his father. 'Cheerio, Dad.'

'Cheerio, son.' Joe's voice was gruff, and his grasp had a desperate firmness in it.

'Cheerio, Neil.' Wanting to hug him too, Patsy held back. Further demonstrations of affection would embarrass him.

'Cheerio, little sister.' He ruffled her hair, aimed a mock punch at Queenie, lifted his suitcase and went out.

The family gathering in King Street on New Year's Day 1941 was rather too large for comfort. When everyone sat down for the meal, the kitchen-cum-sitting room was crowded with so many chairs round the extended table that it was virtually impossible for anyone to move freely.

'I wish we were still at the Gallowgate,' Gracie sighed, squeezing into her seat after dishing up the thick broth. 'I miss having a dining room.'

49

Joe held out the plate of bread to Hetty. 'I've told her a dozen times, the place was going to rack and ruin, that's why it was condemned, but she'll not listen.'

'You don't understand, Joe,' his wife said, sadly. 'All my memories are in that rambling old house – my childhood, with my brothers and sisters, Neil and Patsy as babies . . .'

He patted her hand. 'You can't keep hankering after what you'll never have again, lass, and wherever you are, you'll always have your memories.'

To cheer his sister-in-law, Martin asked, 'Have you heard from Neil lately?'

She brightened considerably. 'We'd a letter last week. He says his feet are hardening up now. The boots nearly killed him at first.'

Martin chuckled. 'I know all about army boots. They're not the kindest of footwear.'

'Football boots aren't so bad,' Raymond observed, leading the men to their favourite topic. Patsy and Queenie were whispering and giggling together but Olive felt apart from them all. She had been anxious to hear about Neil – what he was doing, not about his feet – and nothing else interested her.

As soon as they were finished one course, the next one was set down and the meal ended with tea and cakes. Laying his cup down, Joe stretched his arms lazily, narrowly missing Martin's eye with his elbow. 'I could do with a kip, I'm that full up.'

'Joe, we've got guests,' Gracie reprimanded him.

Martin smiled. 'I feel the same, but how about walking it off? The ladies can join us, if they like?'

Hetty jumped to her feet, but Gracie looked doubtful.

'Go on, Mum,' Patsy smiled. 'Don't worry about the clearing up, we'll do it. I'll wash the dishes and Queenie and Olive can dry.' She knew quite well that Olive wouldn't help – she never had before.

The adults could not have reached the foot of the stairs when the argument began. 'If nobody else wants it,' Raymond said, politely, 'I'll have that last bit of black bun.'

'I'm oldest, so I should have it.' Olive's hand shot out an instant before her brother's.

He drew back, muttering, 'You always have to get your own way, haven't you?'

Patsy acted as mediator. 'You've had more than your share already, Olive. I'm sure Neil wouldn't let you off with that if he was here.'

Olive's eyes flashed. 'Neil would never say anything nasty to me.'

Her haughty tone riled her normally even-tempered cousin. 'Yes, he would. He doesn't like you any more than I do.'

'He does like me! You and Queenie are both jealous of me, I know that. You can have the rotten old black bun, Raymond. I don't want it now.'

Beaming, Raymond picked it up and took a bite before she could change her mind. 'Neil doesn't like you,' he declared, his mouth still full. 'I've told you that as well.'

Assuming a dignity she did not feel, his sister said, 'The trouble with you lot is you're too young to understand about things like that. Some boys are too shy to show how they feel about a girl, but I can tell Neil likes me by the way he looks at me when nobody's watching, like the hero in a film before he plucks up courage to tell the heroine he loves her.'

51

Raymond and Patsy burst out laughing, and a crimson-faced Olive was more annoyed still when she noticed that while she'd been arguing, Queenie had taken the last, small triangle of shortbread from the cake stand. 'You greedy little pig!' she shouted. 'I wanted that.'

Undismayed, Queenie popped it into her mouth whole, and Patsy, ashamed at what she had said before, smiled at Olive. 'Mum baked a whole lot of shortbread, so there's more in a tin, if you want?'

'No, thank you.' Olive bit off each word separately, as if she were spitting it out. 'You'll laugh on the other side of your face, Patsy Ferris, when I'm your sister-in-law.'

This made Raymond and Queenie splutter with mirth, but it wiped the gentle smile off Patsy's face. If Olive had set her mind on marrying Neil, nothing and nobody could stop her . . . not even Neil himself.

# Chapter Four

When Neil came home on his first leave, his family listened with interest as he regaled them with tales of his infantry training, going into great detail about the rifle drill and the marching. 'They were strong on discipline and tidiness, as well,' he laughed. 'A button not fastened properly was like a red rag to a bull to the sergeant, and everything had to be perfect when he came round on kit inspections.'

'It hasn't done you any harm,' Gracie said. 'It was time you learned to look after your things properly. You were an untidy monkey before.'

'Well, you should see me now. I can box my blankets with the best of them.'

'Box your blankets?'

'We've to fold them up every morning, and set them at the foot of our beds,' he explained. 'It's what they call boxing them, and if they're not done properly, we've to open them out and do them all over again. Alf Melville – that's a lad from Elgin that I've palled up with – well, he fell foul of the sarge the first day, and he's been in hot water ever since. I got a bawling out sometimes as well so thank God we won't have to put up with him any more. Four of us are going to a technical college in London when we go back. We were the only Ordnance Corps lot, so Alf and me'll still be together.'

As he chatted on, Gracie took stock of him. She had been prepared to see a change in him, but she hadn't expected the broadening out, the maturity. In six weeks, he'd become a man, and her heart ached for the boy who was gone for ever. When Neil's stories came to an end, she said, 'You'll have to go to Rubislaw Den tomorrow. I told Hetty you were coming home today.'

'Must I? I never answered any of Olive's letters and I bet she goes to town on me.'

'Oh, Neil, you should have written to her.'

'What could I have said? "Wish you were here?"'

'Don't get cheeky, my lad. You're not too old for me to give you a scud on the lug.'

Both Patsy and Queenie giggled at this, and Neil held up his hands in submission. 'OK, then. You can phone Hetty and tell her I'll see them tomorrow.'

When Hetty answered her door the following afternoon, she exclaimed at the sight of the khaki figure. 'Aren't you the handsome one?'

'It's just the uniform,' Neil said, delighted but trying to appear modest. 'The minute you put it on, you're different. It makes you . . . I can't explain it, but it makes . . .'

'Makes you feel like a man?'

'I suppose so. You're proud to be in the British Army, to be fighting fit, to know you're needed. It's better to think you've done it off your own bat, though they order you about the same as if you'd been conscripted, but you don't resent it . . . there has to be discipline, or nobody

54

would care.' He stopped, embarrassed at having been so frank.

His aunt smiled encouragingly. 'You like the army?'

'I wouldn't say like, exactly. There's times when you hate the bloody sergeant, and the corporal, and all the officers. Sometimes you even hate the man in the next bed for sleeping when you're lying wide awake with throbbing feet, but when the square-bashing's finished, you've a satisfaction in you. You made it. You didn't break down. You're as good as any of them. D'you see what I mean?'

'Yes, I can understand. What about making friends?'

'Just one, really. Alf's from Elgin and we're the only two Scotsmen in our platoon. That's why we got pally, but he's a good mate and we've had some great laughs.'

Neil enjoyed his aunt's attention, and Raymond's, when he came in, but Olive's entrance spoiled it. He never knew what she might say. At first, it wasn't too bad, even if she went on at him as if he'd to account to her for every minute he'd been away and he felt like telling her that what he did was none of her business, but then came the moment he had been dreading.

'I was disappointed that you never answered my letters . . . but maybe you didn't have time?'

'No, I didn't. When we weren't drilling, we were so tired we fell asleep.' It wasn't exactly true, but near enough to sound honest.

'Oh, my poor Neil.' She laid her hand sympathetically on his arm for a moment. 'Never mind, you won't be so busy when you go back.'

Neil gritted his teeth. He would never feel like writing to her, whether he was busy or not. It was a great relief to him when Martin appeared and he could turn away from her.

'Olive's like a tiger waiting to pounce,' he told Gracie when he went home. 'One false move, and she'd eat me up.'

His mother's laugh was a trifle brittle. 'She's not as bad as that. She's just interested in what you do, that's all.'

'Well, I wish she'd interest herself in somebody else and leave me alone.'

After her son went to bed, Gracie turned to Joe. 'I hope Olive's not serious about Neil. They're first cousins, and inbreeding causes imbeciles. You've only to think about the kings and queens of long ago to prove that.'

'What a woman you are for worrying,' her husband laughed. 'You know as well as I do that Olive's the last girl in the world Neil would think of marrying.'

'Maybe, but it's her that worries me. She never rests till she gets her own way and if she wants Neil . . .'

'Ach, she doesn't want Neil, not in that way. She likes to be made a fuss of, that's all.'

'I hope you're right.' Mainly to show Joe that she had stopped worrying, Gracie made Neil pay another visit to his aunt before his leave was up, and he was pleased that Olive wasn't so overpowering as before. Maybe she had seen how annoyed he had been or maybe her mother had said something to her, but whatever it was he could cope with her like this. He did feel guilty now for not answering her letters, but he really hadn't had anything to say, so what would have been the point of writing?

January ended with bad storms, and ten days into

February, Aberdeen had the worst snow storm of the winter. Six inches fell in two hours, and the Corporation Transport Department had difficulty in keeping tram lines cleared. 'Lorries can't get through from anywhere with supplies,' Joe sighed. 'If it keeps up for long, God knows what I'll do.'

'You're always complaining,' his wife said, tartly. 'If it was you that had to eke out the rations I get for four of us you'd have something to complain about.'

'You'll get nothing at all in a week or two if the weather doesn't clear up.'

Fortunately for all Aberdonians, and people elsewhere who were in the same dire position, the weather did clear before stocks of food ran out.

Gracie was making the girls' bed when she heard the postman pushing something through the door. She'd been worried that Helene's letter hadn't come yesterday, but Joe had told her the mail had probably been held up, and she had pushed her fears aside. He'd been right, she thought, as she picked the letter off the mat. It was only a day late.

Her heart came into her mouth when she saw that it was not Helene's rounded, backhand writing after all. It was a much older hand, an angular hand, and the envelope was addressed to her, not Queenie. She was shaking all over as she took it into the kitchen, unwilling to open it. Telling herself not to be silly, she ran her thumb along the flap, but her worst fears were to be realised. Thankfully, the letter was direct and not over-sympathetic.

Dear Mrs Ferris,

I am afraid I have very bad news to give you, and I think I had better not beat about the bush. Your brother and his wife were both killed last night when their house got a direct hit. Sadly, George Lowell (Helene's father) died two nights before as a result of the bombing, and Ivy is still on the danger list. She has been a good friend of mine for many years, and she asked me to let you know about Helene and Donnie. I cannot begin to tell you how sorry we all are, they were a very nice couple. My husband has arranged for the funerals, George Lowell's too, and nothing is left of the house and shop, so there is no need for you to come. You will have enough to do looking after Queenie as well as your own family. Ivy says she is glad that Helene got the poor girl away, and asks that you break it to her gently.

I know you will be upset, too, but take comfort from the fact that they could not have felt anything and try not to show your sorrow in front of young Queenie. It will be difficult for you, but, remember, God will be with you. That will make it easier to bear.

Yours truly, Dorothy Bertram

PS I have just come back from the hospital, and they told me Ivy passed away early this afternoon. Perhaps it is for the best. She would never have got over this.

The letter fluttered from Gracie's nerveless fingers down to the table. Her heart felt frozen, her whole body felt frozen and she couldn't even weep. If this was what it did to her, what would it do to poor Queenie? She had no one to go home to when the war ended, no parents, no grandparents. If only Helene hadn't been so determined to go back to Donnie . . .

After several minutes, Gracie dragged herself to her feet. She couldn't sit there all day, but how was she going to tell Queenie? While she carried on mechanically with her housework, she toyed with a few simple sentences, words which would take the sting out of what she had to say, words to help the girl to understand how quickly it had happened. As she prepared vegetables, set pans on the cooker, laid the table – tasks needing no conscious thought – phrases whirled round in her brain, but how could anybody break such bad news gently?

Joe was first to appear at lunchtime and had just read the letter when Queenie came running in, followed immediately by Patsy, who had recently been promoted to typist. 'Miss Watt said this morning that my typing had improved,' she said, a little boastfully. 'I know I wasn't very good at first. She used to hold up whatever I'd typed to the light, to see if I'd scraped out any mistypes and I usually had but I can rattle things out now without any mistakes . . . hardly any.'

Queenie smiled at this, then turned hopefully to her aunt. 'Did Mum's letter come today?'

Joe's hand shot out to cover Gracie's as she leaned weakly on the table. 'Queenie,' he murmured, 'I'm sorry, but you'll have to be very brave. Your mum and dad . . .'

Before he could go any further, she whispered, 'You don't

have to tell me, Uncle Joe. They've been . . . killed, haven't they? I . . . knew it would happen. I just knew it.' She turned blindly towards the door, her hands up to her mouth.

'Oh, God!' Gracie followed the girl, and Joe stretched out a restraining arm to his daughter who had made to go after them. 'No, Patsy, leave it to your mum.'

Gracie sat down on the edge of the bed to take Queenie in her arms. 'I'm sorry, my dear. Your house got a direct hit, and your mum and dad . . .' She had to swallow before carrying on. 'They wouldn't have known anything. They didn't suffer at all. Take comfort from that, if you can. I was trying to think how to tell you and maybe you think Joe was cruel . . .'

'It's God who's been cruel,' Queenie said in a low, flat voice, 'but I knew it was bound to happen. Our house was too near Croydon Aerodrome, that's why we got so many air raids, that's why Mum and Dad wanted me away.' A sob started in her voice. 'Why, Auntie Gracie, why? They were the best mum and dad in the world and what's going to happen to me now?'

'Listen, Queenie. Your Uncle Joe and I promised your mum we'd look after you if . . . this is your home now, and you'll be another daughter to us. That's right, my dear, let it all out, you'll feel better for it.' She rocked the girl to and fro until the harsh sobbing eased. 'Never feel you're alone for we love you as much as we love Patsy, and never be scared to tell me anything or ask me anything, the same as you'd have done with your mum.'

After a short, pensive silence, Queenie looked round. 'Was it my grandma that wrote to tell you about it?'

Gracie had forgotten that the girl hadn't been told the rest. 'Queenie, dear, Joe was right when he said you'd have to be very brave. It was a Mrs Bertram that wrote. You likely know her – she lives beside your grandma and grandpa – well . . . their house was hit two nights before, and they're . . . both gone, too. I'm sorry, Queenie, but I can't hide it from you. It would have been a lot worse if I'd waited to tell you that, wouldn't it?'

She held the girl even tighter as the frail body began to shake violently. No amount of comfort or sympathy could make up for what the girl had lost and only time would blunt the heartache. 'You've had an awful shock, lass, and you need a cup of strong, sweet tea to help you get over it. Will you be all right till I go and make one?' The nod was very weak but Gracie stood up. 'Maybe you'd like Patsy to come through to you till I come back?'

At the second faint nod, she made her way to the kitchen, her legs weak and shaky. 'Patsy, will you stay with her till I make a pot of tea?'

Joe waited until Patsy went out. 'Maybe I should have left you to tell her but I was trying to save you the worry. How did she take it?

'She took it quietly to start with but she got the tears out at last, then she asked if it was her grandma that told me and I had to tell her about Mr and Mrs Lowell. She's in a terrible state now but it's not surprising, is it?'

'Poor lassie. We'll need to be extra gentle with her for a long time.' His face darkened. 'Bloody, bloody war! Why do innocent men, women and children have to suffer?'

When the tea masked, Gracie filled a cup and added three spoons of sugar. 'You'd better take your dinner, Joe, before it's spoiled.'

'I couldn't eat. I'll just help myself to a drop of tea.'

When Gracie carried Queenie's cup through, she found

her and Patsy sitting close together, arms round each other, and she was relieved to see that the younger girl's shaking had stopped and her face had regained a touch of colour. 'Go and get your dinner, Patsy. I'll stay here.'

'I'd rather have Patsy, Auntie Gracie, if you don't mind?'

'I don't mind, but Patsy's got to go back to work.'

'Couldn't I stay off this afternoon?' Patsy pleaded. 'Miss Watt would understand.'

'I'll phone her and explain.' Gracie was guiltily relieved that her daughter had taken over the role of comforter. For years, Patsy's knack of gentle reasoning had smoothed over awkward incidents in their family, had even settled quarrels between Ishbel's two boys when they were little, before they emigrated to New Zealand. Olive was the only one who could hold out against her. Olive never listened to anybody.

'I've left Patsy with her,' Gracie told Joe after she had made her telephone call. 'She didn't want me.'

'Patsy'll cope with her. I've often thought she'd make a good nurse, she's got the right touch.'

'Oh, Joe, don't put that idea in her head. I don't think I could stand it if she went away, as well as Neil.'

Joe stood up. 'I feel awful about not going to London, but there's nothing we can do.'

Gracie poured herself a cup of tea when he went out. There was nothing they could do, but that was another Ogilvie gone now. The tears which had refused to come before rushed to her eyes now. It was terrible to think that Donnie had been the last son – the last who would bear the Ogilvie name, for it was a girl-child he'd had, and Queenie would marry one day and change it, the same as all his sisters had.

Gracie sat up. She would have to let her sisters know, but she couldn't phone Hetty until she came to herself, and she'd have to wait until she could think straight before she wrote to Flo and Ishbel in Wanganui and Ellie in Edinburgh. Ellie, next to Donnie in age, had been closest to him, and would be worse hit than any of them. Telephoning her would be the kindest thing to do, but the call to Hetty would be as much as she could bear.

Concentrating on thinking what to say to her sisters her tears came to an end but, for the first time since their mother's death, she felt resentful that they all looked on her as a mother-figure, even Ellie and Flo, who were older than she was. It had started because she had been living in the family home, but she had left there almost two years ago and she was as vulnerable as they were. That was exactly how she was feeling – vulnerable and alone. The tears flowed again, self-pity mingling with grief for her brother and his wife. She was saddled with Queenie . . . no, responsible for her until she had a husband to take over the duty. But the girl wasn't sixteen till April, and she would have to stay on at school till she passed her Highers, like Donnie had wanted. That would be a year or more yet, and another two or three until she earned enough to support herself. And what if she wanted to go to the university? It would be even longer till she was working.

Gracie's musings came to an abrupt stop. What on earth had got into her? It didn't matter how long it was. Queenie was part of the Ferris family now, not a hated encumbrance but a beloved addition, to be cherished and loved like their own daughter, until they both married or until she herself died. She pulled out her handkerchief to dry her eyes. It wouldn't do to let Queenie see that she'd been crying. The poor thing needed someone to depend on, not an unstable, nervous wreck.

It was almost an hour later before the two girls came into the kitchen, both faces showing signs of the trauma they had been through. 'Mum,' Patsy said, her teeth chattering, 'can we have a cup of tea, please? We're both freezing.'

Gracie jumped to her feet. 'I should have lit the gas fire for you, but I didn't think. Sit down and heat yourselves at this fire and I'll put the kettle on.'

Sitting on one of the old armchairs, Queenie said softly, 'Can I see Mrs Bertram's letter, Auntie Gracie?'

'Do you think you should? Maybe you should wait a while.'

'I'd like to read it now. I want to know . . .'

'Yes, I suppose you do.' Gracie took the letter out of the dresser drawer and handed it over, watching anxiously as her niece read it.

'She's over the worst of it, Mum,' Patsy observed.

After a few minutes, Queenie looked up with moist eyes. 'I . . . I'd like to keep it . . . please, Auntie Gracie?'

'I'm not sure it's a good idea, but . . . well, all right.'

'Would you mind if I spoke about my mum and dad?'

'If you think it'll help . . .'

For the next half hour, Queenie told them how idyllic her home life had been, how her parents had always listened to anything she had to say, how they had discussed together any family decisions which had to be made. 'They never left me out. They never did anything without asking what I thought first. When Dad wanted to change the shop round, Mum and I gave him suggestions or he told us what he was thinking and we all talked it over.'

She went on to describe the shop as it eventually was, and the house above it where they had lived. 'It wasn't as big as the house in the Gallowgate, but it was fine for three of us, and Mum kept it ever so nice. On my thirteenth birthday, Dad let me choose the colour scheme I wanted for my bedroom, and I went round the wallpaper shops for days before I chose the cream with teeny pink rosebuds. Dad did the papering and painting and Mum made curtains and a bedspread to match.'

The catch in her voice made Patsy say, 'It must have been lovely. I wish my dad would do something about my room – I mean our room, but there's no wallpaper to be had now.' She brightened as a thought struck her. 'Mum, would you let us paint on top of the old paper? I've read hints about how to make patterns on plain walls with a bit of sponge dipped in another colour. You can make flowers, or anything you like.'

'We'll see what your dad has to say about it.'

Patsy turned to her cousin. 'What about painting the walls cream and using pink and . . .?'

When Joe came in, the two girls were still working out a colour scheme, Queenie looking more animated than he'd have thought possible, and he was pleased that her mind had been taken off her bereavement for a short time. 'You can paint your room whatever way you like – sky blue and pink with magenta spots, if that's what you want. It's not me that'll have to sleep in it.'

After tea, the two girls disappeared to draw up plans, and Gracie said, 'Patsy's worked wonders with Queenie, so I hope Hetty doesn't come rushing here when I tell her, it'll just upset the poor lassie again.'

'Have you not phoned Hetty yet? Look, you can't put it off any longer, Gracie. I'll wash the supper dishes and you go and do it right now. Just say what's happened, and explain it's for the lassie's sake you don't want her to come. Have you written to Flo and Ishbel and Ellie yet?'

'I won't bother with Ishbel. Flo can pass it on to her. So I'll write the two letters once I've phoned.'

Hetty burst into tears when she heard the sad news, and it took all Gracie's tact to prevent her sister from coming to King Street there and then, but she did make her understand that it would do no good, and might even do some harm. She said that it had been Patsy who had comforted Queenie and was stumped for a moment when Hetty offered to send Olive to help, too. 'It's all right, Hetty,' she murmured. 'Queenie's had enough for one day, and I think she'll be going to bed early tonight, and Patsy, as well.'

Luckily, Hetty did not take offence. 'Poor thing, both her parents killed like that.' She had to suppress another sob. 'I can't believe we'll never see Donnie and Helene again.'

'Is Martin there with you?' Gracie asked, gently.

'Yes, I'll be all right. It's just . . . it was so sudden . . .'

'I know, it's been a terrible shock.'

'Will Queenie be living with you for good now?

'I promised Helene I'd look after her if . . .'

'Well, remember if you ever feel you're at the end of your tether, let me know, and I can have her here for a while.'

The offer took Gracie totally by surprise, but she said, earnestly, 'It's very good of you.'

'You've had more than your share of looking after people, but don't think it hasn't been appreciated.'

Gracie felt chastened when she sat down to write to Ellie and Flo. After feeling so sorry for herself earlier, it was gratifying to know that she had not been taken for granted over the past . . . was it really nineteen years past November since their mother had died?

Snuggling against Patsy in the three-quarter bed, Queenie forced her tears back. She had begun to like it here, having a temporary brother and sister had been fun, but at the back of her mind there had always been the warming thought that she would be going home after the war. Now there was no home to go to; no mother and father to come to Aberdeen and take her back; no grandmother and grandfather to exclaim over how much she had grown.

'Oh, Patsy,' she gulped, unable to bear it in silence any longer, 'why did it have to happen? I've never done anything bad, and neither did Mum and Dad, so why did God punish us? Is it because I've been happy here? Is it because I sometimes forgot London was still being bombed?'

'No, I'm sure it wasn't that.' Patsy had no experience in comforting the bereaved, and wished with all her heart that she could find the proper words to soothe her cousin.

There was a short silence, broken only by small, hiccuppy sniffs, then Queenie whispered, 'I suppose I'll have to live here for ever?'

'Don't you want to live here now?'

'It's not that I don't want to, it's just . . . it's going to feel different, knowing I have to.'

'I'm glad you'll be staying here . . . I mean . . .' Patsy felt confused. 'I'm not glad about why, but I'm glad you won't be going away. I like having you to speak to. Neil's all right, but he couldn't speak about things I wanted to speak about . . . and he'd never have let me put his hair in curlers.'

Giving a faint gurgle of amusement, Queenie said, 'I'm so glad I've got you, Patsy. You make me forget . . . for a little while, anyway.'

'Good. Now, we'd better try to get some sleep, or else we won't feel like getting up at rising time, and I'll have to go back to work.'

Hetty and her daughter arrived at quarter past nine the following morning. 'Olive hasn't got any lectures today till later on,' she said. 'Where's Queenie?'

'I made her stop in bed,' Gracie explained. 'She'll need a while to get over it.'

'We'll all need a while to get over it. I can hardly take it in yet myself. Will any of us have to go to the funeral? You didn't say when you phoned last night.'

After hearing what Mrs Bertram had written, she said, 'It seems terrible that none of Donnie's sisters will be there to see him buried, but I suppose it happens all the time.'

'Joe and me didn't get much chance to speak properly till we went to bed, but he reminded me we wouldn't have anywhere to stay if we went down there, and I couldn't leave Queenie just now, anyway.' Ashamed of how she had given way when she was alone with her husband, Gracie did not describe how long Joe had held her, how he had kissed her tears away, how he had convinced her that their duty to Donnie and Helene lay in comforting and caring for their daughter.

Queenie came through just after half past ten, and Gracie was thankful that Hetty didn't overdo her con-

68

dolences. Olive said nothing until her mother prodded her, then she went to her cousin, shaking hands stiffly and saying, 'I'm sorry,' in a not very convincing manner. Queenie did have a little weep, it was only to be expected, but she was soon talking quite calmly about her parents. It seemed to Gracie that by airing her memories of them, she was bent on inscribing them indelibly in her heart so that she would never forget them.

Olive sat stone-faced, and her aunt wished that she hadn't come . . . she was still a spoiled brat even if she was at the university and should know better. Just after eleven, Hetty stood up. 'Raymond comes home at half past twelve, and I've nothing made for lunch yet. Would you like to come with me, Queenie? Olive's to go to Medical School, and I'll be glad of a hand. I'll take you back in the afternoon.'

Thankful for the respite from having to make conversation when they had gone, Gracie moved into a more comfortable chair and lay back with her eyes closed. She would have to get something ready for Joe's dinner, but there was plenty time. She'd hardly had a wink of sleep last night, and she deserved a wee rest.

Only fifteen minutes later, she was dragged out of a deep sleep by someone shaking her shoulder. 'Gracie, it's me.'

Her brain was still a little foggy, but she sat up to find her eldest sister leaning over her. 'Ellie?'

'I got your letter first post and I was so upset I had to come to see poor Queenie.'

Having heard Gracie's explanation of the girl's absence, Ellie sat down. 'I couldn't stop thinking about Donnie when I was driving up. He was the last of our three brothers . . . though wee James died when he was just an infant. Father was so proud when Charlie and Donnie started working with him in the shop in the Gallowgate. He got a new sign put up above the window, remember? Albert Ogilvie and Sons, it said, then the war came and they both went into the army.'

Gracie wiped her eyes. 'I remember how angry Mother was at Father for being proud of them enlisting. I don't think she ever got over it properly.'

'Charlie was her favourite, of course . . .'

'And you were Father's.' This fact had never rankled with Gracie. She had grown up with it, and had known that it was none of Ellie's doing.

'At least we know Donnie never regretted settling down in South Norwood,' Ellie observed. 'When they were in Aberdeen for Father's funeral, we could all see how happy he was with Helene, and now . . . they're both gone, too.'

The two sisters had a weep together, then went on to talk about their childhood, each remembering incidents which the other had forgotten, and they were both astonished when Joe came in just after one, Gracie jumping up in agitation. 'Oh, is it that time already? I haven't made any dinner yet.'

'It doesn't matter,' he assured her. 'A sandwich'll do, if you've anything to put in it.'

'There's a bit of corned mutton left from yesterday.'

'That'll do fine.'

'That'll do me, too,' Ellie said, rising to help just as Patsy appeared.

Hetty brought Queenie back in the middle of the afternoon. The girl was still very pale and Gracie's heart contracted at the sight of the large, blue eyes so deeply filled with pain. Thankfully, at four o'clock, when Hetty said that she would have to go, Ellie also stood up. 'I'd like to take a look at some of the shops before I go back.'

Gracie saw them downstairs, assuring Hetty that there was nothing else she could do, and when she went back to her own kitchen, she knelt down beside Queenie to put her arms round her. 'You've been through an awful lot this past two days, lass, and you must be feeling lost, but Joe and me'll always be here for you. Remember that.'

The girl nestled her head on her shoulder. 'I know, Auntie Gracie. You've been ever so kind, and I don't know what I'd have done without Patsy, but I wish Mum and Dad hadn't sent me away. I wish I'd been killed along with them.'

'Oh, lassie, don't say things like that. You've your whole life in front of you, and they didn't send you away. They didn't want to get rid of you, don't ever think that. They loved you. They wanted to keep you safe.'

'I know they loved me, but . . . oh, Auntie Gracie, I'll never see them again.'

Holding the weeping girl tightly, Gracie felt angry at her sister-in-law for not listening to reason. Helene could have persuaded Donnie to give up the shop and come to Aberdeen if she had wanted to. They shouldn't have left their daughter to become an orphan, for they knew the danger they faced if they stayed in South Norwood. In the next instant, however, she was overcome with grief at their deaths and ashamed at what she had been thinking. As Joe had said at the time, the shop was Donnie's livelihood, and he couldn't give it up.

When Olive went home at teatime, she glared at her mother, 'It made me sick the way you and Gracie fussed over Queenie. I know her mother and father are dead, but she's not a small child, she's fifteen. Hardly anyone spoke to me. You'd think I had the plague.'

'If you were nicer to people, they would be nicer to you,' Hetty barked, uncharacteristically sharp with her daughter, 'but you sat with a face like a fiddle. Why can you not be like Patsy?'

'I'm tired hearing what a good girl Patsy is. Patsy never complains about anything. Patsy always does what she's told. Patsy helps her mother in the house. If you ask me, Patsy's too good to be true, and she doesn't like me any more than I like her.'

Hetty heaved a prolonged sigh. 'Don't you have any friends to go out with? That might stop you being so self-centred.'

'The girls I know are only interested in flirting with the boys they meet.'

'Well, what's wrong with that? I flirted with dozens of boys before I met your dad, and it didn't do me any harm.'

'I'm waiting for Neil.'

A deep frown creased her mother's brow. 'Don't be stupid. Neil's your cousin.'

Saying nothing more, Olive went upstairs to her own room. She hadn't meant to let her mother know how she felt about Neil, but she was missing him so much that it hurt sometimes just to think about him. But even if he didn't write to her, he must be missing her, too. He must be!

# Chapter Five

Cricklewood, 18 February, 1941

Dear Mum,

I'm sorry to have been so long in writing again, and for not writing much last time. The Technical College is really interesting, a whole course just about vehicles. We're billeted in a private house, two to a room, and I share with Alf Melville, remember I told you about him, he's my mate from Elgin. The food's not bad, better than we got in the mess at Chilwell, and I'll be getting as fat as a pig if I'm not careful. I've had to shift the top two buttons of my trousers already. It's either the food or not having any route marches to do.

Hope you and Dad are keeping well, and give my love to the girls. It was good to see you all, but it will be a while before I get home again.

Your loving son, Neil

PS Just got your letter about Donnie and Helene, and I can't get over them being killed like that. I wish I'd had time to go and see them, for it wouldn't have been far from here, and I was thinking about it. Please tell Queenie how sorry I am. It must be awful for her, losing all her folk, and she's such a nice kid. N.

After Joe had read the letter, Gracie said, 'I don't like him being down there. I've heard there's prostitutes walking about the streets of London, and what . . .'

'Prostitutes walk about the streets of Aberdeen, as well. There's Snuffy Ivy and . . .'

'Och, her.' With an irritated movement of her hand, Gracie dismissed the well-known lady whose nasal manner of speaking had earned her the nickname. 'She keeps to the harbour area, and doesn't bother ordinary men, but supposing one of them down in London accosts Neil?'

Her husband gave a great roar of laughter. 'I wish I was there with him, then, that's all I can say.'

Tutting in exasperation, Gracie snapped, 'Could you just be serious for once? He's too young to . . .'

'He'll likely be kept too busy at that college to meet any girls, prostitutes or otherwise.'

She looked a little happier, but took the final word. 'I hope so, as long as he never gets tempted into doing things he shouldn't even be thinking about at his age.'

23 February, 1941

Dear Neil,

I hope you don't mind me still writing to you, though I think you could force yourself

74

to answer sometimes. What kind of things do you learn down there? I suppose it must be something to do with the mechanical side of things, since it's called a technical college. By the way, I'd be interested to know how you spend your free time. Do you go to the cinema with your pals or have you started drinking?

I am missing you a lot since you went back off leave, not that I saw much of you when you only visited us twice! I was rather hurt at that, but I thought you looked great in uniform. I'm fed up having nothing to do except study for exams, but it should all be worth it in the end, when I get my degree. I'll be Dr. Potter, but that sounds so stupid, I'll have to change my surname. Can you think how I could do that?

I've nothing else to write about meantime, but I will definitely be expecting an answer to this. Mum, Dad and Raymond send their regards. I think about you all the time, and I hope that you sometimes think of –

Your loving cousin, Olive.

6 March, 1941

Dear Olive,

I am glad to hear you are studying hard, and I wish you luck with your exams. I don't mind you writing as long as you don't mind me taking a long time to answer. We are kept at it here and I don't get much time to myself.

Your cousin, Neil

17 March, 1941

Dear Mum,

Thanks for your letter. I'm sorry Olive wasn't happy with what I wrote, but it was difficult to know what to say to her. She could read things into a letter that I didn't mean, you know what she's like. Anyway, she wouldn't understand if I told her what we're learning about army trucks and such like, and I've nothing else to write about. Is there any word of Raymond leaving school? He told me when I was home that he was fed up, and it would be good for him to get out into the world and learn to stand up to Olive.

You didn't say anything about Queenie. I hope she is getting over what happened. Well, that's all for now, and I promise to write a longer letter to Olive next time, though I'm not a great one for writing, as you know.

Lots of love to all, Neil

PS I change my underwear regularly, and I make a good job of darning my socks now, so you don't need to worry about me. I'll make a good wife to somebody some day (joke). N.

Neil had found the infantry training hard going, but he was fascinated by all the different army vehicles, and at nights he and Alf went to the cinema, or to a pub, or to a dance hall if they could afford it. He had never had any time for females in Aberdeen, but the girls here were different, and the uniform, which attracted them like moths round a flame, gave him a confidence he'd never had before. He could take his pick of them.

He had been in London for almost a month when he crossed the great divide. He had seen several girls home before, but had always stopped after a few kisses and had been proud of sticking to the straight and narrow, although it was really fear of the unknown that kept him from going any further. He wasn't particularly attracted to Madge when he met her at a dance one evening, she was too quiet, but Alf had collared the only girl Neil fancied, so, while they were on the floor for the last dance, he asked if he could take her home. She agreed shyly and they set off in the darkness, walking side by side but not touching.

When they came to a derelict building, he led her off the pavement and was pleased to find that she wasn't as shy as she seemed, returning his kisses in a manner which told him that she wasn't inexperienced, either. He soon learned that she was much more experienced than he was. Her tongue probed his mouth, starting up an unfamiliar feeling in his loins, a feeling that grew more urgent as she guided his hand to her breasts. It was the first time he'd ever touched a girl like that, and before he got over the shock of feeling how firm they were – he had always imagined it would be something the same as taking hold of a sponge – she was rubbing her pelvis against him, laughing at his embarrassment as his increasing need became more obvious. 'Do you want to do it lying down or standing up?' she murmured.

He was shivering all over, even his teeth were chattering, though it was a warm night. 'What's best?'

Giggling at his ignorance, she pulled off her knickers and flopped down. He was scared at first, but Madge was a true connoisseur, a master – mistress – in the art of sex, and it turned out to be the most thrilling experience of his life. Even in his bed in the billet much later, he perspired as he recalled it – his first time, but not the last. Definitely not the last! He was on equal terms now with Alf Melville, who often bragged about how he had scored with whatever girl he escorted home. Madge hadn't lasted long. She was always on the lookout for the best chance, and when a Canadian came on the scene, she ignored Neil. At first, he had felt peeved, but there had been other girls just as willing, for he wasn't a greenhorn any more. He had taken Dolly home one night, Peggy another, and . . . he couldn't remember half the names now, but none of them had objected to anything he did – in fact, they seemed disappointed if he didn't go all the way, and who was he to disappoint them?

During the day, he and Alf were anxious to learn all they could about their trade. It was an integral part of their future, and they never let thoughts of girls infringe on it; they were only a pleasurable sideline, a hobby to fill the long evenings. Mrs Woods, their landlady, teased them when they went downstairs after the evening meal with their hair plastered flat with water, and boots polished until they could see their faces in them. 'I don't know what you boys do at nights,' she smiled one day, 'but I bet you don't get up to no good.'

Alf winked, lewdly. 'What I get up to's good.'

'Me, too,' Neil grinned, 'and the farther up, the better.'

She gave a scream of laughter. 'Oh, get on wiv yer. You've got proper filthy minds, you 'ave. That's all you ever think abaht, innit?'

As all good things do, their time in Cricklewood came to an end, and the friends were posted to Larkhill in Wiltshire – Ordnance Corps but attached to the Royal Artillery – and had to face the rigours of army life once again. Luckily, it was not as bad as at Chilwell, and the restrictions imposed on them were amply compensated for by the warmth of the locals, who were bent on assisting them to have a good time. Free dances and concerts were laid on, and if no entertainment was provided on any specific night, some of the housewives issued invitations to their homes. As one young gunner observed, blissfully, 'They're offering their daughters up for sacrifice.' The soldiers took advantage of it, seducing the poor unfortunates – who no doubt considered themselves fortunate to receive so much male attention – wherever and whenever an opportunity arose.

Neil Ferris was no exception, and entered whole-heartedly into the discussions that took place back in camp about the availability and prowess of the girls. They were categorised thus: willing and experienced, with a further breakdown on a scale of one to ten; willing but not exciting; reluctant but worth coaxing; a dead loss; out for a serious relationship – steer clear. The accent was on enjoyment, not commitment for life, and any young man who admitted to falling in love was held to ridicule. Those who made no play for the girls were assumed to be 'pansies' and were left strictly to their own devices – whatever they were.

'I hope the blonde with the tits like barrage balloons is there tonight,' Alf Melville grinned with anticipation as he and Neil walked towards the nearest village hall. 'I'm going to grab her before anyone else gets their paws on her.'

Neil chuckled. 'You're welcome. That wee redhead with the wiggly arse is more my style.'

Their man-talk – as they imagined it to be – grew coarser until they burst out laughing. 'I'll likely land up with the flat-foot floozie that looks two ways for Sunday.' Alf gave an exaggerated imitation of the poor girl's squint.

'At least she's a decent figure,' Neil groaned. 'I usually get stuck with the one like a haystack tied in the middle.' He sketched an outline with his hands.

Their loud cackles as they entered the hall made most of the dancers turn to look at them. 'Oh, shit!' Neil muttered. 'The haystack's spotted me. I'm off to the toilet.'

The next day, Neil had just come out of the NAAFI when he was stopped by a middle-aged woman. 'You're Scottish, aren't you? I heard you talking to your friend the other day.'

'Aye, I'm from Aberdeen.' He spoke with as broad an accent as he could – a lot of the older women seemed to have a soft spot for the Jocks.

'I was sure you were. My sister-in-law talks exactly like you. She belongs to Fraserburgh.'

Neil didn't disillusion her, although the people from the 'Broch' had an entirely different accent from Aberdonians, and she carried on, 'You must feel it, being such a long way from home, and I'm sure you'd like to come to my house for a meal tomorrow night, wouldn't you? I'm Mrs Baillie of Rose Cottage, and I guarantee my cooking's a lot better than the stuff they serve in your mess.'

It was the fifth invitation he'd had in two weeks, but the woman wasn't to know. 'That's very kind of you,' he smiled. After all, she might have a nubile daughter – she looked old enough – and he was always ready for a bit of this, that and the other . . . especially the other.

Mrs Baillie did have a daughter, Neil discovered, when he turned up at Rose Cottage the following evening – a slender brunette with baby blue eyes and cupid's bow lips. She was so beautiful that his spirits sank. Any mother would keep a careful eye on a gorgeous creature like this, and he'd have no chance to get her on her own. Deciding, ruefully, that it was as well to make the best of things, he tucked into the home-cured ham – done in honey and sliced inch thick – and the green salad and roast potatoes which accompanied it. The apple pie that followed had melt-in-the-mouth pastry and was coated in thick, clotted cream.

'My brother has a farm in Devon,' Mrs Baillie explained.

'I can't remember ever having had such a delicious meal,' Neil said, truthfully, wiping his mouth with the starched, damask napkin and leaning back in great contentment. It had been worth coming for, even if nothing else was on offer.

Standing up, the woman said, 'I'll leave you to give Edna a hand with the washing up. I've a meeting at the Institute at half past seven, and I'm needing all my time.'

81

He couldn't believe his luck, not until Mrs Baillie had put on her hat and coat and gone out, by which time he felt surprisingly bashful, but Edna solemnly collected the dirty crockery, 'I'll easily wash up by myself.'

He jumped gallantly to his feet, however, intent on making a good impression on this vision of loveliness. 'When d'your mother's meetings usually finish?' he asked, as he dried the first plate.

'They last a good two hours,' Edna gave a shy smile.

Before he left, Neil was head over heels in love, and was still smiling in a somewhat inane manner after walking back to camp. 'You look like a cat that's been at the cream,' Alf observed. 'I take it there was a girl there? And by the look of you, you must have had a bloody good time.'

Neil rolled his eyes. 'Edna's a real corker! A smasher! An angel in disguise. She took a bit of coaxing, for she's not really a girl like that, but she was worth it.'

Alf's smile broadened, 'Edna? Not Edna Baillie?'

A flicker of doubt hovered in Neil's mind, 'Don't tell me you know her?'

'Who doesn't? And I mean that in the true biblical sense. Every squaddie for miles has laid her at some time. I'd have told you, if you'd said that's where you were bound for.'

His euphoric love evaporating in disgust, Neil exclaimed, 'Bugger! I should have known it was too good to be true.'

'Did Mother Baillie go off to the Institute?'

'Is that what she usually does? What a bloody sucker I've been, falling head first into it.'

Alf let one eyelid drop, 'But you enjoyed it?'

Neil laughed raucously, 'Yes, by God, I did!'

Neil wrote now about the dances and concerts he went to with his friend, which satisfied Gracie that he was happy where he was. 'Alf sounds a decent laddie,' she remarked to Joe. 'He'll keep Neil out of trouble. I was a bit worried in case some girl led him on and he got her in trouble, but I heard somebody saying the army provides against that, something in their food to dull their appetites for . . . sex. It's a really good idea, with the boys so far away from their mothers.'

As usual, when she voiced any fears, Joe just laughed. 'If what I've heard's true, the army's not bothered about them having sex, it's pregnancies the army provides against.'

'Oh, well,' Gracie muttered, 'it comes to the same thing.'

His eyes twinkling, Joe said, 'It's not the same. It means the laddies can have their fun without worrying.'

'But Neil's not like that, so it's all right.'

Olive was not popular with her fellow students – she was a know-it-all whom the lecturers were inclined to hold up as a paragon – but when she mentioned, in an off-hand manner and with the intention of impressing, that she had a boyfriend in the RAOC, the two girls walking along the corridor with her were very interested.

'How old is he?' This was Francis Lamont, affectionately known as Frankie.

'Twenty-four.' Olive hoped that the extra six years would make Neil sound more mature.

83

Pauline Frayne, Polly to everyone, eyed her with a touch of wonder. 'How did you meet him?'

'His mother's a friend of my mother's.' That was true, and there was no need to say that he was a cousin.

'I'd never have guessed you'd a boyfriend.' Looking rather flustered, Polly added, 'I mean, you seem so aloof, and you never speak to any boys. Have you known him long?'

'A couple of years. He did ask me to marry him last time he was home, but I told him I'd rather wait till after I was finished Medical School.'

'Is he very good looking?'

'Oh, yes, he's a darling. He's on a special course at the moment, training to be an officer.' It was as well to tell a whopper as a small untruth, she reasoned.

'An officer?' Polly's eyes widened. 'You're lucky.'

Olive gave a modest laugh. 'He says he's lucky having me.'

Frankie's smile was a little dubious. 'I suppose he has actually kissed you?'

'Oh yes, dozens of times, but I've never let him . . . I want to be a virgin on my wedding night.' Noticing that Frankie looked more sceptical than ever, she added, 'That is, if I can hold out that long . . . or if he can, which is more to the point.'

Polly sighed longingly, 'I wish I'd someone like that. The boys I've been out with can't wait to get on with the job, though I quite enjoy it. I know I am just a body to them, a body to satisfy their needs, but I suppose it's better than giving my body for research.'

Giggling, Frankie said, 'I've been researched a few times. Boys who hadn't a clue how to do the thing properly, and the fumbling's worse than anything.'

84

Having arrived at their lecture room, they trooped in and sat down in one of the tiered rows of seats, Olive now too involved with dreams of Neil actually doing what she'd said he had done to concentrate on anything else. They were white lies, that was all; everything would eventually come true, and she was sure that she had risen in her fellow students' estimation. It might be a good idea to give Neil a hint of how she felt, a little nudge in the right direction?

1 April, 1941

My Dear Neil,

Here I am again with a few lines to let you know I'm still thinking about you. Your mother told me why you wrote such a scrappy letter before, so I forgive you – this time. She said she didn't know where you were now but she gave me your new address, though a Forces Post Office number doesn't tell anyone anything.

Are you lonely, being away from home? I wish I could be there to cheer you up, though I really need cheering up myself, so I expect a nice long letter back from you. I took a night off studying on Wednesday and persuaded (forced) Raymond to go to the Majestic with me, and we had to walk all the way home because no buses or trams run when there's an alert on. But it was dull going to the cinema with my brother, so I pretended that it was you sitting beside me, and that you were holding my hand. I suppose you think I'm silly, but

I often imagine you're with me and it gives me a lovely warm feeling.

Raymond wants to leave school in the summer, but Dad says he has to stay on and try for the Varsity. I don't think he'll pass the Highers, neither does he, but Dad has set his heart on having another solicitor in the family. Thank goodness he didn't expect me to follow in his footsteps, because I like Medicine, and I'll concentrate on Psychiatry if I get the chance. I'm quite interested in how people's minds work.

I will have to stop now, but I am going to tell you something first, and it's not an April Fool joke, in spite of the date. I THINK I LOVE YOU. There, I've told you, and I wonder how you will feel about it?

Your loving cousin, Olive,

Neil was horrified and felt compelled to confide in Alf. 'My cousin says she thinks she loves me.'

His friend raised his eyebrows. 'Very nice!'

'It's anything but, she's a bloody nuisance. I can't stand her. She's always made sheep's eyes at me and tried to get me all to herself, but this is beyond a joke.'

'Why don't you give her the brush off?'

'I've tried, but nothing works.'

Alf ran his hands through his sandy hair, his round face thoughtful, but after a moment, he said, 'What does she look like? Is she anything decent?'

'I suppose she's pretty enough, but . . .'

'Is she, though?' Alf pondered over this, then a slow, sly smile crept over his face. 'I noticed that we'll both be on leave at the same time, so how about asking me to your house before I go home to Elgin. I won't stay long, maybe a couple of nights or so, but you can introduce me to Olive, and I'll make a play for her, and with my irresistible charm, she's bound to transfer her affections to me.'

'That would be great, but are you sure you don't mind?'

'I'd do anything for a friend, especially when he's got a pretty cousin he wants rid of.'

'You'll maybe regret it.'

'I'll easily give her the old heave-oh when I want to, but maybe I won't want to.'

Neil blew a loud raspberry. 'You'll want to, believe me.'

10 April, 1941

Dear Olive,

Thank you for your letter. I'm glad you take time off sometimes, for you must get very bored of studying. Raymond did tell me when I was home that he wanted to leave school, but if your dad says no, I suppose he'll just have to stay on. You asked me if I was lonely, well, the answer is no. I'm having a great time with all the girls here, a different one every night I'm off duty, though there's nothing serious. It would do you good to go out with boys once your exams are past. We were on manoeuvres again last week, and it's not much fun when the rain is teeming down, I can tell you. Army greatcoats and trousers take ages to dry. I got a chill the first day, and I've been sniffling ever since.

Regards to all your family, Neil

Neil's letter made Olive livid. He'd had the cheek to ignore her declaration of love, had even insulted her by saying she should go out with other boys. Surely he couldn't really be telling her to look for somebody else because he didn't love her? No, no, that was impossible. As she had said to Raymond and Patsy at New Year, Neil was too shy to tell her he loved her, and he must be bluffing when he said he'd been out with other girls. Anyway, he had said that there was nothing serious, and if he was here, she would convince him that she was the only girl for him.

Joe closed his eyes to listen to 'Garrison Theatre' on the wireless, but Gracie was interested in an advertisement in the newspaper. 'I see Raggie Morrison's have a sale on just now – winceyette nightdresses for three and eleven. I could be doing with a new nightie.'

Raggie Morrison's – or Morrison's Economic Stores, to give it its proper title – was a rambling emporium which stocked most things from alarm clocks to bedsocks, fireside rugs to men's combinations, and which had a sale almost every week, as both Joe and Gracie were well aware. 'You're not needing a winceyette nightie when it's coming on for the summer?' he muttered. 'You'll sweat like a pig.'

'Ladies don't sweat like pigs,' she retorted. 'Anyway, I'd keep it till the winter.'

'You're old fashioned, Mum,' Patsy smiled. 'It's only old women that wear winceyette nighties. It's interlock pyjamas you should get.'

'I feel the cold something terrible in bed, though.'

Joe sniggered, 'I can vouch for that. She sticks her cold feet up against my legs and has me shivering as well.'

Gracie looked embarrassed at this intimate detail of her marriage coming out, but Patsy said, 'Interlock pyjamas are actually warmer than nighties, Mum, so you'll be doing Dad a favour as well as yourself if . . .'

'No, no,' Gracie interrupted. 'I've been wearing nighties all my life, and I'm too old to change. I'll buy a nightie tomorrow morning, and I'll start getting Neil's room ready for him in the afternoon.'

Joe frowned. 'His room's fine the way it is.'

'Oh, you men! I've the bedding to air, and give the place a good clean, and I'll only have a day and a half.'

'I'm sure Neil wouldn't worry what it's like.

'Maybe no', but I do.'

Having not seen Queenie since her tragic loss, Neil felt ill at ease with her, but felt that he had to make some sort of commiseration. 'I'm sorry about your mum and dad, Queenie . . . and your grandmother and grandfather. I could hardly believe it when Mum wrote and told me.'

Her face muscles tightened, 'I can still hardly believe it myself, but . . . thank you, Neil.'

She was clearly near to tears, and he wondered if it would have been better not to say anything, but he hadn't wanted her to think he didn't care. He did care. His heart ached to see her so unhappy, and he felt like putting his arms round her to comfort her, but that would probably make her worse. Remembering that his friend was waiting to be introduced, he said, 'This is Alf Melville, folks,' and was relieved to see, when he glanced at Queenie again, that she was smiling at something Patsy had said.

Hetty and Martin took to Alf straight away, as had Joe and Gracie, but Olive felt annoyed by his presence. Every time she tried to talk to Neil, his friend butted in and spoiled it. Thank goodness he wouldn't be in Aberdeen for long she thought, giving up all hope of speaking to her cousin. As the evening progressed, she realised that Alf was looking at her with some admiration, and it occurred to her that a spot of jealousy would do Neil no harm; it might even make him realise that he did love her. With this in mind, she turned her full attention to Alf, agreeing when he asked her to go out with him the next night.

'It worked like a charm,' Alf remarked to Neil on the way back to King Street. 'I like big breasted girls and Olive's got the best pair of tits I've seen in a long time. Are you sure you want me to go on with this?'

Neil didn't take time to consider. 'I'm sure, and you're welcome to her, if that's what you want.' For an instant, it crossed his mind that they were being unfair to Olive, but she had asked for it, and she had jumped at the chance of a date with Alf.

Olive did have second thoughts when she went to bed, but the carrot of making Neil jealous was too tempting to pass, and she was strangely attracted to his friend when he called for her the following evening. Alf was very charming as they strolled out Queen's Road into the countryside, and he was quite good looking in a rugged sort of way, with twinkling eyes that suggested he might be good fun. He was a little shorter than Neil, with slightly broader shoulders, and his manner towards her was much more flattering than the boorish way Neil always treated her.

When Alf stopped and pushed her gently against the dyke, she felt uneasy, but his tender kisses made her forget her fears, and she slid her arms round his neck, hoping that he would become more passionate, but in a few minutes, he drew away and they resumed their walk. A little farther on, Olive said, 'Instead of turning and going back the way we've come, we could go by the Switchback and the Lang Stracht. It's not much longer – just like going in a circle, really.'

As she had hoped, the hollow at the foot of the Switchback was so secluded that Alf stopped again, and several times on the long, straight stretch of country road, so that it took them much longer to get back to Rubislaw Den. After a last, lingering kiss, Alf said, 'Tomorrow night again?'

'Oh, yes.' Olive felt lightheaded as she went inside. Alf was good fun and had behaved like a gentleman – although she half wished that he hadn't – and a double dose of jealousy should teach Neil a lesson. Not that she was caring what he thought now, but he deserved it.

Neil eyed Alf with some curiosity when he returned to King Street, but waited until they were alone before he put the question. 'Well, what did you think of her?'

Taking off his boots, Alf said, 'She's a bit forward.'

'I know that, but how did you get on? Did you kiss her?'

'She didn't know how to kiss. She's a dead loss . . . but I've asked her out tomorrow again.' He struck a pose and went on, 'It is a far, far better thing I do now, than I have ever done before, and it's all for you.'

Neil rubbed his hands gleefully. 'That's my boy! As long as you take her attention off me, that's all I ask.'

On their second date, Olive returned Alf's kisses with an ardour which pleased yet disquieted him. Awakening love for him was stirring in her heart, and she believed that he was more than a little in love with her, so it came as a great disappointment when he broke away from her abruptly. In the next instant, she felt triumphant, assuming that he had been aroused by her and hadn't wanted to defile her.

That night, in bed, she couldn't picture Neil's face, try as she would. It was Alf she kept seeing; the twinkling blue eyes which had turned serious just before he kissed her; the strong mouth that could be heavenly tender against hers; the sandy hair with just a tiny kink on one side of the parting. Why had she ever thought she was in love with Neil? Drowning in a sea of unfamiliar emotions, Olive did not realise that her feelings stemmed from having received her first kisses, and would have been mortified to know that Neil himself had had a hand in arranging the whole episode.

Neil was already in bed when Alf went back to King Street. 'How did you get on this time? Did you score?'

Alf looked uncomfortable. 'I might have if I'd tried, but I couldn't . . . she's your cousin, after all, and I didn't know how you'd feel about it.'

Screwing up his nose, Neil said, 'I wouldn't have minded. Olive needs a bit of a shake up. It would do her good, take some of the starch out of her.'

'Aye, she's a bit too toffee-nosed.'

'I bet she's a virgin.'

'She's not my type.' Grinning, Alf gave him a push, 'Move over, you lazy bugger. You're taking up all the bed.'

Alf went home to Elgin the following afternoon, and when she had her son on his own, Gracie took him to task for not writing as often as he had done before, but he looked at her unrepentantly, 'I've been going out quite a lot lately, and I didn't have time to write.'

'Was it a girl you were out with? Are you going steady?'

'It wasn't always the same girl. Connie, she's the current one, well, she's quite a good sort, but I'm not ready for anything serious yet.'

'I should hope not. You're still only eighteen.'

Considering it wise to change the subject, Neil said, 'You and Dad both look well. Is the shop still doing OK?'

'It's doing fine. Your Dad's pleased with himself, though he girns on about the rationing.' Gracie would have liked to know more about this Connie he had been going out with but didn't ask.

At lunchtime, Neil said, 'I think I'll take a dander up to Rubislaw Den this afternoon.'

'Hetty'll be pleased to see you. I'm glad Olive went out with Alf. She could do a lot worse than him.'

Recalling his friend's amorous adventures both at Larkhill and Cricklewood, Neil grinned. 'I doubt it. I'd like to have a natter with Martin as well, so I likely won't be home at teatime.'

93

He left the house with his father and, as they walked up the street, Joe looked sideways at him. 'What's this your mother was telling me about . . . Connie, was it?'

Neil laughed. 'She's one of many. Let's say I'm sowing my wild oats, the same as you, likely, when you were my age.'

'No, I didn't go with any girls before I asked your mother out, and that took me all my time. I'm right surprised that you're going back to see Olive, though. I thought you didn't like her.'

'I don't.' He considered telling his father about the plan Alf had thought up, but decided that it was too risky. 'I just wondered what she thought of Alf.'

'What did he think of her?'

'Oh . . . I don't think he was too struck with her.'

'But he went out with her twice?'

Neil smiled, a little nervously. 'That's Alf all over. He can't leave the girls alone.'

Stopping at the door of his shop, Joe said, slowly, 'She's one girl I'd advise both of you to leave alone. I sometimes think she'd never let go if she fell in love.'

His father's words had made Neil think, and by the time he rang Hetty's bell, he was wondering if Alf's idea had been such a good one, after all. His aunt welcomed him warmly and took him into the sitting room, where they chatted until her son and daughter came home. 'Look who's here,' she cried to them, skittishly.

Raymond rushed over, but Olive hung back until her mother said, 'Aren't you going to say hello to Neil?'

She came forward shyly, which was so unusual that Neil did not like to ask her any questions, and when Martin appeared he monopolised the young serviceman until Hetty told them to go through to the dining room. To Neil's relief, Olive took her seat at the opposite side of the table, and because his uncle talked to him all through the meal, he did not have to look at her. Back in the sitting room, however, their eyes did meet occasionally, but he couldn't place what he saw in hers . . . it surely couldn't be pity? Whatever it was made him look away uneasily, and he prayed that when Alf eventually gave her the cold shoulder she wouldn't decide to latch on to him again.

# Chapter Six

Queenie, sixteen now, was beginning to think about boys. She had quite liked Alf Melville while he had been there, but he had been too smitten with Olive to notice her. Good luck to him, Queenie mused, grinning as she reflected that he would need all the luck he could get if he were serious about her cousin. She hoped that he was, and that Olive felt the same way about him, because she'd stop being so possessive about Neil. Queenie's heart gave a tiny leap. She didn't think of Neil as a brother now, and wondered if it was very wrong of her to dream about him as a sweetheart. It was a vain dream, in any case – he was still treating her like a sister – and she had better put it out of her mind. There were other boys around; boys who seemed to find her attractive and whistled at her when she passed. She enjoyed that, especially when it was Callum Birnie, who had gone even further and asked her out twice . . . though she had refused him both times. Maybe she should accept if he asked again. If Neil knew she was going with a boy, he would realise that she was no longer a child, that she was actually a desirable young woman.

Spotting Callum standing near the door when she arrived at school, Queenie gave him her sweetest smile – he was quite nice, really, just a bit too young for her liking – and his glum face cleared. 'You're later than usual. I was wondering if you were sick, or something.'

She was thrilled that he had been waiting for her. 'I was just dawdling.'

'I wanted to ask you something. My dad gets complimentary tickets from His Majesty's for displaying their playbills in his window. He can't use them this week, so . . . would you like to come with me?'

Queenie had never been to the theatre – she sometimes went to one of the cheaper cinemas with Patsy, but that was all – so this was too good a chance to miss. 'I'd love to.'

His blush, which had started when he asked her, grew much deeper at this. 'Would you? Honestly?'

'Honestly, and thanks for thinking about me.'

'Tonight, ten past seven outside the door to the stalls?'

'OK.'

Gracie wasn't too happy about her niece going out with a boy, but Joe said, 'Let her go. She needs some enjoyment.'

Patsy teased her a little, but not unkindly, then offered to make up her face, at which Gracie said, sharply, 'I don't want her looking like a tart. That would just be asking for trouble. What kind of boy is this Callum, anyway?'

'He's nice, Auntie Gracie, he's in my year at school.'

'Oh, he's the same age as you? I was a bit worried in case he was a lot older.'

Joe shook his head. 'They're just a couple of youngsters. They'll not do anything wrong.'

'I should hope not.'

Gracie's mind would have been easy if she'd been a fly

on the wall of His Majesty's Theatre that night. Callum handed Queenie a small box of chocolates as they took their seats, but she forgot about them until the interval. 'I was carried away with the play,' she apologised.

'So was I,' he laughed.

Over the next fifteen minutes, they discussed the plot and how it would end, commented on the scenery and had a look at the rest of the audience. The box of sweets was empty by the time the lights dimmed, and they sat back in their seats to be enthralled all over again.

Out on the pavement afterwards, Queenie heaved a sigh. 'I don't think I've ever enjoyed anything so much. I'm glad you asked me.'

'So'm I, though I didn't really think you'd come. I can't let you walk home on your own, though, so where d'you live?'

'In King Street, and I'll manage by myself. I'm not afraid of the dark.'

'My dad said I had to see you home.'

Laughing, she said, 'Then I can't congratulate myself that it was your idea?'

'Well . . . no, but I do want to. I couldn't help noticing how . . . different you looked tonight.'

'It's my cousin's make up,' she chuckled, adding, a little apprehensively, 'It's not too much, is it?'

'No, it makes you even prettier than you usually are.'

A warm glow spread through her. 'Little grains of powder, little drops of paint, help to make a lady look like what she ain't. That's what my grandma used to say.'

'You suit it, though. Um . . . Queenie, this won't be the only time you'll come out with me, will it?'

She was pleased by the uncertain pleading. 'Maybe not.'

Callum slid his arm round her waist. 'I think you're the nicest girl I ever met.'

'Only think?' She had to tease him; she didn't want him to get serious about her.

They had come to the foot of Schoolhill, and had to let a tramcar on St Nicholas Street pass before they could cross over to go up Upperkirkgate, so Callum took the opportunity to pull Queenie round and kiss her. 'I've been wanting to do that all evening,' he whispered.

She was bitterly disappointed. She had sometimes wondered how it would feel to get her first kiss, but was that all it was? Two sets of dry lips touching for a moment? It had done nothing for her . . . not even the hint of a thrill. They walked on silently, and she wondered if Callum felt as let down as she did. But her natural ebullience did not let her brood for long, and she was soon telling him about Neil and Patsy, and how Auntie Gracie and Uncle Joe had accepted her into their family after her parents died. There was no self pity in it, not even when Callum murmured that he was sorry about her mum and dad. 'I was lucky,' she assured him. 'I couldn't have a better home than I do now and a ready-made brother and sister, as well. Do you have any brothers or sisters?'

He groaned. 'A twelve-year-old sister, that's all. She's a proper pest at times.'

He went on to air his innumerable grievances at his sister until they arrived at King Street. His goodnight kiss did no more to Queenie than his first, and she climbed the tenement stairs thoughtfully. Was something wrong with her, or was it Callum's fault? Perhaps it was the first time for him, too, and he didn't know how to kiss. Well, it didn't matter, she decided as she went into the house. Her first real kiss was still to come.

Her aunt gave her a critical stare then obviously relaxed. 'Did you enjoy your night out?'

'It was great. Callum gave me a box of chocolates, but I was so interested in the play that I forgot about them until the interval.'

'Any left?' Patsy asked, smiling hopefully.

'No, it wasn't a big box, and we ate them all.'

'That's romance for you,' Joe declared, winking at Gracie, who just said, 'It's time you were in bed, Queenie, and you too, Patsy. You've both to get up in the morning, remember.'

As soon as they were in the bedroom, Queenie asked, 'Have you ever been kissed?'

Shaking her head, Patsy smiled. 'Did Callum kiss you?'

'If you can call it a kiss. It was like a little peck you give a baby.'

'So there isn't any romance? Better luck next time.'

'I think I'd prefer an older boy . . . a man with experience.'

Patsy frowned. 'Some older men have too much experience.'

'Have you been out with a man?' Queenie said, eagerly.

'I wouldn't want to go out with an older man, I've enough of them at work. They come up behind us and before we know where we are, their hands are all over us. It's horrible.'

'I wouldn't mind letting a man do that once, to see how it feels. Why don't you like it?'

'I might like it if it was somebody nice, somebody a bit younger, but they're all over forty, and I just smack their

100

fingers. They're a lot of creeps,' Patsy shuddered. 'One of the other typists went out with the manager once . . . she hoped he'd put her up for promotion . . . but she swore she wouldn't go again.'

'What did he do?'

'She said he nearly tore the clothes off her. She managed to get away from him, but half the buttons were missing off her blouse and she'd to buy a new set and sew them on before her mother washed it. He doesn't look at her now, and she's sure her promotion's up the spout.'

Queenie got into bed. 'Struggling with him must have been exciting while it lasted?'

'She said she was terrified. She thought he'd go mad with lust and kill her. You'd better watch yourself, Queenie, you haven't a clue what men are really like.'

'But all men can't be like that?'

Switching off the light, Patsy lay down beside her. 'All the ones I know are. Now, you'd better stop asking questions or Mum'll be through telling us to be quiet.'

Queenie closed her eyes, but could not still her curious brain. Why did older men behave like that? Had they been the same when they were young, or did lust develop with age? But Uncle Joe was old, and he didn't show any sign of it. No, it must be just some men and it would make no difference what age they were, so some young men must also be consumed with lust. This was more disturbing. How could a girl tell? She couldn't ask a boy if he was liable to attack her, she'd have to wait and see. Neil had never touched her . . . except to tickle her, and that was in fun, as any brother might do to his sister, and Callum had done nothing out of place. He hadn't excited her, and he

101

hadn't seemed excited either, but it might be safer not to go out with him again.

When Alf said that he'd had a letter from Olive, Neil felt a surge of elation – she had stopped writing to him at last. 'You've done it,' he crowed. 'How long are you going to wait before you break off with her?'

Alf considered briefly, then said, 'If I do it too early, she'll just start on you again.'

'Aye, I suppose you're right. OK, you'd better carry on. I don't want her turning to me on the rebound from you. She'd be even worse than she was before. Now, are you coming with me to that dance tonight, or are you keeping your body pure for darling Olive? Every man to his own poison.'

'Cut out the sarcasm! Of course I'm coming to the dance. You should know me by this time . . . always ready for a bite at a fresh cherry.'

'Even at Olive's cherry?' Neil teased.

'Hell's bells! I just took her out as a favour to you, and if you don't stop harping on about her, I'll write and tell her everything.'

Neil looked aghast. 'You wouldn't?'

'I would, so just watch your step, my fine lad. Will you help me to write to Olive tomorrow? I don't know what to say to her. It can't be too lovey-dovey, just enough to make her think I care for her a little bit.'

'You don't, do you?'

'Christ, no!'

Reading Alf's letter again, Olive wished that he wasn't so far away; if he was stationed somewhere near Aberdeen, they could see each other more often. He had begun by writing 'My Dear Olive', but did he really mean it, or did he think that it wasn't so formal as just putting 'Dear Olive'? Anyway, he said that he had enjoyed her company and looked forward to seeing her again, so he must like her. Her heart speeded up as she read the next sentence. 'I live in hope that we can repeat our kisses and maybe even improve on them.' He could really worm his way into a girl's heart. This was something else to tell Frankie Lamont and Polly Frayne, although they thought her boyfriend's name was Neil, and she would have to be careful not to make a slip.

At the first chance she had, she looked for the two girls, and began by crowing, 'I'd a letter today.'

'Oh yes?' Frankie sounded sarcastic. She had not believed Olive's exaggerated description of 'Neil's' kisses when he was on leave, and was not prepared to believe anything else.

Polly, however, was agog to know what was in the letter, and Olive allowed her to take a quick look at the relevant part. 'Could he improve on his kisses?' she asked, then.

Olive gave a coy smile. 'I don't think so, but maybe he's meaning something else would be an improvement on kisses.'

'Yes, that's what it'll be,' Polly exclaimed in delight. 'He must really love you, and I bet you'll treasure this for as long as you live.'

'Yes, it's the first love letter he's ever written to me.'

If Olive had known how Alf and Neil had laughed together as they made up the flattering phrases, she would not have been so happy and would probably have scratched their eyes out but, in her ignorance, all that concerned her was answering the letter. Should she tell Alf that she longed to see him, that she was in love with him, or was it too soon for that? They had only been alone together twice, and it might scare him off, but surely it would be all right to admit that she had enjoyed the kissing as much as he had.

Callum Birnie had looked so downcast when Queenie refused to make another date that she had given in, and although his kisses hadn't swept her off her feet, they had been quite an improvement on his first one, and they were always getting better. Thinking it over as she went to meet him again, she remembered having heard her grandma saying, 'Practice makes perfect,' and it seemed to be true. . . unless he'd been taking lessons. She giggled at this idea. She liked him very much, but she wasn't sure that she loved him, and if she wasn't sure, she probably didn't. She enjoyed being with him – they had the same sense of humour and could talk easily together – so it would be best to let their relationship drift along. Perhaps love would come in time.

Callum was waiting for her outside the Picture House – he was always first – and his chubby boy's face broke out in a grin when he saw her. 'I was wondering if we should go for a walk tonight? It's too hot to be inside, isn't it?'

'It is hot. Where'll we go?'

'Where our feet take us?' He took her hand and turned her round to go down Bridge Street. 'I like that dress, Queenie. It suits you much better than the school uniform.'

'Thanks, and you look quite good yourself.'

'It's a new sports jacket. I pestered Mum till she gave in and bought it.'

'It makes you look older.'

He seemed pleased. 'That was the idea. Nobody'll know that we're still at school. I look stupid in a blazer at my age.'

She couldn't resist teasing him. 'I'd say looking stupid comes naturally to you.'

He laughed. 'We're a pair, then.'

It didn't annoy her; she knew that he didn't mean it, any more than she had. They often swopped insults this way, and Patsy had said it was a sign of affection, that no one could make fun of a person they didn't like – not to their face.

Their walk, which he had planned before meeting her, took them through the Arches, underneath which no one could 'lay' on the cobblestones, like Flanagan and Allen sang, because they were occupied by fish houses, with scales and pieces of fish lying about the road. Queenie curled up her nose at the stench. 'This is a beautiful place to take a girl, I must say.'

'Watch your feet,' he warned. 'It's slippery here.'

In a few minutes, they came out on Riverside Drive, with the Dee flowing swiftly and silently on their left, the last lap of its journey to the sea. At the opposite side of the water, on the crest of the steep bank, a squat building was silhouetted starkly against the setting sun. 'What's that?' she asked, a trifle uncertainly. 'It looks eerie.'

'That's Craiginches, the prison,' Callum laughed, 'so you had better behave, or they'll drag you inside.'

'I wondered why there was such a high wall all round it.' She shivered. 'Do any of the prisoners ever escape?'

'I think some have but they're always caught.'

'I don't really like being here.'

Sliding his arm round her waist, Callum held her closely. 'I won't let any of the nasty men catch you.'

She had to laugh, and felt better for it. When they came to the gate to the Duthie Park, he said, 'We can go in here and have a seat, if you like?'

'Yes, I wouldn't mind.'

There were few people about, and they found an empty bench with no difficulty. Sitting down, they both stretched their legs out and kicked off their shoes, the simultaneous timing making them laugh. 'It's impossible to be grown up,' Queenie said, in a moment. 'We're still kids, taking off our shoes because our feet are hot.'

He turned to her slowly. 'I don't feel like a kid when I'm with you.'

She enjoyed his kisses for some time, until he shifted his hands from her shoulders to her breasts. 'No, Callum,' she said sharply, drawing back from him.

'Why not? I'm not going to do anything wrong. I just want to feel them.'

She pushed him away, and searched for her shoes with her feet. 'I think we should go back now.'

Gripping her arms, he pulled her up. 'We're not going back yet. Come on, Queenie, let me. . .'

'No!' But his lips came down hard on hers, and his quick breathing alarmed her – he was consumed with lust! If she'd managed to put on her shoes, she thought, distractedly, she would have kicked him, but she would only hurt her toes if she did it now. When one of his legs tried to prise hers apart, she lifted her knee and, with full force banged it into his groin, making him yelp with pain and let her go. It was her chance and she took it, grabbing her shoes off the ground and running as quickly as she could.

He was doubled over and didn't attempt to follow her, but she kept running until a stitch started in her side. After she got her breath back, she leaned against a wall to put on her shoes, thankful that she wouldn't have to walk over the fishy scales in her stocking soles. To make sure that Callum wasn't coming after her, she took a quick glance behind her before walking on. The sun had gone altogether, although it wasn't pitch dark yet, but it was still frightening to be on her own in this deserted area. She imagined that she saw a man cowering in the shadows of one of the Arches and broke into a run again to get past, but it was just a few wooden fish boxes, stacked rather higgeldy-piggeldy. Slowing down, she gave a hysterical giggle. She was being paranoiac, but she hadn't far to go now until she reached civilisation and could relax.

Patsy had been right. All men, young and old, were tarred with the same brush. Even Callum, whom she had thought was a nice boy, had turned out to be as bad as the men in Patsy's office, wanting to touch, wanting to claim her virginity. If she hadn't got away from him, she'd have been in desperate straits. He might have made her pregnant, and what would she have done then? Auntie Gracie would probably have thrown her out and Neil would have been shocked that she had let a boy do such a thing to her. Yes, Neil was different; he was a nice boy. He would never touch any girl like that.

Well, that was the end of Callum, and she wouldn't go out with another boy for as long as she lived. She would remain a spinster . . . not a vinegary spinster, but maybe like Miss Thomson at school, gentle and kind. Teaching would be a good career, Queenie decided, as she left South College Street and carried on up Bridge Street, feeling safe amongst people. To give her face time to cool down before her aunt saw it, she walked very slowly along Union Street, looking in shop windows but not seeing anything. Noticing that the Town House clock showed only five past nine, she realised that she would have to wait a little longer before she went home. If she went in too early, Auntie Gracie would want to know why, and she wasn't in a fit state to tell a convincing lie just yet.

It was almost ten when she finally climbed the tenement stairs, tired out from all the walking she had done to pass the time. 'What did you see tonight?' Gracie smiled.

Queenie was ready with her answer, although her heart was hammering as she voiced the half truth. 'We didn't go to the pictures, it was too hot. We . . . met two girls in my class, so we all went for a walk.'

Joe grinned. 'Didn't Callum object to having three females on his hands?'

'No, he was quite happy about it.'

'Come to think of it, I'm quite happy with you three.'

Gracie snorted. 'Aye, you haven't to lift a finger, have you? You get everything done for you. You wouldn't know what to do if you'd to fend for yourself. I'm sure you don't even know where I keep the tea.'

'In the caddy on the mantelpiece,' Joe said, triumphantly.

'That's about all you do know, then.'

'It's all you need to know, isn't it, Dad?' Patsy smiled affectionately at her father. 'Well, goodnight, I'm off to bed. You'll be taking a cup of tea first, Queenie?'

'No, I don't want anything.'

The two girls left the room together, and Queenie was glad that Patsy asked no questions as they undressed. She would tell them all in a day or two that she and Callum had had a quarrel at school, to explain why they weren't going out any more. It would be awful to face him tomorrow, but he would probably keep out of her way. She smiled in the darkness. She had surprised herself as much as him by the knee-punch, but even though it had been a reflex action, it had done the trick and nothing had actually happened.

The pseudo love letters continued to flow, much to Alf's and Neil's amusement, but Olive believed every single word and was delighted that each one was more affectionate than the last. She tried not to show how deeply she cared, but her feelings did intrude on what she wrote. 'I'll only be half alive until you come back to me,' she said in one letter.

Neil howled at this, but Alf said, guiltily, 'She's going to be real hurt when I tell her it's all off.'

'Oh, come on! Don't go soft on me now. Olive's too full of her own importance to care.'

'It doesn't look like that to me.'

'She'll be angry, not hurt, and you won't be there for her to shout at. She's not fully hooked yet, so wait till after our next leave, then you can call it a day.'

Alf straightened his shoulders. 'OK, I'm game if you are. It's not me that'll end up on the chopping block.'

'She doesn't know I've got anything to do with it.'

'Maybe not, but I bet she'll take her spite out on you.'

The laughter left Neil's eyes. Had he built up trouble for himself in his attempt to be rid of Olive?

# Chapter Seven

Over the long summer, Neil and Alf notched up many 'scores' in the little villages near the camp, vieing with each other in their descriptions of how they had succeeded. Sometimes, they discovered that the girl one was describing had already been 'done' by the other, but it only had them helpless with laughter. There was no animosity.

'This war's the best thing that ever happened to me,' Neil observed one morning.

Alf nodded eagerly, 'Me, too. I just hope we don't run out of steam.'

'Come off it, man, we're young yet.'

'I'll be twenty-one in December.' Alf made it sound as if he were on the border line of senility, and Neil patted his hand sympathetically. 'I forgot how old you were. Aye, you'd better go canny.' Dodging a sham right hook, he went on, 'I just hope we get posted, I quite fancy a change of girls and I wouldn't even mind if we were sent overseas, for it would solve our problem with Olive.'

'Our problem? It's your problem, Neil boy, I can pull out whenever I want. To be honest, I was going to call it off the next time I wrote, for her letters are getting a bit too serious for my liking.'

'Ach, that's the way she is. It's you she wants now, thank God, and I know how her mind works. She'll go all out to get you to say you love her, so make her believe you do – that's all I ask. Come to King Street with me again . . . just one last time, Alf?'

'It'll definitely be the last. It's gone on long enough.'

Because it had been raining the day before, all the washing was still hanging on the pulley and Gracie was depressed at the sight of it when she went into her kitchen first thing in the morning. Joe would complain, as he usually did, about 'clothes flapping round his lugs', and she didn't care much for it herself – it wasn't healthy – but she hadn't time to feel if any of the thinner articles were dry, so they would all just have to put up with it.

She was brusque with her husband when he came through and snapped at Queenie and Patsy for 'scuttering about' instead of eating their breakfast, but fortunately for her family, a letter from Ellie banished her blues.

'Kathleen was married last Saturday,' she told them, after she had read it. 'I was beginning to wonder about her, for she was twenty-four last month, and I've never heard of her having a lad. She didn't get that off her mother, for Ellie had lots of lads before she married Jack Lornie.'

'I never knew him,' Joe observed.

'No, he was killed in 1917. He was a nice boy but he went and enlisted in 1915 when Kathleen was just months old, so she never knew her real father.'

'Gavin was a good father to her though. Ellie was lucky there.'

'He was too old for her, but they were happy.'

111

'We've been happy too, haven't we, lass? I have, anyway.'

Gracie looked self-consciously at Patsy and Queenie, then smiled, 'Aye, we've been happy, and we've got two daughters now as well as a son.'

'Did Kathleen have a big wedding?' Patsy wanted to know.

'No, it was in the registry office. It's not the same as a church wedding, or having the minister coming to the house, but I suppose it's just as binding.'

Patsy looked thoughtful. 'I think I'd rather be married in a church.'

Queenie nodded, 'Me, too.'

Gracie had been glad when Queenie stopped going out with Callum, though she didn't know what had gone wrong, but now she looked fearfully at her daughter. 'You're both far too young to be thinking of marriage. You haven't got a steady lad, Patsy, have you?'

'I haven't got a lad at all. I just meant I wouldn't feel really married if the wedding was in a registrar's.'

Joe changed the subject, 'Does Ellie say anything else?'

'She says Morag's joined the Wrens, and she'd to report at Portsmouth on Monday. At least she got to be at her sister's wedding, but that means Ellie'll be all on her own now, for Kathleen's gone to Chatham with her new husband.'

'You could ask her to sell her house and come here,' Joe suggested. 'We've a spare room now Neil's away, he could aye sleep on the settee when he's on leave.'

'She wouldn't come. I asked her after Gavin died, and she wouldn't hear of it. Anyway, Neil's things are still in his room, and he'll need it again when the war's finished.'

When her husband and daughter went out, Gracie turned to Queenie who was on holiday from school. 'Will you manage to make the dinner? I want to go and tell Hetty about Kathleen, for it's not the same over the phone.'

'Off you go,' the girl smiled. 'I'll manage the housework and the cooking, so you don't need to hurry home.'

'I'll likely be back before Joe and Patsy come in.'

Hetty was delighted to hear that Kathleen was married, but Olive's nose screwed up in disdain. 'A registry office?' She couldn't have put more disgust in her voice if it had been a place of ill repute. 'I wouldn't dream of being married in a registry office.'

Gracie's hackles had risen. 'What's wrong with it?'

'It's not really legal, for a start.'

'It's quite legal, and it's what Kathleen wanted.'

'Oh, well,' Olive sneered, 'if it's what she wanted, it'll be all right . . . I suppose. Did she have a white dress?'

On the verge of losing her temper now, Gracie said rather stiffly, 'She'd on a navy costume with a dusty pink blouse, and Ellie says she looked really lovely.'

'Maybe she wasn't entitled to wear white?'

'Olive!' Hetty warned.

The blatant slur on Kathleen's virginity was too much for Gracie. 'You've a nasty mind, you spoiled brat! Ellie would have said if she was pregnant and, even if she is, it's none of your dashed business.'

Olive's smirk was more annoying than any reply and Gracie turned away, still seething. Hetty, looking helplessly from one to the other, eventually ventured, 'I think Gracie's due an apology, Olive.'

113

'What for? She should apologise to me for saying I was a spoiled brat.'

Gracie's eyes twinkled suddenly, although she did her best to keep a straight face. 'I'm sorry you're a spoiled brat, Olive, it's a terrible handicap for you.'

Hetty drew in her breath, and it came as no surprise to Gracie when Olive spun round and stalked out, angry that the tables had been turned on her. Almost in tears, Hetty said, 'I'm sorry, Gracie, it's my fault she's spoiled.'

Her sister nodded, 'Aye, we all know that, and don't worry about me. I won't lose any sleep over what she said, and I'm sure Ellie wouldn't bother, either, though I'll not tell her anything. She's happy that Kathleen's happy, and that's what matters, isn't it?'

After another hour of conversation which was less strained as time passed, Gracie took her leave, but waited until she and Joe went to bed before she told him what had transpired.

'That girl's going to cause a lot of trouble some day,' he remarked. 'Hetty's going to wish she'd been harder on her.'

Gracie looked at him keenly. 'That's what I've thought for a long time. I used to worry that it would be Neil she would make trouble for, but she's hasn't bothered with him since she started going with Alf Melville. I can't think why she was so nasty about Kathleen though, unless her own romance isn't coming on as fast as she hoped, or maybe she's annoyed that Kathleen got a husband before her. Aye,' she ended, in great satisfaction, 'that's likely what it was.'

The following morning brought a letter from Neil, telling his mother that he would be home at the end of the

114

next week and asking if it was all right if Alf came to King Street again before going to Elgin. 'Neil's going to be here a few days before Alf,' Gracie observed. 'D'you think I should ask him to warn Alf about the kind of girl Olive is?'

Joe grinned. 'He'll find out for himself soon enough.'

'Alf's coming a week on Sunday!' Olive told her mother after reading his latest letter, her excitement too great to hide. 'He says he'll call for me at seven, and I hope you've some clothing coupons left so I can buy a new dress.'

'You've used all mine, and your father's, and Raymond's, and anyway, you've plenty of things that Alf's never seen.'

'I'd have liked something new,' Olive said petulantly. 'I won't feel good in anything old, but I suppose the blue slub linen will just have to do. I've only worn it once.'

Her frustration at the strictures imposed by wartime had evaporated by the time she went up to her room again and her mind was entirely on Alf. Each time he wrote, he said he was missing her but he always stopped short of telling her that he loved her. She almost swooned when a new thought struck her. He was so romantic, he must be waiting until he could tell her in person! She was hurt that he was going home to Elgin on the Tuesday – he could have waited another day or two – but he probably felt duty-bound to see his parents.

Olive let her mind drift ahead. An engagement party on his leave after this one, and he would take her home with him to introduce her to his mother and father, and it would be the leave after that before they could actually be married. Her father would probably want a big wedding . . . a white dress and a church ceremony – definitely not in a registry office like her cousin Kathleen McKenzie – a reception in the best hotel in the city. Excitement rippled inside her at the thought of how marvellous it would be, and all that was only the lead up to the wedding night! She had planned to give herself to Alf this time, but it would be best to wait until they were on honeymoon. It would be all the sweeter for them both if he took her virginity legally. The rippling thrills merged and formed a huge shivery knot in the pit of her stomach as she tried to picture what would happen.

'Olive! Breakfast's on the table!'

Her mother's voice shattered the dream, but there would be plenty of time to think before the big event. 'Coming!'

Looking up when Queenie came through, Neil was amazed. Having taken a few hours in bed after he arrived home, Neil was back in the kitchen only a few minutes when Queenie came throught, ready to go to the pictures with Patsy. The difference in her amazed him. She'd been a schoolgirl when she went out in the morning, but now . . . what a transformation!' Her long fair hair had been swept up at the sides in the latest style, emphasising its gold tinge; the touch of lipstick she was wearing outlined her mouth in delectable curves; whatever she had on round her eyes made them look larger and an even deeper blue; the bodice of her dress – last summer's by the look of it – was so tight that the points of her nipples were straining upwards against the thin cotton. God almighty! She was the most gorgeous girl he had ever seen, and he was glad he was sitting down. If he'd been standing, his arousal would have been in full view.

He had never thought of her as desirable before, had even smiled contemptuously when his mother wrote that Queenie was going out with a boy from her school – a couple of innocent kids, he'd thought – but now he prayed that the boy had done nothing to spoil that innocence.

'What d'you think of our Queenie now?' his father asked, a proud smile on his face.

Neil had to swallow. If he said what he had been thinking, everybody would be embarrassed, including himself. Luckily, Patsy came through and saved the situation. 'Are you ready, Queenie?' she asked.

Queenie appealed to her aunt first. 'Do I look OK?'

'You look fine, both of you.'

When the girls had gone, Joe looked at Neil again. 'She's quite the young lady when she's all dressed up, isn't she? I bet you got a surprise.'

He was able to laugh now. 'I sure did. She could pass for eighteen with the make up on. Is she still going with that boy?' He had to find out.

'She stopped going with him weeks ago. She never said why, but I'm sure there was never anything serious between them. It hasn't bothered her, at any rate.'

Satisfied, Neil started telling his father about problems he'd had with some of the vehicles he had to repair, and it wasn't until he went to bed that Gracie had the opportunity to voice to her husband a new fear which had arisen in her mind. 'Did you notice how Neil's eyes lit up tonight when he saw Queenie?'

'Aye, she looked a right wee smasher. If I'd been thirty years younger, I'd have . . .'

Gracie frowned. 'It's nothing to joke about. I was

117

pleased when Olive started going out with Alf, for it meant Neil was free of her, but if he falls in love with Queenie . . . oh, Joe, I hope there's no . . .'

'Queenie would be better for him than Olive.'

'But she's still a cousin,' Gracie pointed out.

Hetty held Martin back from going to the door with the young soldier after his evening visit. 'Can't you see Olive wants to get Neil on his own so she can ask about Alf?'

'I never thought . . . but Alf'll be here himself on Sunday.'

'Oh, you! Have you no romance left in your soul?'

Trying to sound fully convincing, Neil told Olive that Alf could hardly wait to see her and had to stifle a laugh when she asked, 'Does he say nice things about me?'

'He says you're wonderful. He's always speaking about you, wondering what you're doing and if you think about him as much as he thinks about you . . . the usual rubbish when a man's in love.'

Olive's eyes sparkled. 'He is in love with me, then? He's never said, but I was almost sure he was. D'you think he'll tell me when he's here?'

'I wouldn't be surprised, if he can pluck up the courage, that is. He's really quite shy, though he maybe doesn't give that impression.'

'He doesn't. I'd have thought he was full of confidence . . . but being in love makes a difference, I suppose?'

Neil couldn't hold back a giggle and covered up by saying facetiously 'Never having been in love, I wouldn't know.'

'Has Alf ever been in love before?'

'Not that I know of.' That was true, Neil thought. Neither he nor Alf were serious about any of their conquests.

'You know,' Olive said, dreamily, 'I used to think that I was in love with you, but that was when I was still just a silly schoolgirl. True love is nothing like that.'

'I'd better go. Cheerio, Olive.' Neil hurried away before his control snapped, but he had to collapse against a garden wall in a few seconds to give vent to his laughter. When he got over it, he wondered how his pal would cope with Olive in this state, and hoped that he hadn't gone over the score. It would be awful if Alf took cold feet now.

On Alf's first night in Aberdeen, Neil took him to Rubislaw Den, and they had giggled all the way home at Olive's flirtatious behaviour. They were still laughing about it when they went out for a walk the following morning.

'Hey, you two! What's the joke?' Scuffling out of Back Wynd on his lethargic way to Gordon's College, Raymond Potter had heard the laughter before he saw the soldiers, but when he recognised them, he ran across Schoolhill to talk to them.

'Oh, hullo.' Neil looked surprised. 'It's funny us running into you – we were laughing about Olive.'

'Oh, her!' All the contempt of a sixteen-year-old for his elder sister was contained in these two words. 'What's she done now?'

Neil chortled again, 'It's what we've done to her.'

Alf shot him a warning glance, 'Watch it!'

This only served to whet Raymond's curiosity. 'Go on. What have you done to her? She was going on at breakfast time like she'd come into a fortune.'

119

Neil nodded wisely, 'I bet she was. She'll be hearing the tinkle of wedding bells after last night, for Alf here told her he loved her.'

'Great! When you marry her, you'll be my brother-in- . . .'

'No, no,' Alf interrupted, panicking. 'It wasn't true. She practically forced it out of me.'

Raymond was confused now, 'Tell me what's going on.'

After Neil told him, the boy was beside himself with glee. 'So you've pulled a fast one on her? Goodoh! When are you going to tell her the truth, Alf?'

Neil explained, 'When he goes back to camp, he's going to write and tell her he's found somebody else. He's going home to Elgin now – we're on our way to the bus – and I go back to Larkhill tomorrow, so none of us'll be here when she gets the letter.' He paused for a moment, realising the danger of what he had said. 'For God's sake, Raymond, don't tell her!'

His cousin looked offended. 'What d'you take me for? I can keep my trap shut.'

'You'd better, or else . . .' Neil drew one finger across his own throat, menacingly.

'Scout's honour!' Raymond vowed, then looked at his wrist watch. 'I'll be late for school. Cheerio.'

A worried frown gathered on Alf's brow as the boy ran off, 'You shouldn't have told him.'

'Ach, Raymond's OK. He won't say anything.'

'Famous last words,' muttered Alf darkly, as they turned the corner past the granite lion erected as a memorial to the dead of the previous war outside the Cowdray Hall.

The Elgin bus was already standing in Blackfriars Street,

so Neil walked off as soon as Alf was seated. It was strange meeting Raymond but he was a sensible kid, and he was just as keen to see Olive get her comeuppance as they were. He would keep his tongue between his teeth. Remembering that he hadn't told Alf how he'd felt about Queenie that night last week – it wasn't something he could joke about – he decided to consider it carefully before he jumped in with both feet and did something stupid. He'd never felt anything like this before about a girl . . . but was it love?

# Chapter Eight

Unable to banish the memory of Neil's face when he had seen her all 'toffed' up, Queenie Ogilvie wondered once again if she had imagined the admiration. She knew that she had looked good – Patsy had assured her of that, and even Uncle Joe had seemed proud of her – but Neil must meet some really lovely girls in Larkhill. It could easily have been surprise that he had registered not interest. Nevertheless she was delighted that he had noticed how she looked, and perhaps next time he came home, he might ask her out, maybe even fall in love with her. She was certainly well on the way to being in love with him.

'Have you got another boyfriend, Queenie?' Patsy inquired one night. 'You've been looking kind of dreamy for days.'

'I don't know what you're talking about.'

Her cousin's rising colour told Patsy that she was on the right lines. 'Yes, you do. Come on, tell me. I won't say a word to Mum or Dad.'

'There's nothing to tell.' Why couldn't she just get some peace? She couldn't tell Neil's sister that she was dreaming of him. Patsy would think it was so funny she'd likely tell Auntie Gracie and Uncle Joe, though she'd promised not to.

Looking disappointed, Patsy slapped some Pond's Cold Cream on her face. 'I thought we weren't going to keep secrets.'

'I'm not keeping any secrets. I'd tell you in a minute if I'd a boyfriend, but I haven't. Callum was enough.'

'You never said what happened with him?

On terra firma now, Queenie giggled. 'He was the same as the men in your office.'

Whipping round eagerly, Patsy said, 'Out with it, my girl. What did he do?' She, too, ended up giggling at how Queenie had fended off the unwelcome attentions and forgot what she had asked in the first place.

Looking up at his friend, Alf chewed the end of his pencil – his fountain pen had been lost, or more likely stolen, long ago. 'We haven't got very far. "Dear Olive, I regret having to tell you . . ."'

Neil frowned. 'It sounds more like a business letter. We'd better start again. What about . . . "I am very sorry . . .?"'

Alf blew a raspberry. 'I'm not sorry.'

'She won't know that. OK, then. "Dear Olive, You're such a bloody pest, I . . ."'

'Och, be serious. I wish to God I'd never got involved in anything like this.'

Smiling wickedly, Neil laid his finger against his nose. 'It's your own fault. I'd never have thought of it.'

'You'll have to get me out of this mess, though. If you don't, I could end up having to marry the bally girl.'

Neil gave a howl of laughter. 'I can just see you in a top hat and tails . . . and what a wedding night you'd have. I could bet Olive wouldn't give you a minute's rest.'

'D'you want your face punched in? You're asking for it.'

Straightening the threatened part of his anatomy with some difficulty, Neil gave the letter further thought. 'You could put, "This hurts me as much as it will hurt you, but . . ."'

'That doesn't sound right. It has to be more delicate.'

After scribbling down and discarding several more phrases, Alf was finally satisfied. 'Read it out,' Neil prompted, 'so I can hear what it sounds like.'

Clearing his throat, Alf began, 'Dear Olive, I trust you will not be hurt at what I am going to say, but I know you would prefer me to be honest, though I feel awful about it. The truth is, when I was in Elgin, I ran into a girl I used to go with and I discovered I still loved her. What I felt for you was just deep attraction, not love, and it would be wrong of me to let you go on believing it was. Please don't think too badly of me, Olive. I couldn't help what happened, and I will never forget you. I hope that you find a man more worthy of you some day soon. Yours sincerely, Alf Melville'.

Neil nodded gravely. 'Just the job! That shouldn't put her back up, though you never can tell with her. But I'm free of her now, thank God.'

'As long as she never finds out it was you I did it for.'

'Nobody knows apart from us . . . and Raymond, and he'll never tell her. Anyway, she'll have got over it long before I go home again.'

'It maybe won't be long before we get embarkation leave,' Alf told him. 'There's word we're being sent overseas.'

'Thank God for that, I'm sick fed up here, and even if

124

she still feels angry at you, she won't take her spite out on me if I'm going abroad. It couldn't have worked out better.'

Olive had given her two student acquaintances – they were not as close as friends – a detailed account of all that Alf had done and written to her, using him as a pattern for the boyfriend she had deceptively created. It sounded much more convincing when what she was saying was actually true and Polly, at least, listened eagerly. She had been longing for his first letter since his leave, and when it arrived, her heart accelerated as she ran her paper knife along the top of the envelope. This would be a proper love letter, since Alf had told her how he felt. The first two words alarmed her. 'Dear Olive'? She had expected to see 'My Darling', or 'My Dearest'. He hadn't written a love letter, after all, he was preparing her for something nasty. Having worked this out, she was not so shocked when she read it. She was angry – no girl likes to be told that she's been replaced in her boyfriend's affections – but there was no misery, no feeling suicidal. Granted, she had thought that she loved him, even planned for a wedding, but she only felt let down, probably because she had not known Alf for very long. Well, that was that! She would have to resort to invention again to regale Frankie and Polly.

Giving a small sigh, she placed the letter on her dressing table, to be answered some time – it would serve Alf right to be kept in suspense for a while – and picked up her comb. As she ran it through her hair, she was glad that she hadn't told her mother of Alf's declaration of love. At least none of her family knew how far things had gone, and she would have to play down her resentment at being thrown over.

In the dining room, Hetty looked up with an arch smile, 'I suppose Alf got back to camp all right?'

Sitting down, Olive nodded, a little bleakly. 'Yes, he got back OK.'

'Is anything wrong? You're usually full of beans after a letter from him.'

'He's found another girl.' Olive hadn't meant to tell them just yet – she didn't want any sympathy and Raymond would likely gloat – but she hadn't expected her mother to be so quick to notice. 'Somebody in Elgin he used to go with.'

'Oh, I'm so sorry.'

'It's OK. It happens all the time, doesn't it? Now, can I just get on with my breakfast?'

Her father, engrossed in the morning paper, had not looked up, her mother seemed very concerned, but it was Raymond's expression which disconcerted Olive. It wasn't derisive – as she had expected – nor sympathetic, it was amused. When he realised that she was staring at him, the amusement vanished from his eyes, but there was still something there that she couldn't place. 'Don't feel sorry for me,' she said, with as much dignity as she could muster. 'I only went out with him a few times. There wasn't anything in it.'

Nothing more was said on the subject, so she finished her breakfast and left the house, proud that she had handled the situation so well.

Her mother, however, was not so happy. 'Olive's had quite a shock,' Hetty observed to Martin, whose head was still hidden behind the *Press and Journal*. 'She's pretending not to care, but she's far too calm. She thought a lot of Alf, and she must be upset.'

126

'Mmmm.' Her husband turned a page.

'I'd have thought she'd have flown into a temper, and it's not natural, the way she's taking it.'

'Mmmm,' Martin repeated.

Giving up, Hetty looked at Raymond. 'It's like speaking to a stone wall, trying to tell your father anything.'

An enigmatic smile on his face, her son stood up, 'See you at lunchtime.'

Alf was astonished by the way Olive had accepted what he had written. He had thought that she would answer straight away, calling him every bad name she could think of, or pleading with him to change his mind, but it was ten days before she wrote that she understood, that she forgave him and that he was not to feel guilty. His relief was so great that he felt like jumping his own height, and Neil was equally relieved that she hadn't started writing to him again. 'That got her off my back,' he laughed. 'I'd say Operation Olive was a big success and nobody got hurt.'

'We were lucky. It could have ricocheted on us.'

'Aye, but it didn't. All's well that ends well.'

Alf grinned. 'And the last one to the mess pays the beer tonight.'

Neil had been occupied for most of the day trying to find out what was wrong with the Royal Enfield he had been told to repair, but he had found the trouble at last and it was ready to be taken on a test run. It was no hardship to him, for he loved the feel of a machine like this under him, the thrill as the countryside rushed past, the exhilaration when the wind was whipping his face. All the other vehicles

– the trucks, the officers' cars, whatever he had to repair – were just routine. None of them could beat motor bikes! Revving up the engine, he listened for any alien noises and, hearing none, he engaged the gear and negotiated his way out of the workshop, waving to Alf as he passed.

Once on the open road, he opened the throttle and watched the speedometer climb higher and higher. She's going like a bird, he thought happily, and his life was running just as smoothly these days, with Olive neatly disposed of, although Alf sneered at him occasionally for seemingly giving up his old philandering ways. 'I can't understand you, Neilly boy. If I didn't know any better, I'd think you were in love.'

Content to laugh it off, Neil never rose to the bait. He wasn't exactly in love with Queenie, but he didn't want any other girl. He still accompanied Alf to dances, but he was too aware of his own failing to be as foolish as take any of his partners home, despite their blatant hinting.

He often wished that he had asked Queenie to write to him, but his mother would get ideas and he didn't want that . . . not until he had diagnosed his feelings for the girl properly. He was sure that she had known he was attracted to her, and was almost sure that she'd felt attracted to him, but attraction wasn't love, though love could develop from it, and he would wait until she left school before he said anything.

Realising how far he had come, he slowed down and turned the motor cycle round. If he followed his inclination, he'd be carrying on to Aberdeen to see her again, but if he did, he would be court-martialled for being AWOL or at the very least incarcerated in the glasshouse.

Laughing out loud, he let the engine roar back along the road again.

Alf frowned when he coasted into the workshop. 'Where the hell have you been?

'To heaven and back,' Neil smiled and removed the gloves with a theatrical flourish, adding, 'Don't take any notice of me, I'm just a silly bugger.'

Alf rolled his eyes. 'You never said a truer word.'

Renewed rumours that they were to be posted made Neil think. It wasn't definite, but it was more than probable that they would be sent abroad and he was quite pleased. He had been stagnating in Larkhill for too long, and he would welcome a change. The drawback was that he'd be separated from Queenie for longer than a few months at a time if they were sent to North Africa or the Far East. He was certain in his own mind now that he did love her – she was all that he could think of, dream of – but even if they got embarkation leave before they left, it was too soon to tell her.

Having thought about it from all angles, Neil wrote his first love letter one night. He had no intention of mailing it, but he had to get his feelings down on paper. He would carry it with him always, and if he were unlucky enough to be killed, it would be sent home with his other belongings and Queenie would know how he had felt about her.

My Darling Queenie,

I am writing this because there is word we will be sent abroad. Maybe this will be a big surprise to you, but I don't regard you as a sister any longer. It came as a shock to me, too, but I love you with all my heart. I can't stop thinking about you, and your lovely face fills my dreams every night. I was going to tell you next year, but I might not be in this country, so I am doing the next best thing and writing it down.

I don't know when you will get this or if you will ever get it, but if you do you will know that you mean everything to me. If I survive the war, I will marry you as soon as I come home, and thinking about that will carry me through whatever I have to face. Goodnight, my darling.

Yours till the end of time, Neil

He read it over – it was no literary masterpiece, but he had never meant it to be – then put it in an envelope, wrote Queenie's name on it and, as he slipped it into the pocket of his battledress wondered if any of the other men also writing letters were pouring their hearts out like he had done. Probably not. He had been over-sentimental as if he were sure he was going to be killed, but that was not how he felt – just the opposite. He was looking forward to the future . . . a future with Queenie. Positive, not negative.

As the weeks passed, Olive Potter began to think of Alf as having been just a pleasant interlude. His attentions had flattered her, had made her forget, but it was Neil she wanted

. . . it had always been Neil. He must have been jealous when she was out with his friend, though he hadn't given any sign of it, and she had better make it up to him and show how sorry she was. It would be some time yet before she saw him again, but it would give her time to plan her campaign.

Although Olive prided herself on having kept calm when she received Alf's letter, it was that very calmness which had set her mother worrying, and with her daughter remaining so quiet, as if she were trying to come to terms with herself, Hetty suspected that she was still pining. 'I wish there was something I could do to buck Olive up,' she remarked to her husband one day.

Martin looked baffled, 'What's wrong with her?'

'You wouldn't see sand supposing you were standing on the beach,' his wife retorted indignantly. 'She hasn't got over Alf, that's what's wrong.'

'Oh, that! She hardly knew him.'

'I hardly knew you when I fell in love with you.'

'Olive wasn't in love with Alf. You're imagining things.'

'I'm not, and she's needing to be taken out of herself. I think, when Neil comes, I'll get him to take her dancing or to the pictures or something.'

'Good idea.' Martin lifted a book.

'The only thing is, she used to be so fond of Neil. Maybe throwing them together again would be asking for trouble. It might escalate into something deeper than she could handle.' Hetty waited in vain for an answer, and went on, 'I suppose we'll have to cross that bridge when we come to it . . . if we ever come to it.'

Gracie had been disappointed that Olive's romance with

131

Alf had come to nothing and, after worrying for some time, she decided to confide in Joe one night, 'I'm scared that Olive starts with Neil again, for she'll be more possessive than ever, and he'll stand no chance against her.'

As usual, her husband laughed at her fears, 'You're always worrying about something or other. Neil's not the raw laddie he was before, he's had more experience with girls. He won't knuckle down now, he'll tell her straight out that he's not going to stand any nonsense from her. Alf had the right idea, he's well shot of her. Anyway, you're maybe barking up the wrong tree. Now Olive's been out with one lad, she'll likely have got Neil out of her system. The next thing we'll be hearing is she's got another boyfriend.'

'I hope so,' Gracie breathed.

'It's usually their daughters women worry about, not their sons, but thank goodness our two lassies are sensible.'

'Aye, you're right there. I was wor- . . .' She caught herself before Joe laughed at her again. 'I wondered, the last time Neil was home, if he'd ideas about Queenie, but she doesn't look at boys nowadays, not since that Callum.'

'She's young enough yet to have a steady lad, so's Patsy,' Joe grinned. 'That's when your worries'll start.'

Their posting had come as an anti-climax to all the soldiers involved. Like all first-time travellers abroad, the thought of being in a foreign clime had filled them with a thrilling anticipation, and Northumberland was not what anybody could call exotic. Most of them, however, soon got back to the old routine of picking up willing girls, their libidos getting an unnecessary boost from the new variety of faces

132

and figures. Most of them, but not Neil Ferris, although Alf Melville was always chivvying him to hunt with the pack and he could not explain why he wouldn't. He felt a little foolish now about having written the letter to Queenie, but surely they would be sent overseas soon – he hadn't been out of England and it was nearly a year since he joined up – and it would be best to keep it in his pocket . . . just in case.

Their camp was between Alnwick and Morpeth, with Newcastle not too far away, so there were many interesting places to see on their twenty-four-hour passes, not like Salisbury Plain, where the dominant feature was a circle of standing stones, though there had been several picturesque villages in the area. Both Neil and Alf had been raised in fairly close proximity to the sea so it was natural that they often landed up on the coast of Northumbria, watching birds and boats, and breathing in the bracing ozone of the same North Sea. Neil was fascinated by the causeway across to the Holy Isle, Lindisfarne, which was cut off twice a day by the tide, but when he suggested visiting the island, Alf said, 'No bloody fear. We could be marooned for hours.'

Inevitably, on their walks, they met girls who stopped to talk to them. Alf, of course, was in his element when this happened, choosing his partner and walking off in front, leaving Neil with the other one. A few, accustomed to the procedure, took his arm and kept up a steady stream of talk which required little or no answer, but some were as embarrassed as he was, which made things difficult. On one such occasion, the girl was so shy that Neil had difficulty in getting her to speak at all, but he did eventually learn that her name was Alice, and that she lived in the village of Seahouses – 'back there a couple of miles'.

Her shyness drew him to her, not in any romantic way, more as a friend who would pose no problems and she appeared to feel the same, opening up to say, 'Betty and I came out for a picnic, it was such a lovely day.'

He responded to the overture. 'We hitch-hiked to Bamburgh Castle, and we're walking back a bit to shove in our day.'

A little farther on, they saw Alf and Betty sitting on the sands, unpacking the girl's haversack. 'You could have some of our sandwiches,' Betty giggled.

The picnic let all of them get to know each other a little better, and when the empty paper bags and lemonade bottles had been stowed away, Alf took Betty behind one of the dunes but the other two stayed where they were, facing the wide expanse of gently rippling water which only ended where it met the sky, and letting the warm breeze ruffle their hair. Neil was completely relaxed with Alice now – she had turned out to be a good companion – and after a while she suggested taking a walk along the sands to search for seashells. 'My mum makes pictures with them,' she explained. 'It keeps her busy in the winter.'

They chatted idly – about her work in the bank in Alnwick, about the stupidity of some army drivers which resulted in the burned-out gearboxes and cracked cylinder blocks Neil had to replace – the girl bending down occasionally to pick up a shell that had taken her fancy – but eventually, they turned to something more personal. 'Have you a boyfriend?' Neil asked, purely to make conversation.

'Yes, Bill's in the navy, and I haven't seen him for eight months. We're going to get engaged when he comes home again. Do you have a girlfriend?'

He hesitated for a moment, but the atmosphere was so easy between them now, and the balminess of the early evening so conducive to confidences, that he said, 'Queenie's not long sixteen, and I haven't told her yet that I love her. I think she knows, though.'

Alice nodded, 'A girl always knows that. Bill and I grew up together, and I knew he loved me long before he told me, and I was only fourteen at the time.' Seeing the question in Neil's eyes, she added, 'We haven't done anything wrong, but we nearly did, the night before he went away the first time. That's why I didn't let him go beyond a few kisses the twice he's been home since.'

'I'd never dream of doing more than kissing Queenie though I might feel like it. She's still too young.'

It did not occur to either of them that this was a strange topic between two young people of different sexes, nor that, if they had been at all attracted to each other, it could have erupted into something they wouldn't have been able to stop. 'How old are you, Alice?'

'Seventeen past May. How old are you?'

'I'll be nineteen in November.' Elation was surging up in him. He had actually voiced his love for Queenie, and even though it was to a girl he hardly knew, he felt as if he had sworn it on oath, legalised it, made certain of the outcome. Catching Alice round the waist, he whirled her into the air. 'Oh, it's great to to be young and in love, isn't it?'

When their friends came into view, a few minutes later, it needed no clairvoyant to tell what they had been doing over the past half hour. Betty's thin dress was dishevelled, her face flushed, and Alf wore a hang dog, but satisfied, expression. 'I've promised to walk Betty home,' he said, 'so you can go with Alice, and we'd better put a step in, or else it'll be dark before we get there.'

The sun was dropping behind the horizon, but Neil had been enjoying himself so much that he hadn't noticed. 'You don't have to see me home,' Alice murmured.

'I'd like to.' They waited until Alf and Betty went ahead before they followed, walking at a quick pace to keep up. It was only two miles to Seahouses, but another fifteen to the camp, and the soldiers dared not be late. When they reached her village, Alice pointed out a fishing coble, one of the many small craft tied up in the harbour. 'That's my dad's.'

'He's a fisherman, is he?'

'They're nearly all fishermen here, and I'm sure he was a bit disappointed I wasn't a boy to carry on after him.'

'My dad was disappointed that I didn't want to work in his shop, but I was more at home with engines than groceries.'

Alice lived in one of the terraced houses which overlooked the harbour, standing out starkly against the darkening sky, and looking just as grey and dour to Neil when he came close to them. 'Can I see you again?'

She turned to face him, looking at him earnestly. 'I don't think so. I've had a really great time, but . . . I've got Bill and you've got Queenie.'

Her skin was brown with sunburn, her black hair was short, she was as tall as he was – everything that Queenie was not – but in some way, some indefinable way, she reminded him of Queenie, which made him ashamed of what he had asked. He had no romantic intentions towards Alice, though he had enjoyed the time he had spent with her, and it was probably best not to spoil it. 'Cheerio, Alice, and I hope you see Bill again very soon.'

'Thanks. Goodbye, Neil . . . Queenie's a lucky girl.'

He walked to the end of the row of houses, where Alf was already waiting for him. 'It's been some day, eh, Neil? That Betty's a humdinger. How was Alice?'

'She's very nice . . . a really decent girl.'

'So you didn't score?'

'I didn't try.' He hadn't even wanted to try, Neil thought in some amazement. He'd had Alice in his arms at one point, and had let her go without feeling a thing, when not so very long ago, holding a girl so closely would have aroused him into making at least some attempt. But that was before he'd fallen in love. He was a changed man now – sex was secondary to him . . . until he married Queenie.

Alf, forging on ahead, turned round impatiently. 'Come on, or we'll never make it back to camp in time.'

They hurried on, praying that they could hitch a lift once they were on the main road – they couldn't depend on getting a bus, and luck was with them. They had just left the side road when a van pulled up. 'Thanks, mate,' Alf puffed. 'I'm bloody sure I couldn't have gone much farther.'

'Been out on the randan?' the driver chuckled as he let off the brake.

Alf snorted. 'I have, but this dozey blighter's either in love or he's lost his touch.'

Grinning, Neil winked. 'Don't you wish you knew?'

# Chapter Nine

It was a cold, but dry, November evening when Neil next came home. 'What a journey,' he moaned, as he took off his greatcoat. 'It gets worse every time.'

Gracie was already opening the oven. 'Your supper's ready, I kept it hot for you.'

'Thanks, Mum, I'm famished.' Sitting down at the table, he looked at his sister and cousin. 'You two not out?'

'I'm broke,' Patsy laughed, and added, 'till payday.'

'I know the feeling.' He sat back as his mother laid down his plate. 'And how are you two old folks?'

Joe pretended to scowl, 'Less of the old folks, you cheeky devil. Your mother and me are still in our prime.'

'Speak for yourself,' Gracie said, a shade sourly. 'I feel like I'm ninety some days.'

As Neil demolished the huge pile of potatoes and the much smaller mound of rabbit stew, he watched Queenie darning the elbow of her jumper. Her head was bent over it, but she had looked up at him once or twice and he thought she was still beautiful, even with no make up and wearing an old felted cardigan. His eyes travelled down past her industrious hands to her legs, the streaks puzzling him until he recalled a girl once telling him that she painted her legs because she couldn't get stockings, not even when she did have clothing coupons. Queenie's leg-paint was quite obviously in need of touching up or replacing – whatever the girls did – and a thrill ran through him at knowing this intimate detail about her. Well-worn slippers with one pom-pom missing encased her feet, making them look like massive blobs. He smiled at this thought; nothing about Queenie was massive at all, not even her feet. He would love to be alone with her, to get to know her as a boyfriend not as a cousin, somewhere that he wouldn't be constantly aware of his mother's eagle eye on him . . . but he couldn't ask her out.

In obedience to Gracie's command Neil went, much against his will, to Rubislaw Den the following evening, hoping that Olive would not blame him for Alf's defection but assuring himself that she knew nothing of his hand in it. His welcome was the same as usual from Hetty, Martin and Raymond, but he did think that Olive was a little restrained, though it was maybe just his imagination . . . or guilty conscience? All she said was, 'How's Alf these days?' and when he told her that his friend was very well, she sat back and let her family do the talking.

He had just glanced at the clock and decided that he could get away shortly without causing offence when Martin said, 'I suppose you've a girlfriend now? Or more than one?'

Without even looking at her, Neil was conscious that Olive was holding her breath, and decided to make a joke of what was no longer the truth, 'Dozens. All the nice girls maybe love a sailor, but the bad ones love a soldier, and that's a lot more fun.'

Martin slapped his thigh. 'I bet it is. Seriously, though, what do you do with yourself when you're off duty?'

'Oh, go dancing, to the pictures or stay in the hut and play cards for matchsticks if we haven't any money. Not that we're supposed to gamble, and to let you know what happens, the boys in the next hut to us were playing pontoon for ha'-pennies one night and somebody reported them. They'd no idea who it was, but they'd to go in front of the CO, and this creeping Jesus of a sergeant was there as well.'

Martin nodded. 'So he'd been the one who reported them?'

'Aye, he was a right bast – ' Remembering that there were ladies present, Neil broke off then grinned sheepishly and went on, 'Well, the CO says, "How did you know the men were gambling, Sergeant?" – I don't think he liked the Sarge very much – and the blighter says, "I was walking past their hut, sir, and I heard one man saying, 'Twist', then a second later the same man said, 'Oh, bugger it! Bust!' They were playing pontoon, sir." The CO frowns and says, "You didn't actually see them?" "No, sir," says the sergeant, and the CO turns to the men and asks if they have anything to say, so one bright lad pipes up, "I can't deny we were playing pontoon, sir, but only for matches. We would never play for money."'

Laughing fit to burst, Martin said, 'So they got off?'

'Aye, they got off but the best bit was the sergeant got a bollocking for not making sure of his facts so, of course, he picked on that hut for weeks.'

'Olive needs to be taken out of herself,' Hetty remarked, suddenly. 'She studies far too much.'

His aunt's eyes semaphoring an urgent signal to him, Neil realised, in horror, what she had meant. Oh, damn! How could he get out of this? He couldn't! 'How would

you like to come to the pictures with me one night, Olive?'
He hoped that he sounded more enthusiastic than he felt.

'I'd love to, if you don't mind taking me.'

Yes, he minded. He would rather take a boa constrictor
to bed with him than be a whole evening alone with this
beastly girl, but they'd all be offended if he said so. 'I'm
looking forward to it. I should have thought of it before.'

Her eyes lit up. 'When?'

'Tomorrow?' It wouldn't do to put it off; it would look
as if he didn't want to. As if? That was a real laugh. 'Well,
I suppose I'd better go home, or Mum'll think I'm lost.'

The girls were in bed by the time Neil got in, and when
he told his parents how Hetty had press-ganged him, Joe
joked, 'An evening out with your favourite cousin? Just
what you're needing, isn't it?'

'Like a hole in the head,' Neil muttered darkly.

'Well, it's done now.' Gracie was dubious about the
wisdom of it, but tried to comfort her son. 'Olive's not as
bad as she used to be, she was hurt at Alf, so be nice to her.'

Neil shrugged, but didn't promise anything. If she
played fair, he would force himself to be nice, but if she
tried to start anything, he would walk out on her. He had
thought, in his innocence, that he'd got rid of her but he
was lumbered with her worse than ever by the look of
things. To be fair though, it was her mother's fault, not
hers. At their door, Hetty had whispered, 'She hasn't got
over Alf, and maybe you could take her out once or twice
every time you're home . . . just till she finds another boy?'

That was what bothered him. Would Olive look for
another boy if she thought she had him? Had all the
plotting he and Alf done been a complete waste of time?

Olive lay down in bed, hardly able to believe how things had worked out. She had intended to start writing to Neil again after he went back, to try to make him realise that Alf had been only a passing fancy and that she still loved him, then her mother had actually arranged a date for them. She'd have to be careful not to antagonise him by being pushy. A spot of reluctance might spur him on to take the initiative.

In the Palace Cinema, Neil was very conscious of his cousin sitting beside him. She had grown up, and she wasn't such a bad sort, after all. Why shouldn't he treat her like all the other girls he'd been out with? Lifting his arm, he let it come down gently on her shoulders. Her coat was lying across her knees, and he could feel the warmth of her skin through her blouse. If he wasn't careful, he'd . . . oh, damn! Too late! He removed his arm and crossed his legs to hide his arousal, but his eyes had found a target that drew them in spite of himself. As Alf had said once, her tits were huge, and he was practically sure that she was wearing nothing under her blouse. Had she purposely left off her brassiere?

He tried hard to keep his mind on the film. This was Olive, the brat, the pest. She was no filly for playing around with. If he laid a finger on her, he might as well say goodbye to bachelorhood, and he wouldn't do that for anything less than undying love. His desire died down, but he kept his eyes resolutely turned away from her. She gave no sign that she wanted him to put his arm round her again, so maybe he'd been wrong about her not wearing a brassiere . . . maybe he was just too randy for his own good?

Olive did most of the talking while he walked her home, chattering on without seeming to notice that it was a one-sided conversation and when they arrived at her house, she turned to him with a smile. 'Thanks, Neil, I've had a lovely evening. The main feature was great, and the B film wasn't too bad either.'

'It was a good show.' The words were forced out of him. He couldn't get over the fact that Olive, of all people, should make him feel like this and it was nothing she'd done. 'How about showing me how much you enjoyed it?' he mumbled.

'What do you mean?' She looked up at him innocently.

'The girls I take out usually let me kiss them goodnight.'

'Oh, I see. Well, kiss me if you want to.'

It was anything but encouraging, but he pulled her towards him feeling her tensing at first then melting against him. In a second, however, she drew away. 'No, Neil, don't.'

Dropping his arms, he said, 'Will you come dancing with me on Tuesday?' The minute he said it, he wished he hadn't but luckily she said, 'Thanks just the same, but I've lost too much studying time already. Maybe next time you're home?'

Left standing on the doorstep, Neil turned away abruptly. He had got Olive all wrong. If she had ever cared for him in the way she had once written, she didn't now, which pricked his ego rather badly though he felt no affection for her. The only things that appealed to him were the rounded rear end and the swinging breasts that cried out to be squeezed and fondled. It could have been gratifying to have initiated her in the pleasures of sex – he had a feeling that she'd be a real good lay – but she was taboo.

On his way up the tenement stairs, Neil was struck by an appealing idea. His mother hadn't objected to him going to the pictures with Olive – she hadn't been too happy, but she hadn't objected – so she surely wouldn't say anything if he asked his other cousin out – it was worth a try. Queenie, of course, was a different kettle of fish from Olive, and he'd have to go easy. Knowing his own weakness, he wouldn't even kiss her . . . one kiss from that sweet mouth and he'd be lost, throwing caution to the winds. The only reason he'd stopped with Olive was fear that she might wind her tentacles round him again, otherwise he wouldn't have thought twice about forcing her, but Queenie was too young and innocent to muck around with. He respected her as much as he loved her.

Late the next evening, Joe gave a groan. 'Oh, damn! I'm near sure I forgot to switch off the slicer. Well, I'll not sleep if I don't go and check.'

Gracie rose too, 'I'll come with you. I need a breath of fresh air, I haven't been over the door the whole day.'

When they went out, Neil turned with a smile to Queenie. 'Would you like to come dancing with me tomorrow night?' He had thought about it all day, but hadn't liked ask in front of his mother and this opportunity was too good to miss.

'Oh yes, thanks, Neil!'

He was pleased by her eager acceptance until it occurred to him that Olive might not be happy about it. She would be jealous more than likely and it was unwise to give her any cause to be angry. When his parents came back, he told them what he had done, half hoping that his mother would forbid Queenie to go, but she just shot a troubled glance at Joe who shrugged as if to say, 'Don't involve me.'

The girls went to bed first, Neil following them about ten minutes later, and Gracie said, 'I'd have felt better about it if he'd asked Patsy to go with them. I just hope he's not attracted to Queenie.'

Joe shook his head, 'He's needing company, that's all, and it'll do the lassie good to go out with a laddie again.'

'But what if she thinks he's serious about her? It's not a good idea, Joe, she's his cousin too.'

'Ach, you. You've got some right funny notions. Queenie's a sensible lassie, she'll know he's just being friendly.'

'Olive's not going to be pleased about this.' Gracie felt angry at her son for stirring up a hornet's nest. 'Mind you, I don't like him taking Olive out either, not after the way she used to carry on over him, and it's not as if he cares tuppence for her. There's going to be trouble there.'

Joe yawned, 'Never! They're all just youngsters, for God's sake. I wish you'd stop worrying about things that'll never happen. Give Neil credit for having something between his lugs. He just wants company and you should be pleased he's not picking up some whore off the streets.'

'Joe!'

Neil felt quite protective towards Queenie. She was so young and so inexperienced that he didn't dare to give her a clue as to how he felt, but as well as having a figure that most girls would envy, she was so beautiful it took his breath away. Her silky fair-gold hair curled round her neck, her startlingly bright blue eyes made his heart turn over every time she looked up at him and he longed to run his fingers over her velvety cheeks. He was certain that all the other men were wishing they were in his shoes.

Unconsciously, he tightened his hold on her and when she looked up at him, questioningly, he nuzzled his chin against her brow and murmured, 'You've turned into a real beauty, do you know that? I wish . . .' Common sense made him stop.

'What d'you wish, Neil?'

'Oh, I just wish the war was over, and I could be at home all the time.' It wasn't exactly what he'd had in mind but he couldn't go too fast.

'I was supposed to be going home after the war,' she said, softly, 'but now . . .' Her eyes filled with moisture.

He cursed his insensitivity. 'I'm glad you won't be going away. I mean . . . I'm sorry you've nobody left in South Norwood to go home to, but if you were there I'd never see you.'

Their positions were reversed. He was so confused that she felt protective towards him with the emotions of a mature woman. She wanted to pull his head down, to tell him with a kiss that she too was glad that she would be here for him when he came home, but it was so disloyal to the memory of her parents that she felt ashamed. 'Can we please change the subject, Neil?'

'I'm sorry, I shouldn't have said anything like that. What do you think of this band?' At the final, resounding chord, he swung her round several times before leading her off the floor. 'I love dancing. I went to all the hops with Alf when we were in Wiltshire.'

'Did Alf still go to the dances with you after he started seeing Olive?'

'I don't think Alf was ever really serious about her,' he said, cautiously. 'I think that was all in her mind.'

'Hetty says she still hasn't got over him.'

'I know. That's why I took her out.'

This was a surprise to Queenie as Gracie had kept silent about it and she was thankful that she hadn't told Neil how she felt about him. She was just another cousin with whom he had to do his duty, that was all. Stifling her hurt, she put on a brave show of enjoyment for the rest of the evening.

They walked home to King Street almost in silence but as they entered the communal lobby, Queenie said, 'Is anything wrong, Neil? You've hardly spoken since we left the Palais.'

Halting, he put his hands lightly on her shoulders. 'I say too much sometimes Queenie, and do too much.'

'I won't be angry, whatever you say or do.'

In the soft moonlight filtering through the transom window above the street door, her eyes were luminous and pleading, melting his resolve not to put a step wrong. 'You'd hate me if I did what I want to do.' But his lips could not resist hers and his hands slid down meeting in the small of her back to draw her against him, until he was forced to break away. Holding her hand resolutely, he dragged her upstairs.

Patsy had been in bed for some time, but she was waiting to hear how the evening had gone and Queenie happily obliged while she was undressing. 'It was perfect. I've never gone dancing before but Neil showed me how to do the steps. The slow foxtrot and the quickstep were more difficult than the waltz, but the Palais Glide was easy.' Stepping out of her knickers, she pulled on the trousers of her pyjamas. 'I'd a marvellous time and Neil's ever such a good dancer.'

Patsy sighed, 'I wouldn't have minded going with you but he didn't ask me and, anyway, three's a crowd.'

Fastening the buttons of her jacket, Queenie flopped into the double bed. 'D'you think he'll ask me again? He said he went out with Olive . . .'

'I didn't know that, but I can tell you she's going to be sick with jealousy about you.'

The vivacity vanished from Queenie's face. 'She did tell me once to keep away from him, but I thought she . . . she went out with Alf . . . does Neil like her, too?'

'Like her? He hates the sight of her.'

A ray of hope appeared in Queenie's face 'If he doesn't like her, maybe he won't take her out again. I think he does like me, and I know I like him. If he . . . wanted me to be his girlfriend, I wouldn't refuse.'

Two days later, Neil bumped into Olive on Union Street and knocked her off her feet. He did his best not to show his displeasure when she stood up . . . an offended Olive was far worse than a normal Olive. 'I'm glad I met you,' she said, 'I was wanting to talk to you.'

The tone of her voice warned him that she was about to say something unpleasant but he smiled, 'Fire ahead then.'

'Does your offer still hold?'

'What offer?'

'You asked me out again and I refused, but I've changed my mind. Aren't we girls awful?'

It was more than awful, Neil reflected, it was disastrous, but what could he say? 'Well, I go back tomorrow so there's only tonight left.'

'Can we go dancing? At Miss Oliver's, we were taught all the dance steps, tap, ballet and ballroom, so I wouldn't be a disgrace to you.'

Now he understood. She must have found out that he'd gone to the Palais with Queenie. His mother had likely told Hetty this morning on the phone. 'OK, if that's what you want.'

He arranged to meet her at half past seven, and went home seething with anger which he couldn't vent on anyone. It was his own fault. He should never have suggested another date.

His ill humour lifted as soon as they went into the dance hall. Even Olive was better than no partner.

It was their third dance when she said coyly, 'Is Queenie a better dancer than I am?'

He might have known that she couldn't let it pass without some comment, but he wouldn't let her know that Queenie had been an absolute beginner. 'Much the same.' But it hadn't been the same, he thought. He hadn't minded when Queenie's small, firm breasts pressed against him but he was repelled by Olive's large bosom now, though he had been aroused by it before. Her hair was coarser than Queenie's, her eyes were a lighter blue and not so soft; yet the admiring glances she was getting from other men proved that she was attractive. She wasn't his cup of tea, that's what it was.

Afterwards, he walked her home, thankful that there was no communal lobby at Rubislaw Den where he might make a fool of himself but she turned into the open gateway to one of the large houses in Queen's Road – the gate and the railings had been taken as part of the war effort – and dragged him into the shadows under the mature trees in the garden. 'I'd like you to kiss me goodnight properly this time,' she whispered holding her face up to him.

149

Her lips parted as his met them – a sign that Alf had done some groundwork – and the devil suddenly broke loose in him. Viciously forcing her mouth farther open with his tongue, he was dismayed by a familiar ache in his loins which increased when she pressed her body against him but when he tried to pull away, she clung to him like a limpet, 'Don't stop now, Neil. I know you want me.'

His body would not let him deny it, and he thrust her from him in anger – at himself as much as at her – whirling out of her hold. In a brooding silence, he accompanied her to her door then strode off without looking back.

Before he reached home, Neil had decided not to issue any further invitations to either of his cousins. With Queenie, he could easily get carried away and tell her he loved her and if Olive went on the way she'd done tonight, he might do something he would regret for the rest of his life. He'd be better with the floozies he used to pick up, who were only out for one thing and expected no commitments. He could take his pick of them and devil take the hindmost.

He was laughing when he went home and his father looked up smiling, 'Olive must have been in good form.'

Neil exploded. 'Bloody good form. She's a praying mantis, d'you know that?'

Joe's smile broadened, 'You'd better watch her, though. If you start anything there, you'll be a goner.'

'You don't need to tell me that.'

In the girls' bedroom, Queenie said, 'Neil was late in.'

'He took Olive home,' Patsy didn't want to discuss Neil's association with Olive; she knew how Queenie felt about him and the poor girl had been hurt enough already.

150

Queenie, however, persisted with her questions, 'You said he didn't like her.'

'He couldn't let her go home in the blackout on her own.'

'I feel sorry for her. It must be awful going out with a boy who doesn't like you.'

Patsy snorted, 'Don't feel sorry for Olive, she has a hide like a blinking rhinoceros. Remember last New Year, how she said she'd be my sister-in-law one day, even though Raymond and I both told her Neil didn't like her? I don't think she was ever really in love with Alf and it wouldn't surprise me if she wore Neil down one of these days.' The distress in the other girl's eyes made her qualify this, 'No, I'm sure she won't, for he knows her. He can see through her.' Patsy had meant to console Queenie with this last remark, but she could see that her cousin had not been taken in.

Olive was annoyed at herself. She should have stuck to her original plan and played hard to get but she'd been jealous of Queenie. She had wanted to show Neil that she was still in love with him, to kindle a love in him, but she had only put him off. She would be more careful in future but it would be best to leave Miss Ogilvie under no misapprehension as to his intentions. Queenie might think she stood a chance with him and she was pretty enough to be a serious rival. Neil belonged to her, Olive, and no chit of a Londoner was going to take him from her.

# Chapter Ten

'I'm bloody freezing,' Alf Melville pulled his greatcoat up round his ears. 'No bugger could survive out here in this.'

Neil shifted his hip round a fraction, 'And a ground-sheet's not much to have between your arse and the ground.'

'Two weeks of this and I'll be black and blue all over and frostbitten into the bargain,' Alf sighed. 'Why didn't they wait till summer before they did this? They might have known what it would be like in February.'

The friends were taking part in a training scheme on the Yorkshire Moors and not relishing it. They had been told to work their way round behind the opposing side's main party in twos or threes, and that they'd have to sleep where and when they could. Alf and Neil had found a ramshackle barn on the first night which afforded them at least some shelter from the weather, and the hay-strewn floor had not been too uncomfortable apart from the awful smell that rose from it. They had shared this dubious accommo-dation, and their rock-hard biscuits, with the barn's sitting tenants, a colony of rats. For the next few nights, they had huddled on the lee-side of a tree or a bush, anything which would give a little protection from the biting north winds, but their present position was barren of anything except stones. They had been too tired to go any farther and had flopped down on the open ground near a crossroads.

Both young men had drifted into a light doze when a great bang, somewhere to their left, jerked them wide awake. 'What the hell . . . ?' Alf's voice quivered with apprehension.

'It sounded like a bomb,' Neil muttered.

'It couldn't have been a bomb, there hasn't been a plane.'

Fearfully, they sat up, all hope of sleep gone now, and in the next minute they heard a faint crack as if a twig had been snapped underfoot. 'Somebody's creeping up on us,' Alf whispered. 'What are we supposed to do if it's one of the other side?'

'We don't let them surprise us,' Neil hissed, but a torch was shone on them before they could stand up.

'You there,' a voice boomed, 'your leg's been blown off.'

'Nobody's been near us,' Alf protested.

'Not you – him! The blues let off a thunderflash, and that stands for a shell, and I'm an umpire, and I say his leg's been blown off.'

A label, to that effect, was attached to Neil's coat. 'What happens now?' he asked in bemusement.

'Wait there and an ambulance'll come to pick you up.' The umpire went to hunt for more, unsuspecting, maimed soldiers.

Alf took out a tin of cigarettes saying, as he handed one to Neil, 'You'll be out of this caper, you jammy sod.'

Neil brightened, 'Thank the Lord for that.'

He stood up when they heard the ambulance, but one of the stretcher-bearers shouted scathingly, 'Lie down, you stupid bastard. You're not walking wounded if your leg's off.'

Neil lay down and waited to be lifted on the stretcher. 'I feel a right twerp,' he told Alf, as yards of bandaging was wrapped round the 'bleeding stump'.

'Where are you taking him?' Alf asked.

'To the school. All casualties have to stay there till the exercise is finished. Meals there, beds there.'

Alf gave a low, hopeful groan, 'You'd better take me, as well. I think I've got a bit of shrapnel in my arm.'

The ambulance driver turned to him impatiently, 'You'll be getting a boot up the backside if you don't shut up.'

'No more hard tack, no more bully beef,' Neil chanted, as he was carried to the ambulance.

Alf retaliated by giving a reversed V-sign which Neil did not see in the darkness, then stood up to search for another companion with whom to share the remainder of the night.

There was a great deal of hilarity in the ambulance as it bumped its way to the local school – one of the 'casualties' lifting his head to say, 'We're on to a cushy number here' – and even more when it arrived and they were shuttled in one by one, still on stretchers. But they soon settled down on the comfortable camp beds that had been provided for them, pulled up the army blankets and slept the sleep of the just.

In the morning they were given a cooked breakfast, then left to lie in comfort, a welcome break after tramping the moors for the past few days. Neil had time now to think

154

about what he had learned while they had been at Queens-bury, a village on a hill between Bradford and Halifax. He had heard of the Marquis of Queensbury of course, whose rules were still being used as a bible in the boxing world, but it had never occurred to him that it was a real place. They had been told that they would be there for four months, two weeks of which would be a hardship course, carried out under battle conditions. Rumours had abounded – someone had heard from someone else who had got it from someone in the village – that all the men on previous schemes had been sent overseas shortly afterwards, and they were ready to believe that, otherwise what was the purpose of the exercise?

Most of the soldiers, Artillery and Ordnance Corps combined, were pleased at the prospect. The volunteers had volunteered for this alone and had been bored by having to while away their time in preparation for it; the regulars had been waiting to prove their skills in the martial arts they had been taught and had never had a chance to use properly; only those who had wives and children at home were less than thrilled at the prospect of being sent to a foreign country.

Although it could mean that he wouldn't see Queenie for a long time, Neil was delighted because the quicker they got stuck in against the enemy, the quicker the war would end. Wherever they were sent, they were prepared to fight to the death and if it meant his death . . . he would have given his life for his country. He didn't feel morbid about it for it was a risk all servicemen took, and the letter in his pocket would let Queenie know how much he had loved her.

The rattle of the lunch trolley made him sit up. Breakfast had been quite good, but it hadn't filled the vacuum caused by not having had a decent meal for days, and he was looking forward to this. Poor old Alf would still be eating survival rations he remembered, a little guiltily, but Alf wouldn't have cared if it had been the other way round, so why should he? He hadn't asked to be one of the injured, he'd just been lucky. He hadn't told Alf how he had been inveigled by Hetty into taking Olive out when he was home, nor that she had been writing to him again, for his pal would likely have said it was the price of him.

As the empty dishes were being collected, one 'patient', a proper wag, remarked, 'What price the ruddy Dorchester now? And we'll be here for eight more days.'

This set some of them off singing, 'In eight more days and seven more nights, I'll be out of the calaboose, eight more days and seven more nights, they're going to turn me loose.'

The school was far removed from being a prison, run more on the lines of a proper hospital and they all blessed the umpire for having chosen them as victims. Neil did think occasionally about Alf – still engaged in the 'war' against the blues, and facing the bitter elements with his usual dry humour and stoicism disguised as complaints – but this was the life and he would enjoy it while it lasted.

A few weeks passed before Olive found an opportunity to talk privately to Queenie. The Potters were visiting King Street one Sunday afternoon, and Joe suggested that they all go out for a walk. 'It's the first sunny day there's been for ages. I know it's cold, but it's not that bad.'

Everyone agreed to go except Queenie. 'I've some notes to write up for tomorrow, and I need peace to do it.'

This was Olive's chance; 'I'll stay with you and give you a hand if you get stuck with anything.'

Hetty gave a laugh, 'Olive's not keen on walks, that's the only reason she's staying behind.'

'Queenie won't mind.' Gracie shepherded the others out in front of her and turned before she closed the door. 'Make a cup of tea for yourselves, you two, if you want to.'

Olive waited until her cousin fetched her books from her room and spread them out on the table, 'I believe Neil took you out when he was home?'

It didn't occur to Queenie that the question was anything other than friendly, 'Yes, to the Palais.'

'Are you expecting him to take you out again next time?'

Still unsuspecting, Queenie said, 'I hope so, I enjoyed it last time.'

'It was the last time for you,' Olive's top lip curled in a sneer.

'What do you mean?'

'I mean that you'll say no if he asks you out again. I'm not having you interfering between us.'

Queenie remembered then what Patsy had said about Olive's attachment to Neil but objected to being spoken to in such a manner. 'If he asks me out, I'll go,' she retorted.

Olive tried another tack, 'You'll be wasting your time. He loves me and he said he only took you to the Palais because he was sorry for you.'

'That's a lie.' Anger made Queenie defiant. 'He told me he was glad I wouldn't be going back to London because he'd never see me and he . . . kissed me before we came upstairs.'

157

'A cousinly kiss, because he felt sorry for you.'

'It wasn't cousinly, it was . . .' Queenie stopped.

'It was what?' The words came out like a whiplash.

Goaded into utter indiscretion, Queenie shouted, 'He took me in his arms and kissed me like . . . it was a proper kiss.'

Olive's face was livid now. 'It's you that's telling lies! Neil wouldn't . . . you don't know what a proper kiss is.'

Queenie knew that she had the upper hand. 'Yes, I do. It's long and loving, and he was hugging me against him and . . .'

'You must have led him on.'

'He didn't need to be led on. He wanted to kiss me and he wanted to do more than that.' Queenie had gone over and over it in her mind and had realised why Neil had stopped.

Jumping furiously to her feet, Olive shot out her arm and swept everything off the table. 'You stupid little bitch! I wish you'd never come up here. Nobody wants you!'

To avoid showing how much this hurt, Queenie bent down to retrieve the scattered books, papers and pencils, but Olive continued, doing her utmost to upset her cousin as much as possible. 'Patsy hates having to share a bed with you, and Gracie and Joe have to pretend they don't mind keeping you but they do, only you're so . . . dense you can't see it. Neil wouldn't have asked you to the Palais unless Gracie had told him to take you out of her way for a while.'

In spite of the cruel things Olive was shouting, Queenie was determined not to give way and spread her textbooks out on the table, laying each one down as if she'd nothing else on her mind. Her studied serenity incensed Olive even more. 'You're living in a fool's paradise, Queenie Ogilvie! You're the . . . biggest fool I've ever seen.'

'Have you never looked in the mirror?' The clever riposte surprised both girls. Queenie had uttered it spontaneously and Olive was speechless at her nerve. 'You're as hard as nails,' she muttered, at last. 'Not a thing gets through to you, does it? But don't think you'll get away with this.'

Although her inside was bubbling up like a kettle on the boil, Queenie knew that she had won and that she would be wise to stop now, to bottle up the words she wanted to spit out, the tears she had almost shed. Olive's threat was empty – she could do nothing – and there was no truth in anything she had said. Taking out her fountain pen, Queenie pulled a jotter out of her bag and began to write, noticing out of the corner of her eye and with some satis- faction, that her cousin was hunched up in the armchair glaring at the fire, her scowling face dark and brooding.

When the others returned, Patsy was the only one who was conscious of the repressed animosity in the room, but could say nothing until she was alone with Queenie in their room. 'Olive looked a bit huffy, like she'd come off second best at something. What had she been up to?'

Queenie shrugged, 'If I tried to find out what was wrong every time Olive was huffy, I'd never be done.'

'Did you get peace to finish your homework?'

Queenie did not look at her, 'Yes, I got everything done.'

'Did you not let Olive help you? That's maybe why she was annoyed.'

There was a small intake of breath. 'She thinks she knows everything, but she's wrong.'

Patsy was satisfied that Olive had been offended because her offer of help had been refused and tired, from her walk, she soon fell asleep. Queenie, however, was still taut with the anger she had not had a proper chance to vent. It wasn't true that Neil felt sorry for her. He hadn't acted as if he felt sorry for her. He had enjoyed himself as much as she had – and he did like her, in spite of what Olive said. It was Olive he didn't like. That's what Patsy had said, and she would rather believe Patsy than that supercilious Olive Potter. Anyway, she would find out when he came home on his next leave. If he didn't ask her out again she would know that he'd been sorry for her before, but she was almost sure that he would.

The kiss Neil had given Queenie hadn't been like the one he had given her, Olive thought in distraction. He had desired her and he wouldn't desire a girl he didn't love. For years she had thought she loved him – Alf had been a passing fancy – but that kiss had awakened her emotions properly, and she knew now what love really was. What did Queenie know about a woman's feelings? She was still a silly young girl, and Neil had likely given her a little peck and she had jumped to the conclusion that he loved her. She didn't know what a proper kiss was and how it affected a girl's whole being.

Olive turned cold. If Neil kept on taking Queenie out and kissed her every time, even lightly, he could easily imagine he was in love with her and that would be disastrous. What could she do? How could she turn him against that sweetie-sweet kid? She'd have to think of a way before he came home again; forget all about making him declare his love for her and concentrate on finding out how he felt about Queenie. It might be that she had made a mountain out of a molehill and was worrying for nothing, but it would be best to make sure.

# Chapter Eleven

Although Neil had not told her that he loved her – not in so many words – Queenie was practically positive that he did. He had asked her out when he was home at the beginning of March, but having thought a lot about Olive's warning, she refused at first, making the excuse of having to study for her exams in May, and it had been Joe who told her not to be silly. 'A young lassie shouldn't be sitting in every night.'

She was glad that he had persuaded her to change her mind. Being with Neil again had been wonderful, even if she'd been unable to put Olive out of her mind. On their way home from the Palais, Neil had said, 'You've been quiet tonight. Did I say something to annoy you?'

'No.'

'I'm sure something's wrong – just tell me.'

'Nothing's wrong.' But she couldn't keep up the pretence. 'Well . . . there is something. Olive said you only took me out because you were sorry for me.'

'Oh, for God's sake! You shouldn't believe anything Olive says. She loves making trouble.'

'It wasn't true, then?'

'No, it wasn't. I did feel sorry for you when your mum

and dad were killed, but that was the only time. I wanted
to get you on your own, to get to know the kind of girl
you were away from the house and I enjoyed being with
you, couldn't you tell?'

'I hoped you did but I wasn't sure, then Olive said . . .'

'Damn and blast Olive! I only take her out because . . .
well, Hetty asked me. Just till she gets another boyfriend.'

'Honestly?'

'As sure as I'm standing here – walking here,' he added
with a grin. 'So come on, let me see you're still my girl.'

The tender look in his eyes had told her that he was only
half joking, and recalling how he had stroked her hair as he
kissed her – such gentle, loving kisses – Queenie knew that
it wouldn't have taken much for him to say that he meant
it, that he did look on her as his girl. It would have been
much better if he had told her he loved her, but he would
surely tell her the next time he came home.

Feeling quite let down because they had been sent back
near Alnwick after their leave, with no prospect of going
abroad, Neil lay on his bed to think about what had
happened when he was home. He hadn't meant to ask
either of his cousins out, but Hetty had slipped him some
money with a pleading look and he had been forced to
make a date with Olive. Nobody had forced him to ask
Queenie out, he just hadn't had the willpower not to. He
was certain now that she loved him as much as he loved
her, but he hadn't said anything to her because she was
still only sixteen. In any case, he had the feeling his
mother would be against it – she often reminded him that
Queenie was his cousin – but what did that matter when

they loved each other? The real fly in the ointment was Olive and he wished he had the courage to tell Hetty that the deal was off, that Olive had no intention of looking for another lad. She had seemed shocked when he told her off for being nasty to Queenie and had sworn blind that she hadn't done any such thing and, while he couldn't altogether believe her, he did wonder if Queenie had misunderstood her.

He was ashamed at the way he had kissed Olive before and had been relieved that she'd been more subdued this time and hadn't expected him to do it again. Her letters since he came back had been chatty and humorous – maybe she was growing up at last. After all, she was nineteen now.

Olive Potter was in a very bad humour. She should never have let Polly persuade her to go the auditions for the Students' Show. It was so humiliating that she'd felt like walking out after the first five minutes, but they wouldn't believe her protests that she would feel a fool cavorting on stage in a skimpy costume and it had taken over an hour to convince them that she was serious. It was after eight and very dark when she reached the tram stop outside Falconer's store, her coat already soaked by the lashing rain. There was a long queue and water dripped on to her shoulder off the umbrella of the woman in front but she was past caring. She had to think. Queenie had gone out with Neil again in spite of the warning, and had told him what she, Olive, had said. She had denied it, of course, when Neil accused her, but she wasn't sure that he believed her. Worse even than that, it had been horribly clear that he cared for Queenie a lot more than he had ever done for her. It must be stopped.

Having been jostled by several people hurrying home to get out of the rain and thinking dourly that nobody ever gave an apology, Olive lifted her head in surprise when a young man said, 'Oops! Sorry.' About to say that it didn't matter, she suddenly recognised the girl walking alongside him. Queenie! It was just as well that her cousin was too busy talking to the boy to look round, for she didn't believe she could have been civil to her. The two young people were soon swallowed up in the darkness of the dreich March night, but Olive was juggling with an idea that had occurred to her. They had not been holding hands, nor walking arm-in-arm, but Queenie had been with a boy! It was all Olive needed and she wondered why she hadn't thought of it before.

When the tram pulled up, the conductor's arm barred Olive from boarding. 'Next tram, please,' he called, giving three bells to the driver to show that the vehicle was full, and she didn't feel in the least annoyed. She was first in the queue now and it gave her more time to figure out what she could write to Neil to put him off Queenie. Just saying that she'd been walking with a boy wouldn't do; it had to be much stronger than that. . . much more condemning.

When another letter from Olive arrived, Neil opened it with expectations of being amused by more tales about patients in Cornhill Mental Hospital, where she had to spend some of her time as part of her medical training, but his smile vanished when he read what she had written.

164

15 March, 1942

Dear Neil,

Here I am again, though I haven't time to write much. I'm kept busy at home writing theses for Medical School, but not too busy to write to you. I'm looking forward to seeing you, as always.

I've been wondering if I should tell you this and please don't think I'm doing it out of spite but I feel it's my duty to let you know. I was waiting for a tram tonight outside Falconer's and I saw Queenie with a boy. I thought it was somebody she knew casually but they disappeared into the Adelphi – you know, the dark little alley that goes through on to Market Street? I thought they might be taking a short cut, though it's not on her way home, but they weren't. This is difficult for me to write because you'll think I was spying on her, but I wasn't. I know you like to keep an eye on her, and I wanted to make sure there was nothing funny going on, so I ran along to the top of Market Street but they didn't come out farther down, and I ran back to the Adelphi. I won't go into the graphic details of what I saw, but I can tell you that Queenie isn't a virgin any longer. I'm sorry if this shocks you, but it's better to know these things, isn't it? Please don't let her know that I've told you, because she would never forgive me.

Now, I'll get on to something cheerier.

Sickened, Neil read no further. Nothing would cheer him now, and even Olive wouldn't stoop so low as put something like that down on paper if it wasn't true. What a fool he'd been to trust Queenie. Ripping the letter and envelope into small shreds, he stuffed them into a rubbish receptacle on his way to the workshop, thankful that he'd be busy over the next few hours, which might keep his mind off it. He wouldn't let Queenie know that Olive had told him – he wouldn't give her the satisfaction of laughing at him. To hell with her. From now on he'd paint the town red. Any floozie would do if she gave him what he wanted for he'd been too long without it, and all for a worthless tart who opened her legs to the very first boy who asked . . . or had that one not been the first?

It gnawed at Neil's mind for days yet even when Alf asked what was bothering him, he couldn't speak about it. His stomach heaved when he thought of what Queenie had done – he knew he should stop thinking about it but he couldn't – and his anguish increased until it was almost more than he could bear. It came as something of a relief, therefore, when Alf said one afternoon, 'That's the third time you've put back the plugs on that ruddy truck without looking at them. Don't tell me love has grabbed you by the balls at last?'

Neil grimaced, 'It did, but not any more.'

'So that's it? What went wrong?'

'She found somebody else.'

'Did you have it bad?'

'Bad enough,' Neil said guardedly.

'I'd the feeling there was some dame in Aberdeen but good God, man, there's plenty of fish in the sea. Forget about her and we'll pick up a couple of dollies tonight. What about it, eh?'

Forced to smile at Alf's solution to his heartbreak, Neil decided to give it a try. 'You're on, boy. Look out, girls, Neil Ferris is on the rampage again.'

Alf slapped him on the back, 'That's the spirit!'

For the next few weeks, Neil went wild, not admitting that it wasn't the same as it had been before. The only times he felt at all happy was when he took one of the motor cycles out on the road. They were what he loved now. They could be depended on not to stab him in the back.

Eyeing her sister's steadily-enlarging figure, Gracie asked, 'How do you manage on the rations?'

Hetty shrugged, 'I get by.'

'How? I'm always worrying about what to have for dinners and the girls and I have had to stop taking any sugar in our tea, haven't we, Queenie?'

'I'm used to it now,' her niece smiled. 'In fact, if I do forget and put in a spoonful, it tastes awful.'

Hetty gave a little smirk. 'I know a man who lets me have two pounds now and again . . . off the ration, you know?'

'Black market?' Queenie suggested.

Gracie looked horrified. 'Hetty Potter! The black market? Fancy you cheating like that.'

'It's not cheating. What's the harm in buying extra when you can? I get butter and eggs from him too and a bit of beef sometimes, or pork. Of course, he charges more than the shops, but they wouldn't give me so much.'

167

Gracie was speechless . . . for a moment. 'Money always talks, doesn't it?' she burst out, her face red with indignation.

Trying to pacify her, Queenie said, 'Everybody does it, if they think they can get away with it.'

'Just them that can afford it, not us ordinary folk that have to make one penny do the work of three.' Gracie turned on her sister again. 'We've to survive on bare rations and we hardly ever see fresh eggs, just that dried stuff Lord Woolton dishes out. Anyway, the black market's against the law. I'm surprised at Martin for letting you do it.'

'Martin doesn't know.' Hetty appeared to think that this excused her but she was clearly a little uneasy now. 'It's nobody's business, anyway,' she added, defiantly.

'Not until you're found out. Never mind, I'll come and see you in Craiginches,' Gracie's laugh was a touch sarcastic.

'They wouldn't send me to prison?'

'Aye would they.'

Queenie was glad when her aunts went on to another topic – they never kept up any quarrels – because the reference to Craiginches had brought back a painful memory. She had not thought about Callum Birnie for ages, but she felt her face growing hot, and hoped that Olive hadn't noticed. The Easter holidays were nearly over and it would be a relief when she didn't have to see her cousin so often. Olive hadn't opened her mouth since she came in with her mother, but Queenie had been only too aware of the hostility in her eyes. Of course, she would still be angry that her warning had been ignored but it seemed to be more than that. Chancing a wary glance at her,

168

Queenie was dismayed to find that Olive was regarding her with a smile of . . . it couldn't be triumph? What would Olive have to be triumphant about?

It was into April when Gracie suddenly burst out at the tea table, 'You'll never guess what Hetty's been up to now?'

Patsy gave Queenie a nudge but Joe groaned, 'I'm fed up hearing what Hetty's been up to. If she wants to buy up all the stuff on the black market, it's up to her.'

'She stopped buying stuff on the black market,' his wife said indignantly as if her own integrity had been doubted. 'She came in, as bold as brass, and said she'd bought black grapes . . . in a shop over the counter,' she added hastily.

'Black grapes? That must have cost her a pretty penny.'

Gracie was quite pleased by the impact she had made now. 'She said they were quite dear, and when I asked how dear, she said . . .' Gracie paused, looking round to make sure that she had captured her audience, then ended grimly, 'She said twenty-four shillings for the pound.'

'Twenty-four shillings?' Queenie gasped, and Patsy, quite shocked, muttered, 'Just for a pound of grapes?'

Wielding his knife and fork again, Joe said, 'Hetty's more money than sense, if you ask me.'

Loyalty to her sister had been overthrown by her own sense of frugality and Gracie came out with her grievance, 'It maddens me to think she can spend twenty-four shillings on something like grapes when most wives don't get much more than that to keep a house and a family for a whole week.'

'Aye, well,' Joe said philosophically and popped another forkful of skirlie and potatoes into his open mouth.

'Of course,' Gracie murmured now, ashamed at having spoken so badly of Hetty, and determined to be fair, 'It wasn't as bad as the black market for she did buy them legitimately.'

The howl of laughter which met this observation made her wish that she had never mentioned the matter.

Walking back to school, Queenie remembered what Gracie had said about Hetty having more money than sense. It explained quite a lot about Olive in a way. She had never known what it was like to be dependant on anyone other than her parents and had got everything she wanted ever since she was born . . . but she wasn't going to get Neil, no matter what she did. He didn't like her, let alone love her, and she would have to give in gracefully – probably not gracefully but she would have to give in – when he told her that he loved his other cousin. Queenie's heart started to thud. The day when Neil revealed his true feelings for her would be the happiest day of her whole life; it would make up for all the nights she had lain awake praying for him to tell her he loved her; it would even go a long way towards compensating for losing her parents and grandparents. It would be wonderful.

Olive had watched for the postman every morning for weeks but he still hadn't brought a letter from Neil. He was bound to have been shocked, she had allowed a few days for him to get over it, but he should have written by this time. He had never been prompt in answering of course and maybe he was stuck for the right words. She might have to wait until he came home to find out how he felt about Queenie now but she was quite sure that the story she had spun would have ended any budding romance. A different romance would blossom – the romance she had dreamed of for years – because she was going to be so sympathetic that he would turn to her willingly for comfort and, oh boy, she would comfort him!

# Chapter Twelve

'I've applied to train as a State Registered Nurse.'

Gracie looked at her daughter in dismay, 'What's happened? Has anything upset you at the office?'

Patsy shrugged, 'No, not really, but I'd like to be doing something more useful and I've always wanted to be a nurse.'

'You never said anything about it before.'

'They wouldn't take me before I was eighteen.'

'I wish I was old enough to do something,' Queenie sighed. 'I don't fancy being a nurse but I'd love to be in one of the services.'

Gracie's frown grew deeper. 'You'll be going to university in October. I thought you wanted to be a teacher?'

'So I do, but it'll be years before I graduate.'

'Your father wanted you to carry on your education and I know he'd be pleased you'd passed for the varsity. Stick at it, Queenie, you'll have a good career when you finish.'

Queenie sat back sadly but Patsy said, 'Nursing's a good career as well. Better than being a typist.'

As Gracie suspected, when Joe came in for lunch he was on their daughter's side, beaming at her as he patted her back, 'Good for you, Patsy.'

Resigned, Gracie gave in, 'At least you'll still be living at home and won't be going away anywhere.'

Patsy looked uncomfortable, 'They told me I might not get in at Foresterhill. I might have to go to Glasgow or Dundee or Edinburgh.'

Her mother brightened a fraction, 'Ellie would make sure you were all right if you'd to go to Edinburgh.'

'I'm old enough to stand on my own feet.'

Joe nodded. 'She'll be fine wherever she is, Gracie.'

'I suppose so.'

In bed, Joe patted his wife's hand, 'You should be pleased our lassie's going into a good profession like nursing. She was getting fed up at her job.'

'I suppose I got a shock that she'd done it without saying anything about it to us and I can't help being sad that she might have to go away. That would be both our children left the nest.'

'We'd still have Queenie.'

'It's not the same, for Queenie's not really ours . . . oh!' Gracie looked ashamed. 'I'm sorry, I didn't mean that.'

Scratching his nose, Joe said, 'I know you weren't happy when Helene left her here but I did think you'd grown to love her as much as I do.'

'Oh Joe, I do love her but my head's spinning that much, I don't know what I'm saying. I'll miss Patsy if she's to go away and, I'll tell you this, if Queenie ever does go into the forces, I'll miss her just as much.'

Raymond Potter, having done something entirely off his own bat for once, came swaggering into the house at five o'clock one evening in May. At his mother's query as to why he was later than usual he announced proudly, 'I went to Market Street for forms to join the army.'

Hetty spun round from the cooker. 'You did what?'

'I got forms . . .'

'I heard you! I suppose it was Patsy going to be a nurse that put the idea into your stupid head but you can tear up your forms – you are definitely not going into the army.'

A little deflated, her son nevertheless stood his ground, 'I bet Dad'll let me go.'

Hetty frowned, 'He won't, he'll be mad. Couldn't you have waited till you got your law degree?'

An expression of disbelief at her gross stupidity crossed Raymond's face. 'I haven't started studying for it yet,' he said peevishly. 'I won't pass my exams to get in and I'd have to go to school for another year and I'll likely fail again. The war could be finished before I get a chance to do my bit. Gracie and Joe didn't stop Neil from going.'

'You're younger than Neil was when he went in.'

'Only a year, and they said I'd be in Boys' Service until I'm eighteen.'

Hetty's patience broke. 'Go into the blasted army then. It won't be my fault if you end up being killed.' She looked at him repentently, 'I'm sorry but I worried about your father in the last war though he didn't come to Aberdeen till early in 1918. He was only sixteen when he went into uniform, he'd lied about his age, and he'd been in for less than two years when the armistice was signed.'

Raymond grinned triumphantly, 'I don't see what you're so steamed up about, then. If Dad was only sixteen when he went in, he'll be all for me signing on.'

'Don't say anything to him tonight, Raymond,' she

pleaded. 'We're going to the theatre and I don't want him to be in a bad mood. We can discuss it tomorrow morning.'

'Oh, OK then.'

Martin did not notice Raymond's repressed excitement while they had their evening meal, but Olive did and when their parents went out, she said, 'What's up with you?'

Happy to tell someone else, he burst out, 'Mum told me not to tell Dad tonight but I'm joining the army.'

'You?' Olive laughed, scornfully. 'The army wouldn't take you, you're too scrawny.'

'They will if Dad signs the forms.' Uncoiling himself from the settee, he stood at attention and gave her an elaborate salute. 'Private Potter, Raymond, reporting for duty.'

She burst out laughing, 'You'll never cut as good a figure in uniform as Neil.'

'You've always got to get one over on me, haven't you?' he muttered, as he flopped down again, 'but your precious Neil isn't as almighty good as you think he is.'

Olive's brows came together, 'You don't know what you're talking about, you long streak of misery.'

Her continued sarcasm about his height and lack of girth stung him. 'I do. I know about the trick he played on you.'

'What trick?'

'Well, it was really him and Alf.'

As he hesitated, she snapped, 'What about him and Alf?'

'Neil was sick of you . . . I told you long ago he didn't like you . . . and he got Alf to pretend he . . . you thought Alf was in love with you but that's what they wanted you to think. He didn't like you, either, and Neil helped him to write all those letters you thought were so wonderful.'

175

Expecting her to go for him tooth and nail, he was alarmed at her ashen-faced silence but at last she whispered, 'It's not true. You're just making it up to get back at me.'

Too late, he regretted his indiscretion, 'Yes, it is true. He told me last time he was here. Him and Alf hatched up the plot together and they were laughing at you.'

Olive's disbelieving eyes clouded briefly, then she said, 'Neil wouldn't make a fool of me and he didn't start taking me out until after Alf told me about the other girl.'

Trapped into it, Raymond mumbled, 'Mum asked him to go out with you till you found another boyfriend. I heard her.'

Her eyes narrowed as the full extent of Neil's treachery hit her and she vented her anger on her brother. 'You pig! You sneaking, dirty pig!' Lashing out at him with her fists, she took him unawares and knocked him off the settee then, hoping to make him admit that it had all been a fabrication, she aimed a hefty kick at his solar plexus. Yelping in pain, he doubled up but she could tell by the way he was cringing from her that every word he had said was true. Raymond would never risk further punishment if he could avoid it.

'Get up,' she said, quietly. 'I'm sorry. I shouldn't have done that, it wasn't your fault.'

He rose slowly, still clutching his middle, 'I shouldn't have said anything and Neil's going to kill me if he finds out. You won't tell him, will you, Olive?'

She considered for a moment, her white face pinched with the shock of what she had learned, then said, 'No, I won't tell him. It might be better to play along with him.'

176

'Goodoh!' Relieved, Raymond eyed her accusingly. 'I bet I'll have sore guts for days.'

A little of Olive's spirit had returned. 'I've said I was sorry. What do you want me to do? Grovel?'

'You could stick up for me if Dad says he's not going to sign the forms.'

A glimmer of a smile appeared, 'I'll think about it. Now, I've got some studying to do.'

When she went into her own room, it was neither the forms nor her books that occupied her thoughts; it was the awful revelation that Neil and Alf had made a fool of her. She had always believed that Neil cared for her, but Raymond had proved that he didn't, that he never had and Alf's old girlfriend probably hadn't existed, either. It had been an excuse for dropping her. Not that she minded about Alf's lies, for he meant nothing to her any more, but Neil was different. To think that he had helped Alf to write the letters she had thought were so romantic . . . they must have laughed themselves silly at her gullibility. It was sickening, degrading, and she wouldn't let Neil off with it, but until she could think how to get back at him, she would give him no hint of the fury smouldering inside her. She would let him believe that she still loved him. . . she would let everybody think that she still loved him. She couldn't fool Raymond, though, and she would have to persuade her father to let him join the army so that he wouldn't be there to gloat over her.

Having spent all day in lecture rooms without absorbing one single word, Olive spent that evening trying to come up with a plan to cause as much suffering to Neil as she could. For two whole hours she racked her brains but nothing would come to her. Exhausted and frustrated, she gave up. Her mind was in too much of a turmoil to plan anything and she would be wise to wait for a day or two until she calmed down. She was pleased now that she had told Neil those lies about Queenie, though she had swithered about posting the letter after it was written. In her confused state, it escaped her that what she had done to him was as bad as, if not worse than, the trick he had played on her. By her reasoning, her action had stemmed from love of him while his had come from dislike of her so there was no comparison. He hadn't answered the letter but that wasn't surprising. If, as she suspected, he had fancied Queenie, he'd have been cut to the quick by what he believed she had done, so she was out of the running . . . but did that matter any more?

As she pondered over this, it dawned on Olive that it did matter, that she still loved Neil, despite what he had done. If he would only return her love, she would forgive him for the contemptible trick he had played and would never reveal that she knew about it – but if he persisted in holding her at arm's length, she would make him regret it for the rest of his life.

His heart beating an unfamiliar tattoo as he went upstairs, Neil walked in as if he owned the world. He was determined not to let anyone see how tense he was – especially Queenie and he ignored her as he spoke to his mother. 'Mum, I could go some bacon and eggs if you have any.'

Gracie, who always kept her own ration in case her son was hungry after his train journey, jumped to her feet at once, 'It'll just take a minute.'

'You look better than you usually do after you come off the train,' Joe observed, 'but I suppose you get used to the travelling.'

'I can get used to anything.' He looked briefly across the table at Queenie. 'Anything at all,' he said pointedly and was pleased to see her smile slip a fraction. 'I think I'll take Olive to the Palais tonight. She said in one letter she was kept busy writing theses, whatever they are, and she'll be glad of a break.'

Gracie turned round from the cooker. 'Will you not be too tired tonight?' She was surprised and puzzled that he hadn't invited Queenie first as he usually did but it would take a weight off her mind if he stopped asking Olive as well.

'I think I'll manage a few turns round the floor.'

'I'm off, folks.' Joe's departure left a deathly silence behind but at last, Gracie said, 'Hetty was saying Olive's been acting kind of funny this week. Did you write something to annoy her?'

Neil shook his head, 'Not guilty. I didn't even answer her last letter.' How could he answer it, when it had contained the most devastating information he'd ever had?

'Maybe that's it but you should have written to her. It's bad manners not to answer when somebody writes to you.'

'She's not noted for good manners herself, is she?'

'That's different. Her mother spoiled her, but you've been brought up to consider other people's feelings.'

Neil let his eyes rest harshly on Queenie for a second, 'I do, when they consider mine.'

Gracie kept probing, 'Did she write something daft?'

'No, she just passed on some . . . information.' He knew

that his mother wouldn't understand what he meant but Queenie might and he was past caring what anyone thought.

He had to force down the bacon and eggs and when Queenie said, 'I'll have to go,' he didn't even raise his head.

Gracie said, 'Cheerio, lass,' then waited until the girl went out before she sat down opposite her son. 'What's going on, Neil? I can tell something's bothering you.'

'Nothing's bothering me,' he snapped. 'Can I not go out with Olive on my first night home without you quizzing me?'

'I'm your mother, remember. I can read you like a book.'

'You've got the wrong page this time.'

'You didn't ask Queenie. You didn't even speak to her and she'll be wondering why.'

'I think she'll know why.'

Deciding that it was useless, Gracie gave up. Queenie must have done something last time to make Neil angry but it was clear that he wasn't going to speak about it. 'Patsy'll be in shortly. She's been on night duty.'

Neil's teatime phonecall made Olive exultant. Her scheme had worked – he had finished with Queenie. She had been afraid that she had laid it on too strongly in her letter, that he hadn't believed her, then she had worried in case he would demand a showdown between her and Queenie – bring them face to face to find out the truth – but he seemed to have taken her word for it. He was hers again, hers alone, but it might be best to go carefully for a while. It would take time for him to get over it but she was in no hurry now.

That night, Olive set out to make sure that Neil enjoyed himself. He was a little quiet at first but some of the jokes she'd heard her fellow students bandying about had him laughing in no time and she took great care not to say anything to upset him. It was heaven to feel secure without the spectre of Queenie looming up between them. She kept the atmosphere light, even when he saw her home, and her reward came when they stood at her door. 'OK for Friday, as well?' he smiled, so she smiled back and said, 'OK.' Nothing could have been easier, and he hadn't mentioned her letter once.

It was so unfair, Queenie thought. Why had Neil treated her like that when he was home? He'd taken Olive out three times and he had practically ignored her apart from passing a few remarks that she didn't understand. He had been so nice when he was home in March, so what could have happened in three months to change him? Then she remembered him saying to his mother, in a peculiar sneery way, that Olive had given him some information. Was it possible that Olive had seen her with Philip Rennie and told Neil in a letter? Philip was the only boy she had spoken to since Callum Birnie. It had been a few weeks ago, when she'd had to go back to school for a debate, and Cathie Leys had asked her to walk home with her for company. Although it had been bucketing rain, they had gone through Belmont Street on to Union Street and crossed to the other side because Cathie lived at the foot of the steps beside Boots the chemist. Stupidly, because they were already soaked, they had stood talking for a while and when Cathie left, Philip had caught up with her and they'd walked as far as the Castlegate together.

There had been nothing more in it, and even if it was what Olive had told Neil, surely he would have given her a chance to explain – he knew her better than to believe she would go out with another boy. Queenie was sure that the information he'd mentioned had been about her and was the reason for his indifference to her, and there was nothing else Olive could have told him . . . unless she had invented something, which was not beyond the realms of possibility.

In late June, Neil was testing a Norton, his ears geared, for the first mile or two to listening for rattles or grinding noises but the engine was going so smoothly that his thoughts started to wander. He knew well enough why he couldn't enjoy himself with girls like Alf did, as he'd done himself at one time, but it was stupid to let Queenie spoil things for him. She was old news, bad news. He should forget her as Alf had advised, but her sweet face kept coming into his mind and it was agony to remember that she belonged to somebody else. He couldn't put it out of his mind. In bed at night, even during the day when he was working on an engine, he was looking into the Adelphi in Aberdeen and longing to knock hell out of the faceless boy who was touching her.

Completely engrossed in his tortured thoughts, Neil would not have noticed if the world had come to an end, for it had come to an end for him weeks ago. He had been along the road so often that he knew it like the back of his hand, but with his concentration gone, he didn't see the huge oil drum that had dropped off a lorry a short time before. He only felt the jolt of the impact, heard the scrunch of metal and knew no more.

# Chapter Thirteen

Gracie's fears that Patsy would be leaving the nest were laid to rest when her daughter was accepted for training in Aberdeen at Foresterhill Hospital. It did mean that the girl had to be away from home if she was on night duty but otherwise it wasn't so different from when she was working in the office.

Patsy, of course, did not tell her mother about the hardships she had to suffer as a probationer, and it was Queenie who was her confidante. 'You wouldn't believe how strict the sisters and staff nurses are,' she told her cousin one night. 'Before any of the doctors or consultants make their rounds, the beds have to be as smooth as a baby's bottom. Once they're made, we've to watch like hawks in case the patients move and make creases in the top covers. You'd think it was our fault, though we don't get told off until after the doctor's away.'

'Why don't you say it was the patient that did it?'

'It wouldn't make any difference. Everything we do is wrong. If we get a stain on our aprons, it's a crime, and we've to go and change aprons and cuffs every time the doctors come round, whether they're dirty or not. I sometimes wonder if I did the right thing going in for

183

nursing. I'm just a glorified wardmaid running with bedpans, cleaning up sickness and up to my elbows in hot water most of the time, but it can't last for ever.'

'At least you're doing something,' Queenie sighed. 'I'm at a loose end just now. All the exams are past but I won't know if I'll be going to varsity until the results come out in July. I hope, sometimes, that I don't pass. I'd go into an office till April, when I'll be eighteen, then I'd go into the forces.'

Patsy laughed, 'Over Mum's dead body, if I know her.'

'I wouldn't mind being a WAAF. I thought Raymond looked quite smart in his RAF uniform when he was home after his training.'

'Don't tell me you're falling for him?'

'Oh, no.' Queenie hesitated, then said, 'It's Neil I care for and I thought he felt the same about me until he was here last time. Didn't you notice how he avoided speaking to me? I don't know why he changed, but I've a sneaking feeling Olive had a lot to do with it.'

'There's been something queer about her for a while,' Patsy said, thoughtfully. 'Since before Raymond went away first, and I thought they were kind of wary with each other all the time he was home. Maybe he's not scared to tell her what he thinks of her nowadays.'

'Maybe she's jealous of him being in the RAF?'

'She'd never want to go into the forces,' Patsy smiled. 'She couldn't stand it, she's had things too easy.'

Why was he lying on the ground? How long had he been here? What had happened? Lifting his head a fraction – it was agony to move – Neil saw the crumpled Norton on the

184

opposite bank and it all came back to him. It was funny how he had been flung one way in the accident and the bike the other, was that how it always happened? But what had hit him? No other vehicle was in his line of vision, so he swivelled his eyes to the left, then right, and at last he spotted the cause of the trouble – a huge oil drum, dented but not leaking as far as he could tell. The motor bike had come off worse – bits of it were scattered all over the place. He'd be for the high jump when he got back to camp, if he ever got back. His entire body was one excruciating ache and the slightest movement of his legs . . .

He slipped into unconsciousness again and when he came round for the second time he decided it would be best to lie still. He had no idea how badly he was hurt but this road was usually quite busy, so somebody should come along soon. He strained his ears for the sound of traffic, but all he heard was a grasshopper clicking away like mad, and the cooing of a wood pigeon calling to its mate. The sun was beating down on him – he could end up with sunstroke, as well as everything else.

Think. He must keep thinking, about anything at all, to keep him from drifting away again. Surely Alf would be wondering why he hadn't gone back? Yes, he'd come looking and if he didn't come himself he'd send somebody else. Good old Alf! But . . . what if he was too busy to notice? The Scammel he was working on was a hefty job. It could take hours. Damn and blast it! Why didn't anybody come? He would still be here tomorrow at this rate.

The sweat trickling down his face annoyed him suddenly, so he made to wipe it away. His right arm was so stiff that it was an effort to raise it but he finally succeeded. Oh

God, it wasn't sweat – it was blood! Well, it wasn't surprising. He was likely a bloody mess all over . . . a bloody
mess, that's a good one! The whole business was a bloody
mess. How bad was he? His right arm was working – just –
but what about his left? Lifting it was a bit tricky but he
didn't think it was broken. He would try his legs again. Oh
no, he couldn't move them! Were they paralysed? No, he
wouldn't feel that terrible pain if they were paralysed.
Smashed or broken?

'Are you badly hurt?'

It was a girl's voice, soft and gentle. Whoever she was,
she was as welcome as the flowers in May. Neil tried to
focus his eyes properly but it was too much of an effort so
he gave up.

'Your face is cut, but there's so much blood it's difficult
to know where. I'll mop it up with my hankie so I can see.'

'I . . . think . . . my legs . . . are busted.' Trying to move
them, he passed out again and when he resurfaced, the girl
was still intent on cleaning the blood from his face. He
could see her better now, in close up. Her skin was creamy
peach shading into the delicate rose of her cheeks; her hair,
almost the colour of burnished copper, was smooth and
curling under at the ends; her eyes, looking briefly into his
before they dropped to attend to his wounds again, were
the darkest brown he had ever seen. What an angel! But he
wasn't really interested in girls, he reminded himself, not in
any serious way . . . not after . . .

The gentle wiping touched a raw spot. 'Ouch!'

'I'm sorry. Your cheek is badly cut, as well as your nose. I
didn't see it at first. Look, I've got my bike. Will you be all
right if I go and phone for an ambulance? I won't be long.'

He was about to say that he'd be fine when a rumbling noise made him stop to listen and the girl jumped to her feet. 'It's a lorry. I'll ask the driver to get them to send an ambulance when he gets back to camp.'

That thing'll never make it back to camp, Neil thought – it was rattling like an old tin can – but she was already in the middle of the road flagging it down with both hands. When it drew up, she talked excitedly to the driver who jumped out and came over to the side. 'What's up, mate? Have an accident?'

Neil managed a grin. 'No thanks, I've just . . .

'. . . had one,' finished the driver, laughing. 'Can you walk?'

'I don't think so.'

'He thinks his legs are broken,' the girl put in.

'I'd better not try moving you then. I'll get them to send an ambulance.'

'Thanks.' Neil relaxed as the lorry moved off. He'd likely have a long wait, knowing the army, but he couldn't get up and walk away. He was as weak as a new-born kitten, his head was pounding like a sledgehammer and he was desperately cold.

'You're shivering.' The girl looked down compassionately. 'I suppose it's shock. I'd better wait till the ambulance comes.'

'There's no need.' But his protest was unconvincing.

'Don't argue. By the way, what's your name?'

'Neil Ferris.'

'I'm Freda Cuthbert. My dad has the market garden about half a mile up the road.'

'I've . . . seen . . .' Reaction had caught up on him now,

187

making it difficult to think clearly enough to speak coherently.

Noticing his discomfort, Freda kept talking, 'I work with my dad, but I've just come from his sister's. She's sprained her ankle, and she phoned to ask if I'd take her some potatoes. She's not too bad, really, but she can't put any weight on her foot so I tidied up a bit, and peeled a few of the spuds. She had some meat left from yesterday so I didn't need to cook for her and she wouldn't let me do anything else.'

She paused briefly, obviously thinking what else to say. 'I'd better tell you something about myself, now. I'll be twenty in August, I've still got all my own teeth, and I've never had a perm. I registered along with my age group but I'm working on the land already so they didn't want me.'

She stopped again to look at him. 'I'm not bothering you, am I?' His faint headshake reassured her. 'I don't usually talk so much but I was afraid for a while there that you were going to pass out on me again. You're not, are you? Good. I don't go out much in the evenings, though my dad's always telling me I should go to the dances. I'm a bit shy, you see. Maybe you'll find this hard to believe but I've never spoken to a stranger before. Some of the soldiers whistle at me if they see me in the fields and one or two stop and try to chat me up but I pretend not to hear, and they go away.'

Neil wondered why her voice was fading and prayed that he wasn't going to sink under again, but that wasn't what it was. In a great, shaming rush, his stomach gave up its contents and he was unable to keep it back. Worse, it was so unexpected that he had no time to turn his head, even if he could, which was doubtful, so the vomit went all down his front.

When he stopped retching, Freda laid a cool, soothing hand on his clammy brow. 'Do you feel better now?' He was too exhausted even to nod, so she said, 'I'll clean you up, but my hankie's covered with blood, so I'll have to take yours, wherever it is. Don't move, Neil, I'll find it.'

The breast pocket of his overalls yielded only bits of paper, scraps of pencils and a few washers, so she dug her hand into his left trouser pocket but had to try the other one before she pulled out a grubby, khaki handkerchief. 'It's a bit oily, but I don't suppose it'll matter.'

Before she started, she used some dock leaves to get off the worst of the mess, then rubbed hard with the handkerchief for a few minutes. 'That'll have to do. The smell won't go away until your boiler suit's had a good wash.'

The ambulance arrived then, and she stood aside until the two men lifted him on to a stretcher, but the movement jarred him so much that he lost consciousness once again.

He came round in hospital. At first, his mind was a blur but little by little it came back to him – the crash, the pain, the oil drum, the girl. The girl? Was she real, or was she part of a delirious dream he'd had? No, she was definitely real. She'd said her name was Freda Cuthbert and she stayed with him until the ambulance came, talking, but he couldn't remember much of what she'd said. A market garden? Her father owned the market garden along the road. It was funny he'd never seen her but he would likely have been going too fast to notice. He would have to go and thank her once he was out of here.

'You're with us now, are you?' A smiling young nurse, her red cheeks shining, was standing beside him. 'Your legs have been set, one was broken in three places, but don't try to move much yet. Your whole body's had a shake-up, and you've had a nasty crack on your nose. That's the bad news, but the good news is that your girlfriend's waiting to see you. Will I send her in?'

'My girlfriend?'

He looked so puzzled that the nurse laughed. 'She didn't say she was your girlfriend, I just thought she must be for she's been here for hours. Her name's Freda, if that means anything?'

'She's the girl who found me. Do I look presentable?'

'Apart from a couple of black eyes and the dressings on your nose and cheek, you're fine. I'll tell her you've come round.'

Freda walked into the ward a moment later. 'How are you?'

'Not too bad, considering. Did you come in the ambulance with me? You shouldn't have waited but thanks for everything.'

'I wanted to know how badly you were hurt, so I cycled after the ambulance, and I'm only allowed to stay a minute . . . would it be OK if I come back when you're fit for visitors?'

'I'd like that, but don't feel obliged to come.'

'I want to.'

As soon as Freda went out, Neil closed his eyes. The allotted minute had been long enough for him but he was grateful to her for waiting. He was sure she wasn't one of those girls who were just out for what they could get but he hoped that she hadn't felt sorry for him, or responsible

190

for him because she had been first on the scene of his accident. He had vowed never to get attached to any girl after Queenie but he wouldn't complain if Freda wanted to be more than a friend.

Gracie hadn't even reached the end of Neil's latest letter when she looked up in alarm. 'He's had an accident on a motor bike,' she told Joe. 'Only a broken leg and scratches on his face, he says, but maybe he's just saying that to save me worrying.'

'If he's able to write, he can't be that bad,' Joe pointed out, quite reasonably.

'But he'll have nobody to visit him, away down there.'

'He's got pals, and he'll be enjoying the attention he'll get from all the young nurses.'

Neither of them noticed how Queenie had reacted. Her face had blanched at the mention of his accident, her fingers plucked at the tablecloth in agitation. Joe glanced at the clock on the mantelpiece and jumped up. 'I never noticed the time, I should be away.' He turned as he went out. 'Don't worry, Gracie, lass. A broken leg'll soon mend.'

Gracie looked across at her niece. 'What d'you think? Is Neil telling me everything?'

Queenie stood up. 'I hope so. I'll have to hurry too.'

As she ran down the stairs, she wished that she could go to see Neil, to find out how he was, but he would likely refuse to see her, if the way he'd treated her last time he was home was anything to go by. He could be dying for all she knew, and she would never find out what had gone wrong between them . . . but he had written to his mother, so he couldn't be dying. The thought did comfort her a little, but she realised that he might still be badly injured and it would be a long time before he was fit enough to come home again.

When a letter from Olive arrived, Neil was tempted not to open it, but curiosity got the better of him.

2 July, 1942

Dear Neil,

I have just heard about your smash and I hope you are feeling better. It must be awful to be lying in hospital in this lovely weather and I wish I could be there to cheer you up. The only thing I can do is to write to you more often so expect a daily visit from the postie. Your mother said your leg was broken and that you just had a few scratches on your face, but I know they wouldn't keep you in very long with just a broken leg. I'm an embryo doctor, remember, so you can tell me, and I promise not to let it go any further. I expect they will let you come home as soon as you can walk but you won't be fit for dancing for a while. Ho, hum, there's always the pictures.

How did your accident happen? I know you were on a motor bike, but did something run into you, or was it vice versa? Your mother said that the girl who found you has been visiting you every day. Watch yourself there, Neil. You're still recovering from shock and it would be easy to get stupid ideas in your head. Don't take long to answer this, because I'm anxious to hear how you are.

Regards, Olive.

She was quite goodhearted in her own way, Neil thought, laying the letter down at his side and stretching across to his locker for his writing pad and pen. She had certainly changed for the better lately. There was nothing out of place in what she had written and she was bound to be curious about his health when she was studying medicine. She had likely sent her last letter with the best of intentions, for she couldn't have had any idea of how he felt about Queenie at the time.

Dear Olive,

Thanks for your welcome letter. Don't tell my mother, but my right leg was broken in three places and my left leg had an ordinary, straightforward break. I'd some scratches and cuts on my face but I'll only be left with little marks, so I'll still be as handsome as ever, says me. Like you said, I won't be doing any dancing for a while but it's not the end of the world, is it?

By the way, Freda's a really nice girl, so I won't need to watch myself like you warned me. I'll stop now, for I'm still a bit weak and I get easily tired.

As always, Neil

He addressed an envelope, then read the letter over and added a postscript. 'I bet you'll be surprised at getting a letter from me by return.'

Long before the afternoon visiting time, his eyes were drawn to the door of the ward and the stream of nurses scuttling in and out with bedpans had his spirits leaping and sinking like the scenic railway at Aberdeen, and just as he thought that he would have a heart attack from the strain of waiting, a sister fixed the doors back to let the visitors in. Luckily for Neil's heart, Freda was one of the first to enter and as she sat down at his bedside, she lifted the letter he had written. 'Do you want me to post this for you?' She gave it a quick glance, then asked, 'Is it to your girlfriend?'

'Olive's my cousin,' he answered, a little stiffly.

Taken aback at his tone, she said, 'Oh, I'm sorry, I didn't mean to be nosey.'

He stretched out his hand to her. 'No, I'm sorry. It was just . . . I didn't want you to think I'd a girlfriend.' Noticing that she seemed happier at that, he relaxed, but wished he'd the courage to tell her that he wouldn't mind having *her* as his girlfriend. It was too soon for that, in any case, so it was as well to keep their relationship light.

Neil's next letter eased his mother's mind – and his cousin's – about his wellbeing but raised other doubts. 'He's going on about a girl now,' Gracie told Joe, in some concern. 'Listen to this. "Freda visits me every day. She's the girl who found me after the accident. She even cycled to the hospital behind the ambulance and waited till I was out of the anaesthetic so she could come in and see if I was all right." What do you make of that?' she appealed.

'Is that all?' Joe smiled. 'I don't know what you're getting all worked up for. She likely feels a bit responsible for him and she just goes to make sure he's recovering.'

'You can't see past the end of your nose!' Gracie declared, a little annoyed at him for making light of her worry. She turned to Queenie now, 'I bet she's after him.' Her niece's woebegone expression made her wish that she had held her tongue.

'He'll be glad of her visits,' the girl said forlornly.

'Aye, like enough, and I'll read the rest out to you, for he doesn't say any more about her. "I'll likely be here for a few weeks yet but don't worry. My leg's mending nicely, the doctors say, and I'll just be left with a wee mark on my nose. It could have been an awful lot worse. I hope you and Dad are keeping well, and not working too hard. Love, Neil." He sounds cheery enough.' Gracie glanced at Queenie again and was pleased that her colour was returning though she was still a bit pale.

Queenie felt hurt that Neil hadn't even mentioned her in his letter, and wondered if Gracie had been right in thinking that Freda was after him, but probably not. It was natural for her to visit him, when she had seen the state he must have been in after the accident. Any decent girl would do the same and it would stop after he got out of hospital.

With his nervous system not fully recovered from the accident, Neil was ripe for overresponding to any sort of kindness and Freda's daily visits had come to mean a great deal to him. She was completely different from either of his cousins – not full of arrogant self-confidence like Olive nor bubbling with life like Queenie – but her quiet, almost shy, manner was as balm to his buffeted spirits and he sang her praises to Alf Melville every time he went to the hospital.

'I think I can smell love in the air,' Alf smirked one day, about six weeks after the accident.

'Nothing of the kind,' Neil blustered then gave a chuckle. 'Maybe you're right. I think I love her, but I don't know how she feels about me.'

Having met the girl on several occasions, Alf's grin widened. 'She's bats about you. I've never seen a more sickening case of love with the lid on and that goes for you, as well. Put her out of her misery, Neil, lad, before I've to knock your stupid heads together.'

Lying back after his friend went out, Neil concluded that he didn't just think, he was so deeply in love with Freda that he couldn't bear the idea of not seeing her again after he got out of hospital. He would have to find out if Alf's assessment of her was true, that she was 'bats about him'. He would have to risk being rebuffed, but he couldn't go on without knowing one way or the other.

'Did you have Alf in last night?'

Neil was too keyed-up to make small talk. 'Freda,' he burst out loudly, oblivious to everyone around them, 'I love you, and I want to know if you love me.'

'Ssh!' Her cheeks pink, she looked around to see if any of the people making their way to other beds had heard but it was the patient in the bed next to Neil who said, 'Go on, then, do you love him? I can't bear this suspense.'

Scarlet now, she nodded shyly and Neil's triumphant yell was followed by his neighbour's sigh. 'Thank God. Maybe now we'll all get some peace.'

'I'm so embarrassed,' Freda whispered.

He grabbed her hand. 'I'm not. I'm so happy I could shout it from the rooftops.'

'You nearly did.'

'I suppose I can't kiss you in here?'

'I should think not. You've made a big enough exhibition of us already.'

She sounded so serious that he said, 'Are you angry with me?'

'Not really. It was just so unexpected but I'm glad we got it sorted out. We could have gone on and on without knowing.'

'That's what I thought.'

They held hands until it was time for her to leave. 'I'll see you tomorrow,' she smiled, as she stood up, then leaned forward and kissed his brow. 'Will that do, darling?'

'It'll do to be going on with.' He watched her walking away, and returned the wave she gave him before she turned into the corridor, then he lay back, smiling contentedly. She had called him 'darling'! He had never felt like this before, never in his entire life. It was true that every cloud had a silver lining. If he hadn't smashed himself up, he would never have met Freda.

# Chapter Fourteen

From what Gracie could gather from Neil's letters now, he had fallen head over heels in love. 'It's Freda this, Freda that, in every one,' she wailed to her husband one night. 'If there was ever anything between him and Queenie, there's nothing on his side now, and that's a mixed blessing, for I can't help feeling sorry for her and I'm none too happy about him being so serious about this other girl. He's not even twenty yet.'

Joe heaved a great sigh, 'Ach, Gracie, you'll find things to worry about when you get to heaven. I hope I go first, so I can warn St Peter not to pay any attention to you.'

Somewhat offended, she snapped, 'And you never worry about a thing, though this Freda's maybe not the kind of lassie you'd want your son to get involved with.'

'If he wants to get involved with her, it wouldn't matter how much we worried. It's his life, so let him get on with it.'

Freda's name cropped up in Neil's letters too often for Olive's peace of mind. After putting Queenie out of the running, it was galling to think that competition was cropping up from another direction and she couldn't ask him anything in a letter. She'd have to wait until he came home and if he really was in love with this girl, he wouldn't be able to hide it. Then she would have to put her thinking cap on. It would be more difficult to deal with a rival who was so far away, but she would have to do something.

When Neil wrote to say that he would be home in a week, Gracie felt the need of advice and her husband was the only one she could ask, 'I haven't said anything to Queenie about him being in love, but should I tell her, to warn her, or will I leave it till we see what he says himself?'

After giving it some consideration, Joe said, 'I think you'd be best to leave it. I know you're concerned for her, but we can't interfere. Anyway, you're maybe imagining things.'

Neil didn't look as bad as Queenie had expected. He was still a bit pale, but that was only natural, and he was walking with a stick, though he told his mother that he didn't really need it. There was a nasty puckered mark on his cheek and a deep scar on his nose, but that was all.

'So the wounded warrior's returned?' Joe was saying. 'I hope you realise you gave your mother an awful fright?'

'I got quite a fright myself,' Neil smiled.

'Well, I hope it'll learn you to be careful on the road. How did it happen, your smash up?'

Neil grinned. 'I'd an argument with an oil drum. It must have fallen off some lorry, and I didn't see it. If I hadn't been in hospital, I'd have been on a charge for wrecking the bike.'

'You'll maybe be put on a charge when you go back.'

'The adjutant says they'll overlook it this time.'

199

'Good.' Gracie pushed him into a chair. 'Your breakfast's in the oven – I'll just take it out.'

Neil turned to Queenie, 'I believe I've to congratulate you on passing all your exams?'

'Thanks, I'll be starting university in October.' She wondered if he could hear her heart thumping, it was going mad . . . just because he had spoken to her again.

'I always knew you were just as clever as Olive.' He did not notice the shadow that crossed her face and picked up his fork and knife to tackle the heaped plate his mother set down. 'No Palais for me this time, but what about going to the pictures with me tomorrow night?'

Gracie raised her eyebrows and shot a worried glance at Joe, but Queenie said, trying not to appear too eager, 'Yes, thanks, I'd like that.'

As usual, Joe had to leave to open the shop at eight and as Queenie helped Gracie with the dishes, Neil said, 'I think I'll lie down for a while.'

'Off you go, then.' His mother could see that he was tired.

Nothing was said for a minute or two, then Queenie observed, self-consciously, 'He's looking quite well, considering.'

Gracie nodded. 'He could do with feeding up a bit, but he's a lot better than I thought he'd be. You know . . . I thought the two of you had quarrelled last time, but . . .'

'We didn't quarrel. I don't know why he was like that but I'm glad he's got over it.'

For the rest of the day, Queenie tried to imagine what Neil might say to her when he took her out. Would he apologise and tell her why he'd behaved in that awful way? Perhaps he would kiss her as if it had never happened? She would be quite happy with that, and happier still if he told her that he loved her, then she could tell him how much she loved him. She went to bed that night with a song in her heart.

It was very wet the next morning but Neil said that he would go out anyway. 'I'll go and have a yarn with the lads I used to work with. Some of them will still be there, the older men, at any rate, and I'll carry on to Hetty's in the afternoon. I'll be back for tea, in plenty of time for the pictures,' he added, smiling at Queenie.

She pottered around all day, helping with the house-work, but her mind was on Neil. Olive was on holiday too and he would see her when he went to Rubislaw Den. Would he ask her out as well? It was more than likely, Queenie thought sadly. She was positive that he didn't like Olive but she didn't trust the girl. She would try every trick she knew to get Neil and she would double her efforts if she found out about tonight.

'Isn't it about time you started getting dressed?' Gracie had been taking her washing in from the drying green – the rain had gone off just before lunch – and her niece's pensive, dejected expression disquieted her even more than the renewed hope that had been on her face when Neil gave his invitation. 'You'd best be ready before teatime, so you can get out early.'

When Neil came back, he said, 'That dress suits you, Queenie. It picks up the colour of your eyes.'

She was embarrassed, but delighted. 'I made it myself.'

Gracie beamed. 'She's good with her hands, and it was a bit of material I've had lying for a long time. She'll make a good wife to some lucky man some day.'

The girl flushed, but Neil laughed, 'Don't forget to send me an invitation to the wedding, Queenie.'

It was as if her legs had been shot out from under her and she sat down abruptly. He couldn't love her, not when he said a thing like that. She had been living in a fool's paradise, like Olive had told her once . . . unless . . . he hadn't wanted his mother to know how he felt? Not yet, when he hadn't told her, Queenie? But he would tell her . . . tonight!

The rain had been spitting again when they left to go to the Capitol Cinema, but the pavements were dry when they came out. Queenie had been disappointed that Neil hadn't taken her hand while they were watching the film but her stomach was churning with anticipation as they walked home. He wouldn't tell her in the street, he would wait till nobody could see them when they went into the lobby of the tenement. 'Does your leg bother you much?' she asked, to take her mind off the joy to come.

'It's a bit stiff after sitting so long without being able to stretch it,' he admitted.

'I'm glad you weren't seriously hurt.'

'So am I.' He laughed for a moment, then looked at her with an expression she couldn't quite place. 'Queenie, I'm sorry I was so nasty to you last time.'

'It's all right, though I did wonder why . . .'

'It's not all right. What you do is no business of mine.'

'What do you mean?' She felt a prickle of apprehension now.

'I was angry before, but I've had time to think, and . . . other things have happened that made me . . . well, I do care about you, like a sister . . . and just be careful, that's all.'

202

She could not grasp what he was trying to say, but one phrase had dashed all her hopes. 'Like a sister.' He thought of her as a sister! He didn't love her. He had never loved her. She kept walking mechanically, wishing miserably that she was dead.

The stony silence was not what Neil had expected and he felt out of his depth. He had thought that she would deny what she had done with the other boy, and had planned to make her admit it and to warn her of the risks she was running, but because she had said nothing, he began to doubt Olive's story. He ought to have questioned her about it when he saw her . . . better yet, he should have done the decent thing and asked Queenie herself if it was true. It was too late for that, so he just said, 'I'm really sorry for what I thought.'

Giving a little sniff, she whispered, 'What did you think?'

He avoided the question. 'I wish I . . .'

Her eyes were swimming with tears when she looked up at him. 'Will you tell me something, Neil?'

'Anything.'

'Did Olive say something bad about me? Is that why . . .?'

He hesitated. What good would it do to tell her? She might go and have it out with Olive and she would likely be more hurt. 'No, Olive had nothing to do with it. I was wrong to think what I did, but let it go at that, Queenie, please.'

'You're in love with Freda, aren't you?'

'Is it that obvious?'

She smiled, wistfully. 'Yes, it is.' There was something she still had to find out, however. 'Did you never love me?'

Her pleading face tightened a screw in his heart. He had been a proper heel to her and she deserved an honest answer. 'I did love you, Queenie, very much, but I got it into my head somehow or other that you loved somebody else, then I met Freda.'

'I know . . . so it's all over.'

He opened the door for her when they reached their tenement, but grasped her arm when she put her foot on the first tread of the stairs. 'I hope there's no ill feeling, Queenie?'

'None.'

'Show me, then. I do still care for you, you know, more than I should. I wouldn't want to kiss my sister, would I?'

'Oh, Neil,' she sighed.

He knew he was mad, he knew that it was unfair to her, but he couldn't help himself. 'You'll always have a part of my heart,' he murmured. It was true, he reflected, as their lips met. She was his first love and he would never forget her.

He made no attempt to stop her when she pulled away from him. 'That's the last time, Neil, the very last,' she whispered, 'so don't ever ask me out again, because I just couldn't bear it.' Turning blindly, she ran up the stairs.

Unravelling an old jumper to get wool for knitting blankets, Gracie looked up in alarm when Queenie burst into the house and went straight to her bedroom. A moment later, Neil looked round the kitchen door. 'Goodnight, Mum,' was all he said, before he too went to his room. Perplexed, Gracie went to tell Joe. 'I'm nearly sure Queenie was crying when she came in, and Neil was a bit upset, as well. I hope they haven't quarrelled again . . .'

Breaking off, she thought for a moment, then went on, 'Surely he wouldn't have tried anything with her?'

'God, woman,' Joe exclaimed, 'the things you come up with. One minute you're saying he's in love with Freda, and the next minute you're thinking he's . . .'

'No,' she interrupted, 'he wouldn't do a thing like that, but maybe he's told her he loves Freda and that's what's upset her so much. She'll get over it, though, and it's the best thing that could happen, when all's said and done.'

Joe cast his eyes to the roof. 'You change your mind oftener than I change my socks. Now are you coming to bed?'

Having arranged the date with Olive the previous day, Neil took her to the Regent, although he hadn't felt like going out with her at all. The main feature was a musical he'd have enjoyed if his mind hadn't kept turning to Queenie. He bitterly regretted what had happened, she had been quite happy until he came out with that sermon. She hadn't understood what he was trying to say, for he hadn't accused her outright, thank goodness, but he must have set her puzzling. Nothing had gone as he had planned; it had escalated into him telling her things he hadn't meant to tell her, but it had taught him a lesson and he'd steer clear of anything personal when he took Olive home, he wouldn't even tax her with telling lies. It was over and done with.

After standing for the national anthem when the show ended, they made their way out and had turned the corner at Holburn Junction when Olive said, 'You haven't said much tonight, Neil. Are your legs bothering you?'

'There's nothing wrong with me or my legs,' he snarled, then felt ashamed. She had only asked out of sympathy.

'I'm sorry I snapped. I'm not very good company some-times.'

She smiled. 'That's understandable. Don't worry about it.'

They carried on slowly – partly because of his gammy leg, but mainly because it was such a beautiful evening – and were in Albyn Place before Olive observed, 'I love strolling along here, maybe it's the the peace and tran-quillity, but it makes me feel good, especially when you're with me.' Trailing her hand along the top of a hedge, she looked up at him coyly. 'Do you think of me at all when you're in Alnwick, or does Freda take your mind off every-thing else?'

Damn her, Neil thought. Was she being nasty or was she just being her usual sarcastic self? He would give her the benefit of the doubt. 'Freda doesn't try to take my mind off anything.'

The softening of his voice told Olive all she wanted to know. He was either in love, or about to fall in love, and she'd have to do something to stop it. He hadn't known Freda very long, so the affair couldn't have gone far yet, and with any luck she could do something to make sure that it didn't go much farther.

When they came within sight of her house, she said casually, 'Will we be going out again before you go back?'

'I don't think I'd better. My right leg seizes up when I've to sit for three hours at a time. I'm not as fit as I thought I was and I took Queenie to the Capitol last night, as well.'

Not by one flicker of a face muscle did Olive reveal how she felt about this. 'Thanks for tonight anyway, and remember, if you feel up to it, you'll be welcome at the Den any time.'

'I'll see how I feel. Goodnight.' He held out his hand.

Things were looking bad, Olive mused, as Neil limped off. She had thought she had cooked Queenie's goose for good, but he was still taking her out and now there was this new protagonist to contend with, an unknown quantity. Freda was the real danger.

Feeling particularly down one afternoon, Gracie decided to pay a visit to her sister and was disappointed that Hetty was not alone. She had forgotten that Olive, like Queenie, would still be on holiday, so they wouldn't be able to speak freely.

'Neil looked quite well when we saw him,' Hetty smiled. 'Have you heard from him since he went back?'

Olive tried not to show her interest. She hadn't heard from him, but maybe his mother had. Gracie nodded. 'Just the one letter, and he's still getting on fine. He says his leg's very tired by the end of a day, but when he went back to the hospital for his check up, they said the exercise should help it.'

'He was lucky to get off with a broken leg,' Hetty observed. 'He took Olive to the cinema, since he couldn't dance.'

'He took Queenie to the pictures, as well.' Gracie felt she had to wipe the smug smile off her niece's face. 'He once said he went out with dozens of girls and I wasn't bothered, for I thought he wasn't serious about any of them, but I'm beginning to have doubts about that now.'

'Do you think he's fallen for one of his girls at last?'

They were both astonished when Olive burst out, 'If you think he's fallen for that Freda, he hasn't.'

Her scarlet face and the passion in her eyes made Hetty frown but Gracie said, very quietly, 'Don't be so sure about that.'

The girl jumped up and ran out, slamming the door behind her, and Hetty and Gracie looked at each other in dismay. Hetty was angry at her daughter for showing how she felt about Neil, and Gracie was angry at Neil for apparently dallying with his two cousins' affections. She was also worried in case he had gone a lot further than that with Queenie. . . and maybe with Olive, too, but she couldn't say that to Hetty.

When Gracie told Joe what had happened, he laughed, as usual. 'So Olive's still hankering after Neil? You'd think she'd have got the message by this time.'

'She wouldn't get the message supposing he told her to go to hell and never come back!'

'I can't see what she can do if he doesn't want her.'

'You don't know her like I do.' Gracie stopped, there was no point in trying to explain. 'Joe, I'm sure Neil likes Freda and it doesn't take much for liking to develop into love, and love to develop into passion. He could end up having to marry her, and forced marriages never really work.'

Catching her husband's look of exasperation, she changed her tune before he could say anything. 'I just want him to be happy and I won't try to stop him if he wants to marry Freda. For one thing, it would put an end to Olive's nonsense.'

# Chapter Fifteen

Neil's feelings for Freda had already developed beyond love; mere kisses were no longer enough, yet every time he was on the brink of unleashing his passion, his conscience held him back. She was so innocent and pure that he couldn't give in to the temptation, not until she gave him some sign that his advances would be welcome.

They had been keeping company – all it really amounted to – for three months when Freda remarked, 'One of my friends is getting married next week.'

'Oh, yes?' Neil hoped that she wasn't suggesting that they do the same – he wasn't thinking of being tied down yet.

'I can't understand her. She was a nice girl, but she let her fellow . . . you know . . . and her father made him marry her.'

'How did her father know he had . . . you know?'

Freda coloured, in spite of his broad teasing grin. 'It . . . it was beginning to show.'

'You mean she's pregnant? What's so awful about that? Even nice girls make mistakes.'

'I'd never make a mistake like that. I'd never let any . . .'

'It's all in the luck of the draw. Some girls fall at the first fence, as you might say, and others get away with it.' The subject was making Neil's needs grow, and he hoped that he could convince Freda that she would be in no danger if she allowed him to do what her friend's 'fellow' had done.

'But they shouldn't be doing anything like that if they're not married! It's not nice.'

Neil couldn't help laughing. 'On the contrary, my darling, it's very nice indeed.'

She looked horrified. 'Have you . . .?'

'Lots of times, but not since I met you.'

'Did you love any of the girls?'

'No, it was just a bit of fun, for them and me both.'

'Did you make any of them pregnant?' Her tone was harsh.

'No, I knew what to do. Look, I'll show you.' He put his hand in his pocket and took out the small, flat envelope he had been carrying, hopefully, for weeks but she recoiled in distaste. 'Put it away. You're filthy, Neil Ferris!'

A tiny seed of misgiving entered his mind, but he ploughed on. 'I'm a man, that's all. Like I said, those other girls were just a bit of fun, but I love you, and when two people love each other, it's natural for them to . . .'

'But it's wrong when they're not married.'

'It's not wrong. Oh, Freda, please let me . . . I swear on my honour that nothing can happen.'

'If you're going to be like this,' she said, icily, 'don't bother asking me out again.'

He fought back the urge to grab her, to force her down on the ground, but there would be no pleasure in it for either of them if she wasn't willing. He had offended her sense of propriety, but there were other nights, and he would work up to it in future, use all the tricks he knew that kindled a girl's desires, and soon she would be offering herself to him . . . begging for it.

Things had not been going smoothly for Olive during the day and she went home in a vile humour, ready to lose her temper at the slightest criticism. Fortunately, Hetty spiked her guns by saying, 'I put Neil's letter on the mantelpiece. It came second post, but you haven't been home since breakf –'

'About time.' Olive picked up the letter and took it up to her bedroom to read, her eyes lighting up at the first three words.

> My dear Olive,
>
> Sorry I haven't written sooner, but you know how it is. I always mean to answer your letters, but I never get round to it. I hope you are still working hard at the varsity, the psychiatry sounds quite interesting, but I wouldn't fancy it myself. I've been thinking tonight about the old days and the picnics we used to go on when we were kids. I guess your psychiatrists would make something out of that but the truth is I was drinking with some of my mates, and beer makes me nostalgic.
>
> Have you heard from Raymond lately? I hope he's not as bored as I am, for I'm fed up to my teeth some days and I wish they'd send us overseas. Still, it's not long till my leave, the middle of December, though I'll have to come

back before Christmas, worse luck. I'll close now, hoping you and your family are all well.

Yours, Neil

Olive's depression had lifted several degrees now. Neil had admitted to thinking about her. Not in so many words, he was too shy, but if he had been remembering the old picnics, he must have been thinking about her too. And another hopeful point, there had been no mention of Freda. Had she just been a flash in the pan?

Reading through the letter again, Olive devoured each word and lingered over the signature. 'Yours, Neil.' It was what she had longed for, it was as good as telling her he loved her. He was on the right lines at last and it would only be a matter of time before he would come right out and say it. Perhaps she should give him a little help, since he found it so difficult?

22 November, 1942

My dear Neil,

Thank you for your very welcome letter. I hope your leg isn't giving you too much trouble, I know it was bothering you the night we went to the Regent, so I wasn't too hurt when you didn't kiss me. I can't stop thinking about you and I don't need to tell you why, but I will anyway. Neil, my darling, I love you with all my heart. I always have and I always will.

I'll never forget how passionate you were on that oh so wonderful night, so I know you love me too, and if you're too shy to tell me, why don't you write it? I'll be the happiest girl in the whole world if you do.

I WILL LOVE YOU TILL THE DAY I DIE. If I can write it, so can you. All my love, Olive

x x x x x x x x x x That's twenty kisses,

x x x x x x x x x x now we're both twenty.

'Oh, Jesus!' Neil dropped the letter he was reading as if it had scorched his fingers.

'Bad news?' Alf looked up from his own letter, the weekly epistle his mother always sent.

'The worst!' His friend's sympathetic face made Neil carry on quickly. 'No, it's not what you think, it's Olive again. She's getting out of hand, really she is.'

'Don't tell me she's till pestering you? After me sinning my unsullied soul to make her think . . .?'

'If you don't believe me, read it!'

Alf bent to pick the letter off the floor, skimmed through it and whistled. 'Short and sweet, but it sounds as if you'd made love to her at some time.'

'She's the last bloody person I'd make love to. I did kiss her once . . . maybe a bit too passionately, and she's trying to make something of it. Her mother thought she wasn't getting over what you did to her and asked me to take her out till she found another lad and I didn't like to say no, but I'm damned sure she's no intention of looking for anybody else. She wasn't so bad for a while, but she's off again. It looks like our little scheme didn't work.'

213

'Why don't you take Freda home with you next time? You've been going steady with her for months now, haven't you, and it would let Olive see you weren't interested in her.'

Alf jumped as Neil thumped his back. 'That's it! Good lad! You've saved my life.'

'You should know by this time I'd do anything for a pal, even take over his cast-offs for a while. Now, will you give me peace to finish my mum's letter?'

Neil sat back. He'd been a damned fool telling Olive he'd been thinking about the old picnics, that's what had set her off again, but he'd been down in the dumps with Freda being so cold to him. She was a little warmer now, though not warm enough, and, hopefully, if he got her away from her mother she might forget her fears. He really was serious about her. It was entirely different from how he'd felt about Queenie, though that had been love, too, an innocent love where he hadn't had to keep fighting down his desires. Not that he hadn't desired her, but the urge hadn't been so powerful.

Thinking about Queenie reminded him of the letter he had written when he thought he was being sent abroad. When he started going steady with Freda, he had put it in his kit-bag, in case he pulled it out of his pocket any time, and it might be a good idea to get rid of it altogether now. Making sure that Alf wasn't looking, he rummaged through his things until he found it and smiled tenderly as he read it. He had meant every word at the time, and he still felt something for her, but he had Freda now. What would she think if she saw this? Grimacing, he stood up and went to the lavatory, where he put a match to the letter. It was safer not to have incriminating evidence lying about.

Gracie had worried all morning about how to tell her niece and as soon as Joe came home for his lunch, she burst out, 'Neil's taking that Freda home with him. What am I going to do? It's going to be an awful shock for Queenie, though she maybe doesn't realise we know how she feels about him, and maybe it's better to happen now rather than have her keeping on hoping, for it wouldn't have been right for cousins to marry, though if Neil hadn't fallen in love with Freda, he wouldn't have listened to what anybody said.'

Her husband had raised his eyebrows at the unexpectedness, and length, of her speech, but it only proved how distressed she was. 'Calm down, Gracie,' he soothed. 'Just tell me, are you pleased about it, or no'?'

'I don't know myself and I wish I knew what this girl's like. She could be common, for all we know, and not the kind of wife we'd like for Neil, but. . .'

'Look, Gracie, if it's her he wants for a wife, he'll take her in spite of us and we'll just have to accept her even though she's as common as cat's shit.'

'Ach, Joe!'

They both turned as Queenie walked in, and Joe said, 'I'd better go to the lavvy before I take my dinner.'

Aware that he was giving her the chance to tell her niece on her own, Gracie felt obliged to get it over as quickly as she could. 'Neil's taking Freda home with him next week.'

There was the merest pause before Queenie said, rather too brightly, 'So she's definitely the one?'

'It looks like it.'

'Well, I . . . just hope she's good enough for him.'

'That's what I was saying to Joe.'

Joe's return was a relief to both women, and Queenie kept up a steady stream of chatter until it was time for her to go back to the university. The lectures that afternoon were completely wasted on her, but she did not allow herself the privilege of tears until she was alone late that night as Patsy was on night duty. There was no hope for her now she thought, mournfully. Neil was bringing Freda home to meet his parents which could only mean that he intended to marry her. But . . . maybe Freda wouldn't fit in. Maybe he would see her in a different light when he was in his own home environment. Maybe there was still hope.

Because Neil never referred to the all-important letter she had written weeks ago, Olive was in something of a quandary. Should she demand an answer or had she scared him off? She had tried to help him out, but it looked as if she'd spoiled things, and she would have to back pedal for a while, play hard-to-get. The magazines said that men always wanted the girls they couldn't have so she would keep all her letters as short and impersonal as possible until he wanted her.

Picking up her fountain pen, she began to write and when she went downstairs on her way to the pillarbox, her mother was laying down the phone. 'That was Gracie.'

'Has something happened to Neil?' This fear was always at the back of Olive's mind.

'Not exactly,' Hetty hedged, unwilling to upset the girl when she had been behaving so well. But what was the use of keeping it from her – she would find out soon enough. 'He's taking a girl home with him next week.'

216

Olive's face blanched. 'A girl? But . . .'

'I think it's the girl who went to see him in hospital.'

'Freda? But he stopped writing about her.'

Sighing, Hetty decided to be blunt. 'I know you've always liked him, maybe you even think you love him, but he doesn't feel the same way about you . . . he never has. This was bound to happen some day and you'll have to face up to it. You'll feel hurt but please don't spoil his leave for him.'

Her pallid face tightening, Olive said, 'I won't spoil it, but I'm glad I got some warning.'

Rushing upstairs, she ripped her letter into shreds, then thumped down on the stool of her dressing table. It was her own fault! If she hadn't tried to force him to say that he loved her, he would never have thought of taking Freda home with him. He was doing it out of spite, he couldn't love the girl. Olive looked at her reflection in the mirror. She was by no means a raving beauty, but she wasn't too bad as far as looks went. Her blonde hair waved at the top and curled round her ears; her eyes were quite a strong blue; her teeth were white and even; her lips . . . the lips that Neil had once found so thrilling . . . He did love her, she thought in anguish. He did! How could he deny it after that kiss?

# Chapter Sixteen

'This is Freda – Mum, Dad, Queenie.'

Neil looked so proud and happy that the weight on Gracie's heart lifted as she shook hands with the girl. 'I'm really pleased to meet you, lass.'

'I hope you don't object to Neil taking me home with him,' Freda said shyly.

'No, I'm pleased he did.'

Joe elbowed his wife out of the way, joking, 'Let the dog see the rabbit.'

'Oh, Joe,' she protested, 'stop saying things like that. I don't know what Freda'll think of you.'

'It was meant as a compliment,' Joe told the girl, making her blush furiously and wince as her fingers were crushed in a vice-like grip. 'If Neil took you home on approval, you pass with flying colours.'

'Sit down, Freda,' Gracie smiled, 'and we'll have a cup of tea before I cook your breakfast.'

'Don't go to any trouble for me, Mrs Ferris.'

'It's no trouble.'

Queenie, who had been dreading this meeting, stood up now to shake hands. 'How do you do, Freda. Patsy said she'd stay at the Nurses' Home so that you could share with me. I hope that's OK with you?'

'I don't mind where I sleep, but I'm sorry if I'm putting Patsy out of her bed.'

'I could have slept on the bed settee,' Neil said.

'No, no,' Gracie frowned. 'It's not handy having to get it made up every night and unmade in the morning, and it causes a lot of dust and fluff. And Patsy's quite happy about it.'

'Fair enough,' Neil agreed, quite glad that he wouldn't be lying on the lumpy mattress.

As everyone sat down, Gracie said, 'Hetty's invited you to supper tomorrow.' She turned to Freda to explain. 'She's my sister, Neil's auntie.'

'He told me, but I'm going to feel as if I'm on show.'

'So you will be,' Joe smiled, 'but it'll not be as bad as you think.'

Neil spoke up, quietly. 'Do we have to go to Hetty's?'

'She'll be offended if you don't.'

'It's just . . . you know.'

'Yes.' Gracie fell silent suddenly. She knew why he didn't want to go. How would Olive react to meeting Freda?

While Gracie fried the bacon she had cajoled from Joe and made an omelette with dried eggs, Neil said, 'Freda knows I used to take Olive out, and what a pest she is, so she's got an idea of what to expect when we go there.'

Joe scratched his head. 'Ach, Olive's quietened down and, once she meets Freda, she'll give up on you. It was just a childish fancy – her being the same age and being brought up with you in the Gallowgate for a few years.'

219

After breakfast, Joe went to the shop and Queenie set off for Marischal College where she was studying for her B.A. degree. Freda rose to dry the dishes, but Gracie waved her away. 'You'd better go and unpack your things. I've cleared two drawers in the dressing table for you. Take her through, Neil, and show her which room it is.'

It was some time before they appeared again, but Gracie didn't tease them. She didn't want to put ideas into their heads, and she didn't think that Neil would do anything out of place in his own home, whatever he did down in Alnwick.

'I'm taking Freda out to see a bit of Aberdeen, Mum. We'll take a snack somewhere at dinnertime, but we'll be back in plenty of time for tea.'

Freda was most impressed with what she saw of Neil's home town. 'I'd no idea Aberdeen was so big, and it's so clean.'

Neil beamed. 'Aye, we're civilised up here, though some of the English folk think we're all red-haired savages in kilts and run about the hills with heather sprouting from between our toes. I bet you haven't seen one kilt today. . . except for the boys in Scottish Regiments.'

She chuckled. 'I don't think you've a very good opinion of the English, either.'

'Oh, some of them aren't so bad . . . one in particular.'

His serious look made her blush and change the subject. 'I like your mum and dad . . . and your cousin.'

'Queenie? Yes, she's a nice kid.'

'She's very pretty.'

Not wanting to get into a discussion about Queenie, Neil said, 'I don't know when you'll see Patsy, but she'll

220

likely pop in some evening, and you'll meet Olive tomorrow.'

'I'm looking forward to it.'

Which was more than he was, Neil reflected. It was Olive's reception of Freda that worried him, but surely she wouldn't say anything to embarrass him . . . or would she? She had never been in the habit of considering other people's feelings.

When they returned to the tenement, he pulled Freda to him before they went upstairs, pushing aside the memory of how he had kissed Queenie, standing in exactly the same place.

'Neil?' Freda's soft voice held a question. 'I wondered why you took me home with you and it just dawned on me. Are you on embarkation leave?

'No, my sweet. Would you worry if I was sent abroad?'

'You know I would. There's no word of it, is there?'

'Not yet, but it could come any day.' He hesitated before going on. 'Freda, I truly love you, but I'd do anything not to be stuck in this country repairing cars and trucks that lunatics drive into the ground. I'd have been better joining the Artillery not the Ordnance Corps . . . not that I'm in that now, either. They transferred the transport section to the new REME when they started it this summer, but it's made no difference to me. I'm still doing the same work.'

'I didn't know you wanted to get away,' Freda said, rather plaintively. 'I thought you'd rather have been with me.'

'You know what I want.' His voice was thick. 'I don't know how often I've pleaded with you, but you always say no.'

'I can't, Neil. Really I can't.'

'Don't you want to show me how much you love me?'

'No, Neil, no.' The soft protest came as his hands touched her breasts.

He dropped his arms hopelessly, 'All the other girls I've been out with let me . . .'

'I'm not all the other girls and I think it's wrong.'

'If I asked you to be engaged to me, would you let me?'

After considering briefly, she said, 'I might let you do some things, but not all the way. I'm sorry, Neil, but it's how I've been brought up.'

'So you won't give in without a wedding ring? And what if I tell you I'm not ready for marriage yet?'

'That's up to you,' Freda said, a little coldly. 'I should never have come here with you. My mother said you'd try . . .'

He whirled away angrily. 'Damn your mother! Haven't you any feelings of your own? If you loved me, you'd let me . . .'

'I do love you and I do have feelings, but if I gave in to them, you wouldn't respect me. I'd be the same as all those other girls you spoke about, and you'd soon tire of me.'

His anger evaporated. 'I'll never tire of you, my darling, and I do understand what you mean. I hadn't planned on this, but will you let me buy you an engagement ring, and we'll be married as soon as I can arrange it after we go back?'

'Yes, darling, as soon as you like.'

His aching need became almost unbearable when she leaned against him, but he kept his arms firmly round her waist as he kissed her. 'We won't say anything tonight to my mum and dad. We'll surprise them tomorrow with the ring.'

In bed, Neil was amazed that he didn't feel trapped. He'd really had no intention of getting married for a long time yet, but he couldn't risk losing Freda. He loved her deeply, in spite of her keeping him at bay for so long – or perhaps because of it. His parents would get a right shock tomorrow, but he was sure that they'd be happy about the engagement.

Gracie and Joe were delighted at lunchtime next day when Freda proudly displayed the ring – a small solitaire diamond which sparkled cheekily in the weak December sun shining in through the window of the kitchen. Joe jumped up to give his future daughter-in-law a smacking great kiss on her cheek, and Gracie hugged her. 'I'm really pleased for you both.'

'Congratulations.' Queenie shook hands with Freda first, then with Neil, who clasped her hand in both of his and held it for a moment longer than necessary. She had desperately clung to the faint hope that he might come back to her once he tired of Freda, but this engagement was the final proof that he had never cared for her as much as she thought. 'I'm very pleased for you, too,' she added.

Neil let out a loud guffaw, 'We're very pleased ourselves, aren't we, Freda?'

'I'm very happy,' the girl murmured. 'I do love Neil, Mrs Ferris, and I'll be a good wife to him.'

'I'll bring up a bottle of wine at teatime,' Joe said. 'We have to drink to our only son's happiness.'

It was Gracie who remembered. 'They won't be here. They're going to Hetty's for tea tonight.'

Neil's eyes clouded. 'Do we have to go? Could we not leave it till another night?

'She'll have everything ready by this time.' Gracie could understand her son's reluctance. He would have to tell Hetty and Martin about his engagement in front of Olive. 'They'll be as pleased for you as we are,' she ended uncertainly.

'And the wine'll keep till tomorrow,' Joe smiled.

Neil was very quiet as he and Freda walked to Rubislaw Den later, but his fiancée was too ecstatic to notice. 'This was the only ring I wanted,' she told him, 'and I'm so glad it wasn't too expensive. My mum's going to be surprised when we go back – she said you weren't really serious about me. I wonder what your Auntie Hetty will say?'

It wasn't what Hetty would say about their engagement that troubled him, it was what Olive would say. Would she have the decency to congratulate them, or would she make a scene? There was no telling with Olive, but his money was on her making a scene.

Olive had rushed home from her last lecture in order to have time to bathe and change into something more attractive than the heavy skirt and thick woollen jumper she had put on in the morning. She had to compete against this girl that Neil was bringing, and she had no idea what the creature looked like. She was probably one of those painted, too-smart-for-her-own-good types, and it would be better to show her up by dressing conservatively and acting like a lady.

Emerging from a half-hour soak in the perfumed bath salts she had been hoarding, she wrapped herself in a large towel and went into her room, eyeing with some distaste the dress she had laid out – a navy flannel with a demure, white Peter Pan collar. Having worn it once before when she was out with Neil, she would have preferred something new, but there were never any clothing coupons left when she needed them. Still, Neil had complimented her on this one, and it was just the thing for her purpose. Now, dab on a little powder, and just a touch of lipstick, give her hair a good brushing, and then it would be watch out, Freda Whatever-the-end-of-your-name is, the gloves are off.

Olive waited until she heard the doorbell and her mother talking to the visitors before she swept down the staircase like a star in a Hollywood musical, her hand caressing the curved bannister. 'Oh, you're here, Neil. I didn't hear the bell.' Her feigned amazement convinced Freda, but not Hetty nor Neil.

'Meet my fiancée, Freda Cuthbert,' he mumbled.

Olive was stunned, but had the presence of mind to say, 'Congratulations.' His fiancée? Why had no one told her?

'Isn't this a nice surprise?' Hetty gushed. She was still recovering from the shock herself, and was praying that her daughter would not disgrace her. 'Don't keep standing here, you two. Come and tell Martin your good news.'

Trailing behind them into the sitting room, Olive tried to tell herself that Neil had got engaged to spite her. He couldn't love this mousey person with the dark red hair that made her pale face look even paler. She wasn't even pretty. Her mouth was too wide, her nose turned up, her eyes were too dark for her hair, and her figure was nothing startling, either. She was too skinny – so neat in her straight skirt and green twinset that Olive felt lumpy and awkward.

Martin was voicing his felicitations. 'You're a very lucky lad, Neil, but you're a dark horse, keeping a gorgeous girl like this up your sleeve. I'd say this calls for the brandy, Hetty.' He leaned back in his chair. 'And when did you take the plunge?'

Thoroughly embarrassed, Neil mumbled, 'Just this forenoon. We hadn't planned it . . . it just sort of happened.'

Martin's grin was threatening to split his face. 'Oh, it's good news, great news.' Becoming conscious that his daughter was still standing near the door as though turned to stone, he said, 'Isn't it great news, Olive?'

She gave a start. 'Oh, yes, great.' It was the worst news she had ever heard, but Neil could have his moment of glory, simpering, dimpled Freda could have her moment of triumph . . . Olive Potter would make certain that it didn't last. In any case, it might just be another of Neil's ploys to put her off him. But he wouldn't get away with it now that she knew the kind of tricks he got up to. 'It's really great,' she said, a little more emphatically.

The brandy helped to restore her flagging spirits, and she joined in the laughter – a little forced, perhaps, but not too noticeably – until Hetty told them to go into the dining room. While they were eating, Olive said, 'Is it OK with you if I keep on writing to Neil, Freda? I've done it since he joined up, though he just sends little notes occasionally.'

Freda smiled beatifically. 'Yes, it's OK with me.' Wagging her finger at her fiancé, she said, 'Naughty boy! You must answer every one of Olive's letters in future. Promise me?'

Clutching his knife tightly, he could cheerfully have slit Olive's throat, but he nodded. Not by one word could he let Freda suspect that Olive's letters were anything other than cousinly, for it would raise doubts in her mind. His panic abated. Surely Olive wouldn't write anything stupid now he was engaged? She must know when she was beaten.

But Olive hadn't finished. 'He always used to take me out once or twice when he was on leave, but I suppose . . .?'

'We're going dancing tomorrow night, so why not come with us?' Freda looked a trifle smug at being so magnanimous.

Before Neil could say anything, Martin objected. 'No, you don't want Olive tagging along. Two's company, you know.'

Casting a murderous glare at her father, Olive turned to Freda, 'Dad's right. I'd only be a gooseberry.'

Hetty jumped in here, 'Yes, you would, when they've just got engaged. Now, does anyone want a second helping?'

For the remainder of the evening, they talked in a light-hearted manner, Olive, having scored one small victory, even going as far as to tell them of the work done in the medical laboratories, but Neil was itching to get away. As soon as he could, he said, 'It's time we were leaving, Freda. These people want to go to bed.'

'It's early yet,' Martin smiled but Hetty frowned at him. 'They want to be on their own.'

'It's not that,' Neil blustered. 'It'll take us a while to walk home and Mum and Dad'll likely be waiting up for us.'

The walk home took much longer than it should have done but even wearing his engagement ring, Freda parried

Neil's attempts to seduce her in the first secluded spot they came to. 'It's not that I don't want to,' she explained, 'it's a matter of principle.'

On fire with need, Neil persisted for some time before he mumbled, 'I suppose I should be grateful. If you won't let me make love to you, it proves you won't let anybody else do it either.'

She seemed horrified at him for even thinking she might, so he gave her one last kiss and they carried on walking to King Street, where his parents were indeed waiting up.

'How did it go?' Gracie asked. She had worried all evening about what was happening at Rubislaw Den and Neil's rather glum face alarmed her.

'We had a most enjoyable time,' Freda smiled. 'They had a pleasant surprise when they knew we were engaged.'

'Pleasant surprise' was not how Neil would have described Olive's reaction, but it was another half hour before he was able to plead over-indulgence in Martin's brandy and they all dispersed to bed. Taking off his uniform, he hoped that Freda hadn't noticed Olive's tension, but what on earth had possessed her to tell his cousin to keep writing to him? It was a foot in the door for Olive, and she was cunning enough to make use of it. She had been prevented from going dancing with them, thank goodness, but if she wanted to get her own back at him nothing would stop her.

He lay down and pulled up the blankets, wishing that his leave was over. He would have to arrange his wedding as soon as he went back – it was the only way to prove to Olive that she had no claim on him and it was no hardship for him. He wanted to marry Freda now, more than anything else.

Olive hauled her dress off and flung it down on the floor in a temper. Damn Neil! She would never forgive him for putting her in such a terrible position. She had primed herself to face his girlfriend, but it had been a thousand times worse to learn that it was his fiancée. She'd had no time to think of anything to show Freda that she wouldn't have things her own way, that she would have a fight on her hands.

Her mood changing, Olive gave a giggle. The trusting fool had played right into her hands though, telling her to keep writing to Neil. It wasn't much of a loophole, but it could be enough. Should she tell him that she was broken-hearted? It might stir his conscience but it might be better not to give him the satisfaction of knowing that she still carried a torch for him. A torch? It was a great, bloody beacon she was carrying. Maybe she should play it slowly and just tell him how much she missed him. . . or would he find that amusing? She would have to think it out very carefully, weighing all the pros and cons, before she did anything.

Engagements were made to be broken, and she would do her damnedest to get him back . . . or to take her revenge for that despicable trick he and Alf had played on her.

# Chapter Seventeen

Freda had told Neil to wait for a while before he asked her father if they could be married. 'I'd like to get used to being engaged first,' she explained, 'and there's no rush.'

As far as he was concerned, there was every need to rush but he let her have her way. As long as it wasn't more than a few weeks, he could wait. She sprang it on him one night less than a week later, when he was not expecting it. It was raining heavily, with a hint of snow in it, when he called for her and she asked him to come inside. Her parents were sitting by the fire in the living room, the woman stout and red-faced, the man wiry and weatherbeaten. 'Dad,' she said, 'Neil wants to ask you something.'

Taken by surprise, Neil stammered, 'I . . . I'd like to marry F . . . Freda as s . . . soon as you'll let us, Mr Cuthbert.'

His hopes were knocked on the head by Freda's mother, who was clearly head of the house. 'She's far too young yet and I wouldn't let her marry in haste, anyway. What would people think? I'll tell you,' she went on, before Neil could open his mouth, 'they'd say she had to get married.' She turned to Freda suspiciously. 'You're not expecting, are you?'

Neil felt like shouting that she would be if he'd had his way but he just said, very deliberately, 'Your daughter is still as pure as the driven snow, Mrs Cuthbert.' The devil, always lurking inside him, made him add, 'Unfortunately.'

Mrs Cuthbert was so relieved that she overlooked this last word. 'She has been brought up to have the same ideals as I had, never to let a man touch her until he marries her, and I insist on at least a full year's engagement, then a church wedding, with all our relations there . . . and yours.'

'Oh, Prissie . . .' her husband began but she rounded on him before he finished. 'I insist, George.'

He said no more, and Neil was hard put to it not to smile at the woman's name. It would be Priscilla, but Prissie was absolutely made for her – she was as prissy as they came. He looked at Freda's expressionless face and felt annoyed that she had shown no spark of independence. If she really loved him, she would be as anxious to get married as he was but maybe she didn't want to marry him. She might be quite happy just to remain engaged, to show off the ring to her friends as proof that she wasn't going to be left on the shelf. One thing was sure, however. He wasn't going to try arguing with her mother – that would get him nowhere.

Walking back to camp, his anger subsided. Freda might give in to him yet, if he caught her offguard, if he plied her with enough drink to make her forget her mother's teachings. She was getting him into such a state that at times he felt like going out and getting drunk himself, picking up a nice bit of fluff and quenching his biological needs. Freda would never know . . . but he couldn't deceive her like that. She was sticking to her mother's principles, doing what she believed was right, and he should admire her for it.

231

The only good result of his engagement, as far as he could see, was that Olive seemed to have come to her senses. Her letter had been so innocent that he had given it to Freda to read and she'd said, 'You told me she was a pest but she's really quite a nice girl. I can't see what you have against her and you should be glad I told her to keep writing.'

On Christmas Day, Queenie was still trying to get over the shock of Neil's engagement, and she was glad when Patsy came home in the evening and gave them an excited account of what had gone on in her ward. 'One of the doctors dressed up as Santa Claus with a sack and he dished out little gifts to the patients. I'd always thought he was snooty, but he isn't really, he can be very good fun.'

'I think you fancy him,' Queenie smiled.

Patsy gave a small giggle. 'All the nurses fancy him, even Sister goes all fluttery when Doctor Repper comes round, but he's married, worse luck. Still, there's quite a few heartthrobs among the young doctors, as well as a few creeps that can't keep their hands to themselves.'

Frowning a little, Gracie said, 'I hope you let them know you're not . . .'

'I let them know, all right. I slap their hands or glare at them so they don't bother me for long, but some of the other girls encourage them. They'd go like a shot if any of them asked them out.'

Queenie waited until they were in bed before she put her question. 'Don't you ever wish you'd a boyfriend?'

Patsy didn't need to consider, 'I do, sometimes, but I'd never go out with anybody unless I liked him and none of the doctors I like have ever asked me.'

'What about patients? Have you ever fancied any of them?'

'One or two, but when they're discharged, I never see them again.' Patsy hesitated, then said, 'Have you fancied any of the boys you meet at the varsity? I know how keen you were on Neil, but now he's engaged . . .'

'I'm still keen on him,' Queenie admitted. 'Not just keen, I can't stop loving him.'

'But . . .' Patsy broke off, then began again. 'I'm sorry. I didn't realise it had gone as far as that. Did Neil know?'

'Yes, and he did love me for a while before he met Freda and . . . oh! I'm being silly, but I can't help hoping he'll . . .'

'Oh, Queenie, it's not silly, but you shouldn't go on like that. I know you've been hurt, and I know it'll be hard, but you should try to forget him and find somebody else.'

'I suppose I should. Maybe . . . some of the girls go to the Students' Union quite a lot.'

'Well, there you go. A ready-made supply of men to choose from. Don't jump at the first one who smiles at you, though. Take your time and wait till you meet somebody who really appeals to you.'

'OK, I'll start looking after the holidays.'

When Patsy fell asleep, Queenie thought over what she had said. Even if she did meet another boy would she be able to forget Neil? She would see him, and Freda, every time he was home on leave, and the agony would start again. If only she could get away. That would be the ideal solution, but where would she go? The answer struck her in a blinding flash. She had almost forgotten that she'd wanted to go into the forces and she would be eighteen in April. Neil would be home again before she could leave but surely she could bear seeing him just once more?

On New Year's Day 1943, Gracie hosted the family dinner once more. Hetty had wanted to have it at Rubislaw Den but had agreed that, with Neil back near Alnwick, Raymond somewhere in the south of England and Patsy on duty for the day, the seating arrangements would be easier.

When the Potters turned up in the afternoon, Joe said, 'I think Martin and me should go for a walk. We'll only be in the road here.'

Gracie, hot and bothered from all the cooking, nodded her head. 'That's a good idea, and take Queenie and Olive with you. Hetty can give me a hand to get everything ready.'

Having gone down Urquhart Road and reached the promenade, Joe and Martin were walking in front of the two girls who, although they were both at university, had only ever had one interest in common – their cousin, Neil. After a protracted silence, Queenie remarked, as brightly as she could, 'It was great about Neil's engagement, wasn't it?'

Olive shot her a suspicious glance, 'I didn't think you'd have found it great, any more than I did, but you never had any chance with him, of course.'

'I'd more chance than you!' Queenie had made up her mind not to quarrel with Olive but had been provoked into it.

'I've told you before. He only took you out because he was sorry for you but you don't want to understand.'

'He was never sorry for me,' Queenie declared, her hackles up, 'and I know perfectly well it was your fault he turned against me for a while and fell for Freda.'

'My fault?' Olive demanded. 'How do you make that out?'

'You told him some lie about me – don't deny it.'

'You've a good imagination, that's all I can say.'

'Anyway, it didn't work the way you hoped. When Neil told me he was in love with Freda, he said he cared for me more than he should. I bet he never said that to you, Olive Potter, so even if you try to break his engagement, and I wouldn't put it past you, it's me he would turn to, not you.'

A bitter north wind had whipped the sea to a churning mass of huge white-crested waves which reared up and crashed down before rushing onto the sands, but the two girls neither saw nor heard, and their red-hot anger saved them from feeling cold. Olive was searching for words scathing enough to banish any hope that might linger in the other girl's mind, and Queenie was preparing to fend off the expected attack. They walked thus until Olive, unsuccesful in her quest, gave a rather high-pitched laugh, 'I'll get him back.'

'How? By telling him more lies? You'll never get him back, Olive, because you never had him in the first place, and I'm glad he's happy with Freda, so you'd better not try anything to drive them apart. I don't believe you could, anyway.'

Stung, Olive tossed her head. 'I could and I will . . . some day soon.'

Queenie, aware that her cousin was unsure of herself, let the matter drop and they carried on without saying anything until they reached the end of the prom, at which point, Joe turned round. 'We'll go back by St Clement Street and up to the Castlegate. That's a nice circular tour, but we'd better put a step in, for it's getting blooming cold. You two OK?'

'Fine,' Queenie assured him and he took Olive's silence as an agreement.

By the time they got back, the dinner was ready, and they took their places at the table while Hetty helped Gracie to serve. The others did not need Joe's order to 'Tuck in,' but Olive, having something less mundane than food on her mind, only toyed with each course, which alarmed her mother but did not bother Gracie who had always thought that Olive was a queer fish. Queenie, still smarting from Olive's remarks, sneaked a quick glance at her and felt gratified that she looked miserable. It had been idiotic to argue with her but it had made her think.

Gracie suddenly caught Olive glaring at her malevolently and wondered what she had done to annoy her. 'Would you like tea, Olive?' she asked as cordially as she could, 'or would you rather have lemonade?'

Olive's lips turned up scornfully. 'Tea, if it's not too much trouble. I'm twenty now, remember, not a kid.'

Feeling like wiping the sneer off her face with a smack, Gracie said, 'I know that. You're the same age as Neil.'

This remark led Martin and Joe to reminisce about the time of the births in the Gallowgate and Gracie breathed easily again. She shouldn't let Olive upset her. It was a waste of time trying to fathom out the imaginary insults the girl was harbouring against her. Olive's thinking had no reason.

At the end of the meal, Joe further upset Olive by saying, 'You and Hetty sit down, Gracie. Let the girls clear up.'

Both Queenie and Gracie expected an outburst at this but none came. Olive just stood up and started stacking dishes although it was clear that she was inwardly fuming.

Gracie had to wait until their guests left before she told her husband what she thought of him. 'Did you have to tell Olive to dry the dishes? She was in a bad humour anyway.'

Joe gave his usual grin. 'I could see that, that's why I did it. She needs to be reined in a bit, that one, and when she finds a man, she'll have to learn to do dozens of things she's never set her hands to before, though God help the poor bugger that ends up with her.'

The swearword made Gracie scowl but Queenie prayed that whoever ended up with Olive, it wouldn't be Neil.

When the new semester began, Queenie threw herself into the business of finding someone to replace Neil. She went out so many nights that even Joe remarked on it. 'I can't see where you find time to do any studying.'

She pretended to laugh at his ignorance. 'We all study in the Common Room when we've spare time, or at the Union at nights, helping each other with notes and essays.'

'Not copying from each other?' This was a crime to Gracie.

'Not really, we've all our own ways of putting things and the lecturers are quite happy.'

'I don't like it,' Gracie said unnecessarily.

Queenie didn't altogether like it herself but she would be leaving in three months so it didn't matter. She had met some nice boys in the Union – a small place in Broad Street, crowded and so smoky that her eyes nipped every time she was there – but hadn't gone out with any of those who'd asked her, although she might start one day soon. Until she left Aberdeen, and probably afterwards too, she would have to pretend that she was having fun, put on a face to the world. She would never stop loving Neil but that didn't mean she should go into a decline. He had found his true love in Freda and they would live happily ever after . . . as long as Olive did nothing to spoil it.

Neil had to put up with much teasing from his friends about his engagement, especially from Alf, who had said, 'She got you hooked, then? She'll have the ball and chain round your neck in no time.'

Neil took it all with a laugh, but he didn't tell Alf that his marriage would be in the dim and distant future – that was what it seemed to him – nor that Freda kept him at arm's length as far as sex was concerned. He couldn't get her to understand that there was nothing rude about it, nothing to be ashamed of. 'If you can't wait till we're married,' she had said last night, 'I'd better give you your ring back.'

That had shaken him, and thinking about it again, he knew that she had meant it. Could he wait a year or would he be better to cut his losses and run? No, by God! He couldn't do that, he loved her too much. He would wait . . . but it might be worth trying again in a little while. She couldn't hold out against him for twelve whole months.

Olive was glad that Frankie Lamont was off with tonsillitis and that she had Polly Frayne to herself. She always got the feeling that Frankie didn't believe her stories, but Polly took every word as gospel. 'Neil wanted us to get engaged on his last leave,' she began, 'but I reminded him that I still hadn't got my degree.'

Polly's eyes darkened, 'I don't know how you can treat him like that. Didn't he get angry?'

'No, he loves me, you see, and he'll do anything I want. I know he's finding it difficult to wait but like I told you before I want to be a virgin on my wedding night.'

'I won't be a virgin on my wedding night,' Polly sighed. 'I don't seem to be able to say no.'

'You should have had willpower, like me. It's not that I don't want him to make love to me, sometimes I want him as much as he wants me but I made up my mind long ago that I wouldn't give in to him and I'm sticking to it.'

'Well, I hope you don't regret it. You'll maybe find, one of these days, that he's gone off with somebody who's not a cold-blooded fish.'

'I'm not cold-blooded,' Olive burst out indignantly. 'I'm just being sensible.'

But she wasn't being sensible, she thought, later. It was anything but sensible to carry on with these lies and she could never let Polly know that Neil was engaged to somebody else. Polly would think that he didn't love her, and while she knew deep down in her own heart that this was true, she didn't want to believe it. He had loved her before and he would love her again, once she found a way to get him back. It was this belief that had seen her through the awful weeks since he had been home, and she was determined not to lose sight of it. It would come true, no matter what Queenie or anyone else thought.

# Chapter Eighteen

Neil had grown more despondent and frustrated as the weeks crept past. Freda, despite the promise in her kisses, never let him go beyond that. She steadfastly refused to have more than one drink, and jumped away like a scalded cat if he tried anything when he walked her home. She made him feel as if he were an unreasonable rotter, though all he wanted was a full commitment on her part . . . just once.

When his leave came round again, he was actually relieved that she had caught a very virulent strain of influenza and couldn't go with him. He had often felt like taking her by force and damning the consequences – what could her parents do even if they found out? Put a gun to his head and force him to marry her? That was what he wanted to do anyway – but if he lost control at home and his mother found out there would be hell to pay. Temptation was better left behind.

The train was late when it arrived in Aberdeen and both Joe and Queenie had left by the time he reached King Street.

'I'm sorry Freda wasn't able to come,' Gracie said. 'I was looking forward to seeing her again.'

'It was just one of those things,' Neil sang, putting on a sad expression and turning the palms of his hands upwards.

Gracie frowned at his flippancy, 'Poor lass, she's likely hurt at you for going away and leaving her when she's ill.'

'I did offer to stay there with her, but she wouldn't hear of it. Anyway, her mother fusses round her like an old hen, and I'd just have annoyed her – Mrs Cuthbert, I mean. She's the boss in that house, and she's too overpowering for me.'

'I'm glad you came home.' Gracie hoped fervently that he wouldn't end up with an interfering mother-in-law.

After a breakfast of toast and tea, Neil went to bed – he had stood in the corridor of the train most of the way from Newcastle. Stretching out on top of the blankets, he looked round his old room. He had occupied it little more than a year before he joined up, so it was strange how nostalgic he felt about it. It hadn't changed much. The floral curtains had been replaced by heavy blackout material, which made the room gloomy, even when they were pulled back. The chest of drawers had a new runner on it – it looked like tapestry though it probably wasn't – but the framed snapshot of Patsy and him as children was still there, balanced at the other side by a matching framed photo, the first he'd had taken in uniform. Between them stood the alarm clock that used to get him up for work, its twin bells shrilling so noisily that he had often felt like hurling it out of the window. . . but he'd have had to get out of bed to do it.

The same reproduction of 'The Monarch of the Glen' hung on the wall and he remembered being frightened of it when they lived in the Gallowgate. The stag was a magnificent animal but it had seemed fearsome to a small

241

boy and the only one he had confided in was his Granda, who had said, 'He's just defending his territory, lad. He'll not attack man nor beast unless they threaten him.' This had eased his fears but he had sometimes worried that boys might not be as immune from attack as men and beasts.

If Granda had still been alive, he'd have been the person to ask about this latest fear, Neil mused. He had begun to wonder if he was unnatural in having such a steady ache for sex but maybe it was just because he'd had too much of it before and was getting none now . . . like a drug addict whose supplies had been cut off, but the craving would surely wear off eventually.

Neil spent that evening talking to his parents – 'Queenie hardly ever stays in,' his mother had said – but he went to see Hetty the next evening and was disappointed to be told that Martin wouldn't be home for a while. 'He's on another of his working late binges,' Hetty said, pettishly 'Well, he says he's working late.'

His aunt's odd manner made him feel uneasy but Olive was speaking to him now and he had to turn his attention to her. While they were having a cup of tea, much later, it occurred to Neil that several empty evenings lay ahead, and that he couldn't impose himself on his aunt too often. He was afraid to ask Queenie out – he couldn't trust himself there because he still felt something for her though she seemed to have got over him – but why shouldn't he take Olive dancing? He let this run around his brain for several minutes, wondering if it would be asking for trouble, then decided to risk it. Surely she'd have given up on him now and he would tell Freda about it when he saw her. She wasn't the jealous type and Olive was his cousin, after all.

He waited until Hetty went into the kitchen before he murmured, 'Olive?'

'Yes, Neil?'

Her old eagerness was gone, he was pleased to note. 'Would you like to go to the Palais with me some night?'

'If you like.'

'Wednesday?'

'OK.'

'I'll meet you at the usual place at eight.'

'Fine.'

When Hetty returned, Olive said, 'Neil's asked me out.'

He felt he had to explain. 'I'm at a loose end and I don't feel like going to the Palais by myself.'

Hetty smiled indulgently. Neil was engaged and would just be needing company. 'Olive doesn't go out very much. It'll be a nice change for her.'

Martin looked tired when he came in, Neil thought, but it wasn't surprising if he worked late so much. 'I was thinking I wouldn't see you tonight.'

'A last-minute hiccup in a house deal,' Martin sighed. 'I got it all sorted out but it took much longer without Evie. She was my secretary,' he explained, 'and she was really efficient but she married a marine and left last week. The new girl's still wet under the collar, she's only just out of a business college but I believe she'll shape up. It'll just take time to train her.'

'Mum was a bit jealous of Evie,' Olive chuckled.

Recalling his aunt's previous remarks, Neil realised that this had been true but Martin said, 'She has no reason to be jealous, of Evie or anyone else. I need a secretary, but I'd never get involved with any of them.'

Hetty had the grace to look ashamed. 'I know, Martin. I've been paranoid about it, but you're so often late home.'

'Pressures of work, that's all, I assure you. Now, Neil, you must be bored with our little differences, and don't let us put you off marriage. It's the best institution there is, no matter what anyone tells you.'

'Nothing'll put me off,' Neil laughed, 'but Freda's mother wants us to wait. She's a dragon and a half, that one.'

'I was lucky,' Martin smiled affectionately at his wife. 'Hetty's mother was a real gem. If it hadn't been for her, I would never have told Hetty that I loved her.'

It was after eleven o'clock when Neil stood up. 'Mum and Dad will think I'm lost. I'll see you on Wednesday, Olive.'

His parents were unhappy about the date he had made. As Gracie said to Joe when they were in bed, 'After the way she used to run after him? He's going to stir it all up again.'

Inwardly, Joe agreed, but his wife looked so troubled that he tried to reassure her. 'Olive's changed. She knows he's engaged, and I can't see her causing any trouble.'

Gracie snorted. 'She thrives on causing trouble.'

Taking Olive home on Wednesday night, Neil felt relaxed. He had wondered, beforehand, what he was letting himself in for but he had thoroughly enjoyed their evening out. She could be good company when she set her mind to it and if she had been like that all along it would have saved him many an anxious hour. Still, that was in the past and a man had to live for the day, hadn't he?

They arrived at her house in a fit of the giggles at a rather risque story she had been telling but she held out her hand and said, more seriously, 'It was good fun tonight, Neil, thanks for taking me. Have a safe journey back.'

He kept hold of her hand. 'I don't have to go back till next Tuesday. You'll come out with me again, won't you?'

There was no coyness, no self-satisfied smirk. 'OK.'

'Saturday, then?'

'Fine. Goodnight, Neil.'

When he went home, only Joe was still up. 'How did you get on with Olive?'

'Great! We're going out on Saturday again.'

Joe scratched his ear lobe. 'Your mother's not too pleased about you taking her out. It's not that long since you were saying you couldn't stand the sight of her.'

'I used to call her everything, but she's different now, no stupid nonsense. I think she's grown up at long last.'

'Maybe it'll be all right, but . . . I'd watch myself if I was you. She's got a . . . what's the word? . . . voluptuous, that's it, a voluptuous figure, and the best of men could be tempted.'

Neil laughed loudly. 'Freda's the only one I want. Olive doesn't appeal to me, not even her big tits.' He looked at his father and grinned. 'Sorry, Dad, it just slipped out.'

Joe shook his head. 'I see you've learned men's talk?'

'I bet if you heard some of the things we speak about, it would make your hair curl.'

Stroking his balding pate, Joe observed ruefully, 'That'd take a bit of doing, these days.'

When he went home on Saturday night, Neil was

245

thankful that both his parents were in bed. He couldn't have faced them, not after what he had done. God, he'd been a bloody fool! It hadn't been entirely his fault but that was no excuse. His mind jumped back a few hours.

When he met Olive, she'd said, 'It's far too nice a night to be in a stuffy hall.' That should have warned him but he had thought nothing of it. It was a nice night, warm and balmy although it was still March, and he fell in with the idea quite happily. They took the tram to Hazlehead and found that the park closed at sunset but they went past the locked gates and carried on along the rather rough road between the trees.

After a few minutes, Olive said, 'This road's making my feet sore. I can feel the stones through my shoes.'

Neil's own feet were uncomfortable, so they moved on to the grass verge and when they saw a gap in the dyke, they went through on to the golf course, the springy turf feeling like a thick-piled carpet. They walked for perhaps half an hour, Olive sometimes running ahead and dodging behind one of the trees, waiting to jump out on him when he caught her up, the twigs snapping under their feet, the fallen needles sending up the fresh fragrance of pine as they capered about in the darkness like fauns.

Neil couldn't recall which of them had suggested having a rest but he was almost sure it was Olive. They had lain down side by side under the gnarled old trees, still breathless, and looked up at the scattering of tiny stars winking in the black sky. After a few minutes, when they got a second wind, they had exchanged more stories and their laughter turned to teasing, the teasing became fun-wrestling, until . . . his hands had accidentally brushed against her breasts and his long-suppressed urges had erupted. Not that she had objected. It was probably what she'd been leading up to from the minute he met her. She had returned his kisses with a passion that drove him wild, pushing him beyond control, encouraging him, helping him, towards the release that was his sole concern.

Instead of the memory setting him aflame again, it made him feel worse than ever. Olive, of all people! It had been her first experience of sex, his first with a virgin, and he groaned now with the bitter shame of it. She had clung to him after it was over, whispering, 'I always knew you loved me, Neil darling,' and he had jumped up, too angry to argue with her. He had felt like walking away and leaving her but he couldn't let her go home alone in the blackout and he'd waited until she made herself respectable.

As they walked back the way they had come, she had crowed, 'You'll have to break off your engagement now,' and had been astonished when he shouted, 'You're a stupid bitch, Olive Potter, do you know that? I love Freda, with all my being.'

'But I thought . . . oh, Neil, you must love me, after that.'

'I've never loved you, and I never will. I'm sorry for what I did and it'll never happen again. A man doesn't have to love a girl to make love to her, though it makes it more satisfying. It's a need he gets and Freda respects her body, so I've never . . .'

'You mean she won't let you?' Olive gave a coarse laugh. 'God, Neil, I credited you with more gumption.'

When they arrived at her door, he snapped, 'Don't write to me again, because I won't answer any of your letters.'

247

'Are you going to tell Freda about . . .?'

'What do you think?'

He had left her and hadn't even turned his head when she called after him, 'Come back, Neil darling.' He was up to his neck in boiling water and he couldn't tell Freda what he had done. She would be shocked, hurt, and so angry that she wouldn't marry him. A tremor of stark fear ran through him. Surely Olive wouldn't be as vindictive as to tell her? Maybe it would be a wise move to get in first, to tell his fiancée everything and throw himself on her mercy, though it was unlikely that she would forgive him. It might be best if he arranged to see Olive again, to reason with her, to make her understand that nothing she could do would make him love her and to make her promise that she would never tell Freda by letter or by word-of-mouth. He would phone her tomorrow.

Olive, too, was recalling what had happened. How could Neil deny that he loved her when he had whispered beautiful words of love all the time they were . . .? But possibly he wanted to wait until he broke his engagement before he told her? He might think that was the decent thing to do and she would have to be patient. Yes, she decided, it would all work out in the long run. Having thus convinced herself, she settled down to relive the most wonderful moments she had ever spent . . . so far. Her whole life would be even more wonderful, once Neil was free of Freda Cuthbert.

She was dressing in the morning when her mother called to her that Neil was on the phone, so she ran downstairs in her petticoat. 'Hello?' she said breathlessly.

'Can I see you tomorrow night? I promised an old pal I

ran into the other day that I'd go for a drink with him tonight and I go back on Tuesday morning.'

Triumph surged through her. She had prayed he wouldn't go without seeing her again. 'Tomorrow's OK. Same place?'

'Same place, same time.'

Worrying about what he would say to Olive, Neil didn't much enjoy his old pal's company and they did not have much in common now anyway as Paul was in the Air Force and thought himself better than a REME. When he went home, just after quarter to nine, he was surprised to find his father on his own again. 'Is Mum all right?'

'She hasn't been feeling great these past few days,' Joe told him, 'but she won't go to the doctor.'

'She should. I'll have a word with her in the morning. She might listen to me.'

They sat for about twenty minutes discussing the war, then Joe said, 'I believe you're seeing Olive tomorrow again?'

'Did Mum hear me on the phone?'

'Aye.' Joe looked pensive. 'I told you before, it's not a good thing. That's three times you'll have been with her and she could start thinking things, you know.'

Neil would have liked to reassure him but couldn't. It was even worse than his father thought. 'She knows I'm engaged,' he muttered, a rush of guilty colour flooding his face.

'That wouldn't mean much to her. Go canny, lad.'

Even though Neil had slept little the night before, he lay awake for some time thinking about the coming confrontation, but he was shaken awake by his father just before two in the morning. 'Neil, phone the doctor . . . it's your mother.'

By the time the doctor arrived, Gracie was doubled up with pain. 'It's worse than being in labour,' she gasped. A few questions and a brief examination resulted in the diagnosis, 'A stone in the kidney. I'll ring for an ambulance.'

Joe accompanied his wife to hospital, holding her hand as they sped across the city to Foresterhill and Neil dressed himself, amazed that Queenie hadn't heard all the commotion, but it was probably just as well. He'd have been left alone with her, both of them worried sick; that would be fatal. He had already blotted his copybook with Olive, and it would be so much easier to make a slip with Queenie. Back in the kitchen, he made a pot of tea, but it was after four when his father returned, grey-faced with anxiety. 'They're going to operate on her and I wanted to wait but they wouldn't let me. They told me not to phone for a few hours.'

'She'll be all right, Dad, don't worry. I'll make a fresh pot of tea. This'll be stewed.'

'Don't bother, I couldn't drink it anyway.'

Joe paced the floor like a man demented until Neil pulled him to a halt. 'You should go and lie down for a while, Dad, and I'll give you a shout about six.'

'I'll not sleep.'

'You'll be resting, though.'

'Aye, that's right.' Joe went out, his shoulders drooping.

Neil stretched his legs out across the fireplace. He had kept the fire going, and it was warmer in the kitchen than it was in his room. It was better not to go back to bed, in

250

any case, because he might fall asleep. It crossed his mind that he had scarcely seen Queenie apart from mealtimes, and he wondered if she had kept out of his way or if she really went out every night, like his mother had said.

Poor Mum. What would they be doing to her at this minute? He had told his father not to worry, but he was every bit as worried himself. What would they do if anything happened to her? Dad would go to pieces, for Mum did everything for him and if Queenie ever left – a lovely girl like her was bound to marry some day – he wouldn't know where to begin as far as housework was concerned. Dad likely hadn't the faintest idea where the sweeping brush was kept, never mind anything else. As for cooking, he couldn't even boil an egg.

But nothing was going to happen. The operation would be a success and Mum would be back home again in a week or two, as fit as a fiddle.

# Chapter Nineteen

Startled by the click of the letter box, Neil looked at the clock in disbelief. Five past seven? He had fallen asleep after all. Stretching his arms, he stood up stiffly and went to take in the post. There were two letters, one from Flo in Wanganui – that would cheer Mum – and the other addressed to him in Freda's neat writing. He tore it open.

> 20 March, 1943
>
> My Dearest Darling,
>
> I've missed you very much this past week. I'm feeling a lot better now and I'm going back to work on Monday, half days only for a start, the doctor says. Nothing has been happening here so I haven't anything to tell you, except I LOVE YOU.
>
> Give my regards to your mum and dad and tell them I'm sorry I couldn't come with you this time. Remember me to Queenie, also your aunt and uncle and Olive. I can hardly wait till I see you again on Wednesday night.
>
> All my love, darling. Freda x x x

A warmth had spread through Neil's chilled body, and he read the love note again. He would be seeing Freda again the day after tomorrow! Laying the letter down, he filled the kettle and was setting it on the cooker when Joe came through, his sparse, uncombed, grey hair straggling on to his brow, his chin dark and bristly with stubble, his hand stifling a big yawn. 'I fell asleep after all.'

'So did I.' Neil lit the gas ring and laid the matches back on the ledge. 'We'd better wash and shave first before we phone the hospital.' He felt surprisingly reluctant about that now that the time had come. He wanted to know how his mother was but he didn't want to hear . . . if it was bad news.

Lifting yesterday's newspaper from Joe's chair, he knelt on the rug to remove the ashpan from the fire, then tipped the contents onto a double page. Next, he twisted the other pages individually in the way he had seen his mother doing, criss-crossed some kindling sticks over them and was placing coal on top when the kettle came to the boil. Raising his head, he saw that his father was gazing vacantly into space.

'You shave first, Dad,' he ordered. 'Leave some water for me and I'll put the kettle on again for the tea. I'll make the toast once I've washed. Will you be going to the shop?'

'I think I will, I can't sit doing nothing.' Joe lifted the kettle and poured some boiling water into the basin in the sink then, with soap lathered over his face, he turned round again. 'I can't wait, Neil. I'm going to phone now.'

He disappeared into the tiny lobby and Neil crossed his fingers superstitiously until he came back. 'They just gave me the usual pap. "She's as well as can be expected."' Joe imitated the impersonal voice that had answered him. 'What kind of thing's that to tell a husband? They won't let me in to see her till seven at night, for it's only on Wednesdays and Saturdays and Sundays you get in in the afternoons.'

'Mum must be doing fine, or else they'd have told you.'

'I suppose so.' Joe pulled off his shirt and ran some cold water into the basin to cool it down.

Standing up, Neil took a taper from a jar on the mantelpiece, lit it from the gas ring then held it to the paper in the grate. He was still blowing life into the flame when Joe looked round, 'You'll come with me tonight?'

'Of course I'll come with you . . . oh, hell's bells! I said I'd meet Olive tonight. I'll have to phone her.'

'You'd better wait till they're up. It's early yet.'

'OK, Dad. I'll leave it till about eight.'

Queenie came through then – she normally waited until Joe had shaved – and had to be told what had happened during the night. 'Why didn't you wake me?' she cried.

'You couldn't have done anything,' Neil soothed.

'I bet she'd have been glad of another woman there, not just two men.'

Joe patted her shoulder. 'But one man was her husband and the other man was her son.'

Understanding why the girl's mouth tightened, Neil said, 'I'm sorry, Queenie. I'm sure Mum would have been glad if you'd been there, too, but they were away in the ambulance before I realised you were still sleeping and there was no point in wakening you then. But you can come to the hospital with us at night.'

'Are you sure you want me to come?'

With a low moan, Joe flung his arms round her,

'Queenie, lass, she'll need all her family round her and you've been a daughter to us as much as Patsy.'

The trembling of his voice made her burst into tears and he held her, his own eyes moist, until she calmed. Watching them, Neil had a sudden longing to have her in his arms, to wipe away her tears. There was nothing sexual in it, but he knew how easily this could change if he dared to touch her.

When he was left alone, he took the wrapped-up ashes down to the rubbish bin in the backyard, then made his telephone call to Rubislaw Den. Martin, after expressing sympathy for Gracie, went on, 'Hetty'll want to visit her, but I'll tell her to wait until tomorrow, when you'll be away.'

'Thanks. Em . . . Martin, I'd arranged to meet Olive tonight, but will you tell her I can't make it after all?'

'I'll call her down and you can tell her yourself.'

'No, it's OK.'

'Right, I'll pass on the message.'

'Thanks again.' Neil hung up, hardly daring to think what Olive's response would be, but he couldn't cope with her on top of everything else.

When Joe came home for lunch, his face was less strained. 'There's nothing like being kept busy to take your mind off trouble. What have you been doing with yourself?'

'I went to the butcher's. I forgot meat was rationed, but he gave me half a pound of mince when I told him Mum was in hospital, and I got two mealy puddings in case that wasn't enough. Then I cooked it, made your bed and mine – Queenie had made hers – and I did some sweeping and dusting.'

255

'He's a good lad, isn't he, Queenie?' Joe observed.

'I'd have done the housework at teatime,' she protested.

Neil laughed, 'I'd nothing else to do.'

'We'll need all our time tonight,' Joe reminded them. 'We have to be at the hospital for seven, so we'll have our tea at twenty to six – Jim can manage on his own till six – just something quick.'

Giving a grinning salute, Neil said, 'Yes, sir! What does sir fancy, sir?'

'I meant to bring up eggs, but I forgot, so just make up a pan of that dried stuff.'

When they arrived at Foresterhill Hospital at ten minutes to seven, a large queue was already waiting, but the door was not opened until precisely seven o'clock. The uniformed doorman, a stout officious individual, allowed in only those who had the cards which were issued to visitors and was adamant that others would not be admitted, even if they had travelled great distances to be there.

'Only two to each patient,' he repeated, and Neil could hear several people near them arranging to come out at half time and hand their card over to a third person so that he or she could get in. He was about to suggest this to Queenie when it was their turn to face the tyrant but didn't have to. 'Members of the forces don't need a card,' the man told them, surprising Neil by smiling at him as they went inside.

When they reached her ward, Gracie's face still bore some evidence of what she had gone through, but her smile was warm and loving. To allow his parents some privacy, Neil and Queenie went to sit in the corridor after fifteen minutes – filling in time by watching the steady stream of nurses and visitors – and went back when the bell rang to mark the end of visiting time. 'Cheerio, Mum,' he said, 'I've to go back in the morning, so I won't manage to come again, but I'll be thinking about you. Get well soon.'

Olive had no time to think properly until she went to bed. She had spent most of yesterday planning what she would say to Neil tonight and he'd actually cancelled their date. To be fair, it was Gracie's fault, not his, but it meant that she had no opportunity to carry out her scheme for his last night. She had meant to act the lovelorn girl, to weep on his shoulder in the hope that he would succumb to her pleas, and if that didn't work, she had intended to turn nasty, to threaten to tell Freda. She had not thought beyond that. She had been positive that he couldn't hold out against her for long, that she could wear him down . . . but this had happened.

When she was given Neil's message, she had said, 'I'll go to Foresterhill to meet him after visiting time,' but her father had forbidden it. 'He'll be wanting to be with Joe since it's his last night. He'll be upset about his mother and you're not to pester him. At least he had the decency to phone as soon as he could to tell you he couldn't meet you.'

It wasn't decency, Olive mused, it was cruelty, maybe even fear, after what they had done on Saturday night. She would never forgive him for not keeping their date, and she would never forgive Gracie. They'd all conspired against her, even her own father. Mum hadn't said anything but she'd been too afraid that her sister might die. Olive's heart gave a leap. If Gracie did die, Neil would need somebody to console him and who better than the cousin who had loved him for as long as she could remember? That could be the answer to the maiden's prayer . . . though she wasn't a maiden any longer.

It was quite late before Neil arrived back at the camp so, as Freda had known, it was Wednesday evening before he went to see her, still undecided as to whether or not to tell her about Saturday. As he neared her home, he was struck anew by the quaintness of the low, roughly hexagonal cottage, which, according to Mr Cuthbert, had once been the lodge for Duffin House, burned down in the late 1800s – the ruins could still be seen in one of the fields. He had also said that the walled part of his gardens had originally been the kitchen garden for the manor house.

When Freda opened the heavy, latched door, her face still looked rather pinched, but her eyes glowed as she gave him a welcome-back kiss. 'We've something to tell you,' she said softly, her voice charged with excitement, and dragged him inside. He was disappointed that she hadn't given him a more substantial sign that she had missed him, but her father was saying, 'Sit down, Neil, and I'll pour out some sherry.'

Obeying, Neil wondered what was going on. There was an air of conspiracy, even Mrs Cuthbert looked less forbidding than she had done before, and her husband was making something of a ceremony of the simple task of opening a bottle. Whatever they had to tell him, it couldn't be anything bad, so he let his eyes travel round the small, cosy room. He had only been inside once before, when he asked if he and Freda could be married, and he had been so much taken aback by her mother's refusal that he had paid no attention to the room, but it was just perfect for such an old-fashioned lodge. The beamed ceiling was low and there was chintz everywhere: the curtains, the loose covers on the armchairs, the cushions on the wicker chair, twin of the one he was sitting on. The table and the dresser, where Freda's father was engaged in filling four stemmed glasses, were of solid oak. It was a homely room, a comfortable room, but he felt anything but comfortable when he met Mrs Cuthbert's calculating eyes.

'Now, Neil,' Mr Cuthbert boomed, handing round the sherry, 'I suppose you'll be wondering what all this is in aid of. We do not often indulge in drink, but we could not let . . .'

'Get on with it, George!' his wife snapped.

Neil gathered that she was not in favour of 'it', whatever it was, but Mr Cuthbert was not to be deterred from making the speech he had prepared. 'We could not let this occasion pass unmarked. It's the only time we will have the chance. I had always imagined myself . . .'

'For heaven's sake!' his wife said, exasperation getting the better of her. 'Can't you get to the point without all this rigmarole?' She turned to Neil. 'I don't often climb down over anything, but you can marry our Freda as soon as you want. She was miserable all the time you were away and . . . my daughter's happiness has always come first with me.'

'B – but,' Neil stammered, 'I thought you said we'd to wait at least a year . . .'

'Have you changed your mind about marrying her?'

'Oh no!' The full realisation of what she had said dawned on him now. 'This is great! Do you still want the wedding to be in the church or have you climbed down over that, too?'

Freda broke in, 'I persuaded her to let us have it in the registry office in Newcastle, and it'll only be your mum and dad and mine there. No fuss, no white dress, no anything.'

'I'm not happy about it,' Mrs Cuthbert stated, needlessly, 'and to prevent you treating the marriage lightly since it will only be a civil ceremony, we will all go to church on the Sunday, so that it can be blessed properly. I trust that your parents will not object to that?'

'I'm sure they wouldn't, but I don't think they'll be able to come. Mum had an operation on Monday morning to remove a kidney stone and she won't be fit to travel for a while.'

'Oh, Neil,' Freda sighed, 'does that mean we've to wait?'

'Mum wouldn't want us to postpone our wedding. I'll write to her tonight and tell her. I'm sure she and Dad won't mind not being here.'

George Cuthbert, having stood patiently with his glass in his hand, had obviously decided to carry on as if there had been no interruption. 'I had always imagined myself leading my daughter down the aisle, but I know times are changing, and I suppose church weddings will soon be a thing of the past. Be that as it may, I now raise my glass in a toast. To Freda and Neil, a long and happy life together, and may all their troubles be little . . .'

'To Freda and Neil.' His scowling wife interrupted in time to stop his indelicacy.

Because Freda seemed disinclined to leave her parents at such a momentous time, Neil remained with them until it was time to go back to camp, but she offered to walk a little way with him. 'Mum was worried about me not picking up after the flu,' she confided, 'and I said I was missing you and that's why she changed her mind.'

'I missed you, too.' His conscience stirred, but perhaps not deeply enough. 'By the way, I took Olive out a couple of times when I was home. I hope you don't mind?'

'No, of course I don't.'

'I was going to see her on my last night, as well, but I called it off because of Mum.'

'That would have been three times, and you always said you didn't particularly like her.'

There seemed to be no annoyance in her voice but, to be on the safe side, Neil spoke firmly. 'I've never liked her. You're not jealous, are you, darling?'

'No, you Scottish chump.' She hesitated for a moment, then said, wistfully, 'You've never actually proposed to me. I'd always dreamt of a romantic . . .'

Neil whirled her round to face him. 'Dearest darling, will you please do me the honour of becoming my wife?'

'This is so sudden,' she said, with feigned coyness. 'I'm only a poor little virgin and . . .'

'I know that!' he exclaimed wryly. 'But not for long now. And that's not the reason I want to marry you . . . well, it's part of it, but I do love you, with all my heart.'

After several ardent kisses, Freda pulled away. 'I'm sorry about your mum and when you write, tell her I hope she'll soon be on her feet again. Now, I'd better go before Mum and Dad think we've eloped.'


'A letter for you, Mrs Ferris.' The auxiliary nurse handed an envelope to Gracie who glanced at it and smiled. 'It's from my son. He's in the REME and he was home on leave when I was taken in here. He just went back on Tuesday night.'

'He'll be wanting to know how you are.'

'Aye.' Gracie had been intending to write to Neil today in any case, because Joe hadn't brought her writing pad in when she asked him. He'd a mind like a sieve and Queenie was as bad. The house would be in an awful state by the time she got home. Sighing, Gracie opened the letter.

Wednesday night

Dear Mum,

I hope you're making good progress and what I'm going to tell you should make you feel even better. Freda and I are getting married! I'm going to arrange it with the registrar for as soon as possible. Freda's Mum and Dad wanted you to be here and I hope you're not disappointed that we're not waiting but honestly, Mum, I'm so happy I couldn't wait. Tell Dad he should be thankful that he won't have to make a speech. That's all I've time for before lights out.

Lots of love, Neil

PS. Freda was sorry to hear about your operation and she hopes you'll soon be well again.

Noticing that Mrs Ferris was wiping her eyes, the kindly nurse hurried over. 'Not bad news, I hope?'

Gracie gave a watery smile. 'No, it's good news, the best I could have had. My son's getting married and I'm so happy I couldn't help having a little weep.'

'You mums! Getting sentimental when your little boy takes a wife. You won't be losing a son, you'll be . . .'

'I know, gaining a daughter-in-law. Freda's an awful nice girl and I'm really pleased about it.'

While she was writing to Neil, Gracie wondered if it would be better not to tell Hetty yet, though there was no point in keeping it from her. Olive had to know, sooner or later.

When Joe came in with Hetty – Queenie waited outside – he said, 'Did Patsy manage to come and see you today?'

'Yes, the same time as yesterday, when she came off duty.'

'Neil phoned this morning to see how you were and I told him you were coming on fine.'

Gracie smiled. 'Didn't he say anything else?'

'Just that he'd had a tiring journey back . . . oh, and he said he'd written to you. Have you got his letter?'

'Yes, this morning. Read it.'

In a few minutes, Hetty was expressing as much delight at the news as Gracie and Joe, and if Queenie's later echoing of their happy sentiments was not quite so honest, no one noticed. She resented the fact that Neil had said nothing to her when he was home. They had been quite close at one time, and he should have told her.

It wasn't until Hetty arrived home that she began to feel apprehensive. Martin was sitting reading when she went in, but he raised his head and smiled, 'How's Gracie?'

'She's a bit better. Is Olive up in her room? Somebody'll have to tell her that Neil's getting married.'

'Good for him! We'll have to send a wedding present.'

Hetty climbed the stairs slowly and unwillingly, angry at her husband for not taking on the responsibility. She had no time to think and it was quite possible that Olive would go berserk when she was told.

The girl was bent over her desk writing furiously, with text books all round her, and she looked up irritably when her mother opened the door. 'Gracie had a letter from Neil today and he's getting married as soon as he can arrange it.' Hetty had decided not to shilly-shally, but kept well back waiting for the volcano to erupt.

'Married?' Olive's eyes widened, but her manner was quite mild. After a minute, she gave a smile. 'We knew it would come, didn't we? People who are engaged usually do tie the knot eventually.'

Hetty's racing heart slowed down. 'You're not upset?'

'Why should I be?'

'I thought . . . you were always so fond of him . . .'

'A person can be fond of someone without love coming into it. Now, will you let me get on with this?'

'Yes, sorry.' Hetty went back to Martin. 'She didn't seem to be bothered.'

'That does surprise me . . . if she's genuine.'

'I think she is. She accepted his engagement. She knew it would only be a matter of time before he got married.'

'Thank heaven for that. I thought I might have to come and shovel you off the hall floor.'

'Shovel me off . . .?'

'I thought she'd throw you downstairs,' Martin laughed.

'You didn't think of telling her yourself, though!' Hetty burst out. 'Everything's always left to me.'

'That's because you're so good at these things and it was a woman's place to do it, not a man's.'

Cooling a little, Hetty said, 'I suppose it was, but she took it like a lamb.'

It was a very fierce lamb who was pitching her papers and books across the room at that precise moment. If Neil had been there, Olive would have struck him down with one blow. He was fiendishly evil, she thought bitterly, kicking her folder from under her feet. On Saturday – less than a week ago – he had given himself to her in the fullest sense, as she had given herself to him, turning her unsure world into a paradise of certainty. He had proved that he loved her. He had even admitted that he'd never made love to Freda, so why was he in such an all-fired hurry to marry the bally girl?

Unscrewing the top of her fountain pen, she removed the outer case and squeezed the narrow rubber tube, watching as the ink spurted over the top of her desk, and wishing that she could squeeze Neil's neck until his blood spurted out of his veins like that . . . God! Was there nothing she could do?

For several minutes, she racked her brain for even a ghost of an idea, until it crossed her mind that Neil had possibly told her a downright lie when he said that he had never made love to Freda. This rushed wedding couldn't be anything but a cover up to pregnancy. Olive was even more distressed by this conclusion. The very thought of him having sex with anyone else made her feel as though a steel spike was being ground into her chest.

Even worse than that, if Freda was pregnant, it scuppered all her own hopes of driving them apart. She had planned to wait a few months then write to Neil that she was expecting his child, in the belief that he would feel honour bound to break his engagement and do the right thing by her, but now whatever lies she told would be useless. He would stand by Freda.

Olive sat for a further few minutes, admitting defeat at last. She had lost Neil, after all she had done to make him love her, after all the hours she had spent scheming how to win him. Suddenly, with a quivering sigh, she dropped down on her hands and knees and began to remove all traces of her temper tantrum.

# Part Two

# Chapter Twenty

On Wednesday, 21 April 1943, twenty-five Dorniers flew out of Stavanger, each carrying more than two tons of bombs. The target was Aberdeen. It was dusk, a little after nine in the evening, when they came sweeping in from the north to wreak their terrible destruction.

Olive Potter – blasé about the alerts since there had been only a few tip-and-run raids lately – remained in her room until she heard the first bombs fall then, galvanised into action, she shot downstairs as though all the hounds in hell were after her. Her father, grim but calm, pulled her into the back hall where her mother was already sitting with her back against the wall.

With the increase in noise level, Hetty whispered, through lips that were trembling fearfully, 'They're coming nearer, Martin.'

'They're still a good bit away.'

'I hope they're nowhere near King Street.'

'Ssh!' Martin was holding his head high to concentrate on the approaching sounds and, in a few minutes, they were all certain that a bomb had fallen in their immediate vicinity. They could feel the vibrations through their feet

269

and they huddled together waiting for the next one, perhaps the last they would ever hear.

Joe, Patsy and Queenie huddled with the other tenants in one of the cellars – the sunks, as they were colloquially known – underneath the tenement. 'I think they're going away now,' Patsy said, in some relief. 'One was close, but they don't sound so loud now.'

Joe nodded. 'They've likely been after the harbour first, but they could be aiming for anything . . . hospitals and . . .'

'Oh, God!' Patsy burst out. 'I hope they haven't got near Foresterhill. What about Mum . . . and all the other patients?'

Mrs Burnett from the top floor was appalled. 'They surely wouldna bomb hospitals?'

'They did it in other countries, trying to break morale.'

'Oh, that's right cruel.' This was Mrs Fleming who shared the landing with the Burnetts. 'But surely the Spitfires'll shoot them doon afore they get as far inland as Foresterhill or Woolmanhill.'

Queenie was still horrified, 'I could understand if they aimed at barracks and places like that, but not hospitals.'

Mr Walker from the second floor – a shrivelled-up, retired railwayman whose wife was curled up with her hands over her ears – tutted in disgust. 'They're barbarians! It's Hitler I blame. Him and that Goering.'

They all looked at each other in fear as several deafening explosions resounded in rapid succession, then Joe shrugged his shoulders, his thin grey hair parting to show his bald patch, and carried on speaking as if bombs were an everyday occurrence. 'They've to obey orders, the same as our boys. I bet the ordinary Germans would be as shocked as us if they knew what was going on.'

'Do our bombers bomb hospitals in Germany?' Queenie asked.

'If that's what they're told to do, but the trouble with bombs is they're not always dead on target and even if they are, whole areas can get flattened, hospitals and houses and schools even, if they're near. War's a dirty business these days. It's not hand-to-hand fighting, or shelling across no-man's-land like it was the last time.'

Each family there had at least one member in the forces but no one mentioned the husband, son or daughter who was at that moment taking part in the defence of Britain and other allied countries, whether on land, or at sea, or in the air. Nevertheless, it was the thought of their loved ones that prevented a show of panic. If *they* could stick it out, the people at home could do the same.

For security reasons, details of the raid were not given in the local newspapers next day – the headlines merely said 'Raid on North East Town' – but the toll gradually emerged. The bombs had been of the phosphorous and oil type, igniting on impact, and seemed to have been dropped indiscriminately on large buildings and densely populated areas – which may have been intentional, if the enemy were trying to undermine morale. Churches, the Royal Mental Hospital and its nurses' home, two schools and the barracks of the Gordon Highlanders had all been set alight. A stick of bombs had even fallen on St Peter's Cemetery in King Street, fortunately missing the Ogilvie family grave. Other planes had attacked with cannon and machine guns, and streets had been raked with bullets.

271

Close on a hundred people had been killed and almost as many were seriously injured. Joe's assistant Jim was one of the fatalities, and it was days before he found a replacement – a widow with two sons in the navy.

Once Gracie got home from hospital, she regained her health slowly. Queenie continued convincingly to be as effervescent as she could and Joe grumbled about the extra work – and the annoyance to his customers – that the rationing was causing, and about his new assistant until she learned the prices and positions of the goods he sold. But in the main, he was as good-humoured as he had always been.

In May, Neil's marriage having finally made up her mind, but having waited until her aunt was strong enough to bear the shock, Queenie took the fateful step. 'I signed on for the WAAFs today,' she announced as they sat down to lunch. She had expected opposition but was dismayed to see the colour draining from Gracie's face.

It was Joe who said, rather sharply, 'Have you thought it over properly?'

'Yes, I have. I've been thinking about it for ages. I'm . . . losing interest in my lectures and it's a waste of time me carrying on. I want do something to prove myself.'

Rubbing his hand across his chin, already stubbling since morning, Joe said, 'I'm not happy about it, but I'll not try to stop you. What about you, Gracie?'

His wife nodded, her face still ashen. 'If that's what she wants to do.'

'It's what I want to do.'

Patsy said very little when she was told, but tackled her cousin when they were in bed. 'If you think going away will make you feel better about Neil's wedding, you're wrong.'

'I won't feel better about it,' Queenie agreed, 'but at least I won't be here to see him with his wife.'

'They'll likely be here before you've to go.'

'I think I can manage to cope with them once.'

'What about your teaching career? Have you given up on it altogether?'

'I can always carry on with my studies after the war.'

Patsy thought for a moment, then said, 'Maybe you'll meet somebody when you're in the WAAFs.'

'Maybe I will.' Queenie thought that it was unlikely that she would meet anyone who would come anywhere near Neil in her affections but let it go at that.

No one referred to Queenie's enlistment in the WAAFs the following day, but at teatime, in an effort to show her that he did not hold it against her, Joe remarked, 'I know you girls can't afford to go to the pictures very often,' here he stuck his hand into his trouser pocket, 'but here's five bob, have a treat on me.'

'No, Dad,' Patsy said, as he held out two half crowns. 'We don't need it. We don't mind not seeing any . . .'

'Take it! I'll be offended if you don't.'

'Well, if you put it like that . . . thanks, but is it OK if we go tomorrow? I told Hetty on the phone that I'd go there tonight . . . how about coming with me, Queenie?'

'I'd rather not. Olive and I have never got on.'

Remembering why, Patsy felt a momentary pang of pity for the other girl. 'Can't you put up with her for one night?'

'Yes, go, Queenie,' Gracie urged. 'Hetty says Olive's a lot quieter and better behaved now.'

Queenie sighed in resignation, 'I suppose I could. Right, Patsy, you've got a chum for tonight.'

The visit turned out to be quite pleasant, after all Hetty and Martin made them very welcome, and even Olive managed to smile.

When they went to bed that night, Queenie said, 'I can't get over Olive being so nice to me. She hasn't had a civil word to say to me for a long time, but she asked how I was getting on with my degree work and even offered to help with anything she could. She certainly has changed.'

'I don't know if I should ask this, but was it anything to do with Neil that made you two fall out?'

Glad to talk to someone who would understand, Queenie told her everything, and when she came to an end, Patsy said, 'I always knew Olive could be nasty, but I never realised how malicious she was. Still, it should be a comfort to you to know she's lost Neil, too. I suppose she felt just as hurt as you when he was married.'

'I never thought of it like that. She must have been hurt for she always thought she would get him in the end.'

'Um, Queenie, seeing you've confessed to me, do you mind if I confess something to you?'

'No, carry on.'

'There was a Canadian Air Force sergeant in our ward for a few weeks and . . .'

'Don't tell me you fell for him?'

'I couldn't help it, Queenie. His name's Jake Corbierre . . . he's French-Canadian really, and he's got a lovely way of speaking, with just a hint of an accent . . . he'd been brought up to speak French, you see, living in Quebec. He's dark and foreign-looking, and his eyes . . . this sounds like something you read in a novel, but his eyes are kind of deep set, a dark, dark brown, and they just look right into you. Some of the things he said made me think he looked on me as a person not just a nurse, and I thought he did care for me, but he was discharged last week and he didn't even say goodbye, and that's that. Exit Prince Charming, so there's no love story. I should have had more sense than . . .'

'Do you know where he's stationed?

'At Dyce. I thought he might come back to see me or write me a letter or something, but he hasn't.'

'Couldn't you write to him?'

'If he wanted to keep in touch, he'd have done something, so it looks like I was imagining things.'

'Oh, Patsy, I'm so sorry.'

'I'll get over it, I suppose, but I did like him an awful lot and I feel let down.'

Next night, the girls went to see Mickey Rooney in 'Life Begins For Andy Hardy' and regaled Gracie and Joe with the whole story when they went home, Gracie studying them as she pretended to listen. 'You know, Joe,' she began when they went to bed, 'I couldn't help noticing how close the girls are. They used to be so different, Patsy was a lot quieter than Queenie, but they're like true sisters now.'

'Aye,' her husband agreed, more seriously than usual, 'but I think they were putting on an act for us. Do you not think the laughs were kind of false and high-pitched, like they were trying to prove there was nothing wrong?'

275

After considering for a moment, Gracie nodded. 'Aye, now I come to think about it. Queenie must have been in love with Neil after all, that could be why she wants to go aways but what would Patsy have to hide?'

'Maybe she fell in love with a boy who didn't love her?'

'She's never spoken about anybody in particular and she's never been out with anybody that I know of, but maybe it was one of her patients. Patsy's not the kind to tell folk about her troubles, but even if they're both covering up a broken heart, they'll get over it some day, and thank goodness we don't have to worry about Neil now. *He's* happy.'

The atmosphere in the small cottage was anything but happy. Neil could see that Freda was pig-in-the-middle between him and her mother, but he was powerless to ease the situation and it was getting him down. Mrs Cuthbert barged into their room at any time without knocking, and paid no attention to all the hints he dropped. For Freda's sake, he did not want to quarrel with the woman but it was difficult to keep his temper. What made things even worse, his wife often refused to let him make love to her in case her mother heard them.

'What the bloody hell difference does it make?' he snapped at her one night. 'We're married, so she must know what we get up to, and she must have done it with your father once. You weren't the result of an immaculate conception.'

Freda looked pained. 'I can't help it, Neil. I can't . . . you know . . . when I'm worrying that Mum might hear us.'

'Might?' he exploded. 'I'll bet my bottom dollar her ear's pinned to the wall every night.'

'That's what I mean, though I think you're exaggerating.'

Regretting having taken his annoyance out on his wife when her behaviour was a result of the circumstances, Neil said jocularly, 'Look, sweetheart, the walls of this house are so thick she'd have to bore a hole before she heard anything and I don't think even Prissie would go as far as that.'

Instead of taking this as a joke, Freda perversely took it as a slight against her mother and flounced round with her back to him. Bugger her, Neil thought, rage overcoming the last vestige of desire. Bugger her mother. Bugger all women.

# Chapter Twenty-one

On her first fourteen nights at Padgate, Queenie had stayed in the hut, brooding about Neil. She didn't want to think of him but she couldn't get him out of her mind even though she had not seen him since his marriage. It had been a relief to her when, instead of coming home on leave, he took Freda on a belated honeymoon to York, for it meant that she could get away from Aberdeen without having to see him with the girl who was now his wife. At the beginning of the third week of her initial training, she decided that enough was enough. If she was ever to get over him, she would have to try to enjoy herself, to mix with boys. With this in mind, she went to a dance that night with some other WAAFs but, as the evening wore on, she found it became more and more difficult to keep smiling. Making the excuse of having to take an aspirin for a severe headache, she went to the cloakroom.

On her own, she gave way to the tears which she had been holding back and let her thoughts turn to Neil again. When he asked her out for the first time, she had believed that he had been sent by God to compensate for taking her parents and grandparents away and it had helped her to bear the bitter grief that still attacked her in the night.

After he kissed her, she had woven wonderful dreams of the future. She had been so childish, so silly . . . but had she really been silly? Her dreams would have been fulfilled if it hadn't been for Olive. Neil had loved her, Queenie, until Olive told him a wicked lie about her. That was when he had changed. He would never have looked at another girl before and, even after he admitted to being in love with Freda, he had told her that she would always have a place in his heart. That had given her fresh hope, until the engagement. She had prayed that it wouldn't last, but his marriage had been the end of all her dreams.

Drying her eyes, Queenie realised that she couldn't go on like this, it was utter stupidity, but she couldn't go back inside the hall. After splashing her face with cold water, she made for the outside door, holding her head down so that no one would see that she had been crying, and cannoned into a young airman. 'Sorry,' she mumbled, without looking up.

'It's OK. You haven't done any permanent damage.'

She did not appreciate the levity. 'I . . . didn't see you . . . I was thinking about something.'

'Wait!' He put out a hand to stop her from walking on. 'It isn't Queenie, is it? Queenie Ogilvie?'

Gasping in astonishment, she lifted her head. 'Yes, but I don't think I know . . .' She broke off, scanning his face in wonder. 'Les Clark?'

His face, older now but still familiar, was too much for her, and tears came flooding again. Taken aback, the young man hesitated briefly before drawing the overwrought girl to his chest and letting her sob against him, not knowing why she was crying. Les Clark – who had started on the

279

same day as Queenie at St Mark's Junior School in South Norwood – had awakened dormant memories she never dared to let loose; memories of her beloved father and mother, of her childhood home where she had been cosseted and cherished, of George and Ivy Lowell, who had doted on their only grandchild and who would have given her the moon if they could. Until she was fifteen, the agonising thought came, she'd been swaddled in love, then everything had been snatched away from her.

Although they were standing in an area where there was a steady stream of people passing on their way to and from the toilets, Les held her for a long time, ignoring the amused, sympathetic glances, and it was Queenie who drew away when her sobbing quietened and stopped. 'I'm sorry, it was seeing you again, Les . . .'

'It's OK.' He was delighted that she had recognised him and presumed that something had upset her earlier. 'I never expected to see you,' he said, heartily, to get her mind off whatever it was.

'I've only been here just over a fortnight.'

'I've been a week longer. I'm glad I bumped into . . .' He grinned suddenly. 'I'm glad you bumped into me. What did you do after you left school? I never saw you around.'

'I was evacuated to Aberdeen in August 1940 but . . . my mum and dad were both killed in an air raid in February 1941.'

'Oh.' Light was dawning in the boy's mind now. 'Seeing me made you homesick for South Norwood, was that it?'

'Yes, I suppose that's what it was.'

'I'm sorry about your mum and dad – I hadn't heard about them – but who do you live with now?'

'Dad's sister and her husband. I stayed on at school until I was seventeen, then I went to university for a while.' She changed the subject before he could ask why she had left. 'I don't remember seeing you at Whitgift. Didn't you go on to the grammar school?'

'No, I went to Croydon Poly, that was in 1937, so it must be seven years since we last saw each other. Where were you bound for in such a tearing hurry?'

Queenie shrugged, 'I was going back to camp. I came with some of the other girls but I wasn't enjoying myself.'

'My pal found himself a girl and I'm on my own, so I'll walk back with you if you like. You'd better go in and tell your friends first, in case they wonder where you are.'

'I'm not one of the gang, they won't miss me. Anyway, I said I'd a headache so they'll know I've gone back.'

'Right, then.' He tucked her arm under his before leading her outside then remarked, 'It's a nice night. Do you feel like having a walk first?'

'I'm not in the mood for talking.'

'I know you're upset about something, and I can guarantee I'm a first-class listener, if you want to tell me. If you don't, I'm also a first-class talker, and you can listen.'

'Oh, Les.' Her voice was slightly tremulous. 'I do need to tell somebody. Maybe I'll get over it then.'

'OK, tell all to Uncle Les, in strictest confidence.'

'There's not much to tell, really,' she began, glad of the swiftly enveloping darkness. 'Just the usual story of girl loving boy and boy marrying somebody else.'

'Unrequited love?' he suggested.

'No, he did love me, until . . .'

'Out with it,' Les ordered, as she broke off uncertainly. 'It's far worse to bottle it up. Who was the boy?'

'He was my cousin, Neil.' Faltering a little at first, but gaining strength as she went on, Queenie told him everything from the time she had been taken to Aberdeen.

Les proved himself a first-class listener by not saying a word until she came to an end, then he squeezed her arm. 'Do you feel any better for having told me?'

'Funnily enough, I do. I don't feel so alone now.'

'Good. Now, do you know what I think? This Olive must have loved Neil as much as you, but being a different type, she was determined to get him whatever happened. Right?'

'Yes, she'd always got what she wanted before.'

'So we can't really blame her for fighting for him. You, on the other hand, being a decent, well-brought up girl, let things drift on without doing anything about them. Did you ever tell Neil you loved him?'

'I thought he knew.'

'If you had told him, he likely wouldn't have believed her lies. By my reckoning, and don't get angry at me for saying this, you were as much to blame for him falling in love with someone else as she was.'

'I never thought about it like that but I suppose so.'

'On the other hand, I feel that he wasn't much of a man to believe lies without asking you if they were true.'

'Oh, but Neil was . . .' Queenie stopped, her eyes clouding.

'You see? I've made you think. I believe you've known that all the time and that's why you've been so upset. He wasn't worthy of your love, Queenie.'

282

They walked some distance in silence then she said, in a small voice, 'I think you're right, Les. He did love me for a while, but maybe not deeply enough, otherwise he wouldn't have turned to Freda so quickly. You've made me see things differently, I was too close to it before. Thank God I met you tonight. You were always able to sort out my troubles, even when we were very young.'

'We'd some great times at St Mark's School, hadn't we? Do you remember . . .?'

After discussing their classmates and teachers for a few minutes, Queenie said, 'I used to be terrified when the big boys teased me, but you always stuck up for me. You punched that Johnny Daker once, because he said I was a cry baby.'

Les grinned. 'He punched me back and you wiped the blood from my mouth with your hankie.'

'He knocked out one of your teeth, didn't he? I'm glad it grew in again. You used to carry my satchel sometimes, too, and I felt good when the other girls were jealous.'

Looking pleased at that, Les said, 'I felt good that you liked me best because I always liked you best.'

'We do some silly things when we're young,' she sighed.

'Liking each other wasn't silly and we're still young.'

Her heart lifted a little. 'Yes, we are, aren't we?'

'How about coming out with me tomorrow?'

'All right, but only as a friend.'

'That's all I want.'

In bed, Queenie could hardly believe that in the space of less than an hour, her heartache had eased. It had not gone altogether, it probably never would – it had been too deep – but she could think of Neil with only a touch of sadness.

He had been a fairweather sweetheart, easily dissuaded at the first sign of a squall, and she would be eternally grateful to Les Clark for making her understand that. It was strange that Les, in a superficial way, reminded her of Neil. He was almost the same build, with the same round face and square jaw, but that was as far as the resemblance went. His hair was bright red, not dark, his blue eyes were lighter and not nearly so serious, his mouth was not sensual like Neil's . . . but it was still a nice mouth.

Queenie caught herself at this. She was too vulnerable at the moment, and she shouldn't have agreed to go out with Les again. They had been bosom pals when they were children but that was a long time ago and, even if he hadn't changed, or didn't appear to have changed, she had. But she had made it clear that there could never be more than friendship between them and he had agreed. They would just be a rather lonely boy and girl spending time together, and she would not say anything about him when she wrote to Gracie. Her aunt would likely start hearing wedding bells.

Olive had told no one her secret. At first, she was unable to believe it herself but there was no doubt now. She was definitely three months pregnant and if ever a well-planned plot had backfired on its perpetrator, hers had. This was how she had meant to ensnare Neil – but only by pretending – if he hadn't taken the wind out of her sails by marrying Freda. What on earth could she do now? Her mother would be shocked and say that she had brought disgrace on the family, but she would likely support her when it came to the crunch. Her father, on the other hand,

284

would probably lose his head and throw her out . . . not that she could blame him.

As each day passed, she worried in case her mother noticed anything – she had heard that pregnancy showed in a girl's face long before it was obvious in the rest of her – but, so far, nothing had been said at home. Polly Frayne had asked her the day before if she was feeling ill, because she was very pale and drawn, but she had offered menstruation as an excuse. When she came to think about it, though, it might be a good idea to tell Polly the truth; she might suggest something. Not that anything she had tried herself had done the trick. She had swallowed spoonful after spoonful of castor oil, despite gagging as it went down, had taken boiling hot baths, had done some strenuous exercises, had even drunk gin, but the foetus was still clinging to her womb like the proverbial ivy to the wall.

The following morning, Olive found herself sitting next to Polly in the lecture room, and decided to take the bull by the horns. 'Can I have a private word with you later?'

'I'm going to Woollies at lunchtime for some pencils and a bottle of ink, so you could come with me if you like. We can talk on the way.'

'OK, thanks.'

That night, Olive gave serious consideration to what Polly had advised her to do. She really could not have this baby and abortion seemed to be the only answer. It was dangerous as well as illegal, but she would have to take the risk and Polly knew a woman who would do it. 'She's terminated quite a few that I know of,' Polly had said, 'with no ill effects. It would be as well if you stayed away from home for a night to get over it, but you can come to my digs, if you want.'

Recalling this, Olive came to the most momentous decision of her life. She could never face Neil again, not after she got rid of his child, and especially not if he had his wife with him, so she would have to leave home . . . she would leave Aberdeen altogether. She would have the abortion, stay with Polly for one night, then go to a YWCA somewhere until she made up her mind what to do after that. Volunteering for the forces might be the ideal solution.

If only Neil knew what she was doing for him, it would be easier to bear, but no matter how much she still loved him, she was determined not to ruin his marriage. If this was the penalty she had to pay for making his life a misery before, she would face up to it, and perhaps, by devoting her life to the service of her country, she could eventually forgive herself for the wicked things she had done. Before she did anything else, however, there was still one thing she had to do for Neil. Sitting down at her desk, she began to write.

Freda was feeling extremely upset about the previous night's quarrel. Neil had been totally unreasonable and it had all started because she had refused to let him make love to her without any protection. It had only been her excuse, though, because she was afraid that her mother would hear them, not afraid of falling pregnant. As quarrels do, it had escalated out of all proportion, ending in a shouting match that her parents must have heard.

As she pulled on the men's baggy trousers she wore to work in the gardens, she remembered yelling, 'That's all you ever married me for! Just to satisfy your cravings for sex.'

'I sometimes wish I'd never married you! I got a lot more satisfaction from the sluts I used to go with.'

That was what had hurt most. He should be pleased that for at least one night a week, she had tried to forget her fear, but he went off the deep end regularly, and the set-to last night was the worst ever. She couldn't help being the way she was, and if he would give her more time, she might come to enjoy his nightly advances instead of dreading them.

Freda was smoothing down her oversized woollen jumper when her mother came in. 'A letter for Neil from Aberdeen,' she announced, laying it down on the chest of drawers, 'but it's not his mother's writing.' Mrs Cuthbert made sure that Neil was not in the room, then added, 'What were you two arguing about last night? Is he . . . making too many demands on you?'

Flushing, Freda shook her head. 'It was nothing like that, and I'd rather not talk about it.'

Not believing the denial, her mother went on, 'Your father was the same when we were first married but I soon put him in his place. Just do what I did – refuse him till he stops bothering you.' Having delivered this advice, she swept out.

Neil came in a moment later, still as angry as when he went to wash, and Freda eyed him coldly. 'Mum took through a letter for you. It's on the chest of drawers.'

'It's from Olive,' he muttered, as he picked it up. 'She never writes anything worth reading, and I haven't time now, I'm late as it is.' Unbuttoning the breast pocket of his tunic, he slipped it inside, and only then did he look at her. 'We'll have to do some serious talking tonight, Freda. You can't go on the way you're doing.'

'The way I'm doing?' she gasped. 'It's you that's causing all the trouble.'

'It's your bloody problem that's the trouble,' he snarled, and stalked out.

She heard him telling her mother that he hadn't time for any breakfast, then she crossed to the window in the hope that he would wave to her like he usually did. She watched until he went out of sight round the corner of the house and waited for him to wheel out the old BSA motor cycle he had bought for taking him to and from the camp. It was five minutes before he appeared again, and she was sure that he had been reading Olive's letter in the outhouse he used as a garage. Why couldn't he have read it in front of her? Olive hadn't written to him since he was married, so why was she writing now? There surely wasn't anything between them? But he had said that he had taken her out twice when he was home on his own and he'd meant to see her a third time, and she'd been naive enough to believe him when he swore there was nothing in it.

Without looking round, Neil leapt on the seat of the BSA, revved the engine and roared away, leaving her seething with what she realised was a black jealousy.

The soft, warm air against his burning face did not have the usual exhilarating effect on Neil – his mind was on other things. He would have to do something soon . . . but what? He still loved Freda, even after last night's barney, but they would never be really happy until he got her away from her mother. He sped recklessly along the narrow, winding road, his knees skimming the rough surface as he took the series of sharp corners at full throttle. Coming to the last but one hairpin bend before the camp gates, he was so involved in his thoughts that he did not hear the rumble of the heavy Scammel coming from the other side, and he only avoided it in the nick of time by swerving on to the bank and coming a heavy cropper against a wire fence.

He was in an entirely different frame of mind when he went home that evening. If he had not had the presence of mind to swerve when he did, he would be lying on a mortuary slab now and his second brush with death had made him see how petty he'd been with Freda. The problem lay at his own door as much as hers.

Mrs Cuthbert looked at him with dislike when he went into the house that night but he walked past her to the bedroom where he threw his arms round his wife. 'Freda, darling, I'm sorry I was so nasty. It's all my fault, and I'll never badger you again. I love you so much, I couldn't live without you.'

Her jealousy having increased the more she thought about it, Freda drew away, stiffly. 'What did Olive have to say in her letter?'

'Olive? What's she got to do with us?'

'I don't know but there's something you haven't told me.'

Drawing the letter from his pocket, he handed it over. 'I don't understand what you mean but read it for yourself.'

Her expression changed as she scanned the single page, and she turned to him in remorse when she came to the end. 'I'm sorry, Neil. I thought there was something between you, but I see it was all on her side.'

Having been apprehensive himself before he read it, Neil had been astounded at what Olive had written. Olive, who had never apologised for anything, who had thought of no one but herself all her life. He took the letter back from his wife and read it through again.

> Neil,
>
> I have known for some time about the trick you and Alf played on me and I was very hurt that you disliked me so much. That was why I did everything I could to make you say you loved me, but I know now that even if I had succeeded it would have been a hollow revenge, because it is Freda you truly love. So, my dear boy, I wish you both every happiness in your marriage, and I trust that you will not think too harshly of . . .
>
> Your Cousin, Olive

'There is one thing more I should tell you,' he said as he tore the letter through the middle.

Freda placed her fingertips over his mouth. 'No, Neil, I don't want to hear. I've been thinking all day about us and I know that it's my . . . failing that makes us quarrel, so I've decided it would be best if we found somewhere else to live. It's been the thought of my mother hearing us that . . .'

'Oh, my darling.' Neil drew her gently towards him. 'Are you sure that's what you want?'

'I'm positive, so we can begin looking for a room. I don't mind where or what, as long as I'm with you.'

Their kiss was interrupted by Mrs Cuthbert, who said, in tones of deep disgust, 'When you've finished your nonsense, your tea's ready.'

'Bugger off!' Neil retorted, kissing his wife again with even more ardour than before as the woman scuttled out, her face scarlet. 'I know she's your mother,' he said, in a few moments, 'but she's asked for that since we were married.'

Freda gave a nervous giggle, 'How are we going to face her when we go through for our tea?'

He grinned. 'I'm not hungry, are you?'

'Not really.'

'Well, I'm quite enjoying this reconciliation business, so I vote we carry on. I'm damned sure she won't come in again without knocking.'

Olive went down for breakfast as her father was making ready to go to his office. 'You're late,' he accused. 'It's time you bucked up your ideas.'

'I'm not going in today, I've a bit of a headache.'

'All you young girls are the same, you stay at home on the slightest excuse. Well, some of us have to work. Cheerio.'

'Goodbye, Dad.'

Disappointed at his daughter's lack of commitment to the career she had chosen, Martin did not recognise the anguish underlying those two words, and neither did Hetty, who was regarding the girl with some concern. 'You don't look well. Should I phone the doctor?'

'No, it's nothing.' Olive ate only one slice of toast with a cup of tea before she went back upstairs. She had packed a few things last night and had scribbled a note of farewell when she rose, which was why she'd been late for breakfast. She knew that by sneaking out she would distress her mother, but she could not bring herself to tell her face to face. There would be tears, pleading for explanation, maybe even realisation, and she couldn't risk that. It had to be this way. A clean break . . . for ever. No letters.

She took her coat out of the wardrobe, then glanced round the room, the bedroom which had been hers since her family came to Rubislaw Den . . . nearly eighteen years ago. She would never see it again – there would be no coming back. Lifting her small case with a shuddering sigh, Olive went out on to the landing to make sure that her mother was safely out of earshot in the kitchen, then crept downstairs and out by the front door.

# Chapter Twenty-two

When Gracie wrote to say that Olive had left home and that Hetty had no idea why or where she had gone, Queenie's heart went out to the cousin who had also loved and lost Neil, but she did wonder if this was another trick. Had Olive really given up on him, or would she interfere in his life again?

Queenie, herself, felt more drawn towards Les Clark every time they went out, but not in any romantic way. He was good company whatever they did on their evenings together, he had helped her to get over Neil, and she hoped that he would ask her to keep in touch when they went their separate ways. It would be a pity to let their friendship lapse once more.

When his time at Padgate came to an end, Les told her that he would write, and before her own leave came up, seven days later, he had sent two letters from South Norwood. She said nothing about him when she went home, in case Gracie and Joe jumped to the conclusion that he was her boyfriend, and she didn't think of him like that – not yet, anyway.

After one unsuccessful attempt to find out if there was a boy on the horizon, her aunt wanted to know what she had had to do on her training, and Patsy was too anxious to tell her about her Canadian to bother about anything else. 'Jake said he didn't try to contact me when he left Foresterhill first because he wasn't sure if I wanted him to, but he'd thought about me so much that he finally had to write. We've been going out for four weeks now.'

'Aye,' commented Joe, dryly, 'Jake's all we hear about day in, day out, and you should think yourself lucky you're not here to have to put up with it, Queenie.'

'Och, Joe, don't exaggerate,' his wife warned. 'It hasn't been as bad as that.'

That evening, as Joe had agreed to take over the duties of an air raid warden who had died suddenly and Patsy was on night duty, Queenie was left alone with her aunt. 'What do you think of Patsy going steady?' she asked.

Gracie shrugged. 'I'm not against her having a lad, but I can't say I'm happy about this Jake.'

'Don't you like him?'

'I haven't met him yet, but if they're serious about each other, he'll likely want to take her to Canada after the war and we'll never see her again.'

'I see what you mean,' Queenie nodded. 'Do you think they are serious?'

'I'm near sure Patsy is, and I wouldn't let her know how I feel if she does want to marry Jake, for he'd be a real good catch. His father's got a big business, three branches round Quebec and two in Montreal, as well.'

Thinking, a little wryly, that no one could say Les was a good catch – his father was only a labourer – Queenie found that there was some truth in the saying that absence makes the heart grow fonder. She was even thinking of him in terms of a future husband now. 'Has Hetty had any word from Olive yet?' she asked, to change the subject.

'No, and she's really worried. She can't think what made her walk out without a word, for they hadn't had a row, not lately, anyway, and she says Olive hadn't been looking well for ages. She thinks she was upset because Neil got married so soon after he went back, but I can't help feeling there's more to it than that, for she took her time about leaving.'

'What about Raymond? Where's he just now?'

'Oh, you didn't know, of course. He didn't tell his mother when he was home that it was embarkation leave, but he wrote after he went back. They were being sent to the Middle East, or somewhere, so it'll be a while before she hears from him again, no doubt. Poor Hetty, she's not had her troubles to seek, has she? I'm lucky, for I know where every one of my family is.'

'I'm being shifted, anyway. I've to report at Dover when I go back.'

Gracie's face fell. 'Oh, no! It's too near the Germans for my liking.'

'It's a bit near for my liking, too,' Queenie smiled, 'but I've got to go where I'm told.'

'Aye, of course you have, but be careful and don't take any risks. You know, I can't get over Neil still being left in this country, though I'm pleased about it.'

'How is he?'

'He's a lot happier now. He wasn't getting on with Freda's mother, so they've rented a room a good bit away from her.'

Glad that she could talk about Neil with only the faintest disturbance to her heart – it wasn't even strong enough to be classed as an ache – Queenie said, 'Is there any word of you being a grandmother?'

'Not yet, but I'm keeping hoping.'

They both laughed at that, then Queenie looked candidly at her aunt. 'I loved him, you know.'

'Aye, I thought you did,' Gracie sighed, 'but it wouldn't have been right for cousins to marry. Believe me, lassie, it was better this way, though I was sorry for you.'

'I was sorry for myself and joining up was the best thing I could have done. I've got over him, honestly.'

'I'm glad, and you'll find the right man for you some day. You never know, maybe you'll meet him where you're going but I hope it's not a Canadian or a foreigner, for I don't want to lose you after the war as well as Patsy.'

'I think I'll stick to an English boy.' Queenie wondered if her aunt would pick her up on that – she should have said British – but Gracie hadn't noticed. All the newspapers were speaking about Britain as England these days; Vera Lynn sang 'There'll always be an England', and even the Scots sang it lustily and patriotically. The war seemed to have broken the old barriers, at least for its duration.

Gracie handed her niece a letter which came the following morning, and looked at her curiously as she read it. 'It's from an old school friend I met at Padgate,' Queenie said brightly, still reluctant to speak openly about Les. 'We had some good times together and we promised to keep in touch.'

'Oh, that was nice,' Gracie exclaimed. 'I bet you were pleased to see her again.'

Feeling guilty for the unnecessary deception, Queenie just nodded, but her aunt went on, 'Will she be going to the same place as you?'

The girl chose her words carefully. 'No, but I think we'll be able to see each other sometimes.'

'That's good, though I suppose you'll make other chums.'

'Oh, yes. I'll be with two other girls I know, so I won't feel so strange.'

'You look older in your uniform,' Joe observed, out of the blue. 'I wondered yesterday what was different about you and it just dawned on me. You've got your hair up.'

'It's rolled round an old stocking,' Queenie giggled. 'We had to keep our hair out of our eyes, you see, and we found it was easiest this way. Kirbigrips kept falling out.'

Patsy gave a loud yawn. 'Don't I know it – we're always in trouble if our hair's not kept back. Well, I'm going to bed if you folk don't mind. We'd a hectic night in Casualty and I'm just about dropping. Will you give me a shout about two, Mum? I'm meeting Jake at three.'

Turning round, Joe said sharply, 'And when are we getting to meet him? I'd like to see what kind of man he is.'

Patsy looked at her mother. 'Is it all right if I ask him to come to tea?'

'As long as he won't expect anything fancy.'

'He won't. OK, I'll take him back for six.'

Flopping down on her bed, Queenie longed for the serenity of the tenement in King Street. Being near the south coast was like living on the edge of a volcano – a constantly active volcano – and they never knew when the VIs that passed overhead would stop and plummet earth-wards. When the buzzing cut out, there was a scramble for cover, the male clerks as well as the female, because no allowances were made for the weaker sex . . . they didn't consider themselves the weaker sex.

She wondered if Les had got back to Ashford all right. She was always worried until she heard from him after he'd come to see her, and he came as often as he possibly could. Last night they had spent four hours together, four wonderful but traumatic hours. When the first buzz-bomb came down, he had pushed her down and lain across her, holding her tightly as the world exploded around them, then, when they sat up, both trembling with fear but relieved that they were still all in one piece, he had whispered, 'Queenie, I love you.'

Because she wasn't sure if that was what he had actually said, she kept silent and he murmured, 'I'm sorry. I didn't mean to tell you, not yet, when you'd made it clear that we could just be friends, but I had to. I love you so much I'm terrified in case something happens to you.'

'I'm glad you told me. We'll always be friends, but I know now that I love you, too. At first, I could hardly believe it, but . . .'

His kiss stopped her, but in a few moments, he said, 'I've always loved you, from the time I saw you in your new blazer and three-quarter socks at the door of St Marks. Of course, it was only a small boy's love then, but as I grew older, I often wondered what had happened to you and wished I could find you again.'

'Thank God you did find me again.'

Recalling this tender moment, Queenie's heart swelled with love for Les again. She'd been in seventh heaven, then their kisses had been interrupted by another VI, although

298

it had fallen some distance away. Being in love in the midst of attacks like that was nerve-racking, but it was something to tell their children, something to remember when they were old and grey.

Before she fell asleep, Queenie's thoughts turned to Patsy and her Canadian. When she had met Jake, he had been as nice as Patsy said he was, and it had been plain to everyone that they loved each other – even Joe had remarked on it the next day. Maybe she should tell her aunt and uncle about Les, now that they'd declared their love to each other, but not in a letter. That would be too cold and impersonal, so she would wait until she went home next time.

When Neil took Freda to Aberdeen again – the first time as his wife – his air of satisfied well-being proved to Gracie that marriage was agreeing with him, and his remark to Patsy that she didn't know what she was missing only endorsed it.

His sister blushed. 'Jake wants us to get married, but I'm not too sure. He could be posted overseas, and . . .'

'Don't waste your life,' Neil told her. 'If you love him, marry him. Make the man happy, for God's sake, even if it's only for a little while.'

Gracie frowned. 'Don't say things like that, Neil.'

'We've got to face facts, Mum, and if she lets him away, she might regret it all her life. In the last war, a lot of women refused to marry their sweethearts before they went to France, and they were left lonely and bitter because they'd lost their chance of a little happiness. You don't want to end up like that, do you, Patsy?'

'You're being rather cruel, Neil,' Freda objected.

'I'm being realistic, that's all.'

'Yes, you're right,' Patsy said now. 'I don't want to be a lonely old spinster. I'll tell Jake tonight.'

'Now look what you've done,' Joe exclaimed, looking at his son with mock severity. 'I suppose I'll have to stump up for a wedding now.'

'Jake said he could get a special licence, and if he does, you wouldn't have to pay for anything, Dad.'

A broad smile crossed Joe's face. 'Now there's a man after my own heart.'

Patsy turned to her mother. 'You don't mind, Mum?'

Pushing her sadness to the back of her mind, Gracie shook her head. 'If you're sure, that's all I care about.'

When Patsy asked Freda to come into her bedroom to discuss what she could wear, Gracie took the opportunity to say, 'I don't suppose you've heard anything from Olive?'

Neil frowned slightly. 'Just a note to say she wished us every happiness in our marriage, and as far as I can tell, it had been written before she walked out. It's got me beat; I can't think why she left like that. It's not like her.'

'Hetty doesn't know, either, and she's had no word, though it's nearly three months now. Martin's furious, but Hetty's really worried.'

'Olive'll be OK. She's fit enough to look after herself.' Neil didn't tell his mother that he believed that Olive had left home because she could not face seeing him with a wife, it would have sounded too conceited. Before he learned that she had left home, he had worried a bit himself about seeing her. Her letter had made out that she had given up on him, but he still hadn't trusted her.

'She should have written to let her mother know where she was, though,' Gracie went on. 'She never considers anybody.'

It occurred to Neil that Olive might have been trying to save embarrassment to him as much as to herself, so he said, 'She likely will write home once she's sorted herself out.'

The wedding was arranged for the Saturday of the following week and Jake asked Neil and Freda to be witnesses. Freda went with Patsy to help her to choose her outfit but when Gracie saw her daughter dressed on the actual morning, she had to keep back her tears. The grey suit, chosen for serviceability, was brightened by a blue blouse – both the result of pooling her parents' clothing coupons. The little pillbox hat with its removable veil was in exactly the same shade as the shirt, picking up the colour of her eyes. She looked so lovely, so radiant, that even Joe had to blink tears away.

When they all returned to the house, Neil said, 'Queenie's the only one left now. I wonder when she'll write and tell you she's got a boyfriend?'

'She's still too young to get serious about a boy,' Gracie snapped, still a bit overcome about Patsy being married.

Joe filled his wine glass again. 'The boys in Dover must be blind, that's all I can say.'

While they were laughing at this, Gracie was struck by an awful thought, but she thrust it from her. Her daughter had noticed her face changing colour, however, and came across to her. 'Are you OK, Mum?'

'Aye, don't fuss. It's just all the excitement and things happening so quick.'

Patsy smiled. 'It was quick, I'm sorry. We shouldn't have rushed it. We could have waited.'

'No, no! I'm glad you didn't wait. Go on, now, get back to your man.'

Believing that her mother was overtired from preparing the special meal, Patsy returned to Jake, who gave her a hug and a kiss before they sat down at the table. Joe and Neil began making jokes about newly-weds and first nights, but Gracie turned on them sharply. 'Don't be coarse. What'll Jake think of us?'

Her new son-in-law surprised them all by rising to make an impromptu speech. 'Mrs Ferris – may I call you Mum? – don't be angry at them. They've made me feel a real part of your family by teasing me. I haven't got to know you properly yet but I do know that you and your husband must be exceptional people to have a daughter like Patsy, and I want to fit in, so please don't make anyone change for my benefit. I'd like you all to let your hair down and behave naturally.' Looking round them all, he let his eyes rest on Gracie again. 'Don't worry, I've heard coarser talk than that . . . in fact, I can be quite coarse myself at times. Now, I know you're all waiting for me to say it, so here goes.

'My wife and I . . .' He waited until Joe and Neil stopped thumping the table before he went on, 'My wife and I want to thank you for the gifts you have given us, but especially for making this a day we will never forget. And I want to swear to my new mum and dad that I'll look after Patsy as well as they have looked after her since she was born. Have no fears about that.'

Their cheers and applause strengthened as he sat down and lifted Patsy's hand to his mouth, and Gracie wasn't the only one whose eyes swam with moisture. The meal was eaten to the accompaniment of light chatter which effectively masked the emotions of all concerned, but at last it was time for the happy couple to leave for the hotel in which they were to be spending one night only; they were to be spending the other six days of their honeymoon in Perth. Freda and Neil sat for a short time then went to bed, and Joe sighed as he relaxed in his easy chair. 'Don't look so down, Gracie, lass, she's nae awa' to bide awa'. It'll maybe be years yet before the war's sorted out and she's to leave for good.'

'It's not Patsy I was thinking about,' she whispered. 'It hit me earlier on, when Neil said Queenie was the only one left. I suddenly remembered about Olive.'

'Oh, aye, but Olive's not our responsibility.'

'I've aye wondered why she walked out like she did and I thought it was only because she was upset about Neil getting married, but what if it was more than that?'

Joe's lined face developed a few more wrinkles. 'What daft thing have you got into your head now?

'Maybe it is daft, but do you not remember? Neil went out twice with Olive the time he was here on his own when Freda had the flu.'

'I remember that fine, it was the time you'd to get your operation. I warned him to go canny, but I can't see . . .' He came to an abrupt halt, his brows shooting downwards, then muttered, 'You don't think he . . .?'

'It would explain an awful lot, Joe.' Having expected her husband to make light of her fears, his comprehension made Gracie more convinced that she was right. 'Hetty said Olive hadn't looked very well for weeks, so she could have been in the family way, and the only boy she was ever with was Neil. She must have been about three months when she went away . . . likely before her mother noticed anything.'

'Oh, but my God, Gracie, she wasn't the kind to go through a thing like that on her own, and Hetty wouldn't have thrown her out.'

'Maybe no', but Martin might. I'm sure that's what it was, and it's Neil's child she's carrying . . . our grandchild.'

Her voice having risen, Joe said, 'Calm down, lass, you're not wanting Freda and Neil to hear. Olive had wanted to keep it secret, and we can't condemn her for that. She'll have a hard road to travel to bring up a bairn on her own.'

'I'd have taken her in if she'd come to us.'

'Martin would have tumbled to it being Neil's, the same as we did, and he'd have kicked up a big stramash. He'd have fallen out with Hetty and us, as well as Olive.'

'I always knew she would cause trouble for Neil . . .'

'She hasn't caused trouble, except for herself, and if you want my opinion, lass, it's better to let sleeping dogs lie. Olive's done a decent thing for once by leaving Aberdeen . . . and we're not even sure there is a bairn.'

Twisting her mouth, Gracie said, 'Maybe you're not, but I am. I could wring Olive's neck, for it's been her that egged Neil on. He wouldn't have done anything like that . . .'

Shaking his head, Joe said, 'Our son's no saint, lass.'

# Chapter Twenty-three

Queenie was almost dreading seeing Les Clark again. The last time he had come to Dover, he had said, 'Didn't you tell me you'd a weekend pass coming up? I've been thinking about it, so why don't you come home with me? I'm sure you'd like to see South Norwood again, wouldn't you?'

The unexpectedness of it had taken her aback. 'I . . . I don't know. I . . . I've never thought about it.'

He had smiled understandingly. 'Start thinking, then. You have till Monday of next week to make up your mind, because I won't see you again before that.'

She had given the matter considerable thought and decided that she would like to see her old home area again, but she knew that Gracie would be appalled at the idea of her going away alone with a boy, even at twenty years old. She didn't need to say anything about it, of course. Lots of the girls she knew went off on 'dirty weekends' without telling their mothers, and she and Les weren't contemplating anything like that. But she had to tell Gracie where she was going in case she made a slip next time she went home. It would sound much worse if it came out like that, as if she really had something to hide. Her heart gave a skip as she remembered that her aunt was still under the impression that the old school friend she'd met at Padgate was a girl. If she wrote that she was going to South Norwood with her friend, Gracie would be none the wiser.

When she next met Les he drew her arm through his. 'Is there anywhere special you want to go?'

'Just for a walk. It's too hot to be inside. It's never as hot as this in Aberdeen in June.' She gave a tiny chuckle as she added, 'Not even in July or August.'

'I've heard some of the boys at the drome speaking about the frozen north. They'd been at Wick. Is that anywhere near Aberdeen?'

'No. I'm not sure how far away it is, but the nearest drome to Aberdeen is Dyce.'

They strolled along for some time, letting the heat spread through them and, as they looked out across the Channel, so calm that it reflected the sun like a mirror and the sky so clear that they could make out the coast of France, Queenie said, 'It's difficult to believe the Germans are over there, it looks so peaceful.'

'It could change in a second,' Les warned, then pulled her to a halt. 'Well, have you decided?'

She needed no explanation. 'I'd like to see South Norwood again, but I don't know if I should go.'

'Why not? Are you afraid of me?'

'It's not that. My aunt would be horrified if she thought I was going away for a weekend with a boy . . .' Queenie smiled suddenly. 'But she thinks you're a girl.'

Les thought this was extremely funny and she broke into his laughter rather apprehensively. 'Would you think it was terrible of me if I didn't tell her?'

'I wouldn't think it was terrible but I'd rather you told her the truth.'

'If I do, she'll forbid me to go.'

'But you're old enough . . .' He broke off with a shrug. 'You feel obligated to her, I suppose, when she's taken care of you since your parents were killed. I don't like deception, but if that's the only way . . . promise me you'll tell her when you go home, though. If she sees you've come to no harm and you've enjoyed yourself, she might not be so angry.'

'I promise.' Queenie crossed her fingers under the table. She probably would keep her promise, but . . .

'Will I write and tell my mum you're definitely going?'

'Yes, I'm definitely going.'

Les whirled her round and gave her a kiss, then they carried on walking towards the castle which Queenie often thought of as a sentinel keeping guard from the top of the cliffs. In a few moments, however, he stopped again and lay down on the grass, pulling her into the crook of his arm. She nestled up to him in great contentment as he told her again how much he loved her, and when he suddenly murmured, 'Darling, there's something I have to ask you and I hope it won't upset you. How do you feel about Neil now?'

She laid her hand over his. 'That's all over, and I never loved Neil like I love you. I was so young, I didn't know what love was, but I do now. It's an ache inside me, but it's not painful, it's the most wonderful feeling I ever had. I can't explain the difference between how I felt about Neil and how I feel about you. It's like trying to compare saccharine and sugar. Saccharine's quite adequate until you taste sugar. Does that make any sense to you?'

'It makes me happy, darling, whether it's sense or not.'

'Neil's just a cousin to me . . . no, he's a brother to me. I hardly ever think of him at all, except when Gracie mentions him in a letter.'

'I shouldn't have said he wasn't much of a man. I didn't know him, and I'd no right to pass judgement on him.'

'It made me think, though, and I've realised that what we felt for each other was only cousinly affection. I'll always think fondly of him but that's all, so there's no need for you to be jealous. I'm glad that he's happy with his wife.'

'Could you be happy as my wife?'

Laughing a little, she pretended to consider for a moment. 'I think so,' she began, then realised that he was regarding her seriously. 'You know I'd be happy, deliriously happy.'

She got no chance to say anything more, because Les kissed her exuberantly then wrapped her in a bear hug that almost left her breathless. Some time later, he said, 'I've dreamt about this for weeks, and I wanted to find out how you felt before I took you home with me.'

Les had to leave fairly early in order to get back to his camp in time, and Queenie thought over what she had said to him. It had come out without thinking, but it was true. She did think of Neil as a brother again, as he probably thought of her as a sister. Nothing much had happened between them, in any case, they had gone crazy for a while, that was all. The war, separation, growing up, it was as simple as that to explain it, but it was all over, thank goodness, because it had been very painful while it lasted.

She studiously avoided having to tell an outright lie when she wrote her letter home that night.

Dear Auntie Gracie,

Once again, thank you for your letter. I'm glad that Patsy and Jake have changed their minds about looking for somewhere else to live, for the time being, anyway. You would have missed them if they'd moved out.

Hetty will be relieved that Raymond writes regularly, but I agree with you that she must be heartbroken about never hearing from Olive. Has nobody any idea yet of why she left so suddenly? I thought it was because Neil had married Freda, but I remember you saying that there must be more to it than that. I don't suppose we shall ever know, unless she comes back.

Speaking about Neil and Freda, please give them my regards next time you write, and tell them I'm waiting to hear that I'm an aunt. Of course I won't really be an aunt, just a second cousin, is that right, or should it be a cousin once removed? I don't know, do you?

Do you remember the school friend I told you about? Our postings weren't too far apart so we see each other occasionally, and we're going to South Norwood together next weekend. I'm really looking forward to it and I'll tell you all about it when I come home next month.

Give Uncle Joe my love and don't worry about me. I'm keeping very well and enjoying my work.

Love to everyone, Queenie

After being somewhat timid about how she would be received by Mr and Mrs Clark, Queenie was delighted when Les's mother said, 'We've heard so much about you from Les, I was dying to meet you, and now I can see why he raves about you.'

Her husband's grin, so like his son's, made her feel even more at ease. 'I'd no idea Les was such a good judge, but he must take after his father. I married the prettiest girl on this side of the Thames.' He threw an arm round his wife's waist and squeezed her, roaring with laughter as she shoved him away. 'Stop your teasing, Bert Clark. Sit down, Queenie, and pay no heed to him.'

The girl did as she was told, studying the two men as they stood together at the side of the fireplace. They were not really alike, but there was a resemblance, and it was easy to see that they were father and son. The older man was not quite so tall, he was a little stouter and his hair was more sandy than ginger, although it could have been brighter when he was younger. Queenie concentrated her attention on his wife now. Mrs Clark was a tiny woman with short fair hair but Les had inherited her bright blue eyes and long sweeping eyelashes.

After a cup of tea and some sandwiches, Les took Queenie out and as they walked up Malden Avenue, past the terraced houses, all identical and built in the early thirties, so Mr Clark had told her, he said, 'That wasn't too bad, was it? I could see Mum and Dad liked you.'

She giggled. 'I like them, too. They remind me of Gracie and Joe, in a way. Not in looks but . . . maybe it was the way your mum reacted to your dad's teasing.' Les was silent for so long that she wondered if she had said

310

something to annoy him, but he burst out, 'I meant to say this in the train and I didn't have the courage but the shops'll be shut tomorrow and we'll have to do it today.' He laughed at her bewildered expression. 'I want to buy you an engagement ring.'

'Oh!'

'I want everyone to know that we love each other.'

A warmth pervading her whole body, Queenie murmured, 'I'd like that. All right, where do we go?'

He took her to a jeweller in Croydon, where the owner, a bearded Jew, was as attentive to them as if they were buying the most expensive item in his shop, although Les had warned him that he couldn't afford anything expensive. Queenie did not take long to make up her mind and when they came out on to the pavement again, Les said, 'What about going to see where you used to live? It would be like telling your mum and dad, wouldn't it?'

His thoughtfulness made a lump come in her throat but she managed to hold back her tears until they were gazing at the heap of rubble which was all that remained of her old home. 'I shouldn't have made you come,' Les sighed. 'I didn't know it would be as bad as this and I've only upset you.'

'I'm not upset, just sad that they never knew you.' Wiping her eyes resolutely, she picked up a jagged piece of wood bearing the inscription DONALD OGIL. 'It's part of the sign that used to be over the door of the shop,' she whispered, a little tremulously. 'Donald Ogilvie, Newsagent, it said, but the rest of it's likely buried underneath somewhere.'

'We'd better leave now, darling. It's too much for you.'

'Give me a few more minutes.' Her voice broke as she went on, 'Mum, Dad, I want to introduce you to Les Clark. He's the boy I used to tell you about when I was at St Mark's. We've just got engaged but when we get married and have our own house, I'm going to put this piece of your sign on our wall, so I'll never forget you. Not that I ever would, but it's nice that I'll have something of you to keep. I'm very happy and I hope you are happy for me.' She turned to her fiancé again. 'All right, we can go now.'

As they walked up the street again, she said, 'You won't mind if I put this on our wall?'

'Of course I won't mind. I'm glad you thought of it.'

'Oh, Les, we are going to be happy, aren't we?'

'We'll be the two happiest people on earth.'

'I'll wait till I go home before I tell Gracie. I want to tell her properly, I think I owe her that.' Brightening, she added, 'We can invite her and Joe to the wedding.'

'You're a forward little minx,' he teased, grinning. 'Who said anything about a wedding? No, I'll be serious. If I can get my leave to coincide with yours we could arrange to be married then.'

'Let me have a few days at home first.'

'You're looking very chipper,' Joe remarked, as Queenie went in. 'Being at Dover seems to suit her, doesn't it, Gracie?'

'She's thinner,' his wife protested. 'I'll bet she hasn't been eating properly. Never mind, I'll soon fatten her up.'

'She's not a heifer,' Joe laughed, 'and girls don't want to be fat.'

'I hope it wasn't going to South Norwood that upset you,' Gracie said, eyeing the girl with some concern. 'I said to Joe it wasn't a good idea.'

Queenie burst out laughing. 'If you let me get a word in, I'll tell you that it was a very good idea, but I think I'd better explain something first.'

Tutting, Gracie set a plate down in front of her. 'You can explain whatever it is after you've eaten your breakfast.'

'I want to do it before Joe goes out. It won't take long. I didn't tell you the whole truth before . . . the school friend was a boy, not a girl.'

Joe kept waiting for further explanation, but Gracie said, sharply, 'Do you mean you were away for a weekend with a boy and didn't tell me?'

'We were staying with Les's parents, but I didn't like to say anything before, in case you were angry.'

'I would have been angry . . . I am angry, and disappointed in you. I didn't think you'd be so underhand.'

'Let her finish, Gracie,' Joe put in. 'I can tell there's something else she wants to say.'

'We were going out together as much as we could before he took me to meet his mum and dad, and . . .' Queenie paused. 'I didn't like going behind your back, but . . .'

Gracie smiled suddenly. 'Well, it's done now, and at least the laddie's mother and father were there to see he didn't take any liberties with you, so we'll say no more about it.'

'I've something else to tell you, though.' Queenie's eyes were dancing at the prospect of surprising her aunt further. 'When we were there, we got engaged. Look.' She held up her left hand.

Gracie could barely see the row of tiny sapphires through her tears, but she jumped up to hug the girl. 'Oh, I'm very pleased for you. I know it was hard on you when Neil married Freda, and I've wished you would find somebody else. What's his name?'

'Leslie Clark, but he's always called Les. He's very nice. He towers above me, though he used to be shorter than I was, and he fought the big boys who tormented me. He was always a good friend, sticking up for me if anyone picked on me, but I never dreamed . . .' Lifting her hand, she took another long look at her ring. 'I'm really and truly happy. I never knew love could be like this.'

Sniffing surreptitiously, Joe said, 'I just hope he's good enough for you. All we want is your happiness. But I'll have to go now, I'm late as it is.'

Gracie sighed when her husband went out. 'I suppose you'll be getting married soon and leaving us for good?'

The girl's radiance faded a fraction. 'On Saturday.'

'This Saturday? But not in Aberdeen?'

'Oh, Auntie Gracie, I know you're hurt, but we don't want to wait any longer and waste our lives and Mr and Mrs Clark insisted that the wedding should be there. I didn't write to tell you, because I wanted to see you and tell you properly. I'll never forget what you and Joe have done for me. I know the sacrifices you had to make to keep me at the varsity . . .'

'It wasn't a sacrifice, don't ever think that, for I love you as if you were my own flesh and blood.'

Swallowing, Queenie said, 'I know that and I'd like you to see me being married. Will you come?'

'I'll think about it but you haven't given us much time.'

Joe didn't need to think about it when he was told later. 'Of course we'll go,' he grinned. 'Our last chickabiddy? We missed Neil's wedding so we're not missing Queenie's.'

She flung her arms round his neck. 'Oh, Uncle Joe. That's made me feel like a real daughter to you.'

Embarrassed, he mumbled, 'I've always thought of you as a real daughter, lass.'

As her niece turned round to hug her, too, Gracie said, 'I can't say I did, not at first, but I have for years now.'

Queenie gave a contented sigh. 'No other girl could be as lucky as me – I've had two sets of loving parents.'

# Chapter Twenty-four

The camp and the market gardens were almost equidistant from the farmhouse where Neil had rented a room, but in opposite directions. Having the old BSA motor cycle, it was much easier for him to cover the five miles and he knew that Freda did not mind having to use her rather ancient bicycle. She never objected to being on her own when he was on night guard duty, not even when she sometimes hardly saw him for two or three days at a time. They had been idyllically happy since they moved in eight months ago, although there was still no sign of a baby. The doctor she had consulted a few weeks earlier had told her that it often took some time to conceive and that she shouldn't worry. 'Enjoy your relations with your husband without thinking of a baby, then you'll stop being tense.'

It had crossed Neil's mind that he might be the infertile partner, but he decided to wait a little longer before he suggested this to Freda. There was no point in suffering the degradation of baring his soul – and his private parts – to a doctor unless it was necessary.

In April, 1944, Neil came home one morning with bad news for his wife. 'We're being posted a week on Monday to the south of England somewhere and the rumour's going that this is the lead up to the big invasion.'

'Oh, Neil, no! We've been so happy in this room, and I . . .' Freda stopped, then added, 'I knew it was too good to last.'

'Look, darling, the quicker we get stuck into the Jerries, the quicker the war'll be over. When I come back, I'll get a job and we'll have our own house, not just one room. I knew you'd be upset, but I'll be on leave all next week, so maybe we can start our family before I go, eh?'

Blushing a little, she said, 'I'll ask Dad if I can have a week off.'

'Smashing! Twenty-four hours a day in bed, for seven days, that should clinch it. That's if my toggle doesn't drop off from overwork.'

'Oh, Neil,' she laughed, 'you're really crude at times. I have to go now, but I'll see you tonight.'

'Give me one last kiss . . . to last me till you come back.'

After Freda left, Neil washed up the breakfast dishes and gave a quick dust round before he went to bed, and having been on duty all night, he fell asleep almost at once.

It was only two hours later when Mrs Smith, the landlady, knocked loudly on the door, waiting until he called a sleepy answer before she said, 'Alf's here to see you.'

As he put on his trousers, Neil wondered what had brought Alf there when he must have known that he, Neil, would be in bed, but one look at his friend's face when he went into Mrs Smith's living room told him that something was wrong.

Alf rose off the settee and said, gently, 'It's bad news, Neil. Freda was knocked off her bike just a matter of yards from the gardens and . . . oh, God, I'm sorry, Neil . . . she died in the ambulance on the way to hospital.'

'No! It's not true!'

'Her father contacted the camp and asked if I'd come and tell you. He can't leave his wife, you see.' Noticing that Neil's chest was heaving, his face grey, his eyes glazed, he exclaimed, 'Here, you'd better sit down.'

For a few moments, Neil sat holding his head in both hands then he muttered, 'She said it was too good to last.'

'Pardon?'

'Freda said it was too good to last when I told her we were being posted. We've been so happy since we came here and she said . . .' His voice broke.

'Aye.' Alf gripped his hand. 'Let it out, Neil. There's no shame in crying.'

'I don't want to cry. Crying won't bring her back.' Neil looked up into his friend's face. 'I wish I was dead, too.'

'Don't say that, man. I know how you must feel, but you've got to keep strong. She wouldn't want you to go to pieces.'

'No . . . you're right . . . I've got to keep strong. I'm not giving her mother a chance to say I can't face up to things. I must keep strong. Thank God we'd a few months away from the old bitch. She used to listen to us through the wall, that's why Freda would hardly ever let me . . . but since we got away, every day's been wonderful . . . every night was heaven, Alf . . . but I must keep strong.'

Alf let him babble on, taking his own way to come to terms with his wife's death. 'We were trying for a baby, but no luck . . . no luck . . . no luck, Alf. She was relaxing, though, and I'm sure she'd have conceived if we'd had

318

more time. If we'd had more time . . . we only had months, not enough time.'

Heaving a great shuddering sigh, he lapsed into silence, and Alf kept gripping his hand. 'We've been pals for a long time, haven't we, Alf?' he said in a few moments.

'Aye, for years.'

'We've had some good times, some laughs, eh, Alf? But that was before I met Freda and my good times were all with her. Oh, God, what am I going to do without her?'

Mrs Smith, having overheard why Alf had come, appeared now with two cups of tea. 'I'm very sorry, Neil,' she murmured, 'and if there's anything I can do . . .?'

He made a superhuman effort to speak rationally. 'Thanks, but there's nothing anybody can do. Thanks.' He watched her going out, then turned to Alf. 'Will you come with me to the hospital? You can ride pillion.'

'You're not in a fit state to be driving that bike on your own. I've got a jeep outside, I'll take you once we've drunk our tea.'

'I couldn't drink anything.'

'You need it, man. Come on now, it'll help you.'

In the jeep, Neil sat with his chin resting on his chest, his back slumped over, and Alf wished that there was something more positive he could do to help. They were directed to the mortuary when they went into the hospital and when Neil saw Freda's parents standing in the corridor, he seemed to pull himself together. George Cuthbert – looking far older after the ordeal of identifying his daughter – put his arm round his son-in-law's shoulders and led him into the place where Freda was lying.

It was quite a time before they came out again and Neil, having obviously steeled himself to do battle, went straight to Freda's mother. 'I know we've never seen eye to eye about things,' he began, 'and I'm sorry for some of the things I said to you, but . . .'

'At times like this,' she interrupted, holding her hand out to him, 'all differences are best forgotten. You've been a good man to her, Neil, I can't deny that, and I'm grateful to you for making her last days happy.'

He had been expecting her to blame him for taking Freda so far away that she needed to cycle to work, to blame him for her daughter's death, and this was so out of character that he could say nothing for a moment, the defences he had meant to put forward dried up in his throat. Then, his voice choked with emotion, he murmured, 'The doctors told me she was two months pregnant.' His eyes filling with tears, he burst out, 'Oh, Christ! Why didn't she tell me? I'd have made her stop working and . . .'

Priscilla Cuthbert's face crumpled. 'She didn't tell me, either. Oh, my poor boy.' She pulled him to her and held him closely, repeating, through her tears, 'My poor, poor boy,' and although he knew that her grief was for her daughter, he drew comfort from her embrace as they wept together.

# Part Three

# Chapter Twenty-five

## *1945*

'A' Company of the Royal Scots Fusiliers had been ordered to extend the bridgehead made by the Gordon Highlanders to go across the Goch-Wesel railway and the stream immediately to the south, in order to provide a place for the 46th Brigade of the 15th Scottish Division to re-form the following day. It was a bitterly cold February morning when the Lieutenant-Colonel concentrated the RSF on the escarpment to the north-east, where all ranks were given a hot meal while he himself reported to the Brigadier for further orders.

Later, after he had made some reconnaissance, the Lieutenant-Colonel returned and took his battalion, with 'A' Company leading, to join the 227th Brigade, and at eight o'clock that evening the RSFs ran across the bridge in the darkness and pushed on a hundred yards to the crossroads beyond, their guns having put up twenty minutes' preparation. The remaining companies followed through, but they met with fierce resistance from small arms and mortars and casualties were heavy.

Arriving vehicles met with some success until they reached mines, when two Wasps were quickly knocked out. The Lieutenant-Colonel saw that he would have to wait until morning to extend his bridgehead, and ordered his companies to dig in where they were. One group of RSFs took advantage of the slight shelter provided by the buildings of an abandoned farm, but morale was low and enemy shelling became even more violent during the night – some of it short-range shelling by tanks which could be heard moving in the wood close by. Grumbles about the non-arrival of the promised support grew stronger, and one captain said to his sergeant, 'Have they forgotten us, or would they have run into trouble themselves?'

McIvor, tall and burly, with almost twenty-five years of service behind him, gave a grunt. 'I'd say they've forgotten aboot us, sir. Them buggers o' English have naething atween their lugs.'

The captain let this go. He knew that his men accepted him as 'one of the lads' because his grandfather had been a Scot although he himself had been born and brought up in a small village in Derbyshire. The Lieutenant-Colonel appeared at that moment, as there was a short respite from the bombardment, and after asking the captain if he knew how many had been wounded or killed, he said, 'I can't contact the Brigadier, none of the radios seem to be working, and the despatch riders have been badly injured, so send a man to let him know our position.'

The captain saluted. 'Leave it with me, sir.' Waiting till his superior went out, he turned to McIvor who said, 'We'd be as weel sendin' ane o' them REME lads that were attached to us when we came ower. They're no' muckle use for onything else at the minute.'

'Good idea. See to it, McIvor.'

The sergeant strode off purposefully to where Neil Ferris

and Alf Melville were sitting close together in one of the smaller sheds. 'Ane o' youse twa'll ha'e to go back to the headquarters wi' a message.'

Jumping up smartly, Neil said, 'I'll go, Sarge.'

Alf pulled him down. 'No, you silly blighter. You've been on a suicide mission since we landed, volunteering for every dangerous job going. It's my turn this time.'

'Look Alf, it doesn't matter to me if I'm alive or dead.'

'It'll matter to your mother, though.'

'What about yours, then?'

McIvor snorted with impatience. 'We cannae wait till you twa stop this "After you Cecil, after you Claude" business.' Pointing to Alf, he ordered, 'You can go, and mind and gi'e them this note. It's to let them ken oor exact position.'

Alf gave a triumphant grin as he rose to his feet and made for the area where the vehicles were kept. 'I'd better take the Norton, Sarge, I know it's in good running order.'

'OK, but mind an' come back. No sneakin' awa'.'

Neil went to the doorway – the door had gone before they took up residence – and watched Alf wheeling the motor cycle out on to the farm road to kick start it, but just as the engine roared into life, his eye caught the glint of metal in a patch of bushes. Without stopping to think, he raced forward and flung himself at his friend, knocking both him and the Norton to the ground. Alf's leg was pinned under the motor cycle, and Neil felt the bullet searing his shoulder a split second after hearing the crack of the rifle.

Struggling to get up, Alf shouted, 'What the hell did you do that for, you stupid bugger?' but Neil muttered, 'It's a Jerry sniper. Keep down, he could fire again.'

The second shot came from behind them and was followed by a long blood-curdling scream, then a voice rang out, 'I got the bastard!'

McIvor ran over to make certain. 'Aye,' he said when he came back, 'he's deid a' right.'

Four willing hands – the sergeant's and the private's, who had saved the day – helped them to their feet, because Neil was bleeding profusely and Alf couldn't get his leg free of the heavy weight. 'You were bloody lucky, mate,' the gunner observed. 'If this lad here hadnae had the sense to shove you ower, you'd ha'e been playin' a harp up there or maybe shovellin' coal doon ablow. That effing Jerry was aiming for the petrol tank, an' you'd ha'e been blawn to smithereens if he'd hit it.'

Flexing his leg to get the blood flowing, Alf gave Neil a slightly crooked grin. 'D'you realise you saved my life?'

'Ach, away.'

'No, right enough, so I owe you one.'

'Give's a fag if you've any left and we'll call it quits.'

Alf passed over the last one in the tin of Senior Service he had been issued and held out his lighter. 'I'd better go now, if the bike's still in one piece.'

'Watch yourself!' Neil called after him, screwing up his face as he tried to lift his arm to wave.

While Neil's shoulder was being bandaged – by the only man left who had any knowledge of first aid – a renewed barrage of fire broke out, and he hoped that Alf was out of range of the German guns. They had been together for three and a half years now and were as close as brothers, if not closer, and he couldn't bear the thought of losing him.

During the next quiet spell, Neil relaxed and let his mind drift back. Less than a year ago he'd been the happiest man in the world, with a wife who loved him as much as he loved her, in their own little love nest, then wham! He couldn't remember much about the actual day of the accident, when the troop-transporter had gone out of control and mown Freda down. He had been in a living nightmare until his mother and father arrived the next day, in answer to the telegram Alf had sent. He had found out later that they had been getting ready to go to South Norwood with Queenie when they got the message.

'She wanted to postpone her wedding,' his mother had told him, 'but we said you wouldn't want that.'

He'd been too numb at the time to make any reply – he had not been caring about anything or anyone else – and it was days later before it came into his mind to hope that Queenie had not allowed his tragedy to spoil her wedding day. He had received a letter from his mother when he was in Brighton being primed for the invasion telling him that Les Clark's squadron was also preparing for it, so Queenie must have had even less time with Les than he'd had with Freda. He had thought, a little bitterly then, that Queenie would have her husband back when the war ended but, after the slaughter he had seen since landing on the beach at Normandy, he thought it was possible that neither he nor Les Clark would ever go home again.

Poor Queenie, Neil mused. He had treated her very shabbily and he was glad that she'd found somebody else. He had once told her that she would always have a place in his heart and it was true. He still felt a deep affection for her which in no way detracted from the great sorrow he felt for Freda. He groaned aloud. Why hadn't Alf let him take that message to headquarters? As long as he'd got there and given them the company's position, it wouldn't have mattered whether or not he got back. Had Alf got through? Alf, always so bright and cheery, always ready for a lark, always there when his pal needed him . . . it would be terrible if he were killed.

When a fresh outburst of shelling began, Neil contemplated walking outside and letting the Jerries finish him off, but his legs refused to move. Was he a coward then, as well as being bitter and self-centred? No, by God! He wasn't a ruddy coward, and if Alf came back, he would show him that he had stopped feeling sorry for himself. He was still young, only twenty-two . . . he must have been in Holland on his birthday, though he hadn't remembered about it. Not like his twenty-first, when Freda had baked a cake and . . . but he should stop thinking about Freda. He should concentrate on the present – and the future, if he had one – not dwell on the past.

It was during another quiet spell when Alf strolled in as if he had just been out for a walk, his tin helmet perched cockily on the side of his head. 'Mission accomplished,' he crowed. 'Has anything much been happening here?'

'A fat lot you care,' Neil grinned. 'You couldn't get away fast enough.'

The sound of gunfire made them look warily at each other, but in another five minutes, McIvor appeared. 'We're getting' support at last, thanks to you, Melville. Anti-tank guns, so that'll put the wind up the Jerry bastards.' That afternoon, at his headquarters, the Brigadier expounded his plan for the 46th Brigade's attack next day through the RSFs bridgehead. This battle, unfortunately, would prove to be long and costly, but one soldier at least, out of the hundreds involved, felt happier than he had done for months. Neil Ferris had passed the crisis of the malady which had affected him for so long. He wanted to go on living.

# Chapter Twenty-six

Although Ellie McKenzie had believed that she was prepared for anything, she had never dreamt that the reality of war could be so horrifyingly fearsome. Isa Green, her ex-cleaner and now co-driver in the Church of Scotland mobile canteen in Edinburgh, was determined to get as near the fighting as possible so they had found themselves practically in the firing line at times. On such occasions, they fought back the fear of being blown to bits and kept their hands steady as they poured out cups of tea. The men they served – English, Welsh, Canadians and Americans, as well as Scots – were always cheery and it wouldn't do to let them down.

They had followed the 15th Scottish Division determinedly through France, Belgium and Holland, longing to stop for the long lines of refugees, but knowing that it would be futile. How could they hope to refresh so many desperate people? It would only cause pandemonium among them and, possibly, even the destruction of their van. They had hardened their hearts and carried on, coming eventually to Tilburg and, like the men involved in this long battle, they had been glad to rest when it was all over. The townsfolk fêted the troops who had liberated them, and there had been a lighthearted carnival atmosphere for fourteen days, until the time came to move on . . . into Germany itself.

It was the last week of March when the two women crossed the Rhine behind the soldiers. The air was softer, the trees still standing had a touch of green on their branches. Here and there, cattle were grazing in the fields and sometimes it was so peaceful that, if they closed their eyes to the evidence of war – the shellholes, the ruined buildings, the burned-out barns – it seemed impossible that they could be in enemy territory, but an instant later, all hell would be let loose again.

Isa had drawn off the road one afternoon to go to a small farm for more water, and Ellie was in the van by herself. One large tea urn was still full, enough until the others were filled. There was no sign of soldiers at the minute but they often appeared from behind hedges or trees, and it was as well to be prepared. When Isa came back, they would be moving on to look for the odd, isolated platoon.

It was quite pleasant here, Ellie mused, filling her lungs with fresh air. She would never have believed, even a year ago, that she would one day be in Germany, sitting outside Mehr – she hadn't even heard of it then – waiting to serve tea. She smiled at the last two words. Serve tea. But not in the way she had done at home in Edinburgh, with a cloth on the table and bone china cups and saucers, plates of home-made cakes and biscuits. The troops had no time to appreciate niceties like that . . . and disposable cups saved on washing up. She glanced at her wristwatch. It was five minutes to six. Allowing for the time difference, her two

331

sisters would likely be preparing supper in Aberdeen about now; Gracie for Joe and Patsy if she was not on duty – Jake Corbierre was on this side of the Channel, too – and Hetty for Martin, because there were only the two of them left at Rubislaw Den. Ellie heaved a sigh. Would she ever see any of them again? Would she ever see her own two daughters again?

'Cup o' char, please, missus.'

The cheeky Cockney voice brought Ellie out of her reverie and she jumped to her feet. 'Rightio, coming up.'

'Bin quiet f'r a while,' the boy observed as she turned the tap on the urn. 'Calm before the ruddy storm, eh?'

Pushing the paper cup forward, Ellie shrugged and smiled. 'No doubt, but we're ready for anything, aren't we?'

'Too right, we'll beat the buggers yet.' Remembering that this was a church canteen and the woman probably a staunch churchgoer, he turned beetroot red. 'I'm sorry, missus, I shouldn't be swearin' in front of yer.'

Ellie chuckled, thinking how incongruous it was that this tough young soldier could blush so easily. 'I've heard much worse than that since I've been on this job.'

Isa, returning in time to hear this last remark, smilingly agreed. 'Aye, we've had our education finished over here.'

'We don't mean nuffink by it – it's just Gawd bless yer to us. I bin up the line wiv a dispatch, an' I took the chance of a kip seein' ev'ryfink was so quiet. Me bike's be'ind them trees.'

Isa's eyes widened. 'You were on a bike?'

'A motor bike,' he explained. 'I'd the bl . . . fright of me life 'arf an 'our ago, though. I goes past the advance, for they were dug in well off the road, an' when I realises I'd gone too far, I gets off me bike an' goes be'ind a tree fer a quick Jimmy Riddel before I turns back, an', s'welp me, I comes face ter face wiv this Jerry wiv a billycan in 'is 'and. I think 'e got as big a fright as me, for he drops 'is can and runs inter the wood, an' I makes for me bike and comes 'ell for leather back, an' by good luck, I finds the advance this time, they're about five mile along the road from 'ere. Jocks, if them's what yer lookin' fer. They'll be glad ter see you, they've 'ad a rough time lately.'

Both women had been highly amused by the boy's story, but now Isa shouted, 'Thanks!' and was into the driver's seat before Ellie had time to pull up the flap of the van. The road was pitted with holes and Isa drove slowly, weaving from side to side to avoid them, but before they'd gone any distance, they were stopped by a small patrol.

'You'll have to turn back, ladies,' ordered the sergeant in charge. 'Jerry's not that far off.'

Isa's derisive snort showed exactly what she thought of the Germans. 'You wouldna grudge oor lads a wee cup o' tea, surely? It's the Seaforths, isn't it?'

'Aye.' A broad smile spread across his face as the other soldiers crowded round, accepting the cups of tea Ellie gave out. 'You ken't the badge, did you? Well, since you're that determined, I'll no' force you to go back, but you'd better get off the road – there's a gap in the trees about quarter o' a mile along, and our lads are in behind there somewhere. Maybe you'll find them without Jerry seein' you. Good luck to you.'

'Thanks.' Isa let off the handbrake, then turned to Ellie, 'I hope you're no' feared?'

'No' me,' Ellie had lived in Edinburgh long enough to have absorbed the dialect. 'If our lads can face it, so can we.'

If it hadn't been for Isa's utter disregard of danger, she thought, she might not have felt so brave, and felt grateful for having such an intrepid partner. Isa Green was the widow of a Leith shipyard worker, and had gone out cleaning and taken in laundry in order to bring up her three sons, while Ellie, her employer in the large house in Morningside, had been well provided for when her doctor husband died.

'Here's the gap.' Isa hung on grimly to the steering wheel as she swung the cumbersome vehicle round to the right, the tea urns rattling as it bumped over the mossy mounds between the trees. 'Can you see any signs o' them yet?' she asked, her own attention concentrated on avoiding boulders, fallen trees and tree stumps.

'No' yet.' Ellie was peering steadily ahead and, in the next minute, she exclaimed, 'Aye, there's something there.'

Her eyes darting to where Ellie's finger was pointing, Isa gave a satisfied grunt. 'Oh aye, I see it.'

When they drew closer, they discovered that it was a field medical station and Isa stopped when she saw a khaki-clad figure coming out of a tent. 'How much farther have we to go to get the Seaforths?' she yelled.

'You can't go any farther. They've been under fire, that's why we're here.'

'That's why we're here, an' all,' Isa snapped, letting off the brake again.

'Wait!' Opening the door of the van, Ellie jumped out and ran towards the tent crying, 'I thought at first you were a man, then I recognised your voice. I never expected to see you here.'

Olive Potter stepped back in amazement. 'I never expected to see you here, either.'

Ellie had never liked Olive, but the strange circumstances of their meeting overrode anything personal and she flung her arms round her niece. 'It's good to see you.'

The wariness left the tired face. 'It's good to see you, too, Ellie. We've been so busy since we came over, I haven't had time to think about home, but now . . .' She wiped her eyes with her hand.

Ellie was shocked by the change in Olive, who had always been so fastidious about her appearance. Her fair hair was dragged severely back but some strands had worked loose; her face was grey and haggard, with dark circles under her eyes from lack of sleep; her battledress blouse and trousers were crumpled and stained; she was thinner than she used to be – far too thin. It was hard to believe it was the same girl. 'How are you, Olive?' she asked compassionately. 'This is a right hell hole you're in, and no mistake.'

'I don't regret joining the Medical Corps.' Olive was on the defensive now. 'I enjoy it.'

'Good for you. I don't regret volunteering for the canteen either, though I sometimes think I must have been mad at my age. I'd better go now or Isa'll think I'm deserting.'

When she joined her partner, Ellie said, 'What a surprise! Olive's my sister's daughter and she used to be a real pain in the neck and so supercilious you would hardly credit she could stick it out here. She's changed, though.'

'She doesna look happy,' Isa observed, taking a glance at the girl, who was waiting for them to leave. 'I suppose we could stop for a while, if you want to find out what's wrong wi' her. Maybe ten minutes, would that do?'

Remembering how worried about her daughter Hetty had been the last time she saw her, Ellie was glad to have a chance to talk properly to Olive. Running back, she said, 'Can we chat somewhere for a few minutes?'

Obviously apprehensive now, Olive said, 'My quarters,' and led the way to a group of small tents behind the large one.

Brevity was essential, so Ellie was blunt. 'I'm not trying to find out why you left home but if there's anything you want to tell me . . .?' She stopped as the girl shook her head, then went on, 'If you think your mother's angry with you, I can tell you she's not. She's worried sick about you, and I think you should write to her.'

'There's nothing to write.'

'Oh, come on, now. Just a little scribble to let her know you're OK, that's all it needs.'

'I'd rather not.'

Ellie lost patience then. 'Good God, Olive, you could be killed any time. Surely you want to patch things up with her before you die?'

The obstinacy fading from her face, Olive said, 'I didn't have a row with Mum, it was something I did . . . something that she wouldn't have forgiven me for . . . I had to leave.'

'Look, Olive,' Ellie said gently, 'I don't know what you did, and I don't want to know, but you can't punish your mum for something that was nothing to do with her.'

The girl hung her head for a moment, then straightened up. 'I'll think about writing home.'

'You just need to apologise for not writing sooner and it would put her mind at rest.' Standing up, Ellie straightened her skirt. 'I'll have to go now, but I hope we run into each other again some time.'

'I hope we do. Thanks for not condemning me, Ellie, and . . . if you write to Gracie, please don't say you saw me. I don't want her telling Mum what I'm doing . . . not until . . . yes, I'll definitely write home, when I get a chance.'

'You won't regret it, Olive.'

'Everything OK?' Isa asked, when her partner returned.

'I think so . . . now. She'd had a bit of trouble, but I think she's seeing sense about it.'

Switching on the engine, Isa said, 'Poor lassie.'

Ellie couldn't help agreeing with this, even if Olive had brought her troubles on herself. Oh, damn! She should have told her about Neil's wife; she wouldn't know that Freda had been killed in an accident.

Ellie's thoughts were interrupted. 'There's some men up there,' Isa told her. 'Can you see, just through this next clump of trees?'

Over the next hour, the two Scotswomen were almost swamped by the avalanche of Seaforth Highlanders who surged towards them when they stopped the van. All the men were delighted to see them and astonished that they'd had the temerity to venture so near the enemy lines.

One scrawny private even said, 'Are youse no' feared?'

'No, are youse?' Isa retorted, her eyes twinkling.

'Naw!' he grinned, 'but we cannae move till we're tell't, an' youse could easy be some place else. Naebody would ken.'

'We'd ken.' Her defiant stare dared him to argue.

'See this twa?' he demanded of the next soldier. 'They're the bloody bees' knees, that's whit they are. Right up to the front line, an' them jist a couple o' auld weemen.'

'No' so much o' the auld,' Ellie smiled.

'You're aulder than my maw.' The boy stretched up, pulled her head down and kissed her. 'Ye're the only weemen we've seen for months, an' ye're a sicht for sair een.'

A great roar of laughter rose up, and Ellie felt her heart swell with the pride of lightening a few moments for these brave boys. When the orders came for the soldiers to move, one officer came back to the van. 'We will be putting up a fresh barrage shortly and Jerry'll be retaliating, so you'd be safer to pull back, ladies. Thank you for coming, you've bucked us all up.' Saluting gravely, he left them.

'We've done no' bad for one day,' Isa said, as they packed up. 'I think we'd better get back to base.'

'I'll drive this time.' Ellie sat behind the wheel, hoping that they would be out of range before the shooting started. To save time, she went out on the road as soon as she saw an opening, and sped back the way they had come. They were well past the area of the Medical Station before they heard the gunfire but by then they were safely out of harm's way. As Isa had said, they had 'done no' bad' for that day – in more ways than one – and Ellie considered that they deserved all the rest they could get.

Olive returned to her quarters pensively, wondering now if she should have confessed everything to Ellie; it might have eased her burden of guilt. Her aunt would never have guessed who had been the father of the child whose existence she had terminated so barbarically, but her mother would have made the connection with Neil straight away. It was better that no one should know of the hour she had spent in the shabby tenement flat with the woman who poked inside her with a spoon-shaped instrument and then told her it might take some time for the abortion to work; of the night Polly had sat with her waiting until it did; of the gnawing emptiness she had felt when the thick clots of blood started to come away. It had all been so shaming, so sordid, that she would never feel clean again.

Polly had let her stay on in her room until she recovered sufficiently to go to Glasgow, where she'd lived in a girls' hostel until she came into the Medical Corps. Not having qualified as a doctor, she was accepted as a nurse, and had gone to the Cambridge Military Hospital in Aldershot for the months until her detachment was sent to France, just after D Day. They had been meant to set up a medical field station at Caen, but the Germans had still been holding the town and they'd had to work alongside some Queen Alexandra nurses near St Lo until they were allowed to go forward themselves.

After days of working round the clock, Olive recalled, of patching up men who would then be sent back down the line to a less transitory, better equipped hospital, she hardly knew whether or not she was still on her feet. When she had done all she could for one casualty, another was waiting for attention – it never seemed to end. She had been a nurse for over a year now, but she would never become inured to the terrible injuries she saw. Even yet, she felt sick at seeing a severed limb, a gaping wound, a shattered or burned face, but she carried on taking and transfusing blood, suturing, clamping, acting as doctor or surgeon if the need arose, her movements automatic. The silent suffering of her patients tugged at her heartstrings, compelling her to treat them to the best of her ability, and they responded by placing their trust in her. When, in spite of all she did, one of them died, she felt a bitter disgust at herself and wondered if there had been something else she could have done for him.

Olive's mind came back to what had happened a short time before. She had just left the bedside of a young soldier who had succumbed to his wounds when her aunt turned up, and she had not been feeling like talking. Having been on duty for thirteen hours, she had felt nauseous when the boy died, and had clung on to the end of his bed. Tina, another nurse, had looked at her in some alarm. 'Are you OK? You look ghastly.'

'I feel a bit squeamish, that's all.'

'Take a break for a couple of hours. We'll manage here.'

'I think I will. I'm no use like this.'

Olive's legs were trembling, her head was pounding, but a few minutes in the fresh air did stave off the sickness, and she had been on her way to her quarters when the canteen van drew up. She must have looked really awful, so it was little wonder that Ellie had wanted to talk to her. She would take her aunt's advice and write to her mother, but only to say that she was alive and well, nothing else. It was impossible for her to go home again . . . ever.

# Chapter Twenty-seven

The company of Royal Scots Fusiliers to which Neil and Alf were attached had been so reduced in numbers that it was disbanded and the men transferred to other units who had no need of the REME, so the two friends had been separated at last. Alf was sent to the Argylls, while Neil had to go to the Highland Light Infantry. They had been so long together that Neil felt as if part of him was missing, but it was a case of every man for himself against the last desperate struggles of an enemy who refused to recognise the writing on the wall. He no longer had any wish to die – realising, after the terrible things he had witnessed, that his wife's death, and his child's, had to be accepted. So many people had lost loved ones, he wasn't the only one and he could do nothing to bring them back.

He determined now to survive the war, to go back home and pick up his life from where he had first left Aberdeen. He would never forget Freda but the agony was lessening, the heartache would ease and would gradually become just a deep sadness. So he assured himself, but it was sometimes hard to believe.

On 1 May, the 15th Scottish Division were given orders to clear the Sachsenwald the next day. This was a large area of forest north-east of Hamburg, and three brigades spent all that day taking up positions for the drive, which began at eight the following morning. The HLI were on the left and had an early, sharp fight with marine cadets from the flak school at Hamburg but managed to overcome them and pressed on. At the end of the day, when they came out of the forest, they met fierce resistance before they reached Neu Bornsen which was their final objective. Neil Ferris, however, never got as far as that.

For the last lap of their advance, unhindered by the enemy who were now in retreat, the men boarded an open truck which had caught up with them, jumping into the rear part of the vehicle with cries of joy. Even standing, packed as tightly as sardines in a tin, was preferable to foot-slogging along the rough road. Neil found himself in the middle of the mass of bodies but what did that matter? The truck had gone only a few hundred yards when they heard the whine of the shell and were flung off their feet when the driver put his foot hard down on the brake. Scrambling over each other in panic, they vaulted over the backboard to run for cover but Neil, being underneath, was last to get off and fell as he hit the ground. He didn't have time to roll away as the truck was hit and the diesel tank exploded.

The Argylls, with Alf Melville amongst them, had been to the south, advancing along the main Geessthacht–Bergedorf road, with Bornsen as their objective. They, too, met some marine cadets with 20mm flak guns, and had difficulty fighting on the almost sheer, thickly wooded hill above the road. Alf was one of the minor casualties, wounded in the right leg but waving away any of the overworked medical team who came near him.

Just before noon, there came a long-awaited, and extremely welcome, change in the situation. First only a few, then an absolute sea of white flags appeared and a steady stream of men in hodden grey uniforms came out with their hands raised high in the air. Very soon, the news had spread that Hitler was dead. The Wermacht had nothing left to fight for.

Ever since her unexpected meeting with Ellie, Olive had done a great deal of thinking. She had written to her mother and told her everything, and just setting it down on paper had helped a bit, but she hadn't had the courage to send it. She had started again, just saying that she was in the Medical Corps and that she was very well, but not giving any address or indication of where she was. She had also said she was sorry for leaving the way she had but that she hadn't been able to face any explanations. She had still been left with the guilt that burned her up even after being on duty for sometimes more than eighteen hours at a stretch but, thankfully, the pressures now were not so great.

From the Mehr area, her unit had moved forward gradually, setting up Casualty Clearing Stations in convents or schools – or tents, if nothing else was available. With the help of some Queen Alexandra nurses, they did their best for all the wounded, enemies as well as allies, until the patients could be sent to the Field Hospitals down the line. Olive treated the Germans exactly as she did the others and most of them were grateful, except one young boy who couldn't have been more than fifteen. The surgeons had worked on him for hours to remove all the shell splinters in his chest before he was brought to her, and she had been bent over him to make sure that he continued to breathe after regaining consciousness. For a second, a flicker of fear had crossed his face, then a hint of a smile when he saw that she was a nurse . . . until he spotted her khaki trousers, then he spat on her. She would never forget the hatred in his eyes but she had wiped her cheek and smiled. He was still a child, after all, and had probably been fed lies about British brutality.

Her unit had been between Frankfurt and the Kiel Canal when hostilities ceased and she had spent most of her last leave by the canal, swimming and sunbathing. There had been so many British and American men and women that it had been a real holiday, peaceful and fun-filled, but the break was over all too soon. She was then sent back to just outside Hamburg and it was rumoured that they might be moved shortly with the wounded to hospitals in England. They would be taken to Bremerhaven or Hamburg, likely, then on by boat.

Fastening her belt as she walked, Olive went back on duty, her feet taking her directly to the bedside of a sapper from Southend who had been shot in the spine and was paralysed from the waist down. Ron White's was a case that interested her. At times, his disability did not seem to bother him then, with no warning, he would rant and scream at anyone who ventured near him. There was no pattern to it and with her psychiatric training, she was itching to find a reason for his erratic behaviour.

'Good morning, Ron,' she chirped. 'How are you today?'

He looked up with a smile, 'It's my Scots beauty come

to light up my day. I'm not so bad, thanks. I'll be walking out of here before you can say Jack Robinson.'

Her pity for him swelled. He knew as well as she did that he would never walk again. 'Ready for breakfast? Boiled eggs on toast this morning.'

He pretended to be disappointed. 'I was looking forward to ham and eggs with sausage and tomatoes.'

Olive gave a little chuckle 'Did you get breakfasts like that at home?'

'Not likely. My dad died when I was small, and Mum had to go out charring to keep the two of us. We were lucky to have bread and dripping most days.' He halted, his eyes clouding. 'Go and attend to your other patients, Scottie.'

Obediently, she walked away, pitying him more than ever, and thinking, mournfully, that his mother would have her hands full when Ron was sent home and wouldn't be able to go out to work. How would they exist? She was occupied for the next hour or so with breakfasts, pills, bed baths for those who could not go to the showers. Some of the boys had been embarrassed at first when a nurse washed them all over but most had learned to joke about it. Making fun of the indignity was the only way they could face up to it. Ron had been here before she came, however, and he still wasn't used to it. Sometimes, his tantrums started while he was bathed but at other times he lay passively, wincing if whoever was washing him was not gentle enough and she was puzzled by the inconsistency.

Olive was drying a broad Cameronian who had lost an arm and a leg when Gladwys, a tiny Welsh QA, joined her.

'I've bathed Ron, but can you give me a hand to make his bed?'

'Half a mo'.'

It took two to hoist him on to a chair until they changed his sheets, and they never knew what to expect. He had been quiet for days but he could take a turn at any minute. They were smoothing the top sheet when he began to shout. 'Why the hell do you take so long? You're so bloody slow, I could die in the time I'm sitting here and you wouldn't give a damn.'

Without stopping what she was doing, Olive said, 'You're not going to die, and we're going as fast as we can.'

'I'd be as well dead for all the use I am now.'

'Don't be so sorry for yourself,' Gladwys ventured bravely from the other side of his bed.

'I'm not sorry for myself,' he growled, 'but I'm no bloody use for anything.'

'You're not the only one who's ever lost the use of his legs,' Olive snapped, somewhat rashly. 'Douglas Bader lost his legs altogether and he was flying planes again not long afterwards.'

Her strategy did not work as she had hoped. 'I don't give a monkey's cuss for Douglas Bader,' Ron screeched. 'He got artificial legs to help him to walk. Can you make me walk again? Tell me how I'm going to find work when I go home.'

The bedspread was in place now but when the two nurses came to lift him back, he struck out at them with both arms, knocking the slight Gladwys off her feet and catching Olive in the stomach. Winded for a moment, she felt furious. What was the good of trying to be kind to a man who acted like this? 'Look what you've done!' she shouted, helping Gladwys off the floor. 'Why can't you be thankful you're alive and stop venting your bad temper on people who are only trying to help you?'

There was a moment's silence but no further outburst. Ron was scowling but allowed them to lift him out of the chair. Neither of the nurses spoke but they were as gentle as they could be, setting him down carefully on the bed and drawing up the covers. Then they went back to the Cameron Highlander to repeat the process all over again with him.

'I'd tak' my bonnet aff to you two if I had it here,' he smiled as he held up his one arm and the stump to let them lift him. 'That lad's a bloody maniac.'

Olive shook her head. 'You know he's not always like that. He's really very nice when he's calm.'

'Aye, but you cannae tell when he's goin' aff his heid.'

'We could see it had started and I should have known not to get too close.' Gladwys rubbed her rump ruefully.

A glint came into the Cameronian's eyes, 'Would you like me to kiss it better for you, Sister?

Blushing, she exclaimed, '*Dyuw, dyuw*! You Scotsmen are the blooming limit.'

Ron made no apology when Olive brought his lunch – she had expected none – but she was relieved that the frenzied eyes were serene again. He could be thoughtful, humorous, serious – it was tragic that the injuries to his spine had caused a kink in his brain that could change him into an animal. His hair was dark and unruly, his cheeks, pallid now, would have been ruddy at one time, his jaw was

347

strong, and as clear cut as a twenty-year-old's, though he was over thirty. He had told her once that he had been six feet two and built like a wrestler before he was shot, and his bone structure verified this, but he was pathetically thin now.

Realising that Ron had started to eat, Olive turned to go. 'Is anything wrong, Scottie?' he asked, as if nothing had happened.

He honestly doesn't remember, Olive thought, but said, 'I guess I'm a bit tired.'

'You must be. I feel sorry for you sisters when you're on during the day – you've so much to do.'

She almost retorted, 'Grappling with a wild animal doesn't help,' but she wasn't so foolhardy.

When the MO had done his rounds in the forenoon, he had said that Ron could be taken out in a wheelchair for half an hour after lunch. 'If anyone feels like pushing him,' he had added. Olive had volunteered – she was taller and stronger than Gladwys and Ron never went berserk twice in one day, hardly ever twice in one week. Nevertheless, both girls were rather timid when they wheeled the chair up to his bed. 'How do you feel about going outside for a wee while?' Olive eyed him hopefully. 'It's a shame to waste all the sunshine and the doc said you could.'

'I'm putty in your hands, Scottie.' He smiled at them as they lifted him out of bed and swung him round. 'I've never liked being inside when the sun was shining.'

'Will you manage?' Gladwys asked at the door of the ward.

Olive knew that the question did not refer to pushing the chair but pretended that it did. 'If I don't, this fella's going to have an unconducted trip down the hill.'

Ron laughed with them, his temperament as sunny as the day outside, and Olive set off, taking it slowly and carefully until they reached the foot of the incline and were on level ground. It was hot work, so when they came to a shady tree, she said, 'Will we stop here for a minute or two?'

'That would be nice.' He inhaled the fresh air deeply as Olive put on the brake, then said, 'If you want to sit down, you can have my shawl. I'm warm enough.' He removed the army blanket she had put round his shoulders, but left the knee rug across his useless legs.

'Thanks.' Taking the blanket, she spread it on the grass and sat down. 'We never get heat like this at home.'

'Home? Where is your home, Scottie?'

'Aberdeen, and we do have some good summers but . . .'

'Before I was called up,' Ron said, rather wistfully, 'the farthest I ever was from home was Southend Pier but I've seen a good few places since then. I was stationed in Redcar in Edinburgh for a while, then we laid out runways at Sullom Voe in the Shetlands, then we were in Yorkshire and we ended up in Brighton for a few months before D Day.'

'I came over on D Day plus six.'

'I was four days before you, and most of them still hadn't got off the beaches. We came through Belgium and Holland.'

'So did I.'

'I must tell you something that happened when we were in Holland. We weren't very far from Deurne when a Dutch family invited three of us in and gave us ersatz coffee and homemade biscuits. We were getting ready to leave when I heard a shell coming down, so I dived to the floor and I happened to cover the youngest daughter – she'd have been about four – and the windows shattered and I got glass in the back of my battledress . . . my back always seems to get it. Anyway, the mother thought I'd deliberately saved the little girl and couldn't do enough for me, though I told her it was just a reflex action. She'd heard me saying earlier on that I'd be thirty in two days and she told me they'd kill one of their pigs and give me a feast on my birthday.'

'That was very kind of her.' Olive was amazed that he was telling her this – he had never spoken about his experiences before – but it might do him good.

'We were moved on ten miles the day after and I thought that was my feast up the spout but one of my mates told the sarge about my birthday party and he let me go back with a jeep, so I'd the feed of my life.' Ron stopped. 'D'you mind if I smoke?'

Olive shook her head and he pulled out a battered tin from the pocket of the scruffy robe he had been given. 'We were between Nijmegen and Arnhem when we saw the parachute drop. The sky was red with dust and we thought it was great. We didn't know at that time the tragedy it was. Then we came through Germany itself – and that's where I got mine – just a couple of months before the end of the war.' His eyes rested regretfully on the rug over his legs. 'When they told me I was paralysed, I wished I'd been killed.'

'I can understand that,' Olive murmured, 'but it wasn't as bad as it could have been. You can use your arms and hands, your eyes are OK, and your br . . .' She stopped in

350

dismay, having almost forgotten that his spinal injury had affected his brain, too, a fact which, thank God, he did not realise himself.

'Aye, that's right, I was luckier than some.' He grinned suddenly. 'Now, I've told you all about me, and I don't know a thing about you, except you come from Aberdeen. Have you always been a nurse?'

'I was training to be a doctor, but . . . something happened, and I left.'

'I bet some man broke your heart. I've often wondered why a pretty girl like you wasn't married.'

She felt annoyed at herself for bringing it up and making him curious but when he said, softly, 'Tell me about it,' a great need rose in her to lay it out in the open, to explain her actions, so she began with her childhood attraction to Neil, stressing how much she had pestered him before she mentioned the trick he and Alf had played on her, how it created a thirst in her for vengeance and the need that had driven her to seduce Neil. She hesitated for a moment before going on to tell him of the outcome. Ron listened, his head cocked to one side, his face expressionless, but when she whispered, 'After I . . . got rid of the baby, I felt so ashamed about all I had done that I wished I was dead, so I know how you've felt,' he laid his hand on her shoulder.

'I worked myself to a standstill sometimes,' she went on, 'doing everything I could to help the sick and the wounded, hoping to atone that way for the terrible things I did.'

She half expected him to contradict her, to tell her that nothing she had done was so terrible, but after a lengthy silence, he said, 'Yes, you were a bitch, weren't you?'

The shock of his condemnation unplugged the hard core that usually stoppered her heart and she sobbed, 'I was eaten up with love and jealousy . . . and hate. I didn't care who I hurt, but when Neil married Freda, I knew it was over. Then, when I found out I was pregnant, the only thing I could do was to leave home.'

'You didn't need to get rid of the baby.'

'I couldn't have it. Every time I looked at it, I'd have remembered Neil and, anyway, how could I make a decent life for myself if I'd an infant to look after?'

'Other girls have managed but maybe you're not like them. I think your mother coddled you . . . does she know yet?'

'I didn't write to her until a few weeks ago, then I told her not quite everything and said I'd never embarrass her by going home again.'

'That was kind of silly, wasn't it?'

'What must she think of me? But it's not really Mum I'm worried about, it's my Auntie Gracie – that's Neil's mother. I couldn't let her know what I did.'

Ron screwed up his face, chewing over how to advise her. 'You'll likely hate me for this, Scottie, but I believe you should go home and tell your auntie, face to face.'

Her tears stopped with outrage. 'I can't, and I don't know how you could even suggest it. Look, Ron, I don't know what possessed me to tell you, but please forget it.' She stood up resolutely. 'It's time we went back.'

While she was replacing the blanket round his shoulders, he said, 'You told me because it was festering inside you. You felt you had to tell somebody and I'm an outsider, not connected with it at all. I bet confessing to me hasn't helped you? Be honest now.'

With her free hand, Olive tucked the blanket behind his back, then gave a low moan. 'You're right, it hasn't. When I began, I thought it would, but . . .'

'If I'd sympathised with you, would that have helped?'

'No, I don't believe it would.' Extracting her imprisoned hand, she turned the wheelchair round. The uphill push back took all her strength and she was relieved when an orderly overtook them. 'I'll take over,' he said, jauntily, nudging her out of the way.

'Thanks. It's hard going.'

When they reached the top, he handed over again, 'I'd have come all the way with you but I'm late as it is.'

'I'll manage now. Thanks again.'

'I'm glad you told me,' Ron observed, suddenly. 'I used to wonder if anything got through to you, you always looked so efficient, so self-controlled. But I've discovered you're as human as the rest of us. Everything you did was because you had a one-track mind.'

'A one-track mind?' Olive repeated, sadly, negotiating the chair round an awkward corner. 'That's putting it mildly. I trampled over everything and everybody to get Neil, and I ended up destroying myself. Oh, God, I don't want to think about it any more.'

The move came just over a week later. Olive and three other nurses were detailed to accompany the remaining patients in an ambulance plane, while the rest of the unit went with the medical supplies by train to Bremerhaven, to be ferried to Dover by boat. An hour before the air passengers were to be collected, Ron took another turn, lashing out at anyone who went near him. Olive got a hefty punch in the face when they were trying to restrain him and the MO ordered that he be given an injection to knock him out. Despite her throbbing cheekbone, she burst out, 'He'll be all right in a minute or two.' She didn't blame Ron; it was all the upheaval that had set him off.

It stopped as suddenly as it had started, and he lay back quietly, beads of perspiration standing out on his forehead. 'It's very sad, isn't it?' Gladwys whispered, when they were making sure that the rest of their charges were ready to be transported to the nearest airstrip. 'Ron's such a nice man when he's normal.'

Olive nodded, bleakly. He was very nice as a rule, and the best thing about him was his complete honesty. He didn't say things he didn't mean because they'd be the correct things to say, and his blunt forthrightness after their little talk had done her far more good than any long-winded, insincere sympathy. She had often considered the advice he had given and maybe she would take it one day. Telling Gracie face to face was probably the only way she could ease her guilt. One day . . . but not yet.

# Chapter Twenty-eight

When Ron informed Olive that his mother had died, her first thought was that he would have no one to look after him when he was discharged from hospital. After making enquiries and being told that he would be sent to a permanent home for the disabled, she pitied him all the more. He would hate it. There must be an alternative.

The solution came to her one sleepless night. He was much more friendly with her than with any of the others but how would he react if she were his only nurse? Would he even agree to it? He would likely accuse her of feeling sorry for him and she would have to swear that she wasn't. After all, she thought, ruefully, she used to be an accomplished liar a few years ago, but surely that did not warrant the sacrifice of devoting herself exclusively to a man who was subject to fits of violence and required attention twenty-four hours a day? Another facet of the problem struck her. Was she really so inhuman that she would allow Ron to be incarcerated in an institution, friendless and embittered?

When Olive rose in the morning, her mind was made up, but she still had not decided on the best way to go about it. She would have to wangle it so that Ron would think it was his idea; it was the only way he would countenance it. There was no immediate hurry, however. She would act only when the powers-that-be began to make arrangements for his discharge, possibly not for months yet, which would give her plenty of time to work out exactly what to say.

Ron had also spent most of the night thinking and tackled her that afternoon. He still had not mastered the art of using the crutches the doctors were determined he would use – he was sure he never would – so the nurses took turns in taking him out in the wheelchair, and it was Olive's turn that day. The June sky over Sussex was quite bright but it was not as warm as it had been, so she wrapped him up well and set off at a brisk pace.

They hadn't gone very far when Ron asked her to stop. 'I want to talk to you, Scottie. I know it won't be long before they put me out of here and I've been wondering about the future. I think I could tackle a sitting job, in a factory, maybe, or an office, but I'm willing to have a bash at any dashed thing. What d'you think?'

She didn't have to think. He might be capable of an easy job, though who would employ him when he might lash out at his workmates without warning? But that wasn't the issue. 'Would you manage to look after yourself? What about getting dressed, bathing and can you cook for yourself?'

'That's what's been bothering me. I could always eat out but I don't suppose I'd be able to afford it on the wages I could make, or pay for a woman to come in. In any case, I'd hate a stranger having to do . . . what you nurses have had to do for me . . . the personal things.'

'Maybe an ex-nurse?' Olive suggested, timidly, paving the way for her plan. 'Some nurses would jump at the chance of having just one patient, and you'd get help to pay.'

'Would you jump at the chance?'

'Me?' She pretended to be astonished. 'I've never thought about it, but . . .'

'It's a bit too much to ask, but I wouldn't mind you being with me all the time. To tell the truth, Scottie, I think . . . I've fallen in love with you. You wouldn't consider marrying me, would you?'

This was something she hadn't expected. 'Marrying you? I don't know. I am fond of you, Ron, but I don't love you.'

'I never thought you did, and it's likely better that you don't. I'm only half a man, don't forget, so I couldn't make love to you, I shouldn't think, but marriage would give you security.'

'You don't need to marry me. I'll come and look after you anyway, if you want me to.'

'I want to marry you,' Ron said doggedly.

'Will you give me time to think about it?'

'I want a plain yes or no right now, Scottie.'

Olive thought quickly. She had planned to tie herself to him anyway and if marriage made him happy, it would be all to the good. 'Yes,' she murmured.

His icy hand enveloped hers. 'Thanks. Now, how about going back inside? It's cold out here.'

'We'd better not say anything to anybody just yet. They'll only tease us and talk about us behind our backs.'

His eyes twinkled suddenly. 'Let's give them something to talk about. You'd make a lovely June bride, you know.'

'But it's June now. We can't be married as soon as . . .'

'We can, if we arrange it tomorrow. Three weeks, and you could be Mrs Ronald Percival White.'

'Percival?' She couldn't help laughing.

'After my mother's uncle – he went to America and made a fortune. I think she hoped I'd fall heir to it, seeing I was named after him, but I never smelt a cent when he died. If you're trying to make me forget what I was saying, it hasn't worked. June's perfect for a wedding.'

She had committed herself to him already, and she couldn't back out now. 'You're on,' she smiled.

Pulling her head down, he gave her a boisterous kiss. 'You can take out the marriage licence and I'll ask the padre to marry us.'

The arrangements were set in motion but Olive suspected that Ron had changed his mind only three days later when he said, looking very serious, 'There's something we'll have to clear up before we get married.'

'What's that?'

'You said once that you couldn't go home and you told me exactly why. Remember?'

Alarmed at this being brought up now, she said, 'Yes, but I can't see what . . .'

'I want you to go back to Aberdeen and face up to it.'

'I told you I'd written to my mother,' she said hastily.

'You didn't tell her, though, and if I remember rightly, it wasn't your mother that was worrying you. Wasn't it an auntie – the boy's mother?'

Olive's stomach churned. 'Yes, but I couldn't tell Gracie, really I couldn't.'

'Look, Scottie, this thing's got to be sorted out. If it

carries on, you're going to end up all twisted inside and two twisted minds together could spell danger.'

His awareness of his mental shortcomings astounded her but what he said was true. 'I'll write to Mum tonight, then, and tell her I'm coming home, and I promise to tell her and Gracie while I'm there.'

'You'll feel much better once you've got it off your chest . . . and so will I.'

Her sister looked so agitated that Gracie was alarmed, 'Has something happened to Raymond?'

'No, he was fine the last I heard. They're still fighting the Japs in Burma, of course, but it's not him I'm . . . I got a letter from Olive today. She'll be home tomorrow morning.'

'Home for good?'

'She didn't say and I don't know if I want her here after she walked out without any explanation.'

'Make sure it's what you want before you let her stay, if that's what she's coming to ask.'

'I can't see her on my own,' Hetty wailed. 'You'll have to come to support me.'

'She'll be too embarrassed to say anything if anybody else is here,' Gracie said, but Hetty's woebegone expression made her feel ashamed. 'You'd be best to see her on your own for a start, but I'll come later on, if like.' She paused. 'Will Martin not want to be here? She's his daughter as well.'

'I'm not going to tell him she's coming. I'm terrified he might start on her and there would be an awful fight, and I couldn't bear that. She's coming at nine, so I'd be grateful to you, Gracie, if . . .'

'I'll be here at ten. That'll give you an hour.'

Olive's heart beat faster as the train sped ever nearer to Aberdeen and she wished that she had stood her ground with Ron and refused to come. This meeting with her mother would be fraught with disturbing memories but it wouldn't be half as bad as confessing to Gracie. Whatever she said – and she didn't intend to whitewash her actions – her aunt would find it impossible to forgive what she had done.

She took a taxi from the station and rang the doorbell of her old home rather tentatively.

'Olive!' Hetty could not stop herself from holding out her arms to the daughter she had loved so much. 'I often used to wonder how you were but you look very well.' As she led the way inside, a tear trickled down her cheek.

Olive was determined not to be emotional. 'You don't look very well yourself. Have you been ill?'

'I didn't sleep much last night.'

Hetty hovered about as Olive sat down, pouring out the tea she had made a few minutes before, and making sure that her daughter had helped herself to sugar and milk before she sat down, more nervous than ever now that the crucial moment had come. 'Olive, I'm not going to give you a lecture, I can't deny that I was shocked when you left though I had a good idea why.'

The girl shook her head ruefully, 'No, you've no idea why and you're going to be so shocked when I tell you, you won't want to see me again.' Taking a deep breath, she began her story, slowly and painfully, missing nothing out.

Hetty's face gradually paled and though she made several attempts to interrupt, Olive carried on and it wasn't until she came to the pregnancy that her mother burst out, 'That's why you weren't looking well. I should have known . . . and it must have been Neil's, because you . . .'

'Yes,' Olive admitted unwillingly, 'it was Neil's.'

'So you went away to have the baby. But where is it now?'

'This is the most difficult part to tell you. You see, I . . . didn't go away to have the baby, I went away to have an abortion.'

Hetty's hand flew to her palpitating heart, 'Oh, my God! How could you?'

'It was the only thing I could do. You guessed right away that it was Neil's and Gracie would have, too, and . . .' The gossamer thread of self control broke at last and she threw up her hands and sobbed, 'I'd made Neil's life enough of a misery before and I just couldn't let anybody know. There would have been such a furore, it would have affected all of you; you and Dad, Gracie and Joe – and Freda and Neil worst of all. At least he didn't know anything about it. You must promise never to breathe a word of it to anybody, Mum.'

Her thoughts in complete chaos, Hetty gave herself no time to consider what she was about to say 'I won't even tell your father, but it's ironic . . . no, that's not strong enough, but it's all I can think of . . . it's ironic that you had that awful thing done to you because Neil was married then Freda was killed just months after.'

'Freda's dead?' Olive gasped, her face blanching. 'How?'

'It was an accident with her bicycle, so you didn't need to . . .' Hetty floundered now, 'You didn't need to . . . you could have . . . I understand why you did it but . . . what I mean is, you could have had the baby, Neil would have married you.' The last part came out in a rush.

It was several seconds before her daughter said with a small, scornful laugh, 'Do you really think he would? Patsy and Raymond both told me years ago that he didn't even like me, and it's true, though I didn't believe them at the time. I didn't know his wife was going to be killed and, anyway, even though he'd been willing, I wouldn't have married him knowing he didn't love me.'

'He might have grown to love you.'

'Oh, Mum, you're living in cloud cuckoo land. I did what I thought was best though, sometimes, when I wasn't too busy, I regretted it and I was plagued by the thought that I had taken a human life. That's why I worked so hard to save as many lives as I could.'

Pity for her welled up in Hetty now. 'Tell me what you've been doing,' she prompted. 'I see you went into the army.'

'The Medical Corps, and that's what kept me going.' Having laid her other troubles out, Olive now gave a heartrending account of the men she had nursed and how she had hated when they were transferred before she knew if they would recover from their wounds. 'Of course,' she ended, with a catch in her voice, 'some of them will never be healed. It was one of them who made me come home and tell you everything. Ron is paralysed from the waist down and his brain was damaged . . . a little, so he takes violent turns. They're not so frequent now, though he does get fits of depression occasionally, but he's a good man most of the time, one of the best.'

Her curiosity aroused by the softness in Olive's eyes and voice, Hetty said, 'You sound as if you love him.'

'I don't love him, but I'm going to marry him.'

'You can't tie yourself to . . .'

'To half a man?' Olive's lips twitched in a semblance of a smile. 'Why not? He's got nobody else, his parents are both dead now.'

'But aren't there places for people like him? A Home? Some kind of institution? A mental hospital? It's where he should be if his brain's damaged, with nurses who've been trained for that kind of thing.'

'I've been trained for that,' Olive said quietly. 'I made a muck of so many lives in my time – Queenie's and Neil's as well as my own – but I know now that my love for him was warped and I won't find peace until I do something positive for somebody who needs me. That's why I'm marrying Ron.'

An electric silence followed, broken only when Gracie came in, stopping when she saw the two tense women, one holding back tears of sympathy, and the other holding her head up defiantly, although her eyes were glittering with moisture. 'Maybe I'd better go away again,' she muttered.

'No, Gracie.' Hetty held out her hand. 'I want you to sit down and listen. Tell her everything, Olive.'

After hearing what her niece had to say, Gracie, too, had difficulty in keeping from weeping. 'You did an awful thing, Olive, killing an unborn babe that would have been a grandchild to both your mother and me, but I can understand why you did it and I'm grateful to you for not making any more trouble for Neil. It seems you do have a heart, after all.'

'Broken and patched up and nothing like as good as new.' Olive gave a tight little smile. 'I came home to confess to you, to try to get your forgiveness before I started my new life with Ron.'

Bending down, Gracie picked up her handbag and got to her feet. 'You have my forgiveness, Olive, and I wish you every happiness in your marriage. I hope you find love with your Ron but even if love doesn't come, I hope you'll never feel you've sacrificed your life in vain.'

Olive gripped her hand. 'Thanks for understanding, Gracie. You know, it wasn't till Neil married that I grew up, and I promise you I'm a different person now, but it's best that I never come back to Aberdeen again.'

'But Olive . . .' Hetty stood up in distress. 'You must come back, I can't lose you again.'

On her way to the door, Gracie turned back, 'I haven't had a letter from Neil for a while but you won't want him to know about . . .'

'He must never know,' Olive implored. 'I couldn't face him again as it is but I'd hate him to know about the baby.'

'He'd as much to do with the making of it as you,' Gracie murmured.

'No, it was all my doing. I forced him.'

'He wasn't blameless, but I'll not say a word. I'd better leave you now to sort things out with your mother.'

Gracie slipped out quietly and, as she went to catch the tram, she let out a long sigh. What Olive had told her had been a great shock but the girl had probably done the best thing for everybody and it showed that, no matter how well you thought you knew people, you didn't really know them at all. She found it difficult to believe that Olive would ever commit herself to a loveless marriage but what the girl had told her had taken her mind off her worry about her son, for a short time at least. Why hadn't Neil written? The war had been over for over a year, so he couldn't still be fighting.

Olive took the irrevocable step on 29 June, 1946. The chaplain performed the ceremony in the ward with nurses, doctors and patients as the congregation and many furtive hands raised handkerchiefs to eyes as the disabled man made his vows in a clear voice that echoed round the room, but Olive's quiet responses were even more moving. She had been lent a proper wedding dress – fitted to the waist then billowing out into a full skirt looped up at intervals by lace strips dotted with tiny pearls. Her head-dress, a stiff band of organdie, was embroidered with the same small pearls, as was her long veil. One of the nurses had said that she looked beautiful and, if she wasn't as radiant as she might have been, she had an inner glow that made all hearts go out to her when she bent to let Ron kiss her after he had slipped the slim ring on her finger.

The padre, a shrewd man, gripped her hand tightly when he was congratulating them, to let her know that he understood and approved of what she was doing. This made her egg-shell control crack, and she had to turn away on the pretext of coughing. When she turned back, Ron looked so happy that she regretted her little lapse and kissed him soundly to make up for it, raising a ripple of applause from the nurses and cheers from the other patients.

When she noticed that Ron was looking tired, she said that they would have to go, although the celebration was at its most convivial. An ambulance had been provided to take them to their new home – a rented cottage on a neighbouring farm estate – and they were left alone for the first time since they had been pronounced husband and wife.

Olive felt shy, but Ron said, 'I was really proud of you today, Scottie. No man could have had a lovelier bride.'

'Fine feathers make fine birds,' she scoffed.

'It wasn't the dress, it was something . . . something about you. I've never seen you like that.'

'Wait till you see me first thing tomorrow morning,' she laughed, trying to stop the compliments, which made her feel awkward. 'You'll get the shock of your life.'

'I don't care what you look like in the morning, I was the happiest man in the world this afternoon.'

She knew that she should return the compliment but he was not expecting it and she couldn't bring herself to do it . . . not that she was unhappy, but she was too nervous about the future. Maybe she would come to love Ron – she did like him very much – or maybe she would come to hate him. It was up to herself which way it went.

Looking round the small room, which had not seemed so tiny when she saw it before without the wheelchair in it, she had a sense of belonging, although it was far removed from the elegance of the large mansion in which she had been brought up. The furniture, which had come with the house, was old-fashioned but she quite liked the look of it. Other young couples had lived here – it had been used by farm labourers before mechanisation had decimated the number of workers – had loved here, had been happy here. It had stood empty for years, the farmer had told her, but he'd had it cleaned up, and now the brasses were twinkling, the range was shining, the soot had been removed from the old black kettle on the hob. When her eyes fell on the table, a scrubbed oblong with side leaves, she laughed out loud at what was sitting on it. 'Oh, look, Ron!' she exclaimed, pointing.

He, too, laughed at the china chamber pot filled with tea roses. 'A gazunder! Somebody's got a good sense of humour.'

'It was very thoughtful, whoever did it.'

'Come and sit beside me, Scottie. You don't mind if I keep calling you that, do you? I don't think I'll ever get used to you being an Olive.'

She pulled a wooden chair next to him. 'I quite like being called Scottie.' She smiled at him when he lifted her hand. It was good to feel loved. 'We'll be comfortable here.'

'I'll be happy wherever I am as long as I've got you.'

'Oh, Ron, you're such a nice man, I wish I could . . .'

He pulled a face, 'I can put up with knowing you don't love me, as long as I know you'll never leave me.'

'I'll never do that.'

He lay back with his eyes closed, and when his grip on her hand relaxed, she thought that he had fallen asleep. She was able to study him now; his strong face was lined from all the agonies he had gone through; his hair, so meticulously plastered down for the wedding, was lying in dark strands; his mouth . . . the lips she had kissed . . .

Her heart stirred a little, then she realised that Ron was watching her. 'Did I pass muster?' he joked.

She nodded. This was not how she had felt about Neil. This was a kinder feeling, a warmer feeling, but it was probably because she was very tired. 'I'd better get you ready for bed,' she said, standing up in her normal, efficient manner. 'You've had a hectic day.'

In spite of her own hectic day, her feet were light when she went through to the only other room in the house to turn down the bedclothes and, as she did so, she was astonished to find that she was actually humming a little tune.

Even knowing that Neil was now a widower, she had carried on with her wedding, and the satisfaction she would get from making Ron happy would compensate for all the heartaches her cousin had caused her.

# Part Four

# Chapter Twenty-nine

Ron was sure that the quiet life they led must be boring to his wife and, after giving it much serious thought, he put forward a suggestion one day about five months after their wedding. 'Scottie, I think you should apply for a part-time job at the hospital.'

Olive gasped, 'Oh, no, I couldn't leave you.'

'Yes, you could. Somebody's always popping in to see me in the afternoons so you could make the lunch early and have something easy for our tea. You could manage say, three or four hours a day?'

'And you wouldn't mind?'

'I wouldn't have said it if I minded and the extra money would come in handy. My pension's not exactly a fortune.'

Having had to juggle each week with their finances to meet all their expenses, Olive could not deny this and she knew that the hospital would be glad of her help. It was only a ten-minute walk away, so she arranged to work from one until five and although she felt guilty about leaving Ron every afternoon, she was sure that he would not be on his own for long because, as he had said, somebody popped in to see him nearly every day, neighbours, nurses and orderlies who knew him. Even doctors who had

371

attended him liked to call in for a chat occasionally. It also did her good to be free of the confines of the tiny cottage for a short time and she soon settled back into the swing of things.

She had been back at work for a month when she went home to find her husband in a most peculiar mood and hoped that it was not a recurrence of the depression which had replaced the old bouts of violence. He had been on a level plane for some time now and if he was distressed by her absences, she would have to stay at home. 'Were there no visitors today?'

'Yes, Driver was here.'

'I bet she'd plenty to speak about, her ward's been pretty busy lately with new arrivals.'

'So I believe . . . er . . . have you anything to tell me?'

It was usually he who was eager to tell her what had gone on during the afternoons and something in his eyes – a hint of accusation? – disquieted her, but she smiled as she said, 'Not really, just the same old routine – dressings and blood pressures, pills and bedpans. You know.'

'You're sure that's all?'

He was plainly accusing her of something, but what? 'Ron, I don't know what you're getting at, but that was all.'

'You didn't see an old friend?'

'I saw lots of old friends. All the girls I work with are old friends.'

'An older friend than that.'

'Ron, what is it? Who are you meaning?'

'Your cousin – Neil Ferris.'

'Neil? Is he here? I haven't seen him.'

Her surprise was clearly genuine but he persisted in the same, rather belligerent, tone, 'Dot Driver told me that she had a new patient who said he belonged to Aberdeen and when she told him that one of the sisters came from there, too, he asked your name. Of course, White didn't mean anything to him but when she said you'd been Olive Potter before we got married, he said you were his cousin.'

Olive tried to hide how shaken she was by this. 'I don't want to see him. I told you he'd no time for me.'

A corner of Ron's mouth curled up sarcastically. 'He had, once, according to what you also told me.'

'That was . . . a mistake, something that just happened. There was never anything between us . . . not on his side, anyway.'

'You loved him.'

'In the past tense, yes, and it is past, Ron, honestly. If you think I'm going to run into his arms, you're wrong.'

'His wife died, did you know?'

'Mum told me when I was home but it makes no difference. I'm happy with you.'

Relaxing, Ron said contritely, 'Oh, Scottie, I shouldn't have doubted you, it was unforgivable.'

Grasping his outstretched hand, she sat down beside him. 'I do forgive you, and I don't blame you. It must have been awful thinking I was deceiving you, but I swear that's one thing I'll never do, no more than I would ever leave you. We belong together, Ron, for always.' Patting his hand, she got to her feet, 'I don't know about you but I'm famished.'

While she cooked the sausages – more bread than meat – she pondered over what Ron had told her. Her heart had given a little jump when she heard that Neil was here but that was only because it had been such a shock, not because she still loved him. That was all over, and she could never face him again after what she had done. Thank goodness there was no likelihood of them meeting accidentally – she never had any occasion to go into Dot Driver's ward. Dot Driver's ward? Mostly for burns . . . and skin grafts!

It was several days before she met Dot in the corridor and would have passed without saying anything, but her colleague stopped her, 'Did Ron tell you your cousin's in my ward?'

Olive's mouth went bone dry, 'Yes, he did.'

'His face is better than it was, he's had a graft since he came in and he'd like to see you.'

Searching frantically for an excuse, Olive was aware that, no matter how reluctant she was, it would look bad if she didn't go. 'We're up to the eyes just now, but I'll try to pop in for a minute before I go home.'

'I'll tell him. It'll buck him up.'

For the rest of that afternoon, Olive thought of what she would say. Neil had never known about the abortion, not even that she was pregnant, and all she needed to do was to find out how he had come by his injuries and sympathise with him. It might be best not to mention Freda, in case he got upset. Her duty over, she went to his ward, totally unprepared for the rush of emotion which swept over her when she saw him. The face she had once loved so deeply and which had been so devastatingly handsome that she had fought desperately to make him return that love, was now a hideous mask, the skin angry and puckered, shining and transparent in patches as if it had been stretched to its utmost limits.

374

'I'm a bit of a mess, amn't I?' he said wryly.

Swallowing, she tried to conceal the horrified compassion she felt for him and managed to joke, 'I've seen worse.'

'Aye, I suppose you have, being a nurse. I believe I've to congratulate you, though. Sister Driver said you got married a few months ago.'

'Ron was one of my patients, he's paraplegic.'

'She says he's a very nice man.'

'Yes, he is.' To get him off the subject of Ron, she said, 'How many skin grafts have you had altogether?'

'The first was in a hospital in Stuttgart, the second was in Paris, I've had one here already and there's more to come. You wouldn't have recognised me before.'

Thinking that she would hardly have recognised him now if she hadn't known who he was, she smiled reassuringly, 'They can do wonders nowadays. How did it happen?'

'I was on a truck when it was blown up. Quite a lot of us were injured and the driver was killed.'

The darkening of his eyes told her that he was remembering the horrors of that time so she said, brightly, 'Does your mum know where you are?'

'I haven't written since . . . I didn't want her to worry.'

'I'd think she'll be a lot more worried about not hearing from you.' Her own mother had told her of the nights she had lain awake wondering where her daughter was.

He considered for a moment. 'I hadn't thought of that but I suppose you're right. I'll wait and see how this next graft goes then I'll maybe write. Don't say anything about me when you write to your mother, though.'

Glancing at her watch, Olive stood up. 'I'll have to go or else Ron'll be wondering why I'm late.'

'Thanks for coming, Olive, and you'll come again?'

His eyes were so humble and pleading that she couldn't say no. 'Yes, I'll look in again.'

When she went home, she told Ron that she had seen Neil and explained how she had been forced into it. 'I'm glad I went though,' she continued, a little defiantly. 'His face had been badly burned and he's very self conscious about it. You don't mind me going to see him, do you? I felt nothing but pity for him.'

'Like you feel for me?' He looked at her with his eyebrows raised, then burst out, 'No, I'm not being fair! Poor devil, go to see him as often as you like.'

'I did promise to visit him again.'

'So you should. He's family, isn't he?'

She went to see Neil every second day, telling Ron before she left the house why she would be a little later in going home, and he gave no sign of being displeased. After Neil's next graft, with skin from his back instead of his thigh, as had happened before, she was delighted to see an improvement on his shrivelled upper lip, telling him so before going on to hold a one-sided conversation because he was not allowed to move his mouth yet. She told him about the work she did, about Ron, about anything she could think of which might be of interest to him, and he listened avidly to every word.

A week later, events were taken further out of her hands. She was telling Ron that Neil was happier with his looks and was looking forward to going out. 'He says he can face other people now, though he's still some more grafts to get.'

376

Ron smiled, 'Take him home for tea as soon as he feels up to it. I'm sure he'll welcome some home cooking and I want to meet him. I haven't met any of your family yet.'

Olive thought carefully before issuing the invitation. Ron had meant it in good faith but she was afraid that when he saw Neil and her together he might brood about the fact that they had once made love and be depressed again. At last, she decided to risk it. Ron would realise that only family ties bound her to her cousin now and any doubts he had would be dispelled.

Walking through the hospital doors, Neil was thinking of his visit to the cottage. Watching Olive attending her husband as if he were a child had been a revelation. Ron's love for his wife had been glaringly obvious and it had been equally clear that, although she cared for him deeply, she did not love him. She had changed completely since he had last seen her, Neil mused, a strange feeling assailing the pit of his stomach when he recalled what he had done on that occasion. She was no longer the spoiled brat she had been, determined to get her own way no matter what; she was caring and tender now, and her manner to him had been quite friendly though, looking back, it may have been a little distant. Maybe she, too, had remembered, with shame, what they had done on that last night they had been together.

Ron had been most hospitable, treating him like an old pal and inviting him back the next week and he had promised to go because he had enjoyed their company. It was good to get out amongst friends. He had never found out if Alf Melville survived the war, though Alf had been his best friend for so long. It was a shame that they'd been separated so near the end, for they'd been through so much together and it hurt not to know what had happened to him. But he would likely be demobbed and home by this time, making a play for every girl in Elgin. Well, that was something he would never be doing again, for no girl would look at him now, not with a face like Dr Jekyll after he changed into Mr Hyde.

Neil's thoughts veered to Olive again, wondering what had made her give up her studies at medical school. From the things that were said while they'd all been talking tonight, he had gathered that she'd gone to France just after D Day, not long after he had gone across himself, so she hadn't had time to qualify as a doctor. She had been absolutely set on it before, so what had happened?

Although she was lying in bed with her husband, Olive was thinking about Neil. Over the course of the evening, she had been forced to admit to herself that she still loved him, in spite of his grotesque face – which did not repulse her now as much as when she had first seen him. This time, she loved him for himself, not for his looks, as she had done before. When she had seen him back to the hospital, neither of them saying anything personal, she had been tempted to tell him how she felt about him . . . but only for an instant. She was married to Ron, she had been happy with him until Neil came back into her life, and she would be happy with him again – when her cousin went away.

A small sigh at her side had her on the alert at once, 'Is anything wrong? Do you want a sleeping pill?'

Touching her cheek with his hand, Ron said, 'I'm OK, stop worrying. It crossed my mind just now that Neil and

I make one complete man between us. If he had my face, or if I had his legs . . . you'd have a real husband.'

She turned to kiss him, 'I have a real husband, one that I wouldn't change for anything. You should know that by now.'

'I can't help feeling . . .'

'Don't, then. If Neil's going to upset you, I'll tell him not to come any more.'

'No, no, I like having him here. It wasn't his fault I got moody. In fact, he cheers me up more than anybody else. I've been feeling a bit down all day, that's what it is.'

'Will I ask Doctor Peters to have a look at you?'

'He was here this afternoon, he often calls in when he's passing. Look, Scottie, I'm fine, so just relax.'

She closed her eyes. She had been quite prepared to stop Neil from visiting but Ron seemed to enjoy his company and she would have to keep a tighter rein on her feelings when he came in future.

Neil's visits, at Ron's instigation, were now twice weekly and Olive looked forward to them as much as her husband. She could talk and laugh with him without revealing anything of her true feelings and it was getting easier all the time to act naturally when he was there. She was pleased that Neil's company seemed to help Ron, whose moods had stopped lately, his good humour carrying over from one visit to the next, and she sometimes found herself hoping that Neil would never be sent home.

'Driver was telling me today that Neil's to be having his next skin graft,' Ron remarked one day. 'I won't see him for a while and I'm going to miss him.'

Olive looked at him in concern, 'There'll come a day when he's discharged, you know, and you'll never see him again.'

'Oh, I know that, and I'll have to put up with it but he makes me feel . . . I don't know, maybe it's because we're both in the same boat, having a handicap we'll never overcome . . . but I feel lucky when he's here. I have a wife to look after me . . . and I shouldn't think he'll ever find a girl to . . .'

'He has a mother who'll look after him,' Olive broke in. 'When Gracie's brother and his wife were killed in the Blitz she was left to look after their daughter Queenie and she put her through school and sent her to university, even if it must have been a struggle for her financially. She never complained once, that I know of.' Recalling the things she had said to Queenie, Olive came to an abrupt halt.

Having already been told about this, Ron grinned, 'I know you were a proper bitch at that time, but by God! You're an angel without wings now.' His smile faded. 'I don't know how I'd have got on if it hadn't been for you. It's a girl like you Neil's going to need but they're not ten a penny.'

She gave a faint smile, 'It's just as well, isn't it?'

Six weeks later, Olive was surprised that Ron was not in the kitchen when she went home but she hung her cloak up on the usual hook before going through to the bed-room. He was lying on the bed but the colour of his face told her that he was not just sleeping. Hurrying over, she felt his pulse, barely noticing the tumbler on the chest by the bed, and her heart came into her mouth when she could scarcely feel a beat at all. Bending over him, she tried to give him mouth to mouth resuscitation, but there was no response. Panicking now, she ran to the farmhouse and asked Mr Lord to phone the doctor and, as he gave the operator the number, his wife, a homely, comfortably plump woman, said, 'Is something wrong with Ron? I'd better go back with you.'

When they went in, Olive felt her husband's pulse again but this time it had stopped altogether, not even the feeble beat she had picked up before. Turning to the farmer's wife, she whispered, 'He's gone.'

'Come through to the fire and sit down, m'dear.' The woman took her arm and led her into the kitchen. 'Have you got any brandy? You're as white as a sheet.'

While Mrs Lord was looking for the bottle of brandy in the cupboard, Olive spotted the letter on the mantelpiece with one word on the envelope. 'Scottie.' Suspecting what it was, she grabbed it and stuffed it into the pocket of her apron.

'Here you are, m'dear.'

The spirits calmed her a little and she accepted the cup of tea which she was handed in a few minutes. 'I should have been here with him,' she said sadly.

'You couldn't have done anything. It's been his heart.'

Sure that it had not been his heart, Olive kept silent. If she could only find out what was in the letter . . . 'I'll have to go to the lavatory.'

She almost ran to the outhouse at the bottom of the small garden and put the hook over the staple to lock the door. With shaking hands, she drew out the letter and opened it.

Dear Scottie,

Please don't feel guilty about this. I've thought it over carefully and it's the best thing for everybody. I know you still love Neil, it's in

381

your eyes every time you look at him and he
loves you, too, and needs you. You have made
me very happy since you married me, and I am
grateful for that, but it's no life for a girl as
young as you. All I ask is that you marry your
Neil and that you think of me sometimes.

God bless you both, Ron

'Oh, Ron,' Olive whispered, feeling that she had been
slowly strangled, 'I'm so sorry!'

After a moment, she went back inside, her heart aching
for a man she had never loved, but who was as dear to her
as if she had.

When Dr Peters came, she went through to the
bedroom with him, Mrs Lord remaining discreetly in the
kitchen, and after hearing that Olive had found her
husband lying on the bed and that she had tried to revive
him, the doctor made a brief examination then pursed his
lips. Certain that he had guessed what Ron had done,
Olive held her breath.

His head suddenly shot up, as if he had been deliber-
ating something and come to a final conclusion. Laying his
hand on her shoulder, he said quietly, 'I think you know as
well as I how your husband died, Mrs White?' Colouring,
she hung her head and he went on, 'Shall we keep it just
between the two of us? I know that I am risking my own
career but I think we can get away with it. Mr and Mrs
Lord have seen me here a few times . . . oh, it was purely
social calls but they don't know that and, to be quite
honest, Ron's heart was not very strong. He could have

lasted another year, perhaps not even that, so . . . do you understand?'

'But you can't . . .'

'It will save you a lot of embarrassment, my dear. I know that he'd been worrying about something for some time and I should state on the death certificate that he died while the balance of his mind was disturbed but I will make it out as "cardiac arrest", which is what it came to in the end, after all, isn't it?'

Olive's conscience wouldn't let it rest there. 'It was all my fault though I didn't think he knew. I fell in love with someone else and . . .'

He held up his hand, 'Yes, I suspected that. Come now.' In the kitchen, he said to Mrs Lord, 'Look after her, she's had a deep shock. I should have told her that Ron's heart was a bit dodgy.'

The woman nodded, 'I did wonder why you kept calling.'

Olive was trembling violently when she sat down. Ron must have taken an overdose of the sleeping tablets that she had got for him once and which he had never used, that was why the empty tumbler had been there. If only she had known what was in his mind, she would have taken them away and disposed of them and now, even though he had taken his own life so that she and Neil could marry, he had driven a bigger wedge between them than ever. For the rest of her life she would blame herself for Ron's death.

# Chapter Thirty

## *1947*

Why was Olive being so strange with him? Neil had posed this question to himself several times in the three months since Ron's funeral. It had started on that blustery, showery day in March, when he had hung back until she thanked the people who had attended – those of the hospital staff who could be spared, long-term mobile patients who had known Ron and some who were conveyed to the cemetery in wheelchairs – and when she finally came to him, she had been very curt. 'Thanks for coming, Neil,' was all she had said, then excused herself to go and talk to the minister.

He had wanted to let her know how sorry he was about Ron but she hadn't given him a chance. He realised that she must have had a dreadful shock when she found her husband dead – a heart attack, Mrs Lord had said – and that she would take a long time to get over it, but he had hoped to comfort her a little, to let her know that she wasn't alone, that he would provide a shoulder to cry on any time she wanted one.

She had started working full time at the hospital a week later and had come to see him once or twice after his last graft but she hadn't invited him to the cottage when he was fit enough to go. He had toyed with the idea of turning up unexpectedly one evening and had discarded it on the grounds that she would probably hate to be pressurised, so he would just have to be patient, give her another few months.

The weeks passed slowly for Neil and he was overjoyed when a young nurse came in one afternoon when he was lying on top of his bed having a rest and told him there was a visitor to see him. Expecting it to be Olive – though she usually just walked in – he was smiling broadly when the door opened once more, but his breath was taken away when he saw who entered.

'Hey, you lazy bugger!' Alf Melville grinned as he walked over to the bed. 'You're always taking things easy.'

His heart too full to joke, Neil exclaimed, 'Oh, Alf, it's good to see you. How did you know where I was?'

Chuckling, Alf tapped his nose, 'It's a long, long story, Neil boy.' Then his mood changed, 'No, it's quite simple, really. On my way home after I was demobbed, I couldn't get you out of my mind, so I popped in to see your mother before I went to get my bus to Elgin.'

Mentally thanking his lucky stars that he had written home some time ago, Neil said, 'So what have you been doing since I saw you last?'

For the next hour, they compared notes about the ordeal of the final weeks of the war, amazed that they had both been injured in the battle for the Sachsenwald. 'I came out of it better than you, though,' Alf said compassionately. 'I was only in hospital for a week.'

'Oh, well, I was luckier than a lot of them,' Neil sighed.

Looking at his watch, Alf made to stand up, 'I'd better go before they think I've taken root here.'

'Stay till you're thrown out,' Neil begged. 'I'm going to tell you something that'll shake the pants off you.'

Alf settled back, his face alight with interest. 'Go on.'

'I'm thinking of getting married again.'

'Ach, is that all? I knew you would, one day.'

'Wouldn't you like to know who the lucky girl is?'

'It's bound to be a nurse, you don't meet anybody else.'

A huge grin transforming his scarred face, Neil was almost hugging himself with glee. 'You're right, it is a nurse, and her name's Sister White and, if you're a good boy, I'll take you to see her.'

'What's she like? Cross-eyed, bandy-legged, or what?'

Knowing that Alf was teasing, not implying that no decent girl would look at him now, Neil spluttered with mirth; he was looking forward to seeing the shock on his friend's face when he found out who the girl was. 'You'll have to wait and see,' he giggled, reflecting that it should be all right to take Alf to the cottage because Olive couldn't think he was trying to corner her if he had somebody else with him.

'Your mother was telling me Queenie got married,' Alf said now, giving Neil a peculiar look.

'Aye, I was happy about that, she was a nice kid.'

'I used to wonder if you . . . well, if you fancied her a bit. Was she the one that let you down?'

Neil smiled, a little sadly, 'I thought she had, but it was . . . a misunderstanding.' And that had been Olive's doing, he recalled, in surprise, but he could understand her motive now and forgive her. 'Anyway, Queenie's very happy being in South Norwood again helping her Les to run a little shop he started, though I believe things are pretty tight for them and she's speaking about trying to finish her BA course so she can get a teaching job to help out.'

'And your mother said Patsy married a Canadian.'

'Yes, I'd the shock of my life when Mum told me that. I'd always thought Patsy would end up being an old maid for she never went out with boys before, that I knew of. Still, she seems to be enjoying married life in Montreal, going to all kinds of parties and nightclubs, would you believe?'

'It takes some believing, she was always so shy. I don't think she ever spoke more than a few words to me any of the times I was staying in Aberdeen.'

'Mum sent me a photo . . . I've got it here some place.' Neil rummaged around in his locker for a moment then pulled out an envelope. 'That's their house.'

A low whistle issued from Alf's lips. 'Some cash there, by the look of it.'

'Aye, her Jake's pretty well off. She landed on her feet.'

After a brief pause, Alf said, a trifle hesitantly, 'Your mum didn't say anything about Olive. I wonder if she's changed as much as the rest of us?'

Neil had difficulty in keeping a straight face but he was saved from having to answer by the entry of two nurses with the tea trolley and Alf rose to leave, 'I told my mother to expect me when she saw me, so I'd better look for somewhere to sleep, but I'll come back to see you after I've got fixed up and had a bite to eat.'

'I'll take you to meet Sister White tonight, then.'

'OK, I'll look forward to it.'

While he was having his supper, Neil thought over the

last bit of their conversation. Alf didn't appear to have changed much but the rest of them certainly had. Pasty, who used to be as timid as a mouse was having a high old time in Quebec; dear little Queenie, once so effervescent, was buried in a little back street shop; he, himself, was much more serious; but the biggest change of all was in Olive. She had been a calculating, pampered madam at one time, but she had roughed it as a nurse, faced the horrors of war, married a man who couldn't have been able to make love to her and had looked after him tenderly until he died.

Neil's reflective mood changed. Alf was in for the shock of his life tonight when he met Sister White.

In the early evening, the two friends presented themselves at Olive's door. 'Good God!' she exclaimed. 'Alf Melville!'

'Christ, it's Olive Potter!'

Laughing fit to burst, Neil corrected him, 'Sister White. Now are you asking us in, Olive, or are you going to leave us standing out here?'

'Oh, I'm sorry. What am I thinking of? Come in, come in. I was feeling a bit down, if you must know, so I'm really glad to have company.'

At first – having realised that Olive must have married if her name was White but not knowing if she was widowed or divorced or waiting for a divorce – Alf was not his usual teasing self and kept his ears open for clues. As soon as he heard her remarking that it was 'six months since Ron died', everything clicked into place. She and Neil must be waiting for a decent time to elapse before they took the plunge.

When Neil went out to the lavatory, Olive looked at Alf

with a hint of mischief in her eyes, 'Maybe Neil hasn't told you yet but I know that you two had great fun at my expense a few years ago.'

'Oh, no!' he groaned. 'How did you find out about that?'

'Neil didn't tell me, if that's what you think, it was my brother Raymond.'

Alf rolled his eyes. 'I warned Neil not to say anything to him, I knew he would blab it out.'

'It was a long time after. We were having a row and he took great delight in throwing it in my face. Don't worry,' she added, 'I forgave you both ages ago though I was hurt and angry at the time.'

'I bet you were. Look, I'm really sorry about it but we were just a couple of silly kids having a lark.'

'And I was a spoiled kid, but we've all been through a lot since then.'

'Aye,' he agreed, 'we've all changed – older and wiser and uglier . . .'

Understanding why he had stopped, Olive murmured, 'How do you think he is? In himself, I mean?'

Alf screwed up his face. 'I'm not sure, but I'd say he's OK. He took it really hard when Freda died but as far as I can tell, this business . . . well, he's bound to feel terrible about it but I don't think it's twisted his mind.'

'I didn't think so, either, but I wasn't sure.' Hesitating for a second, she went on, 'I've always loved him, Alf, and I think . . . oh, this probably sounds conceited, but I'm nearly sure he loves me. That's why I've decided to go away. I can easily get another nursing job somewhere else.' She listened for the familiar creak of the outhouse door, then continued. 'You see, I've got a suspicion that he's going to ask me to marry him . . .'

'He told me he was thinking of getting married though I'd no idea you were the Sister White he was speaking about.'

'I can't marry him, Alf, not now, not ever.'

'You'll get over your husband's death, Olive.'

'It's not that . . . well, it is, in a way.' She felt as if she were entangled in some huge, suffocating mesh. She could never tell anyone how Ron had died – Doctor Peters, in his concern for her, had made that impossible – yet there was no other way to explain.

Perplexed by the hunted look in her eyes, Alf said, 'After I see Neil into the hospital, I'll come back, for I can see there's something you need to get off your chest.'

'I can't tell anybody.'

'I'm not anybody – I'm good old Alf, remember?'

Catching the sound for which she had been listening, Olive whispered, 'Don't leave me alone with him, and come back if you want to.' Then she said, in a loud voice, 'What are you intending to do now that you're demobbed?'

'I'm going to have a bloody good time for a while!'

They were both laughing when Neil came in but he didn't sit down. 'It's time we were going, Alf. This lassie has to go to work in the morning and I'm feeling a wee bit tired.' Turning to his cousin, he held out his hand, 'I'll just say goodnight, then, Olive.' He had hoped that she would ask him to resume his regular visits but she just brushed his hand with her fingertips.

'Goodnight, Neil, and goodnight, Alf, it was great seeing you again.'

Neil was quiet as they made their way down the small

390

path and, after a few minutes, Alf said gently, 'What's worrying you, Neil boy?'

'I'm sure she loves me,' Neil mumbled, 'but you could see for yourself that she keeps me at a distance. She's never asked me to the house once since Ron's funeral and I used to come twice a week.'

Because he didn't know what was bothering Olive, Alf tried to soothe his friend by making a joke of it. 'She's probably worried about the neighbours. A widow being alone with a man in that wee cottage? The tongues would wag and not without cause, if I know you.'

Neil didn't smile, 'She wouldn't care what the neighbours said and, anyway, it's only the folk in the farmhouse that can see who goes in and out. Maybe she's too ashamed of my face to marry me?'

'God, it's not that, Neil. She does love you, that sticks out a mile but . . . she's not ready yet. Give her time.'

'How long does she need? It's six months since Ron died and I know she didn't love him, so what's wrong with her?'

'Take it easy, Neil boy. It'll work out.'

When they arrived at the hospital, Alf waited until Neil was safely inside, then turned and hurried back the way he had come and Olive opened the door so quickly to his knock that he knew she had been standing waiting for him.

Laying his cap on the table, he pulled a chair up to the fire and stretched out his hands to the heat, 'It's getting airish out there. Right then, Olive, out with it.'

'I've been thinking while you were gone,' she began, 'and the only way I could make you understand would be if I told you the whole truth.'

'So go on, I'm all ears.'

'It's not as easy as that, Alf. It's not just me, I've got to consider somebody else, somebody else who's involved.'

'Christ, Olive, you don't mean there's another man?

She shook her head impatiently, 'I told you I still loved Neil. Oh, God, I don't know what to do. I want to marry him more than anything in the world, it's what I dreamed of for years but . . .' She broke off, wringing her hands in despair, then added vehemently, 'I have to get away from him.'

Alf leaned forward and caught one of her hands, stroking it as he said, 'Listen, Olive. I know you've loved him for a long time so why the hell do you want to break his heart?'

'I don't want to,' she exclaimed, her voice cracking, 'for it'll break mine as well, but I have to.'

Alf jumped up and pulled her to her feet, enfolding her in his arms as she burst into tears. 'Tell me,' he coaxed. 'I'm sure I can sort things out for you. It's something to do with your husband, isn't it? Neil says you didn't love Ron but did he love you?'

It felt easier to talk about it when she was being held so tightly and didn't have to look in his face, 'Yes, he loved me, and he married me knowing that I didn't love him. He was a fine man, Alf, and I was happy with him until Neil . . .'

'Did he find out about you and Neil?'

'I didn't think so, but he wrote in the letter that he . . .'

She stopped so abruptly and with such a horrified intake of breath before she began to sob wildly, that Alf knew that the letter had been a suicide note. Understanding fully now, he let her cry, for it looked as if this was the first time she had let herself go.

Several minutes passed before she drew back slightly but he pulled her against him again. 'He killed himself to let you and Neil get together?'

'Oh, God, I've let it out, after all. He was doing it for me, but I can't marry Neil after that.'

'You said there was another person involved.'

'The doctor knew what Ron had done, but because he guessed why, he made out the death certificate as "cardiac arrest". If it ever comes out that he made a false entry, his career could be ruined but he only did it so people wouldn't know about Ron's suicide. He did it for my sake, so please don't ever breathe a word of it, Alf, especially to Neil.'

'I would never have told anybody anyway, Olive, it's safe with me.' Alf's brain was working frantically. How could he convince her that her husband's suicide was pointless if she didn't marry Neil? She was so chock-full of guilt that she wouldn't listen to anything he said, but he had to try and he still owed Neil for saving his life. 'Sit down, Olive,' he said quietly, 'and we'll see if we can thrash this thing out properly between us.'

As he had known, she stuck obstinately to her decision to go away so that Neil would forget her, even when he told her that it was the most cruel thing she could do, until he had a sudden brainwave. 'This doctor chappie,' he began, 'he did what he did for your sake, you say?'

'Yes, to save me embarrassment, that was how he put it. If it's not a natural death, the police have to be called in and there has to be an autopsy.'

'Aye, I understand that, but did he know about Neil?'

'He guessed there was somebody and that was why Ron . . .'

'So . . . the doctor was giving you a way to save your face, a way to marry Neil without folk saying, "That's why her man took his life. She must have been carrying on with this one, and he found out." Do you see what I'm getting at?'

'Yes,' she said slowly, the idea obviously new to her. 'I suppose that's one way of looking at it. Do you really think that's why Doctor Peters did it?'

Aware that she was weakening, he pressed on, 'Certain, and he's made a stand for nothing if you persist in this stupid attitude. Ron wanted you to get together with Neil, and this doctor wanted it, and you and Neil want it, so for Christ's sake, Olive, grab your happiness with both hands as quick as you can. You're a long time dead.'

She gave an uncertain laugh, 'Oh, Alf, I should have known your silver tongue would get round me.'

'So?' he grinned. 'Will I tell Neil when I see him in the morning that you'll marry him?'

'He hasn't asked me yet.'

'He would if he got the chance.'

She drew away now and after a lengthy pause, she smiled, 'You can tell him to come to tea tomorrow but please don't say anything else. I want everything to come from him, the courtship, the proposal . . .'

'But you'll invite me to the wedding when it's fixed?'

'You'll be best man. Neil wouldn't have anyone else.'

'Well, now that's all arranged, I'd better get to my hotel in case they lock the doors at midnight.'

Olive kissed him on the cheek, 'I don't know what I'd have done without you, Alf. Thank you.'

With a twinkle in his eye, he grabbed her round the waist. 'What kind of kiss was that for the best man?'

His was a little more than just a friendly kiss, although there was no passion in it, and he let his arms drop with a prolonged sigh, 'Neil's a lucky blighter.'

Picturing his poor face, she thought that Neil wouldn't consider himself lucky, but she knew what Alf had meant and let him out without saying anything more. Sitting down, she went over all his arguments again and by the time she went to bed, she was happier than she had been for months. Why shouldn't she grab her happiness when she could? It was what Ron had wanted for her, what the doctor had wanted for her, and more than anything, what she wanted for herself.

She loved Neil more than she had ever done, as a woman not a spoiled child, yet she had been prepared to give him up. Would she have been brave enough to go away when the actual time came? Probably not. She'd said nothing to Alf about the baby, but she would tell Neil before they were married and trust that it wouldn't affect how he felt about her. If fate designed people's destinies, they had been meant to come together eventually, and all the troubles of the past had been sent to test them. They had come through, not unscathed – for there would be painful memories for each of them – but just a little tarnished.

Smiling, she stood up and went through to the bedroom.